BOOKS BY SUZA KATES

The Savannah Coven Series
Whisper of a Witch
Conviction of a Witch
Binding of a Witch
Haunting of a Witch
Possession of a Witch
Deception of a Witch
Suffering of a Witch

The She Series
She Who is Hidden

Single Titles
Hallowed Eve
The Penance Stone

SUFFERING OF A WITCH

THE SAVANNAH COVEN SERIES

SUZA KATES

ICASM PRESS

SAVANNAH

Published by Icasm Publishing LLC
5710 Ogeechee Rd. Suite 200 #278, Savannah, GA 31405
www.icasmpress.com

Library of Congress Cataloging-in-Publication Data

Kates, Suza
Suffering of a Witch / Suza Kates
    p. cm.

ISBN-13:978-0-9889809-4-5
ISBN-13:978-0-9889809-5-2 (ebook)
I. Title

Printed and bound in the United States of America

10 9 8 7 6 5 4 3 2 1

For Woody
A good man and wonderful stepfather

ACKNOWLEDGMENTS

I find the process of writing a book to be a little different every time, and I want to take this opportunity to thank those who work with me "behind the scenes." I can't say enough how much I appreciate the editing team that helps me iron out the messes. While we might sometimes disagree about the gray areas of grammar, in the end, our various perspectives make for a better product.

I'd like to thank Mandi Cranson not only for her skill as a content editor, but also as a part-time therapist! Oddly enough, it's the words "You need to re-think this scene" that make me need the therapy in the first place. Ha ha.

Sharyn Cerniglia is invaluable with her eagle eye as copy editor, and there's the added bonus of envisioning her editing on a beach in Belize. Vicarious relaxation. :)

Donna Wood is always ready to proofread the final version and is thankfully very flexible with her schedule. (Actually, so are Mandi and Sharyn.) She has been there since the very beginning—and I mean since I first had the crazy idea to try to write a book.

Brian McCann has also been with us for the whole ride, and I am always amazed by the gorgeous covers he creates. I truly appreciate your taking my ideas into consideration and am so excited about future projects.

And David. Wow. Sometimes when he starts talking about new computer software and programs and formatting issues, I understand where the expression "boggles the mind" comes from. How a book gets from my computer to various sales outlets is PFM as far as I'm concerned. (He'll get that.) And I am so very grateful for your big brain!

As always, I have to thank my readers. The journey up until now has been a learning curve, and I am blessed to have so many supportive people willing to give feedback and commentary.

I'm also ever-indebted to those first few who took a chance on "Whisper of a Witch" and an unknown author, helping make the Savannah Coven Series a success. All of you are who I aim to please, and I will endeavor to make it bigger, better, sweeter each and every time!

THE COVEN

Anna St. Germaine
Hair: Long, straight, sable brown
Eyes: Sapphire blue
Color: Sapphire blue
Cat: "Ivy" gray female with lime green eyes

Anna sees visions of past, present, and future. She is the coven's head witch and is a descendant of the three women who originally banished the demon Bastraal three centuries ago. Her ancestral home is on an island off the coast of Savannah, Georgia and now serves as coven central.

Claudia Grant
Hair: Straight, long, flaming red
Eyes: River green
Color: Coral
Cat: "Rowan Von Ashbi" coloring of an American Wirehair with yellow eyes

Claudia is a history professor who only needs to touch an object to sense its past and previous surroundings.

Hayden Wells
Hair: Brownish red "caramel"
Eyes: Golden brown
Color: Pale pink
Cat: "Daisy" black tortoiseshell with yellow eyes

Hayden is a medium from San Francisco who sees and talks to spirits/ghosts.

Kylie Worthington
Hair: Long, wavy golden-blonde
Eyes: Hazel
Color: Yellow
Cat: Sassafras "Sassy" also a long-haired blonde but with bright yellow eyes

Kylie is a college student who's "on a break" to do her part for the coven and is able to control electricity in any form.

Lucia Ruiz
Hair: Long, wavy deep brown
Eyes: Brown
Color: Red
Cat: "Iris" black Persian with blue eyes

Lucia was born to privileged wealth in Spain and has the ability to find anything that is lost. She is an adventurer, world-traveler, and renowned relic-hunter.

Paige Reilley
Hair: Shoulder-length, white-blonde with ragged bangs
Eyes: Turquoise blue
Color: Turquoise
Cat: Tiger Lily "Tiger" brown and gray with white chest and belly, bright green eyes

Recently discharged from the military, Paige is a soldier in every way with the added abilities of super-strength and speed.

Shauni Miller
Hair: Long, straight, black
Eyes: Emerald green
Color: Green
Cat: "Cuileann" black short-hair with green eyes

Shauni is a nature-loving biologist from Colorado and communicates with animals telepathically.

Viv Sakurai
Hair: Shoulder-length, black, angled bangs
Eyes: Gray
Color: Purple
Cat: Kikoku "Kiko" orange tabby with yellow-green eyes and a grumpy disposition.

Relocated from Chicago, Viv is a physicist searching for an explanation for her own special power of telekinesis.

Willyn Brousseau
Hair: Wavy, shoulder-length, light blonde
Eyes: Pale blue
Color: White/cream
Cat: "Snowball" pure white with golden eyes

Willyn is a nurse, a mother, and a Christian. Raised in Alabama, she uses her healing powers to help those in need. She came to Savannah with an additional package, her young son, Tadd.

THE GUYS

Dr. Michael Black *Whisper of a Witch*

This tall handsome veterinarian fell in love with Shauni in the first book of the series. He has dark blonde hair and gray eyes and is able to read a person's aura. He's a pretty calm guy until someone messes with his witch.

Dare Forster *Conviction of a Witch*

Dark and handsome with deep blue eyes, this male witch came to the coven's island with his own plan. He wanted to partner with one of the women, but he never expected to fall in love. Especially with a gentle, Christian soul like Willyn. Now married, the two have made a family with Willyn's small son, Tadd.

Nick Reagan *Binding of a Witch*

The coven likes to hang out in their favorite pub, and the owner of the bar always liked looking at Viv. His eyes are the color of the whiskey he sells, and his past is one of struggle. One night Nick finally got the nerve to approach the Asian beauty, but he got a lot more than he bargained for. The demon Bastraal had been destroyed once before, and his remains had been buried. Beneath Nick's very own pub.

Trevor Roch   *Haunting of a Witch*

One of Savannah's finest, this homicide detective clashes hard with the coven's ghost whisperer, convinced she's a con artist. Hayden has no choice but to work with the annoying man and find a serial killer who's working with the Amara. Staying true to form and following the coven's pattern, the two fall for each other. Against their better judgment.

Ethan Drake   *Possession of a Witch*

This demon hunter is well-acquainted with evil and has been chasing his own monster since childhood. When he offers to help the coven with their demon infestation, he has no idea he's about to be taken on the adventure of a lifetime. Lucia Ruiz is hard to resist, and is the one woman who might be able to save him.

Cole Lonergan   *Deception of a Witch*

As Trevor's police partner, Cole has been introduced to the coven and all of their secrets. While he admires the women and considers them all good friends, he never expects to feel anything more. But Claudia Grant is a long-legged-wicked-smart witch, and much like his favorite candies, Cole finds himself wanting to take a bite.

Quinn is the younger brother of the coven's head witch, Anna. With sable hair and cobalt eyes, he is the masculine and handsome version of the siblings. His knowledge runs to occult history and magickal languages. He assists the coven in all things, and though he has his eye on a particular witch, he does his best to deny it.

1

"Do you think the killer is in there?" Kylie looked over Trevor's shoulder at the monitoring station inside the police van. Onscreen, a tray of champagne flutes floated through party-goers inside the ultra-posh manor, footage courtesy of an undercover cop and one of the silver buttons on his elegant catering uniform.

The men gathered inside the mansion appeared stately and distinguished, non-threatening. Upon first glance.

But they were all members of a secret society. A club that embraced certain . . . predilections. One that promised to supply. As well as satisfy.

"Haven't caught sight of him yet." Trevor acknowledged her with a chin-notch but continued watching the three screens. His eyes narrowed. "But yeah. He's in there."

"And Dalton?"

"He was just spotted." This came from Cole, Trevor's partner. The two homicide detectives were in charge of the surveillance detail. "If everything goes as planned, Ronja will lose her right-hand man tonight. Maybe for good."

Ronja. The evil witch. And that wasn't just a figure of speech. Kylie smiled viciously in the gray-blue glow of the screens. "I'd like to take her actual *right hand*. After she tricked Claudia into bringing her favorite demon into our world, it would serve her right."

Cole showed a flash of teeth. But he wasn't smiling. "You and me both. Bastraal already hurt Claudia once. I don't intend to let it happen again."

Kylie fidgeted with her top. Part of her "disguise." How was a call girl supposed to perform her duties when she could barely draw a breath? The corset ties wouldn't give, so she dropped her hand with a strained huff. "Ronja and Dalton were always arrogant, but now that Bastraal's backing them up with his . . . underworld powers, they're getting way too cocky."

"And that makes them careless," Cole said before swiveling his chair around to speak in hushed tones to Trevor.

Kylie sat back on her seat. Dalton Morne was Ronja's lawyer, and he'd been the careless one Cole was referring to. He was Ronja's servant in all ways legal and immoral, but he'd finally screwed up. Big time.

He'd propositioned a murderer online—on a website for serial killers—and had given Trevor and Cole an unexpected lead. And a chance for the coven to strike a blow against the Amara.

She tried to adjust her skin-cinching top again. Then, out of habit, her hand slipped up to her throat. Bare. No amulet resting on a silver chain.

The absence of her talisman left her feeling exposed—weaker, vulnerable. And disconnected from her coven.

Each of the witches had identical necklaces, intricately woven silver patterns rimmed with eight small stones of various hues. The center stone of each was more prominent and gleamed with its owner's signature color.

Kylie put a single finger to the place her yellow stone usually rested, and then with a sigh, returned her mind to the topic of clandestine meetings and sex parties. The things she did to help save the world.

Or at least a few innocent women.

Her nostrils flared and she curled her fingers into her palm.

The last serial killer Dalton had recruited had taken three lives and tried to steal their spirits to feed to the demon Bastraal. Trevor and Cole had tracked the man down, and Hayden, the ghost-whisperer of the coven, had saved the women's souls.

That had been part of her challenge. Her trial. And she'd also brought Trevor into their ever-expanding witchy family. Just as Claudia had initiated Cole, falling in love even as Bastraal had burst from a portal to attack the coven within the walls of their own home.

Prophecy. Danger. And love. It's how her coven rolled.

Every witch would have her day, but since Bastraal's invasion, the Amara had been quiet. Disturbingly so. Seven weeks had passed, and the next witch had yet to be called to trial. With Claudia's challenge complete, six of the nine women had fulfilled their prophetic roles. Only three were left.

And Kylie was one of them.

She sat up straighter in an attempt to draw more air. How much longer until they could go in and get this over with? Nervous energy pinged through her system. Every day was full of tension, and every night a restless marathon of tossing and turning.

She'd thought seeing her sisters battle darkness and demons was nerve-wracking. But the stillness of waiting, always being on the lookout for danger . . . somehow, that was worse.

So when Trevor and Cole came across murder-for-hire in a chat room, the coven decided to do something they'd never done before.

They were going on the offensive.

"Okay. This is your last chance to back out." Cole handed a tiny ear bud to Kylie, then repeated the offering to Willyn, who'd been sitting in silence, lost in her own thoughts.

"I'm ready." Willyn put the miniscule receiver in her ear as she'd been shown, adjusting part of her strawberry-blonde wig to hide it. The blunt cut angled sexily to her jawline, but that wasn't the reason for her new look. She and Kylie had both covered up their natural blonde hair.

Because the killer preferred red.

Claudia was the only true redhead in the coven, but she couldn't do this job. The whole point was to be incognito. The witches couldn't risk looking like themselves, or Dalton Morne might recognize them.

So here Kylie sat in long copper waves with Willyn in her strawberry-sexy-secretary look. They were acting as Confidential Informants. CIs for Trevor and Cole. Though their enlistment hadn't exactly been by the book.

"Any information you gather while inside will be legit." Trevor spoke from where he sat, still watching the monitors. "But if anything goes wrong, we want you to get out. No questions, no excuses."

"Do either of you need another look at Cutter's photo before going in?" Cole asked.

Kylie lifted a shoulder and leaned in to study the picture. The man who'd raped and mutilated two teenage girls was deceptively bland in appearance. Cutter was more average than average, so another long look at the grainy photo couldn't hurt.

"If we don't see him, we can always look for Dalton." Willyn tapped the much clearer photo of the lawyer. His silver hair and tall, lean physique would be hard to miss.

Cole shifted his gaze between the two women. "Remember, we've got enough on Cutter to arrest him. The warrant on his apartment is being executed as we speak, so don't do anything heroic. If we can't get Dalton tonight, then we'll keep working at it. But no matter what happens, Cutter's going down."

Cole put away the photos and had them both speak into the microphones hidden in the upper edge of their black corsets. "We've got Cutter dead to rights. All we need to nail Morne for conspiracy is an overt act of agreement to commit murder.

Arrangement of details. A price. A handshake. Anything."

Now Cole fixed his stare on Kylie. "Stay safe. Watch out for each other. And avoid Lady Mure at all costs." The woman providing female "entertainment" at the mansion would know Kylie and Willyn didn't belong. She was the only potential snag in the otherwise smooth operation.

When the van's side door slid open with a low rumble, Kylie stiffened as if the devil were at the gate. She studied the tall figure standing there.

Nope. Not the devil. But a damned close second.

Quinn St. Germaine always made her breath catch in her lungs. Blue eyes that delved deep, a rangy but well-muscled form, and sable hair that always seemed to fall forward in a scruffy, careless sort of way.

He was so freakin' sexy.

Those disarming eyes flicked to Kylie. They filled with judgment as he looked her over.

She firmed her jaw in response, because he was also so freakin' *annoying*.

Disregarding her again, Quinn addressed Cole. "The other women just arrived, and they're all wearing the same outfits. We're good to go."

This time when Quinn glanced at her corset's low neckline and curve-hugging fit, he showed no emotion. No desire or distaste. He was a man of ice.

No one did indifference like Quinn. Especially when he and Kylie occupied the same space.

Kylie felt a tug of dismay. He knew how she felt about him and had turned her down. Flat.

But still she wanted him. He was serious, studious, and delicious.

Not to mention his voice. Quinn was a Southern boy who'd attended Harvard. And that's exactly the way he sounded. Warm, smooth, and articulate, the low timbre had a way of vibrating its way through her until her breaths got confused about which way they were trying to go.

She, unfortunately, didn't seem to affect him the same way.

White-knuckling her fingers on the edge of her seat, Kylie lowered her eyes. *I can't believe we actually made out.*

When she looked again, his blue-dagger gaze locked momentarily with hers. She sucked in one of those confused breaths. *Oh, but I want to do it again.*

"You'd better get going," he said abruptly, dragging his attention from her to address Willyn. "Lady Mure's girls entered through a side door near the garage."

Willyn nodded and picked up one of the two black masks she and Kylie were to wear. Apparently, part of the intrigue of these events was not knowing who your . . . *partner* really was.

Quinn stepped aside to help Willyn out. When Kylie stood to do the same, Cole touched her shoulder. "Don't try to prove yourself in there. Just relax, and as strange as it sounds, try to have fun. You'll blend in better if you do."

Dredging up a smile and trying to ignore Quinn's nearness, she winked at Cole. "You know I always have fun."

Quinn spoke roughly. "Just remember that some people have real responsibilities. Cole and Trevor are going out on a limb to help us."

Kylie's cheeks flamed as the heat of humiliation fired in her belly. "I know what needs to be done. Thanks." Why did he always talk down to her? She'd been chosen to be one of the nine, and regardless of her age, Kylie had done pretty well so far. Her friends had no complaints.

But Anna's little brother always seemed to have a snide remark or "helpful" advice just for her. After their dismal attempt at blanket wrestling, she and Quinn had agreed to work together and nothing more.

Yet he just couldn't contain those barbs. He always had to remind her of how little she meant to him.

Perhaps he needed a little reminding too. "Keep your comments to yourself, Quinn, or I'll do the worst possible thing you can imagine."

He stared blankly at her, unconcerned. "What's that?"

"I'll kiss you."

His eyes widened before he shot a look to the other men. Kylie's smile was smug as she stepped down to the cement driveway and quickly caught up with Willyn, leaving Quinn no opportunity to reply.

Once in stride with her friend, she slowed to appreciate the estate they were about to infiltrate. A high-summer moon lit the sprawling, manicured yards, and the massive white-stone manor shone beneath silvered beams.

"Hard to believe this beautiful home hides such a dirty secret," Willyn said.

Kylie took strident steps, still peeved by Quinn's slur. "Not much surprises me anymore. I think I've become jaded."

Soft laughter floated from Willyn. "You're too young to be jaded."

"Ha. But I'm old enough to be wearing this getup," she said, pointing to her micro-mini, black garter stockings, and needle-point stilettos.

Willyn grimaced. The sweet woman of Baptist faith was wearing a similar ensemble. "Good point."

As they stole across the main section of the drive toward the door Quinn had indicated, Kylie lifted her head to take in a whiff of the sultry evening air. Perfumed by gardenia bushes and freshly cut grass, the scent was pure Georgian summer night.

It was a cicada year, a fact she'd overheard from Quinn. The bugs' erratic and crackling song filled the surrounding forests. She might have enjoyed the symphony on any other occasion, but not now, when she was about to throw herself into a group of men who'd only view her as a toy. A sexual plaything.

She shivered. Once she and Willyn entered the sprawling mansion, they had to be confident and alert. Coy, flirtatious, and oozing the promise of kinky sex. But still alert.

At least two of the men waiting inside were willing, even eager, to take innocent lives. The twisted sort of individuals who enjoyed watching people suffer. They would blend with the others at the gathering, hiding their sordid practices behind wealth, extravagance, and sparkling glasses of Cristal.

With one hand on the doorknob, Willyn paused to look at Kylie. "Are you ready?"

Smoothing her bodice and tossing back a sweep of copper-hued hair, Kylie channeled calm on the inside. "How's my lip gloss?"

Willyn cocked a brow. "Rich and shiny."

"Good." Kylie nodded at the door that would lead them to a secret world of sin and debauchery. "Then let's go."

Gliding with both stealth and seductive strides, they stayed a safe distance behind the line of Ms. Mure's women, not wanting the working girls to notice two stragglers hitching up to the end of the train.

They passed through a room with a pool table and oversized media center. Through another door, and the clatter of multiple high heels on marble echoed through a stairwell as they climbed.

Kylie and Willyn could lose themselves amongst the guests as soon as they made it to the party. Then they could search for either Cutter or Dalton. Or both.

At the top, she and Willyn waited a few minutes to allow the other women to disperse. When she eased the door open, she didn't hear the typical social gathering sounds. No laughter or boisterous conversations.

There was music, however; low and ominous, a dark mix of industrial gothic, the bass pulsing a sinful heartbeat through the space. The lights were dim, and candles flickered around the rooms. The flames danced on tables, across a fireplace mantle, and were scattered amongst the ceiling-high bookshelves.

A slick, provocative aura clung to the mansion. Lust and carnality were the only discernible scents.

Already some of the other women had paired off with men. Sometimes one female with two men, or the reverse. One of Ms. Mure's girls was climbing on top of a gleaming black piano with a man's assistance. She was naked from the waist up.

Kylie froze mid-step as Willyn sidled up to stand with her. She cast a glance to her friend. "Keg parties have got nothing on this."

Willyn flinched when she spotted a couple engaging in foreplay on a sofa. She steered her eyes from the lurid display and gulped. "Why aren't the men wearing masks?"

Surveying several different faces, Kylie gave a discreet shrug. "At least Cutter and Dalton won't be able to argue mistaken identity."

As if on cue, she spotted a tall man with an expensive-looking haircut and a stride that told the world he thought himself superior. She nudged Willyn. "There's Dalton."

Keeping in close proximity to each other but without drawing attention to themselves, the witches followed him through the music room. They ignored the piano-top striptease, in addition to the crowd of men watching, the intense silence more disturbing than if they'd been whistling and calling out encouragement.

Eyes forward. Don't lose Dalton. Kylie trailed behind the lawyer until he walked between two white columns and into a spacious parlor. Intricate black railings lined balconies above.

More male-female couplings were overhead, a few absorbed in hushed discussions. Others engaged in more carnal interactions.

A man approached and pushed past Kylie to latch onto Willyn's shoulder. "I want to talk."

Kylie wanted to knock the offending man's grip away from her friend, but Willyn's soft voice handled the brute efficiently enough. "I'm sorry. I'm expected elsewhere." She lifted a finger, pointing to a man sitting in a dim alcove. "He's just there if you'd care to negotiate."

The bothersome man looked over, as did Kylie. *Cutter.* The man sitting alone had medium brown hair and no distinguishing characteristics, but he held his head at an odd tilt.

Just as he had in his picture.

The man removed his hand from Willyn. Grumbling something unintelligible, he tromped past them. Willyn relaxed her shoulders.

Putting a hand to her stomach, Kylie breathed out. "That was close. But good catch on Cutter. Maybe we can get in good with him before Dalton sees him." The lawyer had veered in a different direction, giving them the opportunity to intercept Cutter first.

"I just want this to be over." Willyn's expression was grim.

Kylie agreed. Hopefully the sex-party participants would cordon off their activities with closed doors or pulled curtains.

Or not. As Kylie and Willyn watched, a man thrust one of the masked women against a table and took full advantage of her facedown position.

"Not looking," she said to herself as much as Willyn. "Come on. Let's do this thing."

Channeling a predatory vixen, she conjured up a seductive smile and swaggered toward the solitary Cutter. When she drew closer, he lifted his head, his distant stare traveling quickly over her and beyond.

Then his dark eyes slammed back to Kylie's face.

Relief swept through her. *Hook successfully inserted. Now reel.*

A leer crawled its way from one corner of his mouth to the other. He didn't speak as she walked to him, only nodded slowly and lifted one hand to wave her closer.

Triumph and disgust warred within her, but embracing the role for all she was worth, Kylie took the last few steps and allowed him to pull her down to his lap. With a throaty laugh, she said, "I hate to see you sitting over here all by yourself." Her tone was soft but laced with innuendo.

She sensed Willyn slipping into the corner of the alcove. Her friend blended into the shadows, wisely removing herself as a possible distraction.

Cutter looked Kylie up and down. "*You* are exactly what I came here for." His hand slithered over the curve of her backside and down to her thigh, where he squeezed a little too hard before finally settling on her hip.

"I've got business to take care of," he leaned in and sniffed her cleavage, "but as soon as it's done, we can get to know each other properly."

Kylie kept her lids hooded as if aroused and pursed her lips in a way she hoped came across as flirty. Whatever she had to do to hide the repugnance crowding her throat. Knowledge of Cutter's crimes crawled through her veins like slime.

But if sitting on his lap and feigning interest helped lock his ass up—far away from adolescent girls—she could deal with roaming hands and lewd propositions.

The psycho was busy trailing his finger down her stockinged leg when someone cleared his throat. Cutter's head snapped up with a jerk.

Kylie remained calm, lifting her eyes in a leisurely manner until they fell upon a distinguished man with silver hair.

"Shall we remove ourselves from the main floor?" Dalton Morne lifted one imperious brow as he looked down on Cutter. He adjusted a cufflink and gazed at both of them with disgust.

"I think here's good," Cutter said. The amusement in his stare had disappeared, leaving only cold calculation. The killer had revealed himself.

And Kylie was in his lap.

"Fine." Dalton sniffed. He tried once more to assume the position of command. "Get rid of the girl."

Cutter rubbed a hand over her thigh again before slipping it between her crossed legs.

Her throat quivered beneath her tongue, but she forced down the urge to gag. Leaning into him, she breathed suggestively near the repulsive man's neck. Then wiggled against him for good measure.

She felt his member rise beneath her. Along with her gorge.

"She stays," Cutter rasped. Her little lap dance had paid off. "I agreed to do a job for you. That's all." The murderer-for-hire stared boldly at Dalton. "But outside of that, you don't tell me what to do."

Cole's low voice came through the tiny bud in her ear, the first time he'd spoken. "Doing good."

Kylie almost answered but caught herself. She lasered her eyes to the floor and sat completely still. No noise, movement, or any indication she was paying attention to the two men and their byplay.

Blowing air through bitterly thin lips, Dalton pulled a folded white envelope from the pocket of his gray pants. "Payment. Along with the details of what will be required. The symbol and its application to the skin must be followed precisely."

The lawyer leaned down and pressed the envelope into Cutter's free hand. "And trust in this—we will know if you don't do it right."

Cutter still wasn't intimidated. He inclined his head in agreement and put the envelope in his own pocket.

"Targets and manner of demise are up to you," Dalton said, standing to his full height, "but we prefer females."

The killer beneath Kylie cut his eyes in her direction. "So do I, friend." His hand crawled northward. "So do I."

Okay, Kylie thought, that envelope had to be an "overt act," but still, she would wait for word from Cole. She couldn't blow this.

The grimy fingers moved higher on her thigh.

But neither could she let this maniac feel her up with a member of the Amara standing there watching.

Kylie was deciding how to play it when Cole's voice came through the transmitter. Just in time. "We're on our way in. Try to get clear of the targets."

She shifted and began to swing her legs to the floor, but Cutter's fingers dug into her hip. His grip held her in place as five points of pain shot into her flesh. "Where are you going? I'm not done with you. Not by a long shot." His tongue rolled over his top lip.

Swallowing to hide her revulsion, Kylie simpered, "Just to make a few preparations. I promise this will be a night you'll never forget." *The night your ass gets thrown in jail, you sick freak.*

She drew a fingernail up the side of his neck and under his chin. "I know exactly what you need."

Now he sucked his bottom lip between his teeth and pulled her down against his erection.

A sliver of electric heat arced in her palm. She'd better get away from him. Now. Because she was fully charged and would love to scorch Cutter's demented balls off.

Gaining her feet, she winked at the unsuspecting man who clearly wanted to do vile things to her. Then she grinned. Because he was the only one who'd be on the wrong side of a cavity search this night.

She'd barely taken a backward step when a hand grabbed her arm and clamped down like a vise. She was yanked around.

Uh-oh. She knew that rat face. Ms. Mure, the only person at the club meeting who could cause Kylie and Willyn real trouble. And it looked like that was her plan.

The irate woman spoke aside to a muscle-bound man in a

stereotypical bouncer uniform of all black. "Get that one there." She sneered in Willyn's direction.

Then her beady eyes swung back to Kylie. "Who the hell are you?"

2

Cutter stood and angled his head in that strange way again before encircling Kylie's wrist with his fingers. "She's with me."

He and the angry madam clashed eyes, both of them now wrestling over Kylie like property they were claiming. And she'd had enough of the manhandling. She sent a small but painful shock of electricity into each of them, and they both let go. Ms. Mure with a surprised gasp and Cutter with an uttered, "Fuck."

Kylie took the opportunity to retreat and crossed her arms over her chest. "Too much static, I guess." She hardened her features. "You probably shouldn't touch me again."

Dalton Morne finally took a good, long look at her face behind the mask. After a stunned pause while his mouth hung open, the lawyer's features contorted and his pampered skin flushed the color of beets. "You!" The single word exploded from his lips, recognition and accusation all at once.

Cutter swiveled his gaze between Kylie and Dalton, sizing up the situation. "What is this?"

The scene was deteriorating from precarious to shitstorm, so Kylie moved farther away, this time looking over her shoulder to locate Willyn. The beefy security guard had both of his hands on the coven's healer.

Speaking clearly and directly to the man, Kylie warned him with her stare. "You should let her go now." His brows knit with confusion, but Ms. Mure shot out the order for him to stay put.

Another glance at Kylie seemed to make up his addled mind. He dropped his hands from Willyn and stammered, "What the—" He edged to one side and gave the group a wide berth, not taking his eyes off Kylie.

She silently cheered herself. *I must have one hell of a game face.*

Her moment of triumph was cut short. A hand clenched around the front of her throat and hauled her in. Her back slammed into Cutter's chest, and she felt a thin, cold edge of pressure on her neck.

The man's given name was grossly appropriate. Cutter had a knife to her throat.

Shock came first with fear close on its heels, but those emotions were only reactionary. Reflexive. Nothing compared to the sizzling heat that rolled from her gut and radiated outward, priming her every cell.

Magic raced faster than adrenaline and came much more readily. This witch was done playing nice.

Her telekinetic powers weren't nearly as good as Viv's, but disgust and rage were exceptional amplifiers. Closing her eyes, she focused on the blade being forced against her flesh. She visualized an empty corner of the room and transformed the heat into pure energy.

A jolt of lightning just for Cutter, then a push from magic to send the knife hurtling against the wall.

The killer let go of her, shaking his hand and staring at the scorch mark on his palm. "What the fuck did you do?" His dark eyes were wild now, darting from Kylie to Dalton. Then his mouth twisted into an ugly line as two cops dressed as waiters rushed in with guns drawn.

Still holding his injured hand, Cutter shrieked like a madman and bolted. One of the cops easily took him down while the other pointed his weapon at Dalton.

The lawyer turned vengeful eyes on Kylie and seethed, his jaw working with restrained fury. "She won't let this pass."

Kylie didn't ask who *she* was. She didn't need to. The lawyer spoke of the merciless witch he served, and yes, Ronja would be royally pissed off by the coven's interference.

Never one at a loss for words, Kylie gave him a succinct and heartfelt response. "Well, *she* can just suck it." Hate for the Nordic witch blasted the underside of Kylie's skull.

Dalton vacillated between a snarl and a smile, like his lips were having a seizure. "Stupid, stupid little girl. You can't even control your own powers. You'll never beat us. *Never*."

"Whatevs, grandpa." Breathing in through her nose, Kylie turned and went to stand with Willyn.

Her friend only frowned, rushing over to pull Kylie into the corner with her. "Kylie, cool it."

"Why? I'm sure Dalton's probably heard a lot worse."

"Not that," Willyn said in a strained whisper. "Your eyes are sparking. Calm down before you give everybody in here a light show you can't explain."

"What?" Bowing her head, Kylie let the red wig fall forward to cover the sides of her face. "But I don't feel anything."

Commotion arose from the front of the house. The cavalry had arrived. Stealing a peek around Kylie, Willyn said, "Cole and Trevor are here with more men."

"Then let's get out of here."

"Okay. I'll ask them if we need to do anything else." Willyn left her in the shadows.

Sparking eyes? Was that what Dalton had meant when he'd said she couldn't control her own powers?

A trickle of unease began to flow. Then her body trembled as understanding became a rushing tide. *No. It can't be my turn. Quinn still can't stand me.*

As the police moved in to arrest Dalton and Cutter, the rest of the crowd gladly disbanded to other rooms in the mansion. But the bouncer who'd held onto Willyn remained.

Kylie dared a glance at the man and found him studying her.

"Unless you want to go downtown with us, you need to leave." Trevor stepped between the man and Kylie, cutting into his line of sight. Willyn returned to her side as well, concern wrinkling her forehead.

"But her eyes, man. I just wanted to see." The bouncer tried to sidestep Trevor. Big mistake, since the only one in the room who could out-muscle him was the cop getting ready to hammer him down.

When Trevor put a hand on the guy's chest and said, "Now," the bouncer's tone morphed to that of a whiny teenager. "I didn't do nothin' wrong. But I saw—"

"You have something you want to report?" Cole joined Trevor, providing more coverage for the two witches. "Because if you do, we'll need to take an official statement. Down at The Barracks."

The mention of the police station in downtown Savannah cooled the man's interest. "No. No. I didn't see nothin'." He shot a worried look to Dalton and Cutter, both now in handcuffs, before spinning around to make a beeline from the room.

Willyn spoke quietly to the detectives. "Can we leave now?" She jerked her head to Kylie. "If not," she added meaningfully, "we uh . . . need to get some air. And some privacy."

Cole and Trevor were both used to the complexities of dating witches. They didn't need to be asked twice. "We can get your statements later," Cole said quickly.

Cocking one side of his mouth, Trevor added, "Yeah. Go ahead. We know where you live."

~~~

Kylie closed the car door and made her way through the

garage, trying to ignore the tingling beneath her skin. She and Willyn were both humming with post-crisis energy and untapped magic.

But the underlying current that zigzagged inside Kylie was a worry. It was impatient, demanding. Desperate for release.

Outside the night was calm, so she let the peace envelop her. The river curving around the back flowed seamlessly, its surface smooth and tranquil. Waters that were olive during the day gleamed a dark onyx in the sun's absence, and golden cones of manmade light stretched across green lawns.

They'd returned to the mainland house, the one Anna and Quinn St. Germaine had inherited upon the death of their parents. It had become a secondary base camp and was being used as such until the island mansion was fully secured again.

Three of the coven's most trusted friends—extended family, really—lived in and maintained the elegant two stories. The outside was frosted in pale lemon stucco, and all of their cars were housed in the matching garages.

Willyn, along with her husband and son, had temporarily relocated to the yellow house until the wards on the island could be repaired. Everyone agreed the small boy should reside where the magical security system was still intact.

Dare met Willyn when she walked into the kitchen, taking her in his arms and giving her a big I'm-glad-you're-home-safe kiss. Six-year-old Tadd, however, was already fast asleep upstairs. "How'd it go?" Dare ran his hand over his wife's shoulder-length blonde hair as if happy to see it back to normal.

"More smoothly than I would have predicted." The coven's healer shot a glance to Kylie. "With a few unexpected twists."

Kylie dropped her purse to the floor, long copper curls spilling from the bag. She too was relieved to be back to her usual self. "Just a short in the circuits," she told Dare, patting his arm as she passed. "I just threw off a few sparks. No biggie."

A light burned beneath the hood of the range, and she

spotted a serving tray covered by plastic wrap. *Score!* Opening the refrigerator, she grabbed some milk to go with whatever baked goodies Claire had left out.

No need to see what was under the cellophane. If it was in Claire's kitchen, it was guaranteed to be a slice of epicurean heaven.

Pulling up one corner, she slipped a hand under to retrieve one of the scones. After a bite, she closed her eyes and sighed. Orange-cranberry. One of her favorites.

"Leave me a few of those for my breakfast, girl."

Kylie's eyes flicked open as Joe smiled from the doorway, resplendent in a royal blue house robe. "Look at you." She grinned and took another bite of her midnight treat. "Pretty fancy for lounging around the house."

Rubbing his hand down the soft material, Joe winked. "Birthday present from Claire. I might not have picked it myself, but the old girl gets a thrill out of seeing me in it." He strolled over to the counter and stole a scone for himself. "And I'd wear red feathers if it put that special twinkle in her eye."

Kylie choked a little, then coughed to clear her windpipe. "Joe. What's gotten into you?"

He simply looked out at the night-laden river with a sly lift of his lips.

"Joe." Claire stepped into the kitchen and turned on the overhead light.

Now it was the older man's turn to cough. "There's my sweetheart."

"Mm-hm." The woman of the mainland house—and the boss of this kitchen—strolled to her husband and took the scone from his hand. Without another word, she retrieved a small plate from the cabinet, placed the pastry on top, and handed it back.

Joe grinned. "Thank you, darlin'. Must have slipped my mind."

With one cocked brow, Claire turned to Kylie who scrambled to the open cabinet and got a plate for herself. "Yes, ma'am."

"Now." Claire chucked Kylie under the chin before echoing Dare's earlier question. "How'd it go?"

"They're both going to jail tonight." Kylie leaned against the counter. "Dalton was caught red-handed paying Cutter off. He even gave him written instructions." She shook her head. "His association with Ronja must have made him feel invincible, but he's tied up with human law and regulations now."

Dare and Willyn took seats at the center island, a rectangle of creamy quartz. "Even if he makes bail, he'll be too busy trying to save his own ass to be much use to Ronja." Dare sent a sheepish glance toward Claire. "Sorry. Covering his butt."

"That imagery isn't much better," Claire said, her cheeks lifting in a smile despite her remonstration.

"Where's Joseph?" Kylie asked as the couple's son entered her thoughts.

"Sleeping," Joe groused. "If I didn't know any better, I'd say he's getting old. He conveniently skipped from adolescence straight to his golden years."

Claire made a *tsk* sound and gave her husband a soft elbow to the ribs. "Joseph drove straight through last night and all day today." Her gaze shifted to Kylie. "He went to visit Sylvie. Can only keep himself from that girl for so long, it seems."

That girl, Kylie thought, had once been thick as honey with the Amara crew. After a bad childhood and a potent gift of true hoodoo power, Sylvie had been ripe for Ronja's picking. Hurt, filled with magic, and angry at the world, the young priestess had done her best to help destroy the coven.

Then she'd met Joseph, and their love had healed deep and myriad wounds, both past and present. But Sylvie's new alliance with the coven remained shaky.

"She's still in hiding with her grandmother?" Kylie reached for another scone, pausing to receive Claire's go-ahead.

"She is. Best place for her until this is all over. Ronja doesn't take betrayal lightly." Claire refilled Kylie's milk glass and tilted her head to study the youngest of the witches. "You feeling all right, sugar? You look . . . different."

"How are my eyes?" she asked, fearing the tiny streaks of lighting had returned.

"Still bright and clear." Claire clucked her tongue. "But the sooner you wash off all that makeup, the better. Makes you look older than you are."

Toying with her pastry, Kylie's voice turned sad as her thoughts drifted to another person. The one who always called her young, immature—a brat. "Then maybe I should keep it."

"You're just fine the way you are." Claire patted her hand. "Just fine."

They heard the front door open and heavy steps resonating through the house. Kylie's gut clenched up, and she lost all taste for the sweet orange and cranberry flavor. She knew his sound, could feel his very presence. Somehow, she always sensed when he was near.

Keeping her head down and eyes on her plate, she didn't see Quinn come into the room. But his voice struck through her center when he said, "Hey," to the gathering.

"Cole and Trevor with you?" Dare asked. Like Quinn, he had brown hair, but his coloring was darker, deeper, and his eyes were ocean blue with fathoms beneath.

Whereas Quinn's held the allure of sapphires. Just like his sister's.

"They're going to be a while. Sent me on ahead." The rustle of his pants told Kylie he was heading to the refrigerator. She heard the door open and close. *Stop being such a coward. He's just a man.*

Feeling foolish, she allowed her stare to travel upward. Her eyes slammed into his and heat suffused her cheeks. Her body.

Yeah. Sure. Just a man.

But the only one who could reach straight in and twist up her heart with a single glance.

He held her gaze. "We can head out to the island whenever you're ready."

Why was he talking to her? She swiveled her head to Willyn, and then remembered her friend would be staying here overnight. With Dare and Tadd.

Kylie and Quinn were traveling back to the island home. Just the two of them. Alone.

A situation they usually did their best to avoid.

"I'm ready." Might as well get it over with. "Just let me put this away." She started to clean the plate, but Claire took it and gave her shoulder a little push. "You g'wan now. I've got this."

Great. No reprieve to be found. No help at all. "Good night and thanks for the scones," Kylie muttered.

Quinn swung out the side door and made his way down the flagstone path. Kylie grabbed her purse as she eased through the kitchen and nodded to Willyn. "See you tomorrow."

With nothing left to stall their departure, she went out into the muggy summer heat. A motor revved in the distance. Quinn had started the boat.

Silently she climbed aboard after removing the rope looped around a post. Once they were clear, Quinn throttled toward the middle of the channel. A minute passed before they were in open water.

Another five, and the flat silhouette of the island came into view. Then the moon ducked behind thick clouds, blotting out all visibility.

Neither of them said a word, honoring a previous agreement to be silently irritated with each other. Which was still better than the alternative.

Whenever they spoke, they argued. When they argued, things heated up. And that heat only ever went one way.

Sexual combustion. The kind they both pretended didn't exist.

Kylie had embraced their natural chemistry before, but the demeaning refusal she'd gotten in return had been too painful. The rejection had knocked her down. Now, stone by stone, she was trying to reconstruct her confidence.

So far, she'd managed a haphazard, crack-filled foundation. Because she just didn't know how to rebuild around a broken heart.

Eventually the boat motored to another pier, this one on the island beach. Quinn made quick work of shutting off the engine and mooring the boat.

Balancing as she took cautious steps, Kylie noted the rough waves crashing against the coast. Had a storm come through? Was one on the way?

Quinn was waiting when she got ready to disembark. He held out his hand. "Come on. It's rough tonight."

You have no idea. He was especially handsome in the dark. All lean muscles and quiet strength. No moon in his eyes tonight, though. Only angry clouds.

She couldn't take his hand. Couldn't stand the heat that always struck deep to her core, making her feel safe and aroused all at once. She was already too amped up.

"Just take my hand, Kylie." He'd read her hesitation for what it was, and the reminder of their strained relationship spurred his annoyance.

Reaching for him, she clamped her fingers around his, but as soon as their skin met, he jerked away from her. "Ow! Damn it!" His look was scathing. "I told you not to use your magic on me."

With the wind kicking up and blowing hair in her face, Kylie chose to jump to the dock before she fell between hard wood and crushing boat. She landed cleanly. "I didn't."

"You shocked the hell out of me by accident?" His brows were scrunched together, his mouth tight.

"I—" She broke off when a searing yellow streak leapt from her hand toward Quinn. Tucking her palm against her stomach, she shook her head. "I didn't. I promise."

Another bolt materialized from the air above, striking between her feet and splintering into tiny white cracks of energy that shimmered into the planks. More roiling clouds barreled in from the east.

Lightning didn't frighten Kylie. Though deadly to most, the strikes caused no pain. No injury. Not to her.

Electricity was her life force. Her special gift.

But she'd never been the center of an uncontrollable, miniature storm.

Magic sparked from her body now, moving toward the water, the wooden pier, and the beach beyond. It flew into the sky and from the clouds, shooting in both directions. The essence of her power was communing with the thunderheads.

The blistering flashes of pure energy didn't have her quaking where she stood. Her trembling hands and heaving breaths were a response to something far more dangerous to her well-being.

Another crack split through her poorly-constructed foundation when her gaze clashed with Quinn's. His eyes filled with recognition, understanding. He knew what the phenomenon meant.

She had to speak before he could cut her down with whatever words were forming in his head. "Quinn." She held out her hands, harnessing the bolts, channeling them into her as they struck again and again. "My trial is starting."

He nodded tightly. And gulped.

She couldn't stay here any longer. "I'm going to the house." Her little tempest was fading, now that she'd opened herself up and accepted her fate. Her calling. Her prophesied challenge.

But considerable damage had been done, and not by the power that pounded from the sky. She couldn't stay with Quinn, because the expression on his face was a dagger to the heart.

Her trial had arrived, and it was her turn to face the Amara. To succeed in her own unique quest. And as destiny decreed—to fall in love.

Quinn knew the prophecy better than anyone. He knew its pattern. That's why Kylie had to run. Why she couldn't bear to see his reaction.

Because there was no doubt that her time had arrived.

And he was terrified.

3

Ronja was in her favorite room in the old plantation home. The walls were papered in fierce blue with dark wood shelves holding her most-treasured books and implements. Many so old, they would be classified as artifacts in today's society.

The art here was her preference as well, featuring elements that were wild, rough, and pitiless. Just as she was. Gilt frames showcased craggy landscapes, imposing cliffs, and the cold bitter seas of her homeland. She felt more at ease in this one room than anywhere else in the sultry city of Savannah.

How she hated the bright sun and tiny bugs that thrived in this wet, marshy place. And the dripping heat that blanketed far too many days out of each lunar year. But this was the place Bastraal had chosen.

And as his servant, Ronja would suffer these mild insults until the night of his full return. Not much longer, yet not soon enough.

She growled low, drawing the attention of the woman next to her. "Keep working," she spat when Scarlett stopped stirring the cauldron. Yes, the black iron pot was a cliché from more recent history featuring those tree-hugging Wiccans, but even a powerful seiðr like her could begrudgingly admit the vessel's usefulness.

Her mood was particularly caustic tonight, as she had yet to hear from her lawyer. She'd expected a report from him hours ago. And no one was ever foolish enough to keep her waiting. Particularly humans.

"I think we've almost got it." Scarlett lifted a small piece of metal, the hardened chunk pulsing slowly with a brilliant blue essence.

A vicious and greedy excitement shot to Ronja's chest as she inclined her head. "Do it."

With a clenched grin, her lover dropped the metal bit into the thick brown muck that simmered in the cauldron. Half-immersed, the metal's blue light began flickering erratically, as if it could feel the mystical attack. As if afraid for its non-existent life.

The dark mixture surrounded the piece, but no matter how much of their potion engulfed the metal, the blue luminescence persisted. "It *is* dimmer than before," Scarlett said. She slid her eyes to Ronja, and the Nordic witch thrilled to see the fear living there.

"Better each time," she allowed, stroking her hand down Scarlett's back. Perhaps she could find a way to occupy the hours after all.

Ronja eyed the high collar of the other woman's pale yellow blouse, style circa 1920. Her Scarlett had a thing for that era, and since Ronja deigned to share her demon-laced blood with the former saloon girl, they both enjoyed the benefits of immortality. They had decades of various fashion to recall, if they so chose. Decades to pleasure each other.

And once Bastraal assumed a human form . . . they would own eternity.

Scarlett put her hand to the top button. "Why do I feel like your mind has shifted from magic to something a little more recre—"

The door opened abruptly, interrupting their conversation. Carson rushed in. "Ronja." The blonde Amazon wore brown, nondescript clothing, and her hair was in its perpetually-matted tangle.

Directing her fury at the intrusion, Ronja sneered and gave Carson a quick head-to-toe. Disgusting. "Must you always appear to have just crawled from beneath a rock?" Beside her, Scarlett snickered.

"You didn't save me because you liked my looks." Carson closed the door solidly behind her. "And I have news you'll want to hear. Dalton just called."

"What do you mean? Why didn't he speak with me? I've been waiting for hours!" She threw her hand back and struck Scarlett across the face, the closest available punching bag.

The barest yelp erupted from the redhead's mouth, but she wisely stepped away and covered her bleeding lip.

"He didn't have time." Carson's muscles flexed. From agitation? Fear?

What was she afraid of saying? Ronja stalked closer. "Tell me."

"He was calling from jail. He's been arrested. The cops." Here Carson swallowed loudly. "The ones who are with the coven. They were there with a couple of the witches. They busted him after he hired that Cutter guy."

Rage burst from behind Ronja's eyes and rushed throughout her shaking body. "And exactly when does he think he'll be returning?" *So I can twist each of his joints until they pop like the bones of a dove.*

"He said he didn't know, but they're holding him." Carson visibly braced herself. "He might not be back at all."

Ronja's roar shook her cherished paintings and the walls on which they hung. "I am surrounded by fools and failures!" This time she sent her wrath into the barren fireplace. Though completely empty, the hearth erupted with blood-red flames.

"Damn them!" She aimed for the bookshelves but held back, drawing the burning need to destroy into the center of her chest where it whirled and churned with discontent. "This insult will be answered. I can promise that." Her need for revenge smoldered.

"How hard can it be to find one man who enjoys killing women? As far as I can tell, there's at least one in every bunch!" She whirled to face Scarlett and was brought up short to find her cowering in the corner behind the table.

Ronja crooked her hand and summoned. "Come here. I have spent most of my anger. Don't fear me."

She spread her fingers, focusing her magic on yellow organza. Invisible forces gripped the front of Scarlett's shirt, pulling her forward smoothly, as if the floors weren't wood but slickened ice.

When the other witch was mere inches away, Ronja spoke. Her voice was firm but laced with apology as she stroked a thumb over Scarlett's bottom lip. "Quiet now. Don't fear me."

Trembling, Scarlett nodded. Few understood the extent of Ronja's power, but her female lover was one of them.

When employing her full strength, Ronja could tear through stone with her mind. But she didn't dare waste those stores of power. Not yet.

She was saving it all for that St. Germaine bitch. Anna, descendant of the three who'd banished Bastraal centuries before. Anna, leader of the coven bent on defeating the demon again, along with Ronja and the small army of supernaturals she'd amassed over the years.

Anna. The same simpering, mewling witch who was surely behind Dalton's arrest. Ronja ground her fingers together, and the iron cauldron crumpled before her. Noxious brown fluid broke free, oozing across the table.

The coven had managed to strike a blow. One Ronja had never seen coming. *Very clever.*

She stared as the concoction dripped to the floor. The loss of Dalton Morne would slow her down. The man had been useful, but still, he was only that. A man. A mortal.

And those could always be replaced.

Ronja stroked Scarlett's ruby-hued curls and allowed the rising scent of rose shampoo to lull her. Her temper could be damaging, and she chastised herself for lashing out at her own possessions. Especially the woman who'd been with her for so very long.

Eventually she calmed, and after a deep breath, she stared past Scarlett to Carson. "I would have preferred to offer our master a few more souls to feed on, but now that Bastraal is here in this realm, spirits are no longer required."

Tossing long blonde hair over her shoulder, she released Scarlett and began to pace. "We might be delayed, but we can and *will* find another murderer to set loose on this city. Injury to poor, little humans just drives those witches crazy."

She laughed lightly, staring up at a depiction of a ship adrift on a violent sea. "And I do enjoy the double blow. Innocents suffer, so the coven suffers." She opened her hands in query when she angled toward Carson again. "What could be better?"

Carson didn't speak, simply nodded.

Smart girl. What the Amazon had said before was true. Ronja hadn't pulled her from the jungle as a child because she was pretty, but because she'd demonstrated ingenuity and the desire to survive.

Even at three years of age, Carson had been teeming with unnatural strength, deceptive wiles, and a brutal lack of compassion.

And she'd liked to bite. Ronja had adored her instantly.

She pointed a finger at Carson. "We have no time to waste on Dalton. He's on his own."

Pleased with the path her new plans were taking, Ronja wandered back to Scarlett. She owed her friend and companion an apology. Leaning forward gently, so as not to startle, she placed a contrite kiss on her lover's mouth.

She tasted the blood. And the fear.

And was suddenly feeling much better.

When she spoke, however, her words were sharp. "I'm entrusting you with a crucial task, Carson. I expect you to get me exactly what I need." Still caressing Scarlett's hair, she threw out an order for the Amazonian warrior.

"Find me a new lawyer."

4

Quinn tore his eyes away from the curvy script on the pages and rubbed the center of his forehead. The documents laid out before him were ancient, of yellowed paper and hand-scribbled writing from darker ages. Yet they looked right at home atop the salvaged wood plank he'd fashioned into a desk.

Even in the full light of his desk lamp, the crinkled material and faded letters made for an especially arduous translation. On top of that, he had to pick apart the antiquated language for magic spells that would not only repair, but also reinforce, the wards surrounding the island and the house where he and the coven community resided.

The headache continued to drum in the forefront of his brain, an angry judge's gavel. He needed to take a break and get something to eat.

The sun was little more than a thin orange line on the sea's horizon when he checked the view from his bedroom window. He'd been at this all day, perusing various documents, searching for the critical missing pieces of magic he needed.

Exhaling, he lifted the glass on his desk to his mouth. No water. Bone dry.

Great. He'd have to make a trip downstairs if he wanted some ice. And it was close to dinner, which meant everyone would be gathering for a meal.

Quinn berated himself for actually considering tap water.

He couldn't stand the way the island supply tasted, but right now, the thought of socializing was even worse.

Yes, he had work to do, and the office adjoining his bedroom was the best place for it. But a security overhaul wasn't the only reason he'd been cloistered up here all day.

He was a grown man, a seasoned witch, and had seen far too many horrors in his twenty-six years. Which made it that much harder to admit the unavoidable truth.

He was hiding.

From a sexy little college coed who sparkled and spit lightning whenever she got cranky. One who—as that pernicious bitch called Fate would have it—fervently believed Quinn was destined to be her soul mate. No matter how he'd tried to disavow the notion.

He pushed away from his desk with a grunt. *Lust due to proximity and convenience. That's all she's feeling.* He was just the only guy around who was near Kylie's age, and it wasn't like he hadn't taken a few long, hard looks at her now and then.

Proximity. Lust. And a tight little body he just couldn't stop—

Enough! His fist met the wood of his desk with a thud. What he really needed to be working on was a charm to protect himself from her alluring female attributes. And they were . . . *many.*

Unfortunately, as Kylie was now well aware, the physical attraction went both ways. It was hard enough to fight his desire, but when she answered with her own, tossing herself and his libido back in his face like she had in her room that night . . .

That night. He closed his eyes. When she'd come sauntering toward him, hazel eyes alight with inner vitality and seductive power.

A groan rolled from his gut. *Goddess, give me strength.*

At times the need was almost painful, and he couldn't help

wondering if it was the same for her.

Quinn understood her youthful yet misguided illusion of romance. He really did. And it certainly didn't help matters that the rest of the coven women were falling in line one by one. Like a bunch of remote-controlled Stepford witches.

But other than his backing them up and serving as all-around assistant, Kylie's foray into love had nothing to do with Quinn. Nothing. And he'd remind her of that fact every day if he had to.

Now was go-time. Her trial was here. And wasting any more effort on him was simply not to her advantage. Or the coven's.

Rising from his chair, he stretched his arms above his head and crossed the spacious room to a wall of bookshelves. There was a huge library on the main level, but he preferred his own private collection.

His chamber was a place of solitude, and most importantly, it belonged solely to him. His belongings. His rules. The only respite left to him on an island gone mad.

And a space apart from the St. Germaine prophecy.

His eyes traveled over a few of his favorite possessions. On one wall hung the shiny medieval sword he'd bought himself with one year's birthday money, unaware it was a reproduction.

Beside it was the grittier and damaged—but authentic—version. He'd eventually acquired it via the Internet. Once he'd understood the difference.

Scattered here and there were bottles passed down from his forebears, forged by hand and used for magic. Most were in the tower, once again being used for spell casting, but these few he'd taken for himself. A reminder of what had gone before, and what was still to come.

He fought to preserve the future, not only for him and his, but for so many others. The ones who had no clue what transpired around them, or what lurked in Savannah's shadows.

Monsters.

So he would fight to end them, and he would battle for the things that mattered. Life, light, and . . . Quinn frowned. Here is where his sister would add the word "love," but he'd prefer to skip that one for now.

He returned his mind to his treasures. Especially what was there, in the corner. His most cherished possession. Of course, it was a book. The great atlas his father had given him rested atop a pedestal bookstand.

They simply didn't make such weighty hardcovers anymore. The 16x14 inch pages were voluminous, and to a child dreaming of adventure, they'd offered the world in more ways than one.

A heavy knock shook his door, jarring him from pleasant reflection. What now? The madness out there just couldn't let him be. Not for one blessed day.

Before calling out for admittance, he grabbed a random book without reading the spine and opened it. He could pretend to be engrossed, too busy to engage. Depending on who was out there.

Am I really so afraid to face her? Nothing has changed. His fingers tightened on the pages. *Except the ticking clock. That part's new.*

Kylie had until the end of her trial to figure it all out. And come what may, she would have to relent. Soon, she'd have no choice but to give up on Quinn for good.

Until then, he would escape by burying himself in work. It was a solid plan, and his very-male id felt absolutely no shame. Kylie might not be scary, exactly, but what she represented left him chilled through and through.

Accepting her love would mean giving up on himself.

And that was the reality that kept him up nights. The thought of the chains, all those chains, was like having his spine drilled. Nice little holes where he could be hooked up and winched down.

A cool sweat formed across his brow. *No. I can't do it.* Even if the one cranking the winch looked and smelled as sweet as Kylie.

The door rattled from pounding this time. "Come in," he answered, his voice an octave deeper than usual. He cleared his throat and scowled for the benefit of whoever was invading his space.

Ethan breezed in with a broad but wary grin. "I've been sent to make sure you're still alive and kicking. Mrs. Attinger is worried you'll waste away in the space of five hours if you don't have sustenance."

With black hair falling to his collar and eyes the color of charred coal, Ethan Drake wore his newfound good humor well. Happiness suited him, as did his partnership with a good woman. Love was Ethan's long overdue reward, and it had been delivered by one very determined Spanish witch.

Once Ethan had allowed himself to fall for Lucia, their devotion had released him from a lifelong curse. Quinn was glad to see his friend free from the constant, nagging worry that had plagued him since childhood.

But still, he would rather be alone right now. So he could agonize in peace.

Ethan indicated the book in Quinn's hands. "You still neck-deep in magic recipes, or is that one of your adventure books? Submarines and an antique Colt automatic?"

Quinn looked down. He held a volume that revealed the secrets of Heka, Egypt's ancient form of mysticism. But at the mention of guns and deep-sea heroics, he glanced at the section of shelves that held his Cussler novels.

He flashed into the past, to all the stories and schemes he'd discussed with his friend when they'd shared a college dorm room. The memories felt like so long ago, and with them came a quick thrill, a sweet nostalgia.

Then Quinn thought of Kylie. The muscles running down his neck and over his shoulder ridge clamped down tight. "No weapons or subs. Just research."

Easing the door closed behind him, Ethan stood far across the room. His dark eyes scrutinized. "Yeah, I can tell you've got something formulating in there." He tapped his temple. "So how's it going?"

Quinn shoved the book back into its slot. "What's Mrs. Attinger making for dinner?"

"Okay then." Ethan's brow wrinkled, then smoothed back out. "Some of your favorites, so I'm told. I volunteered to come pull you out of your cave."

A pent-up breath burst from Quinn's lips. "I've been working." He waved a hand at his desk. "Someone's got to fix the wards, or we're wide open for an attack. If the Amara or their demon want back inside this place, they're in." He nailed his friend with a dark look. "Of all people, you should understand what that means."

"All right, all right. Don't chew my ass." Ethan held out placating hands. "Man, you definitely need to eat something."

"And I will." Quinn sighed. "I'll come down and make a plate."

"To bring back up here." The comment was saturated with implication, but Quinn let it pass.

Ethan moved to a wide, comfortable chair of russet leather and plopped down. "So, speaking of adventures, only three witches left to go. And if I know you, you've got a detailed plan to be boots-up afterward."

Propping his feet on the matching ottoman, he crossed them at the ankles and challenged Quinn with a pointed stare. "Where's the first place you want to go? Once the prophecy is fulfilled and you're liberated."

"I have a few ideas."

"Like I said. Always with a plan." Making himself at home, Ethan relaxed and let his head rest against the supple leather. "You'll be able to travel. Like you always talked about. Nothing to tie you down." The air grew heavy when he paused. "Or should I say, no one?"

Quinn glared at his friend, silently pressing his canines into his lower lip. *Et tu, Ethan?* "Nova Scotia," he said with bite. "Or Greenland, maybe. Somewhere cold."

It was Ethan's turn to narrow his eyes. "I hear Kylie's trial has begun."

Quinn said nothing.

"How do you feel about that?"

Keeping his head down, Quinn pretended to scan the bookshelves as if searching for a particular title. "Did you come up here to try to shrink me, Ethan?" Giving up the ruse, he turned back around. "Because the last time I checked, you specialized in demons. Not psychology."

"That's not why I'm here. And you might also remember that before I ever came to the island and long before I met Lucia," Ethan sat up and put his feet on the floor, "before all of that, I was your friend."

Returning to sit behind his desk, Quinn nodded. "You still are. You know you are. Which is why you should understand if I don't want to pick the subject to pieces." His shoulders moved. "You've settled down, and I'm happy for you and Lucia. But you've already been around the world. The only time you ever stayed in one place for any length of time was at Harvard."

Quinn felt small and petulant, but he gave voice to his complaint anyway. "College was the *only* time I got away."

Laughter was a deep rumble in Ethan's chest. "If I remember correctly, you used it well and did plenty during your university days. Like that night we went to see those girls in Concord?"

Quinn's mouth jerked up on one side. "And we woke up in a lighthouse in Maine? The only problem with that trip is I don't remember any of it." He notched his chin up. "Those chicks were scary."

Ethan's grin was roguish. "But they were fun."

"Hmm." Splaying his hand flat across the documents still lying on his desk, Quinn let his gaze fall on the wall behind Ethan. "I had some good times, but even then, I was always on tenterhooks. Waiting for that call. Every time I started to enjoy myself, I had to rein it in, knowing I could get pulled back to Savannah any day."

"But you didn't."

"I'm here now, though, aren't I? Still waiting to be cut loose."

Ethan frowned. "You sound pretty bitter. I've never heard that in you before."

"Not bitter. Frustrated, irritated, agitated. Take your pick. Don't get me wrong. I know what we're doing here is the most important thing." Quinn stared at his hand as it curled into a fist. "Ronja and Bastraal have to be put down once and for all."

"They do."

"And I'm committed to that. I've always known I would serve a purpose and be required to help the coven. I just never expected . . ." Quinn rubbed his fingers on his scalp. The headache was back. "I never expected the other thing."

"That other thing meaning . . . Kylie?"

The only response Ethan got to that was a middle finger.

"She doesn't have a choice in this any more than you do."

"I know. I know." Quinn's already-strained pulse kicked inside his head now. "There's no rationale or argument you can run on me that I haven't already considered myself. I know it's not her fault, but I've been on this island for most of my life. Training, preparing, and . . . just fucking waiting. Being on standby until this prophecy decided to kick into gear."

Unable to stay still, Quinn shoved his chair back and stood. "There are things I want to do too, damn it. I deserve to have something of my own."

Eyeing him for a moment, Ethan finally gave a slow nod. "I get it, man. I do."

Then he lifted a hand. "But look at the other option. Maybe

there's another guy out there for Kylie. Then you'll be off the hook."

That notion didn't make Quinn feel any better. Just as his friend knew it wouldn't. "Screw you, Drake."

"You sure it's me you want to do that to?" Ethan drummed his fingers on his knee and lifted a raven brow. He was one of the few people who would shove the dismal truth in Quinn's face this way. And his friend did it with such panache.

But Quinn refused to talk about Kylie with anyone. Better to let unwanted emotions lie. To let them die. And surely, given enough time, they would.

Closing the book with more force than necessary, Quinn edged around his desk. "Let's just go get some food."

"Yep, yep." Ethan met Quinn halfway across the floor and pounded his shoulder. Mischief enlivened his dark eyes. "I'm just glad I could help put your mind at ease." Ethan grinned. "Let me know the next time you need a little direction."

Quinn shook his head and blocked the smile that threatened. "Asshat."

"Douche." Ethan backed toward the door. "Look, I'm going to head around to get Lucia."

"Sure." Ethan shared the room with his girlfriend on the opposite side of the top floor. And to Quinn's great displeasure, Kylie's was on this side of the mansion. Just down the way from his.

"I'll see you at dinner." Ethan held up a finger. "If you don't show, I'll be back up here to haul you out myself."

"I'm going. I'm going." Quinn shoved his friend the rest of the way out, latching the door behind them. He watched Ethan trot down the corridor and around the corner. With a quirk of his lips, he muttered, "Asshat."

In no real hurry, he took his time, hoping luck held and that Kylie wasn't in the vicinity. She'd be downstairs to eat, and seeing her again was inevitable. He was going to have to deal with her sometime, but in a group was better than one-on-one.

He hadn't laid eyes on her since her little lightning show last night, when he'd watched her expression shift from fear to grief. Because she'd seen his panic.

She's known how I've felt the whole time. Nothing has changed. And maybe if he kept telling himself that—

Quinn came to an abrupt halt when an unmistakable sensation washed over him. Prickling, ominous. The proverbial hairs stood up on the back of his neck like antennae.

He was being watched.

Whirling on the richly-woven carpet, he searched for whoever or whatever was filling him with such sudden apprehension. But no one was there. The hallway was empty.

After a few deep breaths, he began to settle down. Then he rolled his shoulders to chase out the tension.

He'd been hitting the books for too long, so the best idea was to take this overdue break. He'd go to the kitchen if for no other reason than to refuel. And to get rid of the persistent ache in his head.

A throat-scraping hiss sounded abruptly, bringing his attention to the floor. This time his stalker was in plain sight.

Kylie's cat was baring every one of her fangs, and apparently just for his benefit. The feline was the perfect match for Kylie, with long golden hair and a whopping dose of self-worth.

But the botanically-named Sassafras usually greeted him with a purr and a leg bump. He was one of her favorite humans. So what had gotten into her?

Maybe Kylie'd had a late night talk with her medium. Dissing men in general. Or Quinn in particular.

"Easy, Sassy. It's not as bad as all that."

The cat's hiss morphed into a gargling growl.

"All right. It's enough I have to deal with your mistress spitting at me." He carefully sidestepped the irate cat. "But not you too."

5

For as many times as Quinn felt the need to get away from his island home, there were just as many things he knew he would miss. As he walked through the grand hall, he lifted his face to test the air.

Fried chicken? Oh yeah. Mrs. Attinger had pulled out the big guns.

His taste buds jumped to attention as he entered the kitchen to find it in a state of female-dominated chaos. The spry older woman was doing a supervisory dance between the witches providing her assistance.

In her sixties, Mrs. Attinger kept her silver hair cut in a pixie style, reflective of her vibrant personality. Her blue eyes often gleamed with wisdom or rebuke, and when they swung in Quinn's direction, he felt the latter land squarely on his head. She put one hand on her hip, and his chest pinched with guilt.

"There you are. I was wondering if you were ever coming down." She wagged a wooden spoon in his direction. "I don't care how entrenched in those books of yours you get, you still need to eat a decent meal. Whether using your mind or your body, work is work."

Duly chastised, Quinn smiled at the woman who'd been a mother to him since his own had died in an explosion. He and Anna had been orphaned in their early teenage years, and Mrs. Attinger had stepped in to provide care, a strong hand when appropriate, and all the love she could give to the two children who needed her.

She and her husband had worked for Quinn's family for a number of years, and there had never been a question about their remaining on the St. Germaine island. Not only as caretakers, but as rightful members of the family.

"Keep yourself to the side and out of our way if you don't mind. I've already got more help than I can manage." Mrs. Attinger waved the spoon around the kitchen to indicate the women, but despite her claims, she loved being surrounded by her "girls."

Raised voices drew his attention to where Paige, a tall, fierce ex-soldier, argued with Viv. From what he could hear, the debate ensuing was over the type of milk to be added to the mashed potatoes.

Paige advocated for whole cream, nice and fatty. Viv countered, saying she could eat all the fat she wanted on her own, but the rest of them wanted to keep it light.

Quinn pursed his lips. Typical female crap. "Add the cream, Paige," he called out.

Mrs. Attinger pointed the spoon with menace, so he lifted his hands in a truce and backed into the corner. Where it was safe.

At the other end of the counter, Shauni and Hayden were putting together a vegetarian version of the meal. Since Shauni spoke to animals, she didn't eat meat for obvious reasons. And Hayden was from San Francisco. Enough said.

Realizing the meal wasn't nearly ready, he decided to drag one of the wrought-iron stools from the island in the center of the kitchen. Once situated next to the wall, he sent a sidelong glance to Ethan, but his friend wasn't paying attention.

Smiling like a fool, Ethan was caught up in his favorite activity. Lucia-watching.

The Spanish witch who'd stolen his friend's heart was standing in the doorway that led to the greenhouse. She and

Anna were looking through the square window in the center, most likely talking about the plants his sister was growing.

As he watched, another woman opened the door and emerged with a potted flower in her palm. Claudia had the fire of her hair tamed by a long braid. Her face was radiant.

She had the look of a witch who'd triumphed over the dangerous gauntlet created by her trial. And of a woman who'd found her life mate.

As much as Quinn told himself he didn't want to see Kylie, he found himself searching the room for her sun-kissed curls. He found her at a table on the far side of the kitchen, deep in conversation with Willyn.

Seeing the women together reminded him of the previous night's operation. The two of them had both worn red wigs and clothes designed to make a man look twice.

And he had. He'd never admit to Kylie how good her legs had looked in that short skirt, but he wasn't going to forget the enticing picture she'd made either. Not anytime soon.

Trapped. That's what he was. Caught in the hell created by two driving desires. Two very different paths.

He sighed, knowing he'd gladly follow them both if he could, or at least start walking in that direction. But one route led to commitment, the other to liberation.

In his mind, the two would eventually diverge. They had to.

So he'd stick to the one originally planned. No diversions. No whims. And no carefree flings.

Because he didn't want anyone to get hurt.

Again he studied the college coed as she whispered to Willyn. Kylie spoke in subdued tones but used her hands to animate her words.

He put on an outward show of annoyance and dislike where she was concerned, but more than once, he'd let her glimpse his desire. Hell, glimpse it? He'd let her *feel* it.

Now something stirred in his belly that had nothing to

do with food. Because the mere recall of how Kylie had felt under his hands, beneath his body . . . He began to burn as the memory assaulted.

An aggressive need was clawing at him, but he'd learned to keep it under control. That night he'd barely been able to pull back, to stop. But he'd managed to tear himself away, guarding himself with bitter fury.

Still, the end result had been disastrous. To this day, Kylie was angry. And wounded. He knew this, since she did little to hide her contempt.

Quinn pressed his lips into a fierce tight line. *It's how it has to be.*

Folding his arms across his chest, he glared at the slate floor instead of the woman who caused him such turmoil. He closed his eyes and breathed deep, grateful there was some distance between them.

Because being close to Kylie was like standing in a field of wildflowers on a sunny day. Surrounded by vibrant life that was sweet, fresh, and bursting with color. That's how she smelled. How she made him feel.

And it was why he resented her.

"Okay, everybody fix a plate and find your seat." Mrs. Attinger set a platter of fried chicken in the middle of the island just as Paige and Viv both placed their bowls of mashed potatoes on opposite ends.

"Mine are rich and creamy," Paige said with a cocky smile.

Viv was not to be outdone. "And mine won't clog your heart."

Hayden and Shauni glanced between the two women, then separated, the raven-haired Shauni choosing Paige's offered fare, and Hayden heading toward Viv's. "No sense having a war break out over potatoes," the calm and balanced ghost-whisperer declared.

Quinn didn't waste any time, taking a plate and loading it with what some might consider a double helping. But that would only aid his cause and his desire to avoid Kylie for the rest of the night.

Just as he was making his escape, however, two more joined the gathering. Trevor and Cole stepped through the doorway appearing both weary and excited.

"You've got news?" Claudia asked, setting her plate on the counter to greet Cole. She ran her hand down his arm. Kissed his stubbled cheek. "Get some food, and then you can fill us in."

Cole smiled, but Trevor was the one to answer. "I'll take you up on the food, but we can't wait to tell you what we found."

Quinn's exodus would have to be put on hold. He'd stay to hear what the detectives had uncovered. Kylie walked over and he stiffened. She was close enough for him to smell her natural scent.

But nothing would run him out. Not even her.

He was part of the coven too, if only in an unofficial capacity. His sister was the head witch in charge, as the women liked to call her, and Quinn himself had been raised with stories of the prophecy. His expertise was an asset, and he would perform his sacred duty.

Getting straight to the point, Cole explained, "After Dalton's arrest, we were able to get a warrant for his apartment and," the dark-haired detective gave a dramatic pause and grinned, "for his computer."

"That's why we've been gone all night." Trevor went to Hayden's side and took the plate she offered. The stalwart man softened when he looked at his girlfriend. "We went through all of his contacts, documents, and emails. Let me tell you, that lawyer's made a lot of contacts."

Kylie scooted even closer, hands clasped together and fingers twisting. "Don't keep us in suspense."

"Dalton started his career as an ambulance chaser, but in the last decade has focused more on real estate law." Cole added a roll to his plate of fried chicken, green beans, corn, and of course, the notorious mashed potatoes. "Come five a.m., we were about to throw in the towel, but then we caught a pattern. It seems Ronja's lawyer has shown interest in one property in particular."

"A piece of land," Trevor added, "that he has been unable to acquire for his client. As of yet."

"Why couldn't he get it?" Kylie asked.

"Because of its historical value," Cole said. "Apparently, ruins of an ancient building remain on the land, and Dalton has been battling the city and a preservation society. The place is out in the boonies, but the historians still don't want the place going to a private owner." He shrugged. "I guess they want to protect whatever's out there."

Kylie nodded slowly, then began bobbing with enthusiasm. "And arresting Dalton last night put a kink in those plans, didn't it? Or at the very least, it gives us time to figure out why Ronja wants that land."

Throwing a triumphant smile to Anna, she rubbed her hands together, all prior nervousness gone. "And this gives me an idea about where to go from here. What I'm supposed to do for my challenge."

As Quinn grabbed a sweet tea to drink, he watched Kylie bounce over to Cole and kiss him on the cheek. Then she repeated the gesture with Trevor. "You guys are awesome. Thank you so much, because if we hadn't carried out your plan, I'd be stuck with no idea what to do next."

"Glad to help," Trevor said. "Quid pro quo for you and Willyn helping us bag Cutter. A serial killer off the streets and a roadblock to the Amara's plan. Not bad for one night."

Quinn knew what he had to do, but the words stuck in his throat. His mouth clamped down of its own volition. He swirled sweet tea on his tongue.

There was really no choice, though. As always, the prophecy came first. "I'll help you with the research, Kylie."

Her eyes darted to him, then narrowed with suspicion. "I'm sure helping me is the last thing you want to do."

She apparently didn't care if their drama was shared with everyone else. But he wouldn't add accelerant to that fire. Cool and collected was the only way he was going to survive her challenge. "I've done what I could to help every witch who's come up to trial," he said, meeting her stare for stare.

He ensured his gaze was flat, empty, while hers flared with defiance. "You're no different."

For a split-second, Kylie faltered as something behind her eyes shifted. A look passed through the hazel and tugged at Quinn. It ripped into his secret self as only she ever could.

She swallowed and spoke, despite a quivering bottom lip. "You're right. I'm certainly no different."

His impulse was to soothe her, but the uncomfortable silence reminded him he and Kylie weren't alone. So he bit down on the urge. "We can start tomorrow," he said matter-of-factly before turning to Trevor. "You can get me the details tonight?"

Kylie stepped forward. Her lips were pursed. No longer quivering. "He can get *me* the details tonight. This is my trial, don't forget. I know you don't have much faith in me, but that's irrelevant." Her expression was cold and detached. "It's my call."

The disconnect between them should have given Quinn some relief. He should have been overjoyed by her dismissal. It's what he'd been striving for. What he wanted.

Kylie turned her back on him and returned to the plate she'd been preparing.

Yes, he wanted her to get over him and move on to whatever waited in her future. Her destiny.

So taking his plate as planned, he nodded to the two detectives and headed out. Silently and without further interference. He would leave the coven to their business.

~~~

Anna was grateful when Mrs. Attinger introduced conversation to the kitchen again. Watching Kylie and Quinn trade innuendos had been like witnessing a car crash she'd been unable to prevent.

She didn't know which was worse, seeing Kylie agonize over a man she couldn't have or her brother pretending he wasn't suffering in exactly the same way. She knew Quinn and had never seen him affected by any woman the way he was by Kylie.

But she also knew the dreams he held so close. So tightly. Ambitions he wouldn't give up on.

"Never a dull moment, huh?" Paige said beside Anna, just loud enough for Kylie to hear.

Kylie slid her gaze to the brash soldier but refrained from coming back with a snarky remark. And that was so not like her.

Anna worried for the youngest witch. All of the women did, and even Paige—the one without a filter—had a soft spot for the feisty, barely-legal girl who'd been called to stand and fight against evil. When she should have been going to exciting parties and whispering late into the night with her college roommate.

But now more than ever, she couldn't coddle Kylie or show her any more sympathy than the other witches who'd gone before. Kylie was proud, determined to prove herself, not only to the coven, but more so to Quinn.

The best thing Anna could do was give her room to succeed on her own.

But what of her brother? Tapping her newly-pedicured toes on the stone floor, Anna admired the hue and decided it suited her mood. On the one hand, purple was supposed to embody a sense of good judgment. On the other, it represented romance.

The two things rarely went hand-in-hand.

Well, if she wasn't going to intervene on Kylie's behalf—thereby possibly affecting the witch's fate—she knew of no rule that barred her from giving Quinn a push.

A rather devious smile tickled the backside of her lips before finding its way free.

Shauni noticed from afar and came over. "What's going on in that clairvoyant head of yours, Anna?"

Motioning for Paige and Shauni to walk with her, Anna led them to the greenhouse door. Confident that Kylie wouldn't overhear, she hooked a thumb in the blonde's direction. "I was just thinking about Quinn and how stubborn he can be." She smirked. "That's one thing he and Kylie have in common."

"I know, right?" Paige's eyes rolled heavenward. "I mean, no offense, but are we going to have to deal with those two going at it through Kylie's entire trial? If the two of them aren't going to work it out, then I say they just move on already." She took a swig of her beer. "For our sake, if not theirs."

Anna studied Paige thoughtfully before echoing her sentiment. "They should move on."

"That's what I said."

"Uh-huh," Anna mumbled, her mind busy spinning a new scheme.

Paige didn't notice the silent machinations going on right in front of her.

But Shauni did. "Anna . . ."

"Paige, you're a genius. Did you know that?" Anna snatched the soldier's beer, took a gulp, and handed the can back.

Paige looked blank. "Uh, yeah. Whatever you say." She mulled it over for moment. "Now why am I genius?"

"You just gave me an idea."

Shauni's eyebrows shot up. "And what idea is that?"

"The prophecy has set us all up to fall in love," Anna replied. "But I think it's time we got more involved. You know, lend a helping hand where it's needed."

"Your eyes are doing a dancy-sparkle thing, Anna." Paige's forehead wrinkled now, an exact replica of Shauni's. "Should we be worried?"

"No more than usual." Anna glanced at Kylie one more time. "I just have a feeling I shouldn't sit this one out. It's time to show Fate she isn't the only one with plans."

Turning back to face her friends, she whispered, "And she's not the only one who can play Cupid."

6

A storm had rolled over the island in the early-morning hours and had yet to depart. As Quinn eased down the corridor to the library, he felt the gloominess was appropriate. Brooding clouds and snappy thunderclaps were the perfect backdrop.

He was about to delve into the past, one that would likely be sordid, filled with veiled secrets and ancient evils. Given the night he'd had—restless, filled with doubt and uncertainty—he was more than ready to play the tortured hero and certainly felt doomed for misery.

Kylie was waiting for him in the library. A research appointment. But unless they worked at separate tables, her fresh face and soft lips were going to be far too close.

Well within striking distance. And he wasn't talking about her lightning.

Better control the monster, he told himself. The one who could only think about bending Kylie backwards over one of the solid tables and ravaging her mouth until she was breathless.

He should let his brutality take control instead. The selfish side that would remind him she shouldn't be viewed as attractive or a temptation, but as the one person who could steal his life and freedom right out from under him.

Hostility had been his barrier of choice over the past year and had proven effective. Well . . . mostly effective. And he would have sailed smoothly through her challenge if he'd only kept it up. If he hadn't let his guard down.

If he had never allowed himself that one small taste of her, all warmth and eager innocence.

Even now, as he struggled to remain stoic, his blood ran hot with the memory. *Turn it to anger. Resentment. Chain the beast down.*

Because if he gave Kylie any reason to hope they could have a relationship, they'd both be done for. And so would the coven.

The lift of his mouth felt sour as he reached for the brass doorknob. Funny. He'd spent years doing everything possible to ensure the prophecy went off without a hitch. Now his urge to take one female—out of all the women in the world—put his life's work in jeopardy.

Because if he wasn't meant for Kylie, and he felt sure he wasn't, then he didn't need to inject himself into the equation. She had to be truly free of him if she were going to succeed in her trial.

The heavy door swung open to reveal a vast room shrouded in shadow. On his first pass, he skipped over Kylie entirely, until he noticed a glow in the far corner.

With her long blonde hair tied back in some sort of frilly rubber-band, she sat bent over a book. Next to the huge tome, she looked small and dainty. Fragile.

Lightning flashed outside and Quinn jerked a shoulder. Yeah. About as fragile as a million watts of streamlined fury. He would be wise to remember that.

He rubbed his stomach where a strange sensation had taken hold. He'd felt it before, often when he was foolish enough to look at Kylie. Really *look* at her. And when he allowed himself to appreciate her strengths, vitality, and her never-failing sunny outlook.

He'd never known anyone with more guts than the college girl he studied now. She was reading intently, with lamp-light gold falling across her face.

When the clutch in his gut grew stronger, he slammed the gate down on his wandering thoughts, determined to chop the bastards in two. He couldn't have her, not for the limited period he was able to give. Willing to give.

Damn the awful timing. This just wasn't fair to either of them.

Despite what she believed—what he tried so hard to convince her of—Quinn truly cared about Kylie. He only wanted what was best for her.

And he'd be cruel if that's what it took to make sure she got it.

"Find anything useful?" His voice thundered in the hushed atmosphere, and she flinched. "Tell me yes," he added, "so I can go back to bed."

She turned an expressionless gaze his way and nodded. "It's a good day for sleeping in. You don't have to start now if you don't want to. I'm perfectly capable of sorting through these books myself."

Did he detect a defensive undertone? Of course he did, because he'd put it there himself. Mission fully accomplished. Cheers.

He crossed the room, past goliath bookshelves and massive tables situated with computers and reading lamps. "You don't know Savannah," he said evenly. "Or its history."

"Which is why I'm *reading*." She turned back to the open pages, straightened her back, and tossed her hair. Her body language screamed. And it was telling him to kiss off.

Quinn had sown the seeds of his own poisonous garden, but her blatant dismissal still irked. "Well, at least there's one good thing about your trial coming up." He pulled out a chair. "You'll finally be shooting your bolts at someone else for a change."

"I never used my magic on you. Much." She deigned to shift her head toward him slightly. "If I had, believe me, you would have known."

Leaving the front of his chair angled toward her, Quinn reached over and laid his hand across her book. She sat back with a huff and crossed her arms.

"Look, Kylie. Let's just get this out of the way."

"I don't know what you mean."

With barely restrained agitation, he grabbed the edge of her seat and swiveled her around to face him. "Yes, you do. And if we're going to work together, we need to talk about what happened between us. About everything."

Bearing down on his pride, he said, "I'm fully accountable for my part. I haven't handled our situation well."

Her brows winged up. "What's this? The unimpeachable Quinn is admitting fault?"

"Unimpeach—" He shook his head and breathed deeply. Then he drew another, because no one tried his patience like the blonde lightning bomb in front of him. "You've been learning insults from Claudia, huh?"

She didn't crack a smile, only held herself more tightly. She was shielding herself from him, and he detested being someone she distrusted. Someone she feared would hurt her.

Quinn saw past her annoyance and defensive attitude, all the way through to the young, hopeful woman he'd rejected. Kylie had believed she was in love with him, and he'd cut her down. Ruthlessly.

The skin over her left eye gave a nervous tic, an unintentional sign of anxiety. And Quinn's irritation drained away like fire-blown ice. Gentling his tone, he steadied himself. Forced himself to hold her wounded gaze. "Kylie, don't be this way. Please."

She tried to turn her chair but he held it. He spoke quietly, even while her eyes sparked with temper. "I just wish you would take a step back and try to see things from my point of view."

"That won't make it any easier," she snapped.

"But if you just understood . . ." How could he explain? How could he narrow the rift? Maybe a little truth to salve her wounded ego. "Kylie, it should be obvious by now that I'm attracted to you."

Her laugh was caustic. "Sure. You just don't like me."

"You know that's not true."

"Do I?" She dropped her hands to her lap. "You help me when it comes to magic or the things I need to learn to fight, to become a better witch. But whenever we're not talking about the Amara or the prophecy . . ." She stopped and clamped her lips together.

"What? Tell me." Quinn wanted to touch her, to soothe. She'd always pulled at him, and whenever she'd cried, he'd had to leave the room. Before he broke down and revealed too much.

She looked aside, away from him. "You're always so nice to everyone else, laughing and joking, talking about serious matters, comparing ideas." She shook her head slowly. "If you're so attracted to me, then why do you treat me like I'm such a nuisance?"

Tilting his face upward, Quinn breathed in through his nose. He had to be honest. Neither of them could hold anything back or keep secrets while she was being tested by gods and magic. Now his breath came rushing out. "It's *because* I'm attracted to you that I act like such an ass."

Her head whipped up. "What?" Blonde brows collided. "Are you just trying to confuse me, Quinn? You snap at me, then you kiss me, then you snap again. Now you're saying you're attracted to me?"

She scoffed. "Now that I think about it, *you're* the one who seems to be confused."

Quinn readjusted in his chair. Her observation struck close to home. To the very damn center as if by guided missile. She couldn't have been more accurate.

But he couldn't share how he really felt. Just because he

couldn't get his mind right, didn't mean he should mess with hers any more than he already had. She had to pour all of her energy into her challenge.

Yeah, that was the tack to take. "Your trial is serious business," he said. "I don't want you to operate on half-truths or false hope. Distractions can be dangerous."

She shrugged. "And?"

"I'm going to lay it out for you, so don't get mad at me. I'm only trying to help. The thing is, Kylie, what we have between us . . . is some really intense sexual chemistry." *Say it. Say it.* "But that's not love."

Her lower jaw dropped. "Now you *are* being an ass." She shoved at the hands still holding her chair in place. "And don't tell me how I feel. You think I don't know the difference? There is no amount of," here she made air quotes, "'sexual chemistry' that is going to make me act like the fool I've been for the last year."

She hissed in a breath and held shaking fists in front of her. "I don't want to talk about this anymore!"

Quinn finally relented and let go of her seat. "We have to talk about it, Kylie. I'm trying to do the right thing here, whether you see that or not."

"You don't love me." She slapped a hand to his chest. "Do you?"

Everything inside of Quinn tightened up.

"Say it," she said through gritted teeth. "Tell me you don't love me."

"I'm . . . we're friends. I care."

Her arms were locked across her midsection as she leaned closer. "Be a man, for once. Say it."

"Fine." Frustration and fury over the whole jacked-up situation exploded from Quinn. This is what he had to do. For both of them. For the prophecy. His big sacrifice to keep this fucked-up magic show on its warped and treacherous road.

How much more would the gods take from him?

Locking down the uncertainty that was now shouting somewhere deep inside of him, Quinn made his throat work, forced his tongue to move. His mouth to release the words. There would be no recovery from this. "Kylie, I care deeply for you. As a friend." He saw the light dim in her eyes. She could feel it coming. "But I don't love you."

Kylie stared at him for what felt like minutes. Long, heavy minutes that wracked his psyche. Eventually she inclined her head. "I know." The sound was so small, so defeated.

He had to say something. "I don't want to hurt you or interfere with whatever it is you're meant to discover. Whatever task you're destined to perform. I was careless before, when I kissed you. What happened between us was a mistake."

"So you've said." Kylie's mouth pinched in. "But thanks for your honesty."

"I'm sorry. It's just not in me, Kylie. I'm not in the same place as you." Because it came naturally to him—because she was his friend—Quinn reached for her hand. "We've known each other for a year, and if I was yours, I would know by now."

Wouldn't he? The clench in his gut was back and creeping into his chest.

Kylie's lower lip began to tremble, so she bit down hard, as if unwilling to show any further weakness. Not to him.

And Quinn couldn't blame her. This was ripping him apart. He'd never expected to feel so sick and torn up, so conflicted.

No. He'd been right to push her away. He'd known this would happen one day. He'd accepted it. Now she needed to do the same. Maybe giving up on him was part of what she had to do to succeed in her test.

The notion made him want to hurl all the books on the table across the library and through the windows. Vicious, twisted Fate. She loved screwing with the tiny mortals.

Why had the spirits brought him to this place in his life?

This crossroads between a dream long-awaited and a love that came too soon. For both of them.

"I'm so sorry." As Kylie sat struggling to hide her raw vulnerability, it was all Quinn could think to say.

Slowly pivoting in her chair, and away from him, she swept a blonde tendril from her face. Quinn watched as it fell again, in front of her perfectly formed ear and along the high but softly angled cheekbone. *She's not for me.*

"Please, let's just forget about this. You don't owe me anything." Her words slapped him. "Except to help with all this." She fanned her arm toward the piles of books. "This is why you're here, right?"

Quinn nodded solemnly. "And I'm here, aren't I?"

"Yes." She looked him over, and he couldn't begin to imagine what was going on inside her head. Behind the flat, distant eyes that were without their usual sparkle.

Another sigh from Kylie. "Yes, you're here."

He cleared his throat. What they needed was a swift change of topic. He felt cold and queasy and couldn't imagine what she was dealing with. Embarrassment? Mortification? He wished he could fix it, but he couldn't give her what she needed. What she wanted.

He tapped the open book. "Where did you start?"

"Just some local history." She closed the book to display the cover. "This is the area Trevor mentioned, right?"

"It is. Speaking of which, Cole and Trevor sent me the property records too, but they said they only go back so far. They're incomplete."

Kylie's expression was earnest. "We need to figure out why Ronja wants the land. Maybe past ownership will give us a clue."

"Right." Quinn pulled a note from his back pocket. The paper crinkled as he unfolded it. "The first documented owner was a Mr. Bernard Fairlane. He had been deeded the land by an unknown organization with agreement on his part never to sell the land or tear down the building."

"And did he?"

"No." Quinn shook his head. "The property passed down through his family as stipulated, until the last Fairlane died in 1964. There were no heirs to inherit, so the state seized the land. The place has been in limbo ever since, but a historical preservation society has proposed it remain state property. To protect what remains."

"Good." Kylie said.

She was never so succinct or plain-spoken, and Quinn ignored, or tried to ignore, her deflated sense of self. It pained him. "The preservationists got involved a few years before Ronja first appeared in Savannah and made a bid for the land."

"So am I on the right track?" Kylie tipped her head to the book resting under her folded hands.

"I think we should start with Bernard Fairlane and find out who deeded him the land. There must be a reason they insisted he never sell."

After a quick search through the titles Kylie had already pulled from the shelves, Quinn stood and moved to the wooden ladder. He rolled it to the section on Savannah genealogy and early society.

After tugging out three hefty books, he climbed down and headed back to their research corner. "I think we'll have more luck with these."

He handed a book to Kylie. When he slid his chair under the table, his thigh grazed hers. They both stiffened.

He glanced aside. Saw her mouth fall open. Watched her fingers tighten on the spine of the book. Then her shoulders sagged, and she flipped the cover open to peruse the table of contents.

"You may want to check the index. Prominent people are listed—"

"Got it." Kylie flipped pages as if her very salvation was hidden within them.

From that moment forward, a silent agreement of solitude and distance seemed to be in effect. Quinn inched away from her in degrees, and she did the same, gradually widening the gap between them.

Minutes dragged before finally, a comment from Kylie. "I found some Fairlanes listed here. I'm not sure if they're the same family, though."

She continued to read while Quinn tried to concentrate on his own book. It was hard to focus with the scent of summer wildflowers crowding his brain.

"Here," she said suddenly. Reading to herself, she skimmed a finger over the lines. At last she sat back and plopped her hands on the armrests. "The organization that deeded the land to Fairlane was referred to only as a congregation. That's weird."

"A church?" He slid the book to his side to take a look.

"Apparently, but the author doesn't use that exact word. He's elusive, as if he isn't sure what to call it."

Quinn scanned the paragraph until he found a name. "Hidden Creek Congregation. You're right. Strange name."

"I guess we alter our search now." Without waiting for his confirmation, Kylie went back to the index she'd been using.

"These aren't the books we need anymore." Again he scoured the stacks she had on the desk and pulled a thick volume. When he touched the faded brown leather, his hand tingled. His own magic kicking in.

He was closing in on the answer. The spine cracked as he opened the book. In the table of contents, he found a chapter heading titled "Hidden Creek: Religion or Secret Society?" And the tingle became a blast.

"Look at this." Without thinking, he rolled his chair and sidled up close to Kylie. He was too excited to worry about their dangerous proximity. "There's an entire chapter on this church, or congregation, or whatever they were."

The title page was a photo captioned with the name of the chapter. He flipped to the next page to find a picture of the infamous Hidden Creek ministry.

"That's it," Kylie whispered, excitement threading through her voice. "We did it. If nothing else, I guess we do good work." Her attempt at a smile fell flat.

Quinn quickly returned his attention to the story of the congregation.

The sound of footsteps had them both glancing over their shoulders. Willyn had entered the library but stopped mid-step and held up her hands. "Sorry, sorry. Just checking in."

Quinn motioned her over. "Come see this." He at least felt good about what he and Kylie had accomplished. She was right. They worked well together.

Willyn came up behind them and looked at the open book.

Kylie offered a smile, but her expression slid to worry when Willyn put a fist to her chest.

"Oh my God." Willyn pointed a shaking finger, indicating a portrait on the bottom of the right page. "That's him," she rasped.

A sinister chill danced through Quinn. He knew what was coming next.

"That's the preacher." Willyn was visibly shaken. "In my nightmares, that's the man who killed me."

7

"Can I bring you anything to drink?" The receptionist buzzed around her like an overeager office fairy, causing a weary sigh to slip from Ronja's lips. "No." Her tone was cutting.

But the fairy didn't miss a beat. "Please have a seat, and Mr. Keller will be with you momentarily." The woman indicated two chairs on the visitor side of a contemporary black desk.

After scrutinizing the oddly-angled chair, Ronja sat. And was surprised when it turned out to be more comfortable than it looked.

She made a sound of agreement, hoping the woman would slip away and take her mindless chatter with her. Why did humans feel the need for such useless small talk? She heard the woman exit and walk down the hall, leaving the door open behind her. But leaving nonetheless.

Ian Keller. Not a bad name, Ronja mused. The man, though young, had come highly recommended, and if she approved, he would become her legal representative. A younger, more modern version of Dalton.

The image made her laugh, for Dalton Morne had fallen out of her good graces. He'd been careless, and his errors had affected her mission. So she'd cut him loose.

Now she intended to fill his shoes with another. She just hoped this Mr. Keller checked out and was pleasing to her. She so disliked disappointment.

Assessing the interior space for any indication of the man's persona, she found the clean, minimalist style to her liking. The very opposite of Dalton's law offices. While her ex-barrister may have been reliable, his dark leather and smoking-pipe sense of décor had always made her feel claustrophobic.

And old. Something a woman who'd seen more than a thousand years never liked to feel. Even if she never aged.

In her own environment, Ronja preferred classic elegance. Strong silhouettes and artwork that made a statement. Whether the scene was an ocean view or that of a recently-beheaded farmhand, one was as pleasant as the other. It was all just a matter of perspective.

Regardless, the well-organized and fuss-free workspace supported her choice of Ian Keller as her new advisor. Three skylights embellished the slanted ceiling above his chair, a laptop sat upon a ruthlessly ordered desk, and all books were lined up neatly in glass-enclosed shelves.

She steepled her fingers and gave Carson silent acknowledgement for locating the man. Now she only needed to see for herself. For their relationship would entail much more than simple legal queries and advice.

Ronja had to be sure Ian Keller was up to the task. That he was not only smart enough, but also strong enough. And a little misplaced morality never hurt either.

She crossed her long legs, exposing creamy flesh through her skirt's front slit. If he passed muster, she would have him as member of the Amara. And she would convince him by whatever means necessary. By magic, malice . . . or his manhood.

Again, dependent upon what she saw when she laid eyes on him. Though Carson had assured her he was of pleasing form.

A wicked smile played across her lips as she imagined Tyr's jealousy. He was used to sharing her with Scarlett, but the witch's femininity posed no real threat in her powerful male lover's mind. Another man, however—

A deep voice intruded on her salacious thoughts. "Ronja," the lawyer said, addressing her by her first name, as it was the only one she'd supplied.

The man moved to stand beside her chair, and she detected a hint of expensive cologne. *Hmm. Nice.*

Allowing her gaze to travel casually up long, masculine legs, Ronja admired the lawyer's expensive suit, more evidence of his refinement. All the way up she perused, until her eyes fell on his lean, serious face.

She was stunned by what she saw. Hair the color of sun-bleached wheat and cool, arresting eyes, a mixture of deepest gray and cerulean. Like blue-tinted stones. The same as her own.

All carnal intentions fled. "Vanir." A long lost image of her brother came into focus, and his name rushed unbidden from her lips.

"I'm sorry?" Ian Keller asked, his tawny brows clashing together.

Rarely was Ronja as unnerved as she was at this moment. Seldom did her heart throb with any emotion other than hate. Vengeance. The thirst for innocent blood.

But as she looked upon a face so dear, so cherished, tears sprang to her eyes. A thousand years of bereavement washed through her. Like the tide of medieval Christians who had flooded across her homeland. Those who'd murdered her brother for possessing power. So long ago.

"Are you all right?" she heard him ask, his image wavering through her unshed tears. "Can I get you some water?"

A millennia ago, they'd shared a womb. Here before her stood her twin. Reborn.

He looked at her with such concern and compassion while still standing with strength and dignity. Power emanated from this man, and intelligence. Two attributes Vanir had possessed before he'd been cut down by the swords of the pious.

"Allergies," she said, immediately regretting the ridiculous excuse. Yet she could hardly tell this man he was her brother re-incarnated. He exhibited none of the same recognition and would surely think her insane.

He smiled and edged around the desk to sit in his posh, modern chair.

She would get straight to the point. Discussing business would help conceal her disquiet. "Mr. Keller, you know why I've come. I feel strongly that the Historical Preservation Society has no right to petition for the property to remain with the state."

She produced a file from the shiny black case she carried. "It's taken some time, but I've finally tracked my ancestry back to another Fairlane son. One who'd left the family lands to make his own fortune elsewhere."

The documents were forgeries, of course, but Ian Keller didn't need to know that. Not yet.

"They claim to want to protect the property," she added. "But so far, both they and the state have ignored the place. When I'm reinstated as the rightful owner, I'll be better able to preserve its . . . integrity and value." *And what's been consecrated in his name.*

Ian nodded, eyes narrowing shrewdly. "Ah, I'm glad you were able to find these. With records, you may have a plausible angle." He paused, as if gathering the correct phrasing for what he wanted to say. "I heard about Mr. Morne. It must have been disheartening to have lost his services after such a long association."

"Hmm. Yes. That business was unseemly." But fated to be, she was sure. For now she'd found her beloved Vanir again.

One side of Ian's mouth lifted as if he'd just made a decision. "Don't worry. At this point, it should just be a matter of filing a claim. I'll be happy to do so on your behalf."

Elation fluttered across Ronja's heart. An organ she hadn't

paid much attention to in centuries. "Excellent. I had a feeling you would understand my point of view."

As he made a note inside a thin binder, she folded her hands in her lap and spoke earnestly. "History is what makes us all. It should never be forgotten." She smiled when he glanced up at her. "Don't you agree?"

"I do." Ian closed the file and leaned back in his chair.

Ronja glimpsed his self-assurance in the simple movement and was thrilled that some things remained the same.

"Yes. I believe the property is very important." She rose, her posture as regal as Ian's was confident. "And that land, those ruins, they could serve a very important purpose."

Leaning down to put one hand on his desk, she met the mirror image of her eyes. Her smile was sly as she imagined reigning over the bloody anarchy that was to come. "Gaining ownership is extremely important to me."

Yes, oh yes, she would rule as queen. And now, full circle, she would have her brother by her side. "And I believe," she said with meaning, "it could be equally important to you."

~~~

Angry waves pounded the beach as Kylie, Willyn, and Viv strolled along the sparkling beige sands. The sun had returned to the sky, but the water still spoke of the previous storm's fury.

It had been Kylie's idea to take the walk, not only to get a break from Quinn's nearness, but also because Willyn so obviously needed to clear her head. And she didn't want Dare to see her until she'd calmed down.

Viv had caught them creeping out the front door and after one look at Willyn's face, there was no dissuading her from accompanying them. Now the three ambled barefoot as Willyn battled almost-forgotten demons.

"I can't believe it's affecting me this way. I saw his face and . . . I shouldn't be surprised, really. We always knew the preacher was connected to Bastraal; he wanted the St. Germaine book." She shuddered against assailing memories and lifted her face to the wind. The scent of summer ocean washed over them.

Though bright sun shone down, Kylie was preoccupied with the regret and selfishness pounding at her conscience. She hadn't forgotten the misery her sisters had endured during their own trials, but witnessing Willyn's terror made Kylie's problems seem small in comparison.

She wrapped an arm around Willyn's shoulders. "They were more than nightmares. You were reliving your ancestor's final moments. You're holding up a lot better than I would be. I mean, the guy tied you to a stake, tortured you, and then burned you to death."

Viv nodded sagely. Though absent her usual black glasses, she pushed a finger up as if to adjust her frames, a phantom gesture of sheer habit. "It's understandable that you'd be upset. But you prevailed, even with the preacher and Beth trying to derail you. And Kylie's going to succeed as well."

Viv winked at Kylie before speaking again to Willyn. "But I think Dare would want to know about all this."

"And I'll tell him. This walk is for me as much as for him," Willyn said. She patted Kylie's hand where it rested on her upper arm. "This is your time. I shouldn't be making it about me."

"*Pffft*. Don't be ridiculous." Sensing her friend was on her way to recovery, Kylie released her from the half-hug and walked into the water. Submerging her feet in the cool surf felt wonderful. The ocean was generally warmer this time of year, but last night's heavy rainfall had lowered the temperature.

"I'm guessing you needed a reprieve of your own," Viv said, sending a sidelong glance to Kylie.

"I think I know what you're implying, but I'm going to

pretend that I don't. Why should I keep beating the same drum over and over?" Yes, she knew exactly to what Viv was referring, but talking about Quinn only made her think about . . . well, Quinn.

It was bad enough being stuck on an island and in the same house—on the same floor, even—with her very own blue-eyed fantasy, but he'd made it clear, yet again, that he was definitely, unequivocally, *not* her fated love.

If he were, wouldn't he know it by now? When he'd pointed that out, it had almost killed her, because it echoed the truth she'd always tried to ignore. A couple of angry kisses did not equate to true love.

She and Quinn were both young. They were both filled with magic. It only made sense that their hormones might clash around and complicate things. But even after her best seductive performance—which wasn't all that great, if she remembered correctly—Quinn still managed to deny her.

So what else was she supposed to do? Strip naked and walk to his bedroom in the middle of the night? At least he was right down the hall from her.

But no. Kylie had once valued her pride, maybe more than she should have, but she'd sunk to new lows where Quinn St. Germaine was concerned. The time had come for her to let go of the dream and move on to reality.

A reality that didn't include him. Her sweet, bookish Quinn.

A shock of pain lanced through her chest, more disabling then her own furious magic.

She'd been so sure Quinn would love her by the time her trial rolled around, but now she had to accept the fact that another man would be entering her life.

Please come soon. The plea was out of desperation, and she didn't feel one bit of shame. Oh, it wasn't that her heart wasn't breaking, because it was. The fracture just went so deep that she was ready and willing for anything to help heal it. Even if that meant another man.

Willyn picked up the subtle interrogation where Viv had left off. "The two of you seemed to be working together well when I showed up." A question hid behind the benign statement.

"Yep. We have an agreement to do what needs to be done. No more. No less." Kylie added in a chagrined tone, "Just like he would do for any of you. *Nooo* difference at all." Had that reeked of sarcasm?

She shot her eyes to her friends. Judging by their expressions—Viv's analytical and Willyn's sympathetic—she guessed her cynicism showed.

"It's kind of ironic, isn't it?" She bent to dig a shell from the water-logged sand. "I don't know what I'm supposed to do to complete my challenge or who I'm going to meet, but I already know for sure what *won't* be happening."

Viv laughed deep in her gut, drawing a sharp stare from Kylie. "That's the one thing we should all have learned about the challenges by now."

A slow smile crossed Willyn's lips and she nodded.

"What?" Kylie stopped walking, put her hands on her hips, and dug her toes into the beach. "What should I have learned by now?"

Viv was still smiling, but she tilted her head and softened her eyes. "None of us got what we expected, or did what we thought we'd have to do. And even if you figure out some of the pieces, you won't escape without a surprise or two."

"Well, as it stands now, I'm a blank page. Other than the property Quinn and I are researching and its connection to the preacher," she grimaced for Willyn's sake, "I honestly have no idea what will happen next."

"Just promise me you'll keep an open mind," Willyn said. "It's not going to be easy, no matter what. Just try to take each new turn of events at face value. Don't look any further or try to jump ahead, because you'll just make yourself crazy."

"Well said." Viv had joined Kylie in the hunt for seashells and extracted one of a gorgeous pink that even Venus would adore. "Don't make any predictions or assumptions, because if you rely on them, you'll most likely end up disappointed."

"Great. You two are just filled with rainbows and sunshine. I can't count on anything and whatever I think I know is probably wrong." Kylie squinted into the sun before angling toward her friends. "Have I got that right?"

"As long as you know you're probably confused, you should be safe." With this last piece of useless advice, Viv laughed again and held up her shell proudly. "This is fun. We should take more walks on the beach."

"That would mean you'd actually have to step away from your laptop," Kylie teased.

Viv moved her head back and forth. "Nope. That's why they're portable."

Kylie rolled her eyes and groaned. Another step and her foot came down on something cold and gelatinous. With a yelp, she jerked her leg up from what she thought was a wad of seaweed.

It wasn't.

She jumped backward and commenced rinsing her feet in the surf, wiggling her toes to scrub sand between them.

"Ew. What is that?" Willyn's nose was scrunched up in disgust.

"It doesn't look like a fish," Viv stated in her detached-observation voice.

Kylie was out of the water now, scraping her foot through dry sand for extra measure. "I think it was a bird. But I'm not going back to make sure."

Just then, the tide carried the carcass straight toward Viv, and Kylie took wicked delight in hearing her staid and serious friend squeal before dashing several yards down the beach.

She and Willyn chuckled as Viv made her way to higher, drier ground. Still, Kylie couldn't rid herself of that oily, squishy sensation lingering on the sole of her foot and between her toes.

She cast a mournful glance to the small body as it was carried back out to sea. Dead things made her sad.

"Hey!"

Shielding her eyes from the sun, Kylie looked to the edge of the forest to see who'd yelled. Hayden was waving both arms at them. Alarm leapt into Kylie's still-churning stomach, but Hayden was grinning widely. So all was well.

After a minute or so, they'd walked close enough to speak in normal voices. "Anna said to come round you guys up," Hayden told them.

"Yeah, I guess we should tell her what we found in the research." Kylie guessed the reason for their summoning.

"That's not all." The ghost-whisperer's lips twitched mischievously. "She says she has a surprise for us."

That wasn't at all what Kylie had expected to hear. Hope floated up. Should she dare let optimism back in? Could she take another letdown?

Anna was clairvoyant after all, so her surprises tended to be spectacular. Since Kylie was at trial, and her ego and heart were both still bruised, she'd do her best to follow Willyn's instructions. She'd keep an open mind.

There was one true thing about Anna. Her insights could always be depended on. And just when someone was as lost as they could be, the head witch in charge always seemed to have the answer.

Hope tingled again to let Kylie know it was still there. Yes, Anna often knew what a person needed.

Even when they didn't.

8

Kylie was a huge fan of kitten heels, but as she stepped off the rocking boat with Michael's assistance, she suddenly wished for flat soles. Once safely landed on the dock, she smoothed her hands down the front of her dress.

"Rough waves tonight," Michael observed. With his veterinary practice in Savannah, he'd arrived earlier and had been waiting for the women to cross over from the island.

Kylie moved to the side so others could disembark. "The weather can't make up its mind. I just hope we don't have more rain."

"Don't want to get your party dresses wet." Michael spoke to Kylie and Claudia, but as soon as Shauni appeared, his attention was all for her.

Leaving the two lovebirds to greet each other—and because she was ready to get on with the fun—Kylie edged her way carefully over the planks and the cracks between. Again . . . kitten heels.

Once the estate came into view, she paused to marvel at the changes Claire and Joe had made to the yellow house. The curving walkways were lined with ground lights, and paper lanterns hung from trees.

The atmosphere was one of festivity and frivolity. A celebration of life and human interaction. Socialization. Fraternization.

In short, a party.

Glad to be on the flat flagstones, Kylie followed the path and tried not to feel conspicuous. Considering her trial had begun, she felt a bit strange in the fancy dress. The light-colored fabric fell to mid-thigh and cast a gold sheen when she turned just right.

Self-reproach clashed with bubbling excitement, but she ordered herself to relax. And to enjoy.

Anna had organized a real celebration for them all, and not one of the pigs-in-a-blanket variety. Through the kitchen window on the backside of the house, Kylie spied a young man in a white catering outfit. Claire had relinquished control of her kitchen and Kylie grinned, wondering how the woman was holding up with so many people using her favorite space.

Actually, Kylie was pretty amped up by the idea of mingling with new faces, learning about new people. It would be a relief to have conversations that didn't include prophecies, demons, witches—good or bad—and most importantly, the supernatural forces threatening Savannah.

She climbed the stone steps to the side door and walked into the kitchen. As she'd suspected, Claire was hovering and wringing her hands. Claudia, Shauni, and Michael had come up behind Kylie, and when Claire caught sight of them, she strode over directly.

She stopped in front of them and heaved a great sigh. "I'm so glad y'all finally got here. I need something to take my mind off all this commotion. I keep telling myself they'll clean up all those crumbs and spills, but all I can think about is grabbing my rag and taking care of it myself."

"We are *all* supposed to be relaxing and enjoying ourselves tonight," Shauni said, looping her arm through Claire's.

One of Claire's brows winged up. "But cleaning *is* what relaxes me. Strangers in my kitchen do not." Her husband Joe chose that moment to join them, putting his hands on his wife's shoulders. "How about I get you a mimosa?" If I remember correctly, you used to enjoy those."

Claire patted his hand and smiled wryly. "And as I remember, mimosas are how we got Joseph."

"Why do you think I'm offering?" Joe said with a wiggle of his own brows. "Ms. Anna said to take a night off, and I, for one, have no trouble doing that very thing." He offered his arm to his wife with a gallant bow.

Claire giggled and—if Kylie could believe her eyes—the woman's bronze skin actually reddened. Once the older couple exited, Shauni, Claudia, and Kylie exchanged amused grins.

Claudia looked radiant in her pale peach dress, and the orange stone in the center of her amulet seemed extra sparkly. Shauni's dress was black like her hair, leaving only her green eyes as a reflection of her gemstone.

Each of the witches had a necklace, and now Kylie sensed the warmth of magic in her own yellow stone. Her special color, and one she always associated with the sizzling golden energy that arced through her.

"I want to check out the bar," Kylie proclaimed. She shrugged when her friends turned her way. "I can't help it." She squeezed between them to head down the hallway, but not before she tossed back, "I *am* missing my college days, remember? You can't blame a girl for getting her party on when the opportunity presents."

The hardwood floors stretched before her in gleaming redwood tones, adding to the modern yet tropical flair of the home. Palm fronds waved from oversized planters of Asian design. In some places, the green leaves almost brushed the ceiling.

Back on the island, the mansion was everything classic—richly-hued and dark, evocative of ancient castles. So she enjoyed visiting the newer construction with its buttercream walls and white trim. Taking a trip to Claire's tropical version of luxury.

As promised, she went straight for a drink. There was an inset bar in the den, and another white-vested man was set up behind the marble countertop. After he finished serving wine to a woman Kylie didn't recognize, the bartender turned to her.

"Can you make an appletini?" The man nodded in response, and Kylie barely caught herself before she started bouncing on her toes. Wouldn't want Quinn to catch sight of her and make one of his legendary comments.

She gathered her shoulders up into a dignified posture. His opinion of her didn't really matter anymore, did it? And he was right about one thing—her trial had to be at the top of her to-do list. If romance came her way, so be it, but she was done trying to steer her own course.

Taking her clear green cocktail with a nod of thanks, she searched for Shauni and Claudia. They were standing near the fireplace with Viv, who was decked out in her trademark shade of passionate purple, and Hayden, who wore an elegant pantsuit.

"I can't believe how many people Anna knows," Kylie said, taking a spot at the end of the semi-circle. "Did any of you know she was planning this?"

"Possibly." Hayden pressed her lips together and decided to study the ceiling. "But Paige was more involved than the rest of us."

"Why all the secrecy?" Kylie licked her lips. The appletini was positively *dee-lish*. And she hadn't realized how badly she'd needed exactly this. Not the alcohol, per se, but the distraction of revelry. She'd be sure to tell Anna what a brilliant idea this had been.

More people started showing up, and Kylie noticed an increasing number of men. Young, handsome men, many near her age. She felt the first tickle of disquiet.

As her eyes tracked from one dark-eyed Romeo to a red-haired man with wide shoulders and a quick smile, a tiny voice kept repeating Quinn's name. *Quinn.*

Someone touched her elbow and her pulse quickened. She wrenched her eyes up to meet Anna's face. "Oh. Hi."

Anna winked at her. "The only thing you're required to do tonight is have a good time. No coven business or anything non-celebratory allowed."

"Okay, but are you sure this is such a good idea? I mean, right now?" Kylie's fingers gripped the stem of her glass until she feared it might snap. She forced herself to relax.

"It's the perfect time." Tilting her head down ever so slightly, Anna spoke with the warmth and sincerity, not of the coven leader, and not of another witch, but that of a close friend. A sister. "It's not that hard, is it? I think we all need something to take our minds off of supernatural drama for a while."

Then Anna leaned in. "I've made sure to invite plenty of . . . *people* your age."

Kylie's head rushed. From the drink? Or from having her hopes dashed so solidly? She'd been right about all the hot guys.

And if Anna was trying to set her up with someone, what did she know that Kylie didn't?

Finally, Kylie said hoarsely, "Yes. We've all been under a lot of stress."

Anna blinked. "That's why I plan to enjoy myself tonight." She chucked Kylie's chin softly. "And so should you."

Kylie nodded her agreement. Her acceptance. She was tired of that prickling little pain. The one that stabbed in her center every time she thought of Quinn.

She sensed him then as he filled the doorframe, almost as if he'd been summoned by her thoughts. She turned her gaze slowly to find Quinn staring back at her.

Then his devil-blue eyes shifted swiftly to his sister, as if he'd been caught doing something he shouldn't. Kylie glanced away as well, determined to follow Anna's suggestion. She would have a good time.

It wasn't as though feeling good about herself was against the law. *And it's not like I have a boyfriend or anything.*

Reaffirmed of her innocence, Kylie lifted her head and homed in on the carrot-top with the easy grin. Aside from height, the man was as different from Quinn as he could be. So in her estimation, that made him perfect.

As she approached, bachelor number one subtly checked out her legs but then quickly, politely, looked to her face. His smile was more genuine now, crooked up on one side. He seemed to like what he saw, and frankly, she needed the boost to her confidence.

I can do this. It's not like I've been cloistered on an island for a year with no available men. Well . . . okay. Not such a great example.

Brightening her smile, she shoved aside the negativity, determined not to waste another minute of her life on a man who continually tossed her aside. "I'm Kylie," she said, extending her hand to the man. She thought she sounded strong and self-assured.

She was close enough now to see that his eyes were a nice bottle-green, and his skin was tanned, likely from outdoor work of some kind. An interesting contrast with his deep red hair.

"Jonathan," he told her, giving her a full-wattage smile.

They fell into conversation of the mundane, like the people there that he knew and how he'd heard about the party. It turned out he didn't know Anna at all, but had been invited by an acquaintance of hers.

Because she didn't want to seem overly solicitous, and because she really wasn't paying much attention to the poor guy, Kylie extracted herself from the discussion with the pretext of refilling her drink. Jonathan offered to escort her, so she made a hurried excuse about needing to find a friend first.

Exiting the room, she kept to the front of the house thinking

Quinn would be in the rear, hanging out in the kitchen. The front door was open, so she stepped out to gather her wits. Jewel-green lawns spread before her, and the tree line around the estate was in dark silhouette.

A car rolled down the drive, and when it passed under a light, she recognized Joseph as the driver. Leaning against a column at the top of the dual staircase, she watched him get out of the car along with two other men.

Talking and laughing as men do, they made their way to the house. When Joseph noticed her at the top of the brick stairs, he stopped. Then she saw his Adam's apple bob as he swallowed. What was up? Why did he seem so nervous?

His baritone voice croaked slightly when he said, "Kylie, I want you to meet a couple of my friends from college. This is Dan." He indicated a man with blonde hair and puppy-dog eyes.

"And Andy." The other man, much to Kylie's chagrin, had rich brown hair and light blue eyes. The combination reminded her of Quinn.

She promptly decided to like Dan better.

Together they strolled inside and back to the very room Kylie had just vacated. When Dan asked if she'd like a drink, she managed to murmur, "An appletini, please."

Joseph made small talk with Andy while Kylie pretended to follow along, a soft smile plastered to her face. When Dan returned, she accepted the drink and wasted no time taking a huge slug.

Her mind was ping-ponging between what her heart still wanted and what her pride was urging her to do. There were two eligible and amiable men right here beside her. She had to stop worrying about . . . *he who shall remain unmentioned.*

"Well, I'll leave you all to get to know each other better." Joseph exhaled a great breath and stepped away. He seemed eager to make his exodus. As he passed Anna, he tossed her an odd look, his expression tense.

Then Joseph stopped dead in his tracks, and Kylie followed his stare to the corner. Quinn was leaning against the wall, his arms crossed over his chest, a can of beer dangling carelessly from one hand.

But the glower he was giving Joseph should have burned the man's brown skin from his skull.

Kylie was mesmerized. She couldn't pull her eyes away from the exchange between Quinn and Joseph. What was going on there?

Joseph lifted his arm and shoulders in a what-could-I-do? shrug.

Kylie's throat clutched. Her skin tightened and grew hot. Even Joseph had been part of setting up the Kylie Dating Game.

Dragging her stare back around to Anna, Kylie was shocked when her friend gave a quick, encouraging nod.

Then she angled to Quinn again. His usually serene blue eyes burned. Was he angry? Jealous?

Unsure of what to do or how to proceed, Kylie pushed her jangling nervousness out through her fingertips. Where was Hayden the yoga-master when she was so desperately needed? Kylie couldn't find her center and was doubting she even had one anymore.

"Are you a student?" Dan asked, providing a lifeline for Kylie to grab.

"Yes. No. Well . . . I was, but I'm on hiatus for a while. I'm staying at the St. Germaine home. Um, just visiting."

Dan's eyes were kind and velvety brown. He had a slightly heavy brow and small divot in his chin. She had to hand it to Joseph. If he was in fact lining up males for her perusal, he'd chosen some mighty fine stock.

When panic spread in her belly again, she revisited her pretty green drink. This one was a bit more stout than the last, but as things were going, she would probably need it.

The vodka was going to her head, and her cheeks were beginning to feel numb. But so what? The buzz in her system was blending into that happy place, the high crest of the alcohol hill. At this point, she had no choice but to ride it up, over, and all the way down.

But she was beginning to feel better about this whole scenario. Now that she couldn't feel that stab in her chest anymore. Likely because she couldn't feel her body anymore.

Her conversational skills returned, and laughter began to come more easily. At one point, she put her hand on Dan's arm, enjoying the connection to another person. One who actually returned her interest. A thrill curled in her belly when he wrapped his fingers lightly around hers, brushing the sensitive flesh of her palm.

Out of the corner of her eye, she saw Quinn on the edge of the room. Had he moved closer? Was he watching?

Well then, let him. She wasn't hurting anyone simply by talking, and she wouldn't be leaving with Dan, or anyone else for that matter. She was safe and sound in a home that was protected from evil, both human form and demon.

She was appreciating the company of a handsome, intelligent man who couldn't take his eyes off her. And the sensation made her feel all warm and melty inside.

Besides, she had to reclaim her own life. Her own perspective. One that wasn't tainted by her obsession with Quinn. *Unmentioned! Unmentioned!*

She focused bleary eyes on the blonde hottie beside her. Her time to stand at trial had arrived, and with it, her chance to find love. The least she could do was keep her eyes wide open, and her heart as well.

As Quinn was so very fond of telling her, she was still young. *Hmph.* Then she might as well act like it.

Looking down, she saw her glass was empty. When she

brought her head back up, the earth swayed beneath her. An arm was around her waist then, and a lovely, deep voice was near her ear. "Whoa. I think the floor must have moved on you."

Kylie laughed and Dan laughed with her, still holding on to keep her balanced. She didn't feel the least bit threatened, because any friend of Joseph's would be considerate and honorable.

Still, his arm remained for longer than necessary, and he trailed his fingers down her forearm as he released her and stepped back. "Maybe you should get something to eat," he suggested.

Just as she'd suspected. A true gentleman.

"Actually, I'd prefer another one of these." She wiggled her empty glass. She was past her tiny mental crisis, and her head no longer felt clouded. Yes, she was a little drunk, but hesitation no longer lingered. She had two tools at her disposal. A good-looking guy, and her favorite cocktail.

One way or another, she was getting rid of the ghost tonight. And Quinn of-the-blue-eyes St. Germaine would no longer haunt her.

Dan returned with a brand new appletini, but as he offered it to Kylie, another hand swiped the drink away. Quinn was suddenly between them. Still staring daggers. "You've had enough, Kylie."

"That's not for you to say, *Quinn*." She had to mention him if he was in her face, right?

She grasped the bottom of the martini glass with one hand and put her fingers around the stem above his. She tugged insistently until Quinn let go. "I'm fine," she assured him. "But thank you for your concern."

Now her smile turned feral. "It's so nice to have a big brother looking after me."

When his nostrils flared, she silently cheered. One point to Team Kylie.

Deferring to proper etiquette, she gestured to Dan and Andy. "Quinn, these are friends of Joseph's." She stood up straighter, as if that would make her instantly sober. Or at least look it. "This is Dan. And Andy."

"Hey, man." Andy stuck out his hand and Quinn shook with some reluctance.

Dan, however, didn't repeat the formality. He lifted his chin and met Quinn's hard stare with his own. The two seemed to be speaking that male language. The one that went all the way back to the first two amoebas to ever butt heads over a piece of algae.

Finally Dan spoke. "No need to worry. I'll take good care of Kylie." His hand returned to the small of her back where it rested possessively.

Kylie wasn't sure whether to be pleased or mortified when Quinn gritted his teeth and edged closer to Dan. "That's what I'm worried about."

Dan let go of Kylie momentarily. "Are you trying to start something, man? 'Cause I don't know who you are, and I don't like your insinuation."

Quinn put his hand on Kylie in an attempt to push her away from the heated discussion. "No, you don't know who I am. So let me—"

Kylie was about to intervene when Joseph showed up and did the job for her. "Hey." He put a firm hand on Quinn's shoulder, smiling as if they were all having a great time.

While Joseph settled things down, Dan spoke clearly and directly to Kylie. "How about we take a walk? It's getting crowded in here."

Kylie looked up at Dan, a handsome, charming guy who seemed to want to get to know her better. Then she turned back to Quinn. She stared into the eyes of the one who'd pushed her away more times than she could count.

And she made her decision.

9

Two points of pressure drove into his jugular veins as Quinn watched Kylie walk out of the room with Dan. He didn't see red, exactly. He didn't feel any boiling of blood.

In fact, the only scene playing in his mind was smiling-Dan's nose as it crunched beneath Quinn's fist.

A hand bit into his shoulder, so he jerked his head toward the bothersome pinch. Joseph. Staring wide-eyed at him. "Calm down. I can count your heartbeats in your damned temple. You're either going to stroke out or explode, and I doubt you really want to do either of those things in my mama's house."

White teeth flashed against coffee skin. "Can you imagine the fussing she'll do over you for the next month? Not to mention Mrs. Attinger."

Joseph threw a low blow by mentioning the older women who cared for them all—witches, cats, kids . . . and men included. But the reminder worked.

Breathe. Quinn focused on the creamy yellow wall behind his friend. Just breathe. He wasn't going to enact the violence he was envisioning. He wasn't going to break anyone's face. *Breathe.*

But he wouldn't be held responsible for dislocated fingers if smiling-Dan's hand went much farther south. He'd practically been rubbing Kylie's ass as it was.

"Dude, you've got to cool it. Anna's headed this way."

Quinn's angry musings took a hard left turn. He gave a crooked smile to his childhood friend. "Did you just call me 'dude'?"

Now Joseph patted his shoulder. But firmly. "Anything to break the one-track reel of planned violence I saw flashing behind your eyes." He lowered his voice to a hush. "Anna's here."

Quinn smelled the flowery lotion his sister loved as she came up behind him. "Problem?" she asked.

The smug and overly-sweet tenor of her voice told him he'd played right into her hands. "Why do I sense your witchy fingerprints are all over this?" He spoke to Anna, but his narrowed stare was on the front door. Where he'd last seen Kylie, heading out for a moonlight stroll with her new conquest.

Or was she the conquest? Was she being manhandled as he stood inside talking to his sister? "I'll be back." He started to leave but was stopped by a firm grip on his triceps. The grip turned to a vise.

"Ow." He shook off her fingers. "Damn it, Anna. We aren't kids anymore."

"Oh, really? Because I could have sworn I almost witnessed a schoolyard brawl a few minutes ago." She thrust a cold beer into his hands. "Here. You need this as much as the rest of us."

"What are you up to, Anna? Why do you feel the need to get involved?" Despite the bite of his words, he swiped the beer and downed it. In exact synchronization, a server glided by with a tray of empties, so he deposited his can there.

Then he returned his ire to the one who deserved it. "You're my sister. I don't understand why you would plot this all out. Kylie's an adult, and she and I have handled . . . what needed to be handled."

"So now she's an adult? When she's come around to *your* way of thinking?" She crossed her arms and cocked a hip. "I see how this works."

He'd always hated that haughty tone. "You need to make up your mind. You get mad when I tease her and call her a brat. Then you chastise me for being honest with her. Do you women have any idea what it is you actually want?"

Joseph blew a breath out through pursed lips and stepped slowly away. "Time for me to go get a drink."

"Do you?" Anna demanded of Quinn, her brow displaying two irritated wrinkles. "Do you know what you want? Because you sure are sending that poor girl some mixed signals."

She stepped closer, crowding him. "What is it you want most of all? What do you *really* want, Quinn?"

"You should know better than anyone." He was insulted she even had to ask. Through years of growing up together, he'd always shared his innermost dreams with her.

More than any of his non-witch guy friends, his sister understood the pressure. The inescapable duty they were both barreling toward. So she knew he had plans for after the prophecy.

Assuming the world wasn't overrun by demons and a noxious mix of supernatural creatures.

But that very real threat of apocalypse was why he had to stay. Why he would live up to his promise. One he'd made years ago, under a tent of sheets and blankets. A sacred oath made in the shadows, and the dim glow of a superhero flashlight.

"One day we'll fight the demon," Anna said. *"I had a dream."*

Two years her junior, eight-year-old Quinn gave a solemn nod. "You saw it."

"Yes."

"You'll be the winner." He looked at her flashlight. "Like her. Wonder Woman."

"Wonder Woman isn't real." Anna firmed her mouth into a tight line.

She was always so serious, and it seemed to be rubbing off on him. But he could handle it. He would have to help his sister fight.

She was just a girl.

"Some people say magic isn't real." He wiggled closer to the light's beam and held out his fingers to make a shadow animal. "But it is."

"That's different." Anna rolled her eyes like she always did when she had to explain things to him. "We're witches. There've always been witches. Superheroes are make-believe."

"Then why do you have a flashlight with her picture?" He tapped the dark-haired woman with hands propped on her golden-belted waist.

Got you there, Quinn thought with a grin. Maybe he'd be a lawyer when he grew up. Nah. They had to stay in offices. And he was going to go places. Like Africa and wherever the Tasmanian Devil lived.

Another big sister eye-roll of utter disgust. "You're so stupid."

"Am not. You're stupid. And you can fight the demon by yourself too. I'm gonna go to China when I'm big. You can stay in stupid Savannah and live with all the other old, ugly witches." He flopped over and curled into a ball, hiding his face so she couldn't even see him.

He waited for her to call him a name, or maybe crawl out of the tent and go to her room. But she didn't. She stayed lying beside him on her stomach. Right beside him. "You can't go, Quinn. You have to help me."

He felt her hand on his back, and he knew she was right. Some small flicker of maturity inside told him he would stay. At least until she beat up the demon.

Then he would go to China.

"Okay," he mumbled into his pillow. "I'll stay and help. But only if you don't call me stupid."

And he *had* stayed. Now as Quinn stared stubbornly at Anna, he was sure she was silently calling him a lot worse things. "I've kept my promise, haven't I? Why are you giving me a hard time about Kylie?"

Her face melted into sympathy, but she stomped her foot. "Because I love you. It's okay to want more than one thing. To have them both. One doesn't have to cancel out the other." She shook her head. "I just want to see you have everything in life that you deserve. That you've earned."

This time when a tray passed, he snatched a full beer and lifted it to his lips. After he drank, he nodded. "And I will."

"I know what you've sacrificed, Quinn. I do."

"And this is your way of pushing me into what you believe I should have?" He cocked his head and narrowed his eyes at her. "Don't you think that's up to me?"

"Yes. Exactly." She uncrossed her arms. Crossed them again. "And while I truly do want to see you happy, I'm also tired of seeing her so sad."

The statement kicked him in the chest like a mule wearing steel-toed boots. He drank some more. They were all going to get drunk and sloppy at this rate. "I can't help that. She's young. She has a crush."

His sister sneered. "Oh, you are just so full of shit."

Shauni was passing by when the last flew from Anna's mouth. The animal-whisperer looked stunned but wisely kept walking.

He started to respond, but his sister mowed him down with her continued diatribe. "If you aren't interested in Kylie, then that's your choice." She jabbed a finger in his arm. "But don't you dare diminish her feelings by implying they're a product of her youth. To answer your earlier question, Kylie, young though she may be, is one woman who knows exactly what she wants. She's known for the better part of a year."

She dropped her arms to her sides and exhaled forcibly. "And I thought you did too."

Quinn was sparking inside, incensed by her doubt. "I know exactly what I want, which is why I've been trying to be kind and steer her in another direction. Would you rather I lie to her? Tell her I'll be with her forever, even though I plan to split the very second this prophecy is finished and fulfilled?"

"No." Anna was subdued, her eyes sad as she studied him. "But I don't want you to lie to yourself either. Yes, I wanted you and Kylie to be around other people, and for her, maybe some other possibilities."

Quinn looked again to the front door, where the woman in question had left with Dan. This time as he glared, he questioned his own motives. Why did he want to go out there and protect her? It wasn't like she needed his help, and he'd never acted that way with the other women.

But even if he had some feelings for Kylie, he would not let them deter him from his real goals. From pursuing the things he'd wanted for a lot longer than one measly year.

"It wouldn't be right." He didn't know he'd said the words out loud until Anna answered, "Okay then. That's your choice, and you have every right to go after your dreams."

She touched his hand and brought his attention back to her. "Because I do know, Quinn. I remember all the times you talked about seeing the world. Seeing what else is out there and getting off of that stinky island." She smiled with the last.

"But Kylie needs permission to move on. Her time is up, and she doesn't need any distractions." Anna stepped backward, her blue eyes glistening suspiciously. "Time to choose, little brother. If you don't love her, then you have to let her go."

~~~

A few beers later and the house was feeling overcrowded. Quinn had no idea Anna knew so many people, but the chatter and drone were driving him out. Out of the room and through the door, to a deep dark sky that offered a much-needed hush.

Holding onto the rail, he took slow, cautious steps down the right side of the dual staircase. The fact that the steps curved was less than helpful. A man in his condition needed flat ground and straight runways.

Grateful for the even and unobstructed lawn beneath his feet, he made a beeline for the large live oak tree and the white wooden swing he knew hung from its sturdy branches. There he would find some solace.

He'd been mulling over Anna's warning ever since she'd left him with the ultimatum. Because that's essentially what it was. Love Kylie or release her.

But hadn't he already done that? Multiple times? They'd gone over the topic again just today in the library, and Kylie had agreed, even if somewhat reluctantly.

All right, so maybe stepping in the way he had and taking Kylie's drink had been a freshman mistake. Something a young, brash, and overly-reactive man would do. He was lucky Joseph had been around to instill some common sense into the situation.

Or else Quinn might have embarrassed them all.

Tossing back the beer and his head along with it, he dropped onto to the wooden slats of the swing. Above him, the branches created a twisted labyrinth, blocking his view of the starry sky. The leaves were thick and lush, bursting with summer, but if he leaned his head at just the right angle, he could catch the occasional twinkle.

He'd always been fascinated by the idea of ancient explorers using the stars to guide their journeys. But he would be more than happy to employ a GPS system and save himself some trouble. The old ways still held a certain amount of intrigue, adventure, and—he could admit to himself—even a bit of romance.

But of the exciting kind. Damsels in distress. In garter belts.

Not the say-your-vows-and-have-babies type that he saw in Kylie's bright eyes.

He cursed the demanding prophecy for shoving her into his life just when he was on the brink of finally being set free. Yes, he did want to be with Kylie. There he said it . . . or thought it, through the beer-slushed fog in his mind.

He just didn't have faith in what was between them. No offense to all the other witches and their men, but he and Kylie weren't as old as they were. Why should the two of them be saddled with an oppressive and restrictive destiny?

Even if he could convince himself that twenty-six was an acceptable age for settling down with one person, how could he be selfish enough to ask Kylie to do the same? She was four years younger. Hell, she was barely legal.

"Enough of this bullshit." He tilted the can back and, receiving no libation, shook it back and forth. Empty. Now he'd have to trudge back inside and brave all the smiles and clamor.

He looked again to the hidden sky, listened to the gentle breeze. "Nah. I don't need another beer that bad."

Laughing softly to himself for no other reason than he was buzzing hard, Quinn pushed the swing with one foot and let momentum carry him back and forth. Every so often, he gave another little push.

He sat that way for a good fifteen minutes, vacillating between hazy contentment and spikes of upset whenever he thought of seeing Kylie with another man. And the way he'd reacted over it.

He'd been fighting to keep her out of his head for a year. And he still hadn't been completely successful. Why was he so conflicted?

He came around to the same rigid conclusion over and over again. No love for him. Not now. Then he'd see Kylie the next day, and the cycle of indecision would start up again. Just as soon as he saw her smile, heard her laughter bouncing through the mansion.

When the branches he stared at blurred into one mass of

bark-brown, Quinn decided he'd had enough. Enough beer, enough of swinging and sloshing beer around in his gut, and enough brooding over the girl he couldn't have.

Only because he wouldn't allow himself to have her.

Putting both hands on the edge of the swing, he readied to stand. Then he heard an unmistakable female voice. Kylie was speaking in her animated, lively way as she came around the back corner of the house. She wasn't alone.

Quinn picked up on a deeper male voice. *Get out of here. Go inside.* Despite his internal warnings, he kept his eyes trained on the dark, waiting for the couple to emerge into the light. Then, beneath a paper lantern, the blonde curls he knew so well came into view.

And so did her perfectly-matched blonde suitor. With every muscle locked in place, Quinn sat and watched. He hunkered down and waited, a war raging inside.

Where had they been all this time? What had they been doing? His hands clenched wood.

He had every right to feel this way. Even if he wasn't going to be with Kylie, he still felt the need to look out for her. She was flirtatious, outgoing, and some men would take that the wrong way.

How well did Joseph even know this guy? Could he be trusted? Would Kylie bring him into the fold and tell him what she was? What they all were?

Quinn wanted to puke. He hated the thought of another man filling that role. The one he'd been so determined to vacate.

Gripping his forehead with one hand, he clamped down on his temples with fingers and thumb. What was he thinking? He shouldn't be here. He had better things to do than to sit spying on a silly young girl.

He looked again to Kylie and Dan and was distressed to see they'd stopped walking. They had veered off the path so that only moonlight shone on them now. But the subtle luminescence was enough. He could clearly see their embrace.

Kylie had one hand on smiling-Dan's chest, and in return, he had both arms locked around her tiny waist. Quinn groaned low, diverting his eyes. *I really don't need to see this.*

The two shared a secret joke, and he clearly heard Dan say, "I like your laugh."

Quinn liked her laugh. Hadn't he just been thinking so?

"And I'm really glad we've gotten to know each other." Dan again.

Quinn's top and bottom teeth ground against each other. *I really don't need to hear this.*

But then something far worse than the sickening compliments filled the summer night. Complete silence. And Quinn knew exactly what that meant. *I definitely shouldn't look.*

But of course, he did. The first thing he saw was Kylie standing on her tiptoes, even though she wore heels. Dan was tall, so she had to lift to meet him halfway.

So she could lock her lips with his.

Those pressure points were back in Quinn's neck again. A raging sense of possession gripped his torso with a hundred crushing arms.

What was going on? He gripped the beer can and crushed it in his hand. No good. He was still going berserk inside. His eyes flicked back to the blonde couple. A princess with her prince. No, no. That wasn't right.

Quinn's hand was the only one that was supposed to be on Kylie's waist, on her back. He glared through a view of the world that had begun to pulsate. The fury had moved from his chest and into his head, his jaw, his eyes.

Then smiling-Dan's hand dropped way too low.

Oh, hell no. Quinn was up and off the swing, moving with angry but controlled strides. Friend of Joseph's or not, the guy had crossed the line and was taking advantage. How many of those potent little apple drinks had Kylie had?

At the midpoint between the oak tree where he'd sat in obscurity and their darkened corner, Quinn said, "Kylie." He didn't shout, but the steel in his tone conveyed enough of what he felt to have her head jerking away from Dan.

She whirled to face him, eyes widening, then quickly becoming angry slits. "What are you doing out here, Quinn? Were you following me?"

He didn't answer. Didn't have to. He'd seen enough and knew what he was going to do. An inner force drove him, an instinct he couldn't override.

Once he'd reached them, his arm shot forward to grasp Kylie's upper arm. He tugged her away from Dan as she gaped at him.

"This is as far as this goes tonight." Quinn held onto Kylie as she gasped and pulled back stubbornly.

Another yank and she wrenched herself free. "Have you lost your mind? I don't need a bodyguard, and if I did, it wouldn't be you."

"You're too drunk to know what you need." He lowered his voice. "Or what you want."

"I'm not drunk. You are."

"Come on. We're leaving." Quinn reached for her again, but Dan stepped in front of her. All pretense of civility was gone.

"You're out of line," Dan said. "Kylie has made it clear she wants to spend time with me, and I don't know why you think you have anything to say about it."

Kylie stood completely still, as if waiting for Quinn's response. He almost shook his head as reason battled to return. Why was he acting like this?

Didn't matter. Whatever his reasons, acknowledged or not, he wasn't going to stand by and watch her get groped.

Dan put his hands on Kylie's shoulders. "Let's go. I'll ask Joe if I can borrow the boat and take you home."

Maybe it was his arrogant posture, or the fact he had his

hands on Kylie again. Maybe what really set Quinn off was the comment about taking Kylie home. Just where did that asshole think he was taking her?

The island was Quinn's home. The boat was his too. And Kylie?

The next thing he knew, Quinn rushed forward and shoved Dan, causing the blonde man to stumble backward. And now his smile was gone for good.

Dan bared his teeth and shook out his arms. He stepped away from Kylie, then did the four finger bring-it-on gesture to Quinn.

Who was more than happy to bring it.

Quinn moved in and let Dan land the first punch, thereby giving himself permission and reason to hit back. When Dan threw another, Quinn blocked with his left and uppercut with his right.

To his credit, Dan staggered from the blow but managed to stay upright.

The guy was holding his own. Good. Quinn could vent his anger and not feel too guilty about it.

This time Quinn was ready when his opponent threw another version of his first punch. Big mistake. He dodged and drove his fist into Dan's ribs, darkly satisfied when the other man expelled a grunt.

"That's enough!" Kylie wasn't screaming hysterically as many girls did when a fight broke out, but her voice was tight and furious.

Like two bulls, he and Dan circled each other, breathing heavily and dragging feet. Quinn didn't concern himself with the why of his actions. It just felt good to pound on Dan.

He didn't care to look further or worry over the fact he'd been driven to violence for no good reason. He chose to embrace his most basic, visceral reactions.

And that was the beauty of alcohol.

Kylie surprised him by jumping between the two men. She thrust a shaking finger in Quinn's face. No magic flashed from her hand, but the disgust in her expression hit him harder than lightning would have.

"You are out of control." She dropped her hand, scowling. "Go inside. Now."

Dan was holding onto his ribs. Quinn had knocked the wind out of him, but the guy was doing his best not to show it.

"You're coming with me," Quinn told Kylie, still unwilling to leave her with the man who'd been touching her. Kissing her.

"I'm not—" Kylie began, but she was cut off by another female voice. One that made Quinn cringe.

Anna was beside Kylie then, her arms folded in that casually pissed-off way females did so well. "Do you forget where we are?" She didn't have to say anything else to let Quinn know he was well on his way to embarrassing himself, her, Claire, Joe, and Joseph. Pretty much everybody.

Shame crawled through him, and the full impact of his behavior hit home. But he had just enough fury left in him to cast accusing eyes at his sister. He held out both arms. "Isn't this what you wanted?"

"Of course not. What's wrong with you?"

Kylie moved into his line of sight then, her eyes glistening, her face drained of the irritation she'd shown him just moments before. "Yes. Answer the question, Quinn." She held her breath, eyes never wavering from his. "Why did you do this?"

The stomping bull in him wanted to grab her and pull her to his side. *Because you belong to me.* But he couldn't tell her that. It would only bring on more of the same shit they'd been dealing with for months.

He glanced at Anna, recalling her earlier demand. He wanted Kylie, but it would be wrong to have her. *So let her go.*

He nodded to Dan, too proud and self-conscious to say the words. But as a man, Dan understood the quick, tight gesture.

He inclined his head in return.

Quinn looked back to the woman awaiting his answer. He always kept her waiting. "You're right, Kylie." The words scalded his throat, but he forced them out. "I am drunk."

With that as his only excuse, he turned, like a coward, and he walked away.

10

Kylie killed time until ten o'clock the next morning before making her way to Quinn's bedroom door. She knocked at a moderate level, somewhere between an are-you-still-sleeping? tap of consideration and a you-were-a–drunk-jerkoff-last-night thump. After approximately thirty seconds of no response, she turned the knob and slipped inside.

Curtains were drawn against the morning light, and the office portion of his quarters was somber and still. Stealing a peek through the half-open door to where he slept, Kylie studied one long leg, bared of covers he'd kicked off during the night.

She squinted and bit her bottom lip. *Is he naked under that sheet?*

Stifling an errant laugh, she backed away and turned her perusal to his study instead. She'd only been in here a couple of times, but it was one of her favorite rooms in the mansion.

Because everything here was pure Quinn.

Books everywhere, black teakwood shelving all around. The desk he'd made himself from a large plank of wood and two marble pedestals. She stopped and took a breath. The scent here was both old-world leather and open-ocean clean.

Trailing her hand over the book spines of one shelf, she took advantage of a rare opportunity. Never had she been alone in Quinn's space, and the silent ache he'd left inside of her felt greedy. Selfish.

The constricting need told her to take what she could of him, take it all into her, to keep and remember. So she would drink in the textures and smells found here, in Quinn's room. She'd steal what little she could of the man who didn't love her back.

Shaking off the pervading sadness, she centered her gaze on the titles hinting of ancient magicks and defense against the dark arts. Funny, she wasn't as worried about dealing with demons as she was one scholarly male witch.

More of these books were spread across his desk, evidence he was resolved and wouldn't stop searching until he found a way to secure the island home once again. To restore the protective spells that gave them all at least some peace of mind.

No matter how he'd hurt her, Kylie had the utmost respect for Quinn. He was dependable, loyal. She frowned. And unfortunately for her, he was honest to a fault. *I've decided to move on, remember? I am open to my destiny, whatever that may be.*

Or whoever.

She thought of Dan, but even his puppy-dog eyes hadn't moved her like Quinn's mesmerizing blue always had. Like they still did.

So she'd just keep looking. She'd go out. Dance. Party. *Men of Savannah, I'm officially open for business. Come one, come all!*

She cringed. *Yuck.* That wasn't what she wanted. And after last night's debacle, how could she make herself believe it was what Quinn wanted?

He'd been jealous last night. Kylie felt sure that's what had made him so volatile. Not just the beer.

No wonder she still followed him around like a girl with a crush. The claims he kept making about their non-relationship just didn't correlate with his behavior. So what was she supposed to do?

When her toe began tapping on the floor of its own accord, she glanced around. She was standing on top of the motherlode, and if she ever expected to understand the infuriating man, she needed to learn his secrets.

Because he had them. Of that she was sure.

With untamable curiosity flaring again, she moved to what looked like an atlas, its pages spread open on a tall stand. The carvings in the podium's wood spoke of age, as did the worn and faded pages of the book.

Quinn had been using the maps recently, it seemed. A slip of paper rested between the pages, and Kylie found herself leaning closer to take a look. She was invading his privacy, a tiny—and completely overruled—inner voice objected.

But hey. She'd respected his sleeping in the buff, hadn't she? She'd backed off. So instead of taking at peek at him, she'd snoop out here instead. What harm could come from one quick look-see?

Nothing. Or so she'd believed. The piece of paper was much more than a makeshift bookmark, and the notes she read drove a spike into her stomach. Detailed plans and a travel itinerary. Quinn was leaving. The island. The coven.

He was leaving her.

That couldn't be. As she forced herself to start breathing again, reason returned to triumph over paranoia. She considered the man who'd scrawled the plans in strong, clear letters. Quinn was as reliable as moonrise, and there was no way he'd be deserting them before the prophecy was fulfilled.

No, of all the things she had to say about Quinn St. Germaine, shirking his duty would never be one of them. He was steadfast and grounded.

And obstinate.

She closed the book and edged around the desk. If she wanted the truth, she'd go to the source. Fueled by her determination to get some answers, she strode to the cracked door and opened it wide. "Quinn. Time to wake up." He didn't budge.

She was channeling a drill sergeant, but maybe that's what she needed to be. Perhaps that had been her problem all along. She'd been too nice.

Acceptance and patience hadn't worked. Might as well try the opposite.

Marching across the room, she flung open the heavy drapes. Sunlight exploded into his man cave and fired it up with bright light.

Quinn rolled away from the windows and buried his head under a pillow, still unaware of who was rousting him.

Kylie put both hands on the edge of his mattress and bounced. "If you're going with me, you need to get up. I've waited long enough." Boy, had she.

Quinn groaned and rolled onto his back, draping one arm over his eyes. He mumbled unintelligibly.

"I can't hear you." She stood with arms at her side, carefully projecting the air of one who didn't give a damn. Hopefully her rigid posture would help convince her romantic heart to toughen up.

This time the sound of her voice registered. Quinn sat up, wide-eyed and bed-headed. "What are you doing in here?" He clasped a hand to the sheet, making sure he was covered.

Kylie made a noise that was a scoff-laugh. "Don't worry. I didn't peek at your man-parts. Besides, I'm sure you've got a sign down there that says 'No Trespassing.'" Then she snorted and added, "'Kylie, this means you.'"

The look on his face was worth framing. If only she had a camera. Taking advantage of his shocked speechlessness, she continued. "I'm heading out to reconnoiter the land Ronja's so interested in."

She sat on the edge of his bed now and bit back a grin when he scrambled to an upright position, far away from her dangerous self. "You like that word? Reconnoiter," she said again with flair. "That's what Paige called it. I thought I'd borrow the term."

Quinn held his hands out, fingers stiffly spread, and shook them. "Okay, what are you saying? Because all I hear is a bunch of babble."

"You and I agreed to work together." She enunciated slowly, the implication of his dunce-like state clear. "But you've been sleeping all morning, and I'm ready to go. Plus, I know you'll insist on eating, and plotting the best way to approach the property," she twirled a hand, "and blah-blah-blah."

She pressed her lips together. "Best-case scenario, we'll get there at dusk by the time you're done picking it apart."

"Did I miss something?" He combed his spiked-up brown hair with his fingers. "Is there a good reason you barged into my room and woke me up?" He stared her down with his cobalt aim. "And so rudely?"

"My, we did drink too much beer last night." She got up and stalked back to the doorway, leaning against the jamb to cock one brow at him. "And I don't think you're in any position to call me rude."

She lowered her head to glare at him through her lashes. Willing him to remember.

She saw his neck flash red before he jumped up—making sure the sheet stayed wrapped around the good parts—and glowered. Oh yeah. He remembered.

"I was pretty surprised by your lack of composure." She delighted in jabbing at his superior attitude. The one he'd always lorded over her, since she was the *young* one. "But don't worry. Even though you were quite the barbarian, Dan is just fine."

Time to stop jabbing the blade and start twisting. "In fact, he laughed about the whole thing." She lifted her eyes and sighed. "He's such a great guy." Then back to Quinn. "And I have you to thank for shoving me into his arms."

Kylie waited with a smile dancing over the corners of her mouth. The muscles in his neck corded and strained, and his hands gripped the sheets more tightly than necessary.

Through a clenched jaw he ground out, "I'll get dressed and meet you downstairs. Do. Not. Leave. Without me." He jerked his head, telling her to depart.

Was that all the response she was going to get? Taking note of his heaving chest and burning stare, Kylie wiggled her fingers in adieu, then swiftly turned to cross back through his office.

She'd barely closed the door behind her when a muffled *whump!* came from inside Quinn's room. Oh, he was responding all right. *Temper. Temper.* She shook her head, wondering why she seemed to be the only one who could make Quinn lose his cool.

And whether or not that should lift her spirits the way it did.

She was leaning against the door with a grin on her face when something came thundering down the hallway. It wasn't until the bundle of black sped past her that she recognized Shauni's dog.

"Skid," she called. To no avail. The hound was growling and racing for the backside of the house. So Kylie did what any smart witch would do. She gave chase.

The dog lived up to his name when he tried, too late, to slow down for the corner at the very end of the corridor, skidding instead into the wall before righting himself and carrying on. Did the poor thing have a problem with depth perception?

Passing the elevator and then her own bedroom, Kylie rounded the corner and spotted Skid in the middle of the hallway. He was standing with paws pressed against the door there, howling and barking for all he was worth.

"Skid." Kylie ran over to him, and he dropped to all fours to whine, his eyes rolling between her and the closed door.

"You want in Anna's room?" Kylie envisioned the nice, clean

boudoir and all of Anna's fine things. The peacock blue settee. "Oh, I don't think that's a good idea."

Skid issued three demanding barks. He lifted his ears and tilted his head as if to say, "What's the matter with you, lady?"

"Okay, okay." The dog's apparent upset made her relent. Because the only thing sharper than a witch's instinct, was an animal's.

Chills racked her body as she laid her hand on the knob. What had gotten the dog so bent out of shape? What would they find on the other side?

Before she could get the door open all the way, Skid pushed himself through the crack and barreled inside. He barked once. Twice. Then he cut the third off mid-yelp.

Kylie swept the room with her eyes while Skid trotted around the perimeter of the sitting area and sniffed. Next he walked a smaller circle before finally turning around one final time like a wind-up ballerina and sitting on his haunches.

He looked at Kylie and whined.

She held out her hands. "What now?" She wasn't getting any strange vibes. No tingle to alert her of any supernatural danger. "Is there a treat in here or something?"

Blowing a great huff out through his nose, the dog stood and walked casually toward her, disappointment dragging on him so visibly it was comical.

Once past her and out of Anna's chambers, he leaned solidly against Kylie's legs and lolled his tongue as canines do. He was giving her an I-love-you look.

Or he wanted some food.

Ruffling his head, she told him he was a good boy. Even if the ghost he'd been chasing was imaginary. "Let's go to the kitchen and get a biscuit." His ears perked up. "You like that? You want a biscuit?"

Together witch and dog headed for the stairs, because Skid didn't like the elevator. She'd get him a treat and make him happy. So easy. So simple.

She sighed and rubbed his shiny black head again. At least there was one male in the house she understood.

~~~

Kylie studied the dark brown stream of coffee as it poured from the machine. Every time she used the little pre-packaged cups, she thought of the day she'd presented it to the coven. Her gift to the household after its overnight population explosion.

Shauni had been feeling her way through the very first trial then, and all of the witches had shared her uncertainty. Her fears and insecurities. They'd gone through barrels of coffee, she remembered, but with faith, a bit of luck, and a whole lot of badass sisterhood, they'd managed to come through.

Shauni had gone where no witch had gone before. And she'd triumphed. Now it was Kylie's turn, and all she had to do was hold up her end of the broomstick.

"You sure you don't want me to come with you?" Paige was washing a glass that still sported sticky globs of breakfast smoothie. "I think you're being too stubborn about this. Too independent."

Eyeing the tumbler as Paige stuck it in the dishwasher, Kylie made a face. "I still don't know what you put in there that makes strawberries turn brown."

Paige closed the dishwasher with a snap. "Don't dodge the subject."

"I know you all want to protect me." Kylie waved a hand dramatically, and then she gave Paige a sardonic grin. "Or maybe you just want to keep an eye on me, so I don't screw up. But either way, I need to figure out what I'm supposed to do by myself. I have to pass this test."

She glanced at Quinn as he shoveled eggs into his mouth. *In more ways than one.* "And it's not like I'm going out there alone. We'll be in broad daylight."

"Trespassing."

"On land that does not, at this point, belong to Ronja or the Amara. What's the likelihood they'll be camped out waiting for us?" Kylie doused her coffee with creamer and two packs of stevia. Healthy Hayden was having an effect on her eating habits.

"Anna," Paige called out when the head witch breezed back inside the kitchen, "will you take a look and make sure it's safe for them to go out? I think this idea is cracked. And that's putting it politely."

Anna nudged Kylie aside and reached for her own small cup-o-wonder. She was a true convert and used the machine more than anyone else, eschewing the old-fashioned coffee-maker for a thirty-second brew.

She angled her head to Paige. "You know it doesn't work that way. I can't just pinpoint what I need to see. If I could, our challenges wouldn't be quite so . . ." she gave a sidelong grin to Kylie, followed by a wink, "challenging."

Paige threw up her hands. "I can't believe you of all people would encourage Kylie to go out there alone."

"Hey," Quinn interjected with a slice of bacon halfway to his mouth. "Have I suddenly become invisible or something?"

Paige waved him off, unconcerned with his wounded male pride. "Everybody else had help. They all needed it." Now she channeled pure smartass. "You know, it's why we have this thing called a circle. There's a reason we're called the *nine*. Not just the one."

"They didn't need assistance every step of the way. I've been through six trials." Kylie threw up her hands. "My training wheels are officially off."

She pointed at Claudia to back up her argument. "She went into her visions all by herself." Then Willyn. "And she chased after Beth into that old hospital, leaving her friends behind on purpose."

Willyn was doing a crossword. She opened her mouth, paused, and shrugged before going back to the newspaper. She couldn't really argue, because Kylie was spot on.

"I've had to deal with a lot of comments over the last year about being the youngest, and my lack of knowledge about broken records and age-old proverbs, but I do not need an escort with me everywhere I go."

Deciding she should be offended, Kylie put one hand on her hip. "Maybe I should just go by myself." She flicked a finger at Quinn. "He's hungover anyway."

"All right. You aren't going alone," Anna finally intervened. "Quinn is the best researcher we have. The best historian in regard to Savannah and the surrounding areas." She patted Kylie's shoulder before pointing at Paige. "And you leave her alone. Every trial is unique to the witch. If Kylie feels like she can handle this, then we have to let her."

Her eyes, the same glorious and royal blue as Quinn's, softened as she gazed on Kylie. "We have to let you ride off on your own one day. Even if it terrifies us."

Now Kylie felt the familiar, sneaking shame crawl over her cheeks. Her little fit had been too reminiscent of a tantrum. And even grouchy Paige, bless her, was just worried. "Well, you do have insights, Anna, and I'd be foolish to ignore them. If you have a bad feeling about our going out there—"

"No." Anna sipped her Colombian Dark. "Hmmm. As a matter of fact, I have a very good feeling about today, though I honestly don't know why."

"I know," Willyn volunteered as she scribbled on her puzzle. "Because we won't get put through the wringer by Paige today." She looked up. "I'll take spells and potions over sword katas any day. My arms are still sore from the last time."

"Speaking of spells." Anna moved to the half-moon island of gray granite and leaned on her elbows. She faced her brother.

"I hate to push, but have you made any progress?"

Kylie felt a spike of pain as she watched the siblings speak to each other, their expressions saying as much as their words. They were so close, so in tune, even when they argued.

Kylie had dreamed of having Anna for a sister one day. Though connected by the bonds of magic, a type of kinship that Kylie was grateful for, she'd still longed to be part of a different family.

The St. Germaine family.

She turned to stare out the window, to the green lawn that ran alongside the sprawling home. The woods beyond were thick and ripe with summer, soaking in the sun that made plant life on the island so thick and wild.

Here near the house, farther inland, loblolly pines and live oaks grew tall. They sheltered the yards and shaded the surrounding property. Closer to the ocean, she knew, dune greenbriar, sea-beach croton, and a variety of grasses flourished.

The island was protected, not only by magic, but by the people who cared for the land and all its native species. She cocked an ear to listen as Quinn informed his sister of the other barriers. The warding spells.

"I have one level complete." Quinn's voice carried to her, the richness of his timbre brushing over her like velvet. She loved hearing him explain things to her, like the magical alphabets and languages in which he specialized. She could curl up in the sound, like a kitten, safe and content.

No! Don't go there again. She couldn't be sure he'd changed his mind, even if he had been truly jealous of Dan. He might simply be territorial. Protective, like he was with the other witches in the coven.

But maybe not. Kylie's fingers clutched the coffee mug in her hand. She had to use caution and couldn't afford to let her hopes sweep her away again. She couldn't go through another lecture from Quinn on sex and love and their distinct differences.

She couldn't take another knife to her heart or blow to her self-esteem.

"Right now, the wards will keep out the Amara members," Quinn continued. "Those walking around in a human body, at least."

"And those who aren't tethered by the physical?" Anna asked. "Other entities?"

Kylie faced the two of them again. Willyn and Paige were also listening intently. They knew what Anna meant by those not tethered. By other entities.

She was talking about demons.

Quinn pushed away from the island and stood. "Not yet."

"Maybe we should cancel this outing," Kylie blurted. "If you need to stay and work on the wards, I can go with Paige." She didn't want to be responsible for the continued vulnerability of Anna's house and the loved ones who lived inside.

"No. I'm kind of stuck right now." Quinn downed the last of his orange juice and cleared his dishes. "Taking a break from the problem might help me see the solution. I'm ready when you are."

Kylie finished off her coffee. "So let's go." Just her and Quinn. Together. Alone in the woods.

Oh, boy.

It was then she noticed the flowers placed strategically throughout the kitchen. How had she missed them before? Her blood warmed to see all shades of yellow, in honor of the witch at trial. She'd been waiting eagerly to see her color springing from antique vases of crystal and silver.

Sneaking a glance at Quinn, she felt her chest clutch. But now that her turn had arrived, things were not going as planned.

Pausing to appreciate the flowers again, she attempted to cheer herself, but the longer she looked, the more she noticed a certain . . . lackluster.

"Wait," she popped out. "How come everybody else got roses or tulips? More elegant flowers?" She hated to pick apart a kind gesture, but the asters and mums were . . . well, small. She apparently didn't even merit sunflowers.

And the jonquils were a little droopy. Ugh! Were those roots swimming in the bottom of that one vase?

Paige rolled her eyes toward the ceiling before shooting them to where Quinn still stood. "Mrs. Attinger asked Quinn to 'get you some flowers.' He obviously interpreted that in his own way."

He held up his hands. "What? They were right here and available in the woods and the greenhouse. Why would I go all the way to the mainland to get some from a store?"

Kylie screwed her mouth up, gargling down the sharp retort she wanted to spit at him. Then she turned, set her cup in the sink, and marched out of the kitchen.

Well, Quinn was showing her what he thought of her, all right. He'd gone to so much trouble on her account, ripping flowers out of the ground or poaching them from Anna's greenhouse.

All in support of her special time. That figured.

Overcome, she stopped in the middle of the grand hall and stomped her foot on the stone floor. Then once more before she headed toward the foyer.

Quinn St. Germaine gave her droopy flowers. It just freakin' figured.

11

Kylie brushed a leafy branch to the side so she could pass through the dense shrubbery. They'd traveled north, through a few areas of Savannah she'd never seen before, until the landscape became greener and the woods thicker.

But as a breeze crossed her path carrying the scent of saltwater and an undertone of rotten eggs, she knew the marshlands still held on tight, clutching with their muddy grip. "How close are we?" she asked, fearing the ever-popular "Are we there yet" variation might make her seem like a whiner. And she didn't want to backtrack with Quinn.

He'd been looking at her differently today. One moment he seemed disgruntled, and then she'd glance again to find him watching her, his eyes troubled. With curiosity? Confusion? Usually he had no problem making his feelings clear, especially where she was concerned.

But today she kept wondering how he managed to appear both perplexed and standoffish at the same time. Studying her as if he'd never seen her before. Like she was the new-and-improved Kylie.

Hmm. Maybe she should have made out with another guy in front of Quinn a long time ago. Tacky and contrived? Perhaps. But it sure did seem as if something had been knocked loose inside her favorite sexy witch.

A new perspective that rattled and rolled around his

overworked mind. All Kylie could do was keep her head up and hope it rolled in her favor.

She certainly hadn't meant to kiss Dan in full view of Quinn, but she couldn't have scripted the act better if she'd tried. A tall, handsome stranger. A romantic, late-night kiss in the garden.

And Quinn so jealous he could barely see straight.

Her insides fluttered at the memory. Was it wrong that his bad behavior made her so happy?

Hold on. Wait a minute. She shook her head and swatted at some buzzing thing near her ear. She had agreed to let all things pass into history as far as she and Quinn were concerned. She shouldn't get too excited about this new attitude of his.

For one thing, that night a couple of months ago, when he'd laid her back on the bed—before proceeding to lay one on her— she'd thought for sure he'd changed his mind then too. But no. He'd jumped up and run from her like a . . . what was a good Southern saying?

Like a . . . scalded dog. Yes. Just like that. As if she'd thrown hot grease on him instead of offering him her heart.

Quinn apparently didn't know what he wanted, and she was still a little skittish about putting herself out there again. Should she take a chance and try? Could anything be worse than the "concerned" lecture on love and friendship he'd delivered in the library?

More importantly, what was behind all those looks he was tossing her way now? If he tried to kiss her, should she let him? Did she even want him to?

She watched his long legs move through the weeds. Then she let her eyes travel up to his backside, and it looked just too good in those broken-in jeans. Who was she kidding? *Hells yeah.* She'd let him kiss her.

And more.

When a bird was startled from its bushy hiding spot, she

clapped her hand to her heart. Quinn was standing still, surveying the land. "Are you sure you know where you're going?" she asked.

He only grunted and resumed his traipse through the tall grass. Ignoring her. What else was new? *This is why I shouldn't let my imagination run wild. Or my romantic optimism.*

Quinn had three distinctive Kylie-interaction protocols. One, ignore her. Obviously his current choice. Two, treat her like a kid sister, which was way confusing and her least favorite. Or three, a verbal beat-down worthy of a sworn enemy.

Honestly, she kind of liked that last one. In a twisted way, their most intimate moments had sprung from arguments. She stopped cold when thunder rolled in the distance. "We're lost. Did you get us lost?"

"We aren't lost." Clouds covered the canopy of pines and hardwoods then, darkening an already shadowed trail. But Quinn lifted his arm and pointed.

They'd come to an opening in the forest, and she could barely make out a weathered fence, hidden by overgrown grass and weeds. The posts were sun-bleached gray, and their jagged edges screamed that they'd been crafted by hand.

"This is it. The buildings should be in the heart of those trees. Or whatever's left of them." Quinn lifted a piece of paper and indicated a design on the map.

Kylie had studied the diagram earlier before happily handing navigation duty over to Quinn. The markings were old, and the scenery had surely changed since the property outline had been filed with the courts.

Kylie wrinkled her forehead. "How can that fence be the one? Almost three hundred years have passed. The wood should have rotted by now."

Quinn kicked up one side of his mouth, but the half-smile was sarcastic at best. "Dark magic at work? We know Ronja wants the land that once belonged to the preacher and his congregation. And the preacher was connected to the St. Germaine book, to Bastraal."

He jabbed the paper into a pocket of his jeans. "My guess is this place isn't exactly what we'd call holy."

Unholy land. Kylie shivered as clouds rolled. "Do you think we should have come alone?"

"Anna didn't have any bad feelings about today, and I trust her ability." Quinn stared at her, an odd expression on his face. Then he actually smiled. "We'll be fine. Just keep an eye out for snakes. Other than that, there's nothing out here that will hurt us."

Not true, Kylie told herself. *You can crush me with a single look.*

The stray thought made Kylie frown, but she trailed after Quinn as he strode to the fence and cleared the wooden structure in one jump, vaulting over with his hand on the logs. Putting her foot on the bottom beam to test its strength, Kylie found it solid and levered herself over. When her feet met the ground, she felt his hands encircle her waist.

Her heart stumbled and her skin burned where he gripped her. Quinn held onto her a second longer than necessary. Then two . . . three.

"This way," he said in a brusque voice, releasing her as if she'd scalded him. Like that proverbial dog.

Kylie gritted her teeth. If there were such a place as The Land of Mixed Signals, Quinn would be crowned king.

Their legs made swooshing sounds as they wove through high grass. Here the trees were few and scattered, so they passed through the occasional patch of sun.

She sensed Quinn casting surreptitious glances her way again. Finally, he spoke. "So, you said Dan was fine this morning?"

"Mm-hm." She didn't elaborate. Didn't want to steer the conversation. Rather, she wanted to know where Quinn's thoughts were heading.

"That's good." He sighed, then looked above when what sounded like a squirrel scrambled up a nearby tree. "I shouldn't have hit him."

When Kylie remained silent, he continued. "I've been thinking about the night we all met Michael. How he punched me after he saw Shauni hug me."

Keeping her gaze locked to the forest floor, Kylie made a non-committal sound.

"Michael was jealous. He got the wrong idea." Quinn stopped walking and gently hooked her elbow. "I didn't get the wrong idea last night, but that doesn't excuse what I did. I shouldn't have . . . *intervened*."

Kylie laughed, despite the tightening of his jaw and the great toll she knew this admission was taking on his pride. "Intervened? That's a nice word for being an—"

"And I'm sorry."

The misery in his voice made her clamp her mouth shut and swallow the smart remark on her tongue. Opting to let him off the hook, she lifted a shoulder. "We should just let it go, then. Everyone's fine. No lasting damage."

Quinn's brows drew together and Kylie watched with interest as he seemed to struggle for words. At last, he settled on an intense frown before meeting her gaze. "So you two are seeing each other now?"

"Maybe. I don't know." She squared off to face him, wanting to believe he'd had a change of heart, that he'd realized he'd been wrong. But keeping quiet and fostering useless hope hadn't worked so well for her before.

No more skirting the issue. "Would it matter?" If he had something new to say, he needed to just spit it out. "I mean," she said, brushing hair from her face, "it's not as if I've recently left another relationship. There never was one, right?"

"No," he said. Quick, clipped, cold. "No, and you have every right to pursue your search for the man that will make you happy and complete your trial."

She dug the toe of her shoe into the dirt. He sounded like he was giving her a rehearsed presentation. And people didn't have to practice the truth, now, did they?

Kylie breathed in through her nose, trying a technique Hayden had taught her. But she was overly-enthusiastic and only felt like she was inflating her sinuses.

So she blew back out and ran a hand over her hair. Unrequited love. It really sucked.

"Let's just get to these ruins and look around." She put her hands on her hips, wishing she'd worn shorts, despite Anna's warnings about chiggers. Gross. But she was baking in these long pants.

"We must have walked miles to get out here, and a storm is coming." She looked up. "But maybe the rain will cool things off, at least."

Quinn nodded, one quick eye up to the sky. "This is the rainiest summer Savannah's had in years."

"Maybe the weather feels what's coming." A chill rolled down Kylie's back alongside a drop of perspiration, an unsettling combination. Her words bounced back at her, then around inside as if they were more portentous than she'd realized.

"Maybe," Quinn echoed.

As they forged ahead, the forest began to change, colors subtly shifting to darker browns and deeper greens. Kylie slowed her steps as an aura of foreboding tingled up her arms. "Those trees." She gestured. "The bark has been stripped away."

Quinn gave the bare trunks a perusal but said nothing. As they made their way forward, more of the ravaged wood appeared. The ruined trunks created a path for them. A trail marked by destruction.

Kylie's skin raised in bumps despite the humid day. She

and Quinn followed the route marked by the trees. Gingerly, watchfully. Then all of a sudden, it was there.

Kylie stared at the building, amazed. Russet boards in a clapboard style with a sharply steepled roof. A trio of steps leading up to the entrance, and windows made of glass.

Without a single broken pane. No broken boards. There was no ruin, no decay. No damage or evidence of age at all. The building was in excellent condition. But how? Why?

Unnatural forces were at work out here. "What does Ronja know that we don't?" The question whispered from Kylie, tainted by fear.

"I don't know." Quinn was still and solemn. "But whatever her plans are, at least they've been delayed by Dalton's arrest."

"And as soon as Cole and Trevor took him into custody, my trial began. No coincidence there."

"No." He shook his head and stepped closer. "No, I don't think so."

As she scrutinized the desolate structure, time and distance began to stretch before her. Her vision narrowed until she could only focus on the short flight of steps that led up to the front door. A door painted cherry red.

Dizziness trilled inside her head for a moment, but just as swiftly, it rushed out again. Coming here was something she needed to do, and despite their quarrels, despite whatever went unspoken between them, she was glad Quinn was with her.

"It's at least two stories."

Kylie snapped back to reality. "Huh?"

"There's a window near the roof's apex, probably an attic. We won't know if there's a basement until we go inside."

They both remained immobile. Watching. Waiting.

Or was the house waiting for them?

House, chapel—the design called both to mind. Long and narrow from front to back, like a prim school marm looking down on them in disapproval. Or an evil preacher.

"Let's go." She shook herself and started to move. Quinn's footfalls crunched across the neglected ground behind her.

More of the stripped and tortured trees enveloped the building. The bright red door stood out like a brand new apple amongst the rotted and withered.

By the time they reached the stairs, Quinn had taken the lead, boards creaking beneath his weight as he climbed.

Kylie wasn't insulted by the move. Chivalry was a part of who he was. He was acting as her friend, and for today, her partner. If he occasionally fell into a protect-the-female state of mind, it didn't really bother her.

His actions told her more about his true feelings than he ever had with words. She could count on Quinn and knew he'd protect her if he could. Because he cared about her. But would that ever be enough?

The bright door opened easily enough and without a sound of protest. One main room ran from front to back, but it was empty. Nothing was there. No altar or religious décor, no pews. Not even scratch marks on the floorboards to tell if there ever had been.

"I can't believe no one is using this place," she said, easing forward. "It stinks of dark magic to me, but other people shouldn't be able to detect that. This should be a museum or part of a state park."

"It's tied up in legalities. Besides, maybe anyone who's come out here *can* feel that it's dark. Dirty." Quinn stopped and deliberated. "I want to take a look around, but if it gets to be too much for you—"

"I can handle it, Quinn."

"I only meant that you might be more sensitive to it." He gentled his tone. "You're a much stronger witch than I am."

Pleasure and bittersweet need warred within Kylie's system. He always got to her when he said things like that. Those moments of ruthless honesty when he let her in. All the way in.

Then he'd yank the curtains closed again, so she couldn't look too closely.

Easing away, he left her to run his hands along the walls. In an effort to cover her own emotional state, she went to the far end of the room where an altar should have been. Where the preacher must have stood centuries before, spewing his filth and hate.

He hadn't been a man of God, not really. That was just his ruse.

But how had the people of his congregation been tricked into supporting him? Had they ever learned the truth and tried to leave?

The place was one big bad vibe, and she had a feeling no one had ever left the congregation. Not on their own two feet.

The preacher had served the darkness, that much they knew. And he'd known about the book left behind by the three St. Germaine sisters. The book Willyn had been required to find during her trial.

He'd come to Willyn in her dreams, forcing her to relive her ancestor's persecution and death. The woman had been a St. Germaine witch as well, connecting Willyn to both Anna and Quinn by blood.

Connections. So many connections. And Quinn, a relative of the poor woman hunted so long ago, was here with Kylie today. In the hateful preacher's place of worship. Though *worship* didn't seem to be the right word.

In a back corner, a thin doorway led into darkness. The basement? Kylie went to peer inside, finding a narrow staircase that led up instead of down. "Here's the attic," she called to Quinn.

After a quick glance her way, he headed her direction. "I can't find any evidence of a basement. And there's no trace of people ever having been here." When he joined her, they stared together, gazing up through air that smelled far too clean.

No must or mold, dust or animal droppings. Nothing.

He pulled two small tubes from his pocket. Flashlights. They hadn't dragged anything with them today, no bags or even water bottles. But as she sent a look to the dreary space above, she was grateful Quinn had thought of light.

They started up the stairs one at a time, the width too narrow for them to go together. At the top, they found a typical attic with an angled ceiling, the bottom side of the slanted roof. Here the floor was also bare boards, and the space as empty as the main level.

One lone window was positioned at each end of the room, but Kylie didn't need to look out front. They'd come from that direction.

A persistent tug of premonition centered low in her gut, drawing her toward the back. She left Quinn to perform his search of the walls and made her way to the rear window. No grime or dust marred the glass panes, so she could see the forest clearly.

She blinked her eyes in rapid succession and shook her head, trying to dispel the fog that filled her mind. *It's not right. This place is so not right.*

The pines and hardwoods seemed to part before her, opening up to show her what lay beyond. Words came to her unbidden. "Vacuous. Deep." Sounds rolled from her lips, and she couldn't tear her eyes from the view. "Old. So very old."

"Kylie." Someone spoke beside her. Had he moved up close? She hadn't heard a sound. "Kylie? Do we need to leave? You sound strange."

As if immersed in syrup, she turned her head to him, a slow, heavy pivot. She saw blue, blue eyes. Hair the shade of coffee beans. Quinn. She was with Quinn. "Where are we?" Her thoughts wouldn't connect. Her head felt thick.

He shook her then, and the contact broke the trance.

"You're with me, Kylie. You're okay." His fingers gripped her hard.

"I'm fine," she told him, though the experience had unnerved her. "We're still in Georgia, aren't we? In the Low Country?"

He nodded. "Yes. What's going on, Kylie?"

"I just wanted to make sure." She turned back to the window, clamping a hand over Quinn's because she was afraid to lose the connection. The warmth and security.

She inclined her head toward the woods out back and drew a shaky breath. "Then what the hell is that?"

12

Keeping his eye on one craggy peak, Quinn blazed a trail through the dense underbrush, set on seeing the thing for himself. He understood Kylie's confusion. The towering monolith couldn't exist here. Not in Georgia.

A hundred yards in, they encountered a dense line of high shrubs, an almost impenetrable fence of sharp green needles. Perhaps that's what it was supposed to be. A blockade.

He took Kylie's hand, unreasonably afraid they might get separated as they passed through the living wall. But after only a few long strides and some light scratches on his arms, the two of them broke out on the other side.

Quinn didn't know what to make of what he saw. Here in the heart of the Low Country, not far from flat and wide marshland, there stood a mountain of granite, a sheer rock face of unnatural proportions.

"I'm freaking out a little," Kylie said, eyes glued to the towering ton of stone that did *not* belong. "You'd think after what we've seen and experienced, a little old rock wouldn't faze me."

Quinn's lungs shuddered, struggling to function as the sheer impact of what they were witnessing crunched his entire reality. He'd been raised in a family of witches. He was one himself.

But the level of power rolling over the site was staggering.

The bleak energy undulated not only from the huge monument, but also from the other stone structures in the clearing. From the encircling greenery. From the very soil beneath their feet.

He stepped forward, mystified by the different sizes and shapes of the rock formations. Some were similar in shape to crypts but with no apparent entrances. Others were tall and looming, while some were simply great boulders erupting from the earth.

Again he scrutinized the soaring megalith at the far end of the open area. Its height was probably less than five-hundred feet, but there was an aspect of aggression to its lines and sharp, jutting crags.

"What is it?" Kylie's whisper shook. "Where did it come from?" She moved to a nearby column, reminiscent of those surrounding the famous Stonehenge. Before he could stop her, she placed her palm against its surface.

But jerked her hand away just as quickly. "Not from here. My God, Quinn, the strength of this place . . ."

"I know." His instinct was to flee. To grab Kylie and drag her away from here. Maybe it was selfish and short-sighted, but he didn't want her here. He didn't want her facing this.

"We should take a closer look." Kylie cast a wary glance to Quinn before facing the massive structure again. She was nervous, but so was he. She'd already been affected by the forces that slithered through this place, and he was afraid of what might happen if they moved even closer to what was surely the core of the malevolent power.

He'd been dreading Kylie's trial for so long, but for much more selfish reasons. Now he found himself inexplicably alarmed. The putrid fear bubbling inside of him was all for her.

Quinn forced his jaws together, refusing to acknowledge the underlying root of his fear. He loved all of the witches, like sisters.

But the thought of Kylie being hurt was different. It was the source of the cold sweat breaking out on his brow.

"You should stay back. I'll go." He made a move to block her with one arm.

But instead of anger, she grasped his wrist and spoke gently, with patience and acceptance. And with more bravery than he'd ever seen. "This is for me, Quinn. We both know that. I need to deal with whatever's out here. I need to prove we're stronger."

Her voice was more rigid than the formidable rock. "Because you know we'll have to come back out here. One day," her gaze traveled the expanse of the rock-covered yard, "we'll *all* be here."

"Yes." And he did know. Damn it all. His obligation to his family, the coven, and the prophecy reared its head, and he knew they had to face the noxious power that lived here. The darkness that had been waiting centuries. For them.

As they crossed the wide stretch without any trees—or any verdant, living thing for that matter—they came across a circular plane of stone, its circumference approximately fifteen feet. The edges were haphazard and uneven, but the overall shape was round.

"What is this?" She put one tennis shoe on the black-speckled stone and tapped carefully.

The flecks in the material were silver and gray, sparkling as if imbued with microscopic crystals. "I have no idea," Quinn answered. He'd never encountered anything so profane, yet somehow, still so beautiful.

Quinn tilted his head and glanced at her. "It seems to be the prominent piece." He stared past her to the granite monument. "Other than that."

Quinn's eyes latched onto a darker area near the base of the rock face. Was it an opening? Expelling a breath, he felt a battle within. One side pressed him to carry on and complete the day's task.

But his instinct screamed for him to get Kylie away from

this treacherous, unholy ground.

She was already squinting toward the place he'd just spotted. "Is that a door?"

Quinn made his choice and started walking again. If he tried to dissuade her, she'd only fight him. Whatever he had to say about her, she was one determined and loyal witch. She would never let her sisters down by bailing out because she was scared.

So neither would he.

Thinking it was better to just get this done while the sun still hovered—albeit behind a layer of shifting clouds—they covered the rest of the open ground until they drew close enough to make out the entrance. A smooth archway opened into the rock itself. "You ready?" he asked.

"As ever." She untied her long ponytail and retied it in a tight knot at the base of her skull. Preparing for battle? Quinn couldn't help smiling at her. His petite golden warrior. Fearless.

And had he just thought of her as *his*? He swallowed against the panic climbing, the anxiety that always surfaced when he considered taking that path. The one that led to a forever with Kylie.

Only this time, the taste wasn't as bitter as it had been before. He pressed his mouth into a tight line. What irrational sense of possession had been unleashed last night? Was he still riding that chaotic wave of jealousy?

If so, his emotions couldn't be trusted.

So he'd concentrate on what he *was* certain of. His duty.

Darkness overtook them as they stepped under the archway, but when he turned his flashlight on, he was relieved to find only one great cavern inside. The walls were inscribed with pictures and symbols, traveling from the stone floor and all the way up, far past the length of his flashlight beam. "Definitely not your average Georgian historical site."

"No," Kylie said. She'd gone to examine a slab of rock, formed like a rough gravestone and etched with lines of script.

Quinn recognized the marks as writing, because that was his specialty. Yes, he could make flames leap from candles and perform a handful of other parlor tricks, but his true gift was for ancient languages, particularly magickal alphabets.

"Those are runes." He went to stand beside Kylie, shining his light directly at the stone she was running her hands over. She just couldn't seem to stop touching these revolting slabs.

"Like Celtic runes? On the little square tiles?"

"In a sense. The word has changed over time but is associated with vocabulary that refers to a secret, or a whisper. Traditionally, runes were used for divination and decision-making. Known as Futhark, the origin of the runic alphabets is believed to have been derived from a script used by the Etruscans." Quinn peered more closely at the etchings.

He shook his head. "These are like none I've ever seen. They have similarities to Celtiberian alphabets, yet a few pre-runic symbols are intermixed."

Kylie grinned up at him. "I love it when you spout all that linguistic stuff. " She winked. "It's pretty sexy."

"Stop." He tried to come across as stern, but he found himself wanting a taste of that smiling mouth. But if he were ever to kiss her again, which was unlikely, it wouldn't be in this filthy place.

He cleared his throat and kneeled. "See here? This one is often referred to as 'thorn' because," he shrugged, "well, because it resembles a thorn."

"And this one?" Kylie asked. "Maybe I'm biased, but it looks like lightning."

"You are biased." He grinned at her through their shared tunnel of manmade light. "But yes, that is the *kennaz* or *kienspanhalter*. The sixth rune, and an early representation of lightning."

Kylie rubbed her arms. "I'm getting more used to the way

this place feels, but I'm still ready to just take a few pictures and get out of here." She hugged herself and stared dismally at the inscriptions. "My skin is actually beginning to feel like it's crawling."

Between both her discomfort and his overwhelming urge to vacate the premises, Quinn was in full agreement. He pulled his smart phone from his back pocket and turned on the camera. Taking several close-ups and a few from farther back, he stopped periodically to check the images to ensure the script was legible.

When he returned home, he'd transcribe the writing onto paper. Given the mixture of pictographs and pre-runic symbols, he would have to commit extensive time and study before he'd have any sort of viable translation.

"Are you finished?" Kylie was rocking from heel to toe, her desire to leave the dark cave apparent and growing with each minute they remained. As if to emphasize the foreboding atmosphere, a loud clap of thunder boomed outside.

"I think I have what I need." Quinn jerked his head to the arched doorway, and she scurried, beating him to the exit before he had a chance to take a step. Another thing he admired about her. She wasn't cowardly, but she wasn't shy about admitting when she was afraid either.

Once outside, Quinn paused to check the time on his phone. The skies had darkened considerably, though it was still early afternoon. Rushing thunderheads spread across the sky as far as he could see, which meant he and Kylie could be caught in a downpour at any moment.

Nuances of evil, sinister stone monuments, and now a thunderstorm. Quinn took Kylie's hand. It was definitely time to go.

"We should hurry." He jogged across the clearing, pulling her with him without resistance. They purposely avoided contact with any of the stone markers, but especially the flat black disc.

With hands still clasped, they pushed their way through the surrounding wall of bushes before racing toward the backside of the congregation's meeting place. Veering in a wide circle around the building, they ran toward the corner of the fence line where they had originally crossed.

The first drops began pelting the leaves in the trees as soon as they entered the forest on the way back to their vehicle. "Here it comes," he said when the drops came down heavily enough to fall through the canopy and hit his face. "Think you can run? Or would you rather get soaked?"

Kylie's smile was quick and sharp. "Do I want to run away from that place? Oh yeah. I thought you'd never ask."

With a laugh, she broke into an easy sprint, dodging the occasional wide oak tree and side-stepping pines like some sort of nature-made obstacle course. Quinn followed eagerly. Before long they were racing, enjoying the distance they were putting between themselves and the wicked stone yard. It also felt good to exert some pent-up energy.

Quinn eventually took the lead, but he was also the first to stop for a break. "As much as it pains me, I'll admit you have me beat when it comes to endurance." He panted and bent over to put his hands on his knees. "And I'll never make fun of aerobics again."

A light sheen of perspiration glistened across Kylie's brow, and the knot of her hair had fallen free. The hazel of her eyes was bright with exuberance and youth.

Quinn thought she'd never looked more beautiful.

He stared a moment too long, and saw when the flash of recognition came over her. She knew what he was thinking. Maybe she'd always known. And that's why she'd never given up on him.

He was saved from explanations when the bottom dropped out and the storm decided to get serious. Rain started to pummel down, drenching them almost instantly.

Gasping and turning in a quick circle, Kylie said, "I don't remember this area. I would have remembered that fallen tree." She pointed to a huge trunk that had collapsed and been trapped in the crook of another tree's branch.

She blinked as water splattered her face. Quinn did the same.

And now that she mentioned it, he couldn't be certain they were headed in the right direction after all. "We should go back that way." He indicated the path behind her. "I think we veered off course."

"Perfect time for us to get lost," she said with a giggle. "It's not that I mind getting wet, but if this is going to be like the storms we've been having lately, I prefer not to get washed all the way to Florida."

Quinn couldn't agree more. They were already soaked but continued jogging. All the while he searched for a break in the pine savannah that would indicate the service road he'd driven in on.

Another five minutes, and he had to face Kylie's earlier allegations. This time, he had gotten them lost.

"Shit. I'm sorry, Kylie. I wasn't paying attention." The land here was so flat with no landmarks to follow, and even the sun had been blotted from sight. "Let's keep going this way."

Kylie didn't complain. She didn't bemoan their fate or blame him for their misfortune. She simply nodded and trudged ahead.

He was trying to make heads or tails of the terrain when Kylie patted his shoulder. "Hey. I see something." She took off and Quinn chased after her.

Soon they came upon a miniscule cabin sitting alone. Based on its size and apparent lack of residents, Quinn surmised it was a hunting shack.

Kylie walked ahead and climbed onto the porch to knock on

the front door. It swung open with the first rap. "Hello," she called out. Then she turned back to Quinn. "It's empty. Do you think the owners would mind?"

"I doubt it. This land is for sale too."

"That means you know where we are now?"

"Yeah. Lot of good it does."

A bright light lit up the sky before thunder rolled with warning. Quinn flinched visibly. "It shouldn't be a problem for us to shelter here until the storm passes."

Kylie cocked one leg to the side, hands on her lovely hips. "Quinn, are you afraid of lightning?"

Grinning like a minx, she ran a hand through her long, wet curls. She pivoted and stepped into the cabin, but looked back over her shoulder to wink at him. "That explains a lot."

13

Inside the dim, one-roomed cabin, Kylie saw a single cot against a wall with a rolled-up mattress sitting on top of its bare springs. The middle of the floor was covered by a navy blue area rug. And aside from that, the room was empty.

If anyone still used the hunting shack, they apparently brought any necessary amenities with them. A visual scan of the room revealed a small door in the back, through which she spied a basic toilet and sink. *Thank goodness.*

A nudge on her right shoulder blade let her know Quinn was eager to come in. She stepped aside and performed a realtor's arm-sweep. "All you could need or ask for in a twelve-by-twelve foot . . . box."

"Regardless, it will get us out of the rain." He closed the door just as a gale blew in behind him, but a fine mist doused their faces just before he got it shut. "The storm has officially arrived."

Through a moderately clean window, Kylie eyed the pewter skies through gaps in the tree line. Quinn was correct. They'd found shelter just in time. She was particularly fond of lightning, but getting caught in a downpour in the middle of the woods was a different matter altogether.

At least the rug looked clean, she mused, taking in the only soft place to sit. As she kneeled to check it out, she caught a just-out-of-the-store smell. "Someone's been here recently. This rug is fairly new."

"Oh good. That means no fleas." Quinn laughed when she leapt to the side. "I'm just kidding. It's fine. Better than the hard floorboards, that's for sure."

He squatted and leaned back to sit, so Kylie did the same. "Too bad we don't have any hot dogs," she said. "Then again, we don't have a fire."

"Are you hungry?" Quinn asked, wiping stray droplets from his forearms.

"Not really." She glanced around at the four bare walls, out the window to a virtual sheet of rain, then back to Quinn. Several uncomfortable minutes crawled by until she finally sighed. "So, what should we talk about?"

"The usual?" His brows beetled as he hurriedly added, "The coven, Ronja, et cetera. That's what I meant."

What did he think she thought he meant? Then his twitchiness registered and understanding donged like a big, clear bell. With her hands locked beneath her knees, she rolled back and lifted her face to the ceiling, exhaling in a great rush of exasperation. "Oh, stop worrying."

"Worrying about what?"

She dropped the flats of her feet back to the floor and gave him an even stare. "Nothing. Never mind." But maybe he *should* be worried. She was already getting antsy, being all cooped up with Quinn this way.

Not to mention how the layer of dampness on his hair, clothes . . . *his skin* . . . made him look more dangerous. Predatory. And the moisture only amped up his natural male scent.

Quinn had always smelled so good, and the tease of it now made a place beneath her heart swirl warmly. She breathed him in again, and the warmth became heat.

It was totally unfair how sexy he was. No wonder she couldn't get him out of her head. He was the perfect midpoint between broody troublemaker and cool academic.

As she bemoaned her lack of Quinn-love, she amused herself by admiring his jawline, the long, steady fingers and serious expression. Oh, he was a hottie, all right.

And he was just Kylie's type.

"So," she started, trying to level out her sudden fidgets. She wasn't sure what to do with her hands. "I hope you can translate that text from the rocks back there."

He grunted.

"Yeah. That's probably the only reason you're even part of my trial."

He jerked his face toward her.

"You know," she rushed on, "to apply your special skills. With languages, I mean."

"I know what you meant." Now he scowled. "And I also caught your tone."

Clearing her throat, Kylie blinked. All sweetness and innocence. "No tone. I'm just bummed about being stuck in here." *While every hormone in my body screams for me to latch onto your delicious pair of lips.*

She tried for a jovial, encouraging demeanor. "All I'm saying is that's likely why you're involved in my trial, and you shouldn't be concerned with . . . what we talked about yesterday."

"Now that you've moved on to Dan?" he shot out.

Kylie's brows hit her hairline. Where had that come from? "Dan has nothing to do with anything." Or did he? "I don't know why you keep bringing him up."

Quinn opened his mouth to throw a rebuttal, but she blocked him by leaning over to put a finger to his lips. Wow. They felt so soft and warm, but firm, like a man's should be.

She swallowed and hoped the hot shivers climbing up her chest and neck weren't visible in a blush. With regret, she took her hand from his mouth, rubbing her fingers together where they still tingled.

"Let's not argue," she said softly. "Today we proved we can

get along when we have to. So, if we both try, maybe we can make things like they used to be. Except no arguing."

Why was his jaw still clenched? Isn't this what he wanted from her?

"Right. Now you want to be friends." He threw a glance to the window, as if he too wanted out of the confining cabin. And away from her. "I can't help but notice the timing."

She lifted both hands, held them aloft, and then let them slap back to her knees. "What are you talking about?"

"I'm saying you've embraced the idea of us not being together." He looked at her, to the window again, then stared smoothly into her eyes. "As soon as you met another guy."

"What?" She should have been offended, but instead her belly felt light and airy. There was a thrill of hope mixed with the nervous need to laugh out loud. So she did.

Quinn continued to glare.

Once she'd come down from the burst of laughter, she shook her head. "I don't get you, Quinn. I'm finally agreeing with you, going along with what you said you wanted, and you still find a reason to be angry?"

She pursed her lips. "Did you really think I'd let my trial pass without at least trying to look for whoever I'm supposed to be with? Why should I?"

"No . . . I just . . ." Quinn stuttered, and his jaw tightened again. "You didn't have to kiss him in front of me."

"I had no idea you were even there." Now this was really getting interesting. "Besides, I would've thought you'd be cheering. Free at last." Her voice grew strained. "You know, that you'd be happy you no longer had to deal with me."

Again, he turned away, hiding his reaction. Always hiding, or running, or pushing.

Well, he was stuck with her now, and it was time to ante up. So she pounced. "Why do you care if I'm with someone else, Quinn?"

"I don't."

"Liar." She held his gaze when he dared to appear stunned by her accusation. "It's my trial, and I know you won't purposefully add to my anxiety and confusion by lying to my face." She tapped his knee. "Again."

Angst darkened his eyes, and for a split-second she felt bad for him. Then she thought of her challenge and the precious time that was passing daily. Here, at last, was the moment she'd been waiting for.

Quinn tensed. He was teetering on the edge and only needed one tiny little push. Luckily, Kylie had just one more left in her.

And she had to know. "Tell me the truth. The actual truth this time." Blood flowed quick and hot as she readied herself. "You said you don't love me." Emotion tightened her throat and clutched her lungs. "I want to hear it again."

Quinn clenched his eyes shut, rubbing his hands over his face then through his hair. "I told you I care about you, and I do." He heaved a sigh. "And there's no question about the chemistry between us."

She remembered his hands on her stomach, her neck. His mouth on hers, more savage than the rain that now beat down on the tin roof over their heads. "No," she rasped. "No question there."

"But giving in to those basic needs would be wrong, for you and me both. I know what you thought would happen between us, Kylie." He still wouldn't look at her. "But I can't give you what you want. I have other plans, things I want to do."

When he did return her gaze, the agony in his eyes ripped straight through her. "I've held onto one dream my entire life, the only thing that was ever my own. Then you come along, and I'm suddenly supposed to give it all up?"

"I never asked you to give up anything." *Talk to me, Quinn.* Kylie longed to reach for him. *Open up to me.*

"But I would have to do exactly that if we . . . if you . . ." He trailed off, then spoke as if truly pained by their situation. "This is all just bad timing. Neither of us needs an obligation like this."

"No obligation, Quinn." She inched a bit closer. "No promises." Her heart panged beneath her ribs. "But if we're in this together, then maybe we should embrace that. Use our connection—even our sexual chemistry—to bring us closer. Make us stronger. If only for a short time."

She leaped off that cliff and hoped Quinn would follow. "Being close to you, Quinn, it's been so hard for me, but I believe it's been equally hard for you. What's so wrong with giving each other comfort?"

His head tilted, and the smile he gave her was full of remorse. "It's not that simple."

"But it is. I need you." She transitioned to her knees, edging herself even closer. "I need your strength. And whatever happens later, I know," she put a fist to her stomach, "I just *know* this is meant to be. Even if only for a while. If only for now. Maybe that's all it will ever be, but I'm not afraid."

She closed the last bit of distance between them and stared into those eyes of his. They didn't waiver. "I won't take anything from you. I promise." She kissed the side of his jaw, and he shuddered.

Kylie held her breath, afraid he would reject her. When he didn't move, she rested her cheek against his, nuzzling into his rain-dampened hair. She breathed in the tantalizing sensation of being so close to him.

His arm wrapped around her, hesitated, then tightened to crush her against his chest. For several seconds they remained locked in the embrace, both perfectly still, silent. The only sounds were their thudding hearts and the steady rain.

Quinn loosened his grip, and when Kylie sat back and opened her eyes, she saw that his were dark and heated. His pupils were deep with need, his back stiff and straight as a lance. She recognized the signs of desire, as well as his attempts to control it.

Her own body responded as lust swamped her, heady and thick. It tightened her breasts, pooled in her belly where it ached, it throbbed. This was such a delicate moment, too sweet to be spoiled by words. But she wanted him to know everything.

They might never have this again. "Quinn, I've always wanted to tell you something."

He stayed quiet, but his eyes blazed when she stroked her hand over his face.

"I've always connected to energy. It's part of me." She dropped her hand to encircle his wrist. The pulse she felt there was a hammer, and it quickened when she brushed her lips against his. "Harnessing the lightning, letting it flow through me." Her fingers were in his hair. "Nothing in this world ever made me feel more alive."

Deepening the kiss, she teased with the tip of her tongue before angling to whisper in his ear. "Until I met you."

His muscles bunched beneath her hands, but she only leaned into him, praying he stayed with her. That he didn't push her away like last time. That he wouldn't leave her.

With one hand, he cupped the base of her skull. Then he did something that shook her to the very bottom of the heart he'd trampled time and again. Holding her tight, he slowly leaned forward and brushed his mouth over her neck. His tongue flicked out lightly, as if to test.

Then he pulled her into his lap. "Come here," he growled before capturing her mouth for their first meaningful kiss.

They'd kissed before, and it had been its own kind of wonderful. Hot and desperate, with a current of anger running just beneath the surface. But much more than passion sparked between them now.

They'd arrived at a place that was fraught with honesty, and vulnerability. This time when they came together, there was purity, sincerity.

And her deep respect for this steadfast and loyal man only made her want him that much more.

With a shift of her leg, she straddled him. He answered by pinning her to him, forcing her down against his erection. Then he rolled his own hips slowly, languidly.

And she almost exploded.

Kylie would have pulled her mouth away to gasp her pleasure, but now that Quinn had her, he wasn't letting her go.

So she moaned into his mouth instead, appreciating the rhythm of his tongue, because even that was unique to Quinn. One moment aggressive and consuming, letting her know he was in charge, then altering the pace and backing off, so she could take the lead.

Kylie, however, wasn't in the mood for slow. She was greedy, aroused, and too long deprived of him. She wanted to take it all before the chance got away again.

Still astride him, she did the undulating this time, and was rewarded when he groaned his approval. He took her breath when he rolled them over as one, as if they were fused together.

With any luck, they soon would be.

"You smell so good," he whispered against her lips before kissing the sensitive spot just below her ear. Her legs tightened around him as the ache inside her became almost unbearable.

Her hands roamed over his back, up under his shirt to smooth, hot skin. His rangy physique was thick with muscle, and having every inch of him pressed against her made her head go light.

Then he forced himself against her core, until she whimpered from the sweet intensity.

When his open mouth grazed her neck again, she thrust her chest against his. Her breasts were incredibly heavy and needy now, as were parts farther south. Suddenly there was too much fabric between them.

She put one hand on his shoulder and pushed him far enough away to meet his eyes. The brilliant blue fired like never before. Grasping the hem of his shirt, she pulled upward, and he didn't waste any time helping her get it all the way off.

Kylie's breath splintered with a shock of nerves when he started to return the favor. As if sensing her need for reassurance, he held his eyes on hers, then cupped her cheek. "Kylie." The timbre of his voice trilled into her, bolstering her courage once again.

Lifting her arms, she made it easy for him and put her fingers on the button of his jeans.

Quinn's smile turned carnal as he stared at her lacy yellow bra. "Do you always dress like that under your clothes, or is today a special occasion?"

She hooked a finger under the waistline of his jeans and ran her finger underneath, delighted when he sucked in a breath. "I'll never tell. And if you really want to know, I guess you'll just have to find out for yourself. On another day."

She tore open his pants and let her gaze wander down, over ripped abs to his taut lower belly, and then to the first hint of happiness. Hmm. Her smart guy worked out, all right. And it had paid off in spades.

Soon his jeans were tossed aside and his hands were tugging at the rest of her clothes. The remaining items seemed to disappear, as the two of them got lost in a blur of rubbing flesh and moist tongues.

They'd both been simmering for too long, and their need for each other ran rampant. *Quinn. My Quinn.* She sighed when he ran a finger over her hip. *I love you.*

Kylie stilled and looked at him in alarm before realizing she hadn't actually said that out loud. It would be too much. She might scare him away.

And if Quinn stopped touching her right now, she couldn't be held responsible for her actions.

When they were both fully naked and entwined on the rug, Kylie took a bracing breath, ready—no, eager for what was coming next. But Quinn was still tracing her curves, in no apparent rush.

He kissed her stomach, then laid his head on her chest as if listening to her heart. With a subtle move, he placed his lips there. Softly.

And Kylie almost came undone. She hadn't expected the tenderness.

His gentle kisses trailed up over her shoulder and to the side of her face. With his eyes on hers, he eased her thighs apart and positioned himself. Her stomach clutched and her heart pistoned. She was so enthralled, so nervous, she could barely draw a breath.

Quinn seated the head of his erection, nudging against her sensitive flesh so lightly, yet so erotically. He held himself still and used one hand to brush her hair away from her face. "Kylie," was all he said.

A sound that was half-gasp, half-sob escaped her as she felt herself fade into his deep blue gaze. The one that had teased her, haunted her for so long. She nodded, aware that the words she couldn't say must surely be in her eyes.

She lifted her legs to aid his entry, amazed by how . . . *full* she already felt, though he'd only begun easing himself into her. Abruptly, Quinn growled again and his gentle manner changed.

He lowered his head to ravish her mouth, clasping his arms around her to keep her close. He pushed again, gently, and then he thrust.

Kylie gasped when she felt the first real sting of pain. Quinn immediately stilled.

With his breath on her neck, then another kiss to make her melt, she relaxed and opened for him. She whispered against his cheek, "Don't stop."

This time he moved with more force, and the pain intensified tenfold. A cry broke free, and too late, she bit down on her bottom lip to stifle it.

Quinn didn't just still this time but froze in place, poised above her like a statue. He looked down on her with a mask of confusion, then disbelief.

Kylie trembled but stared readily back at him.

Finally he shook his head, still refusing to move any other part of his body. "Kylie, what the hell? You're a virgin!"

14

The tiny cabin seemed to pulse around Quinn. He was stunned for a moment, hovering in a cloud of disbelief.

And then he crashed back to clarity.

He heard the rain pattering on the metal roof. Saw his arms shake. Felt his labored breathing.

And the soft warmth of the woman beneath him.

"Don't be mad." Kylie's eyes glistened, brilliant hazel pools. Her hand fell on the angle between his neck and shoulder.

Quinn lowered himself slowly, not wanting to hurt her any more than he already had. Why hadn't she told him?

"I'm sorry, Quinn." She still trembled, afraid.

That he would be angry? Pull away? Because she knew he would have held himself back if she'd told him this wasn't only going to be their first time, but her first . . . *ever*.

"Just give me a minute." His conscience battled with irritation, but overlying it all, was the volatile need to be deeper inside of her. And a primitive, darker part of him was roaring his male domination.

Kylie was his in a way she'd never been another's. And he grew harder just thinking of it. She was truly *his*.

When his chest settled atop hers, the supple firmness of her breasts against him ignited a new and riotous lust. He couldn't contain it, and so with one smooth stroke, he filled her completely. The sensuality of her tight, silky grip was unimaginable.

When he was seated deep, he was finally able to draw a breath. "I thought we were being honest with each other."

"I know, but I was afraid if I told you, you would've just used it as a reason to say no."

Quinn mentally winced. Because he would have.

Her fingers knotted in his hair, her expression pleaded. "Don't make me beg, Quinn. I was wrong not to tell you, but this . . . this is right. Can't you feel it?"

Yes, he could, and it was all too much. That was the problem.

Kylie's voice became an emotion-choked whisper. "I'm glad you were the one." She lifted to kiss him, and as their tongues tangled, she raised her hips to entrap him with her legs.

And he was lost.

He wasn't strong enough to resist her, not when she used her lips, her hands, and her body on him that way. She pulled back then, lids heavy with desire, and he couldn't stop himself from devouring her pretty pink lips again.

He swallowed her sigh as she matched her rhythm to his. As she kissed him so sweetly. And moved so wickedly.

The smell of wildflowers in high summer overtook him. He reared back and stared down at her. Kylie. All golden and warm and offering herself to him. Only to him.

And as the rain continued to fall outside, Quinn was drowning in sunshine.

"We will talk about this," he said through raspy breaths. "But after."

"Mm-hm." She undulated beneath him, arching her back as a small sound of ecstasy slipped from her lips. "I never knew . . . couldn't imagine what this would feel like."

Her complete abandonment was enthralling, binding him to her as surely as if she'd cast a spell. He slowed his strokes, carefully withdrawing, only to plunge into her again.

When her cry shattered through him, he could sense the

release of her magic. It swirled and danced, and then joined with his own.

And that was a first for *him*. A hot, sensual, mind-blowing first.

Everything about Kylie just felt so damn good. So . . . perfect.

"Quinn," she said with wonder, before blasting him with one of her smiles. "I would tell you how amazing you are, but since I don't have anything to compare—"

She moaned when he thrust again, and he surprised himself by wrapping her hair around his hand and pulling her head to the side to bare her throat. His mouth razed her flesh, nipping and teasing from the hollow beneath her chin down to the cleft between her breasts.

And with every kiss she grew wilder in his arms. "Oh, yes!" she cried, but then she opened her eyes to look directly into his. "I mean, oh *Quinn*," she corrected with a devilish smile. "Because I know exactly who I'm with."

Lifting her arms over her head, she arched her back gracefully, gazing at him with hazy eyes. He saw no fear or doubt, only provocation. And maybe a tinge of smugness.

Quinn accepted her challenge and hooked his arm under one of her knees. He'd show her exactly what she'd been missing. Driving harder now, he brought them both closer to that bright white moment of rapture.

When her muscles tensed and quivered, as her back bowed even more, Quinn closed his eyes and simply felt her. He sensed her taking him in, deeper into her gorgeous body. And deeper into her tender young heart.

Fears pricked at the back of his mind, but nothing would stop him now.

Kylie was beneath him, and she was everything summer. Heat. Beauty. Freedom.

Life.

He roared when she clenched around him in climax, as her

cry of release pulled him with her. She wrenched everything from him that he could possibly give.

Then he collapsed onto her small frame, adjusting his weight to keep from crushing her. He lay half on top of her with one knee on the floor, catching most of his bulk.

When his breathing leveled out and sanity returned, he looked around until he saw his jeans. Kylie's shirt was tangled with the pants in a pile, so he retrieved it and tossed it on her chest.

Grasping the material to cover herself, she gazed at him and tried for another smile. Then she got those clouds in her eyes, the ones that made him want to squirm. That made him want to wrap her up and tuck her away.

And that was a dangerous way to think while his head was still swimming. He was drunk on their lovemaking and needed to take some time. Hell, he needed to take some breaths.

As the overwhelming passion dissipated, so did the forgiveness he'd found while they'd been wrapped up in each other. Turmoil reared in its place and drove Quinn to say the first thing that came to him. "Well, if you wanted to surprise me," his laugh was tight, "you did it."

He couldn't say exactly where the anger came from, but it was riding his back now, digging in its long, sharp claws. Jerking on his jeans, he cocked up one side of his mouth. "But then again, who ever heard of a twenty-two-year-old virgin?"

Her mouth fell open and her brows collided. She sat up, attempting to hide behind the petite shirt. "A general's daughter. That's who. And you don't have to make it sound like a bad thing."

"Just unexpected, especially from you. I mean, you're the one who joked about calling all guys, 'Oh, yes,' so you wouldn't get them confused."

"And you naturally assumed I slept around. Well guess what?" Her eyes narrowed. "There's more than one way to get to an *oh-yes* moment."

Quinn just clamped his lips together and shook his head. So many emotions clashed inside him—release and relief, recriminations. And worse, he felt like he'd been played. Tricked into stealing something he could never give back.

Turning away, he gathered his shoes and shoved them on. Still without words, he scanned the empty room and located his own discarded shirt. In an effort to give her privacy, and himself some time to recover, he went to the window and stared out.

She'd given him a gift, he knew, but how could she wrap up something so important in the package of a lie? Was getting what *she* wanted all that mattered?

He heard her sigh, though he couldn't tell if it was out of frustration or sadness. Then she called his name.

He turned his head, giving her only his profile.

"What are you thinking?" she asked, standing dead center of the dark blue rug that had borne witness to their colossal mistake. "Please tell me you don't regret what just happened. Because I think it was beautiful."

Now he was the one to heave a sigh. "I'm not going to tell you it was the right thing to do." He waited but when she didn't speak, he added, "I'm afraid we only made a messy situation even more complicated."

"Why? What's changed?" Her tone hardened. "I'm still throwing myself at you, and you're still scared and confused." She threw her hands up. "Seems exactly the same to me."

He heard the pain beneath her sharp reprise but refused to engage in an argument. Too many raw feelings stifled the air in the room, and he had to get his own emotions under control.

The storm outside was thinning out, providing him with a quick and easy getaway. "Looks like we can leave soon. It's only a light drizzle out there now."

"Then what's keeping us?" She marched to open the door.

"It's not like we have anything left to say to each other."

"Hey," he barked, stopping her short. "I'm the one who's been tricked here, so don't make this about your hurt feelings." He fell back on old defenses. Cruelty and jabs to push her away.

Just until he could get his head straight and figure out what all of this meant. Figure out what he was feeling, or finally acknowledge that he felt it at all. "I can't help wondering if you thought this would make a difference. Change my mind."

"I told you." The sides of her jaw tightened from where she gritted her teeth. "I'm not asking you for anything, and now more than ever, I realize you were right the whole time."

"Good." He moved to stand in front of her. To glare down at her, so she would understand him once and for all. "Because you should focus on your role in this war, and stop trying to make me love you. I won't do it."

Quinn recoiled inside, because his claim sounded more like insistence than fact. *I don't love her. I can't.*

"Not a problem." She shoved the door the rest of the way open. "I can finally say without hesitation that this thing between us will never work out. It doesn't matter how hard I try."

She shook her head as she looked him straight in the eye. "Because I'm obviously too mature for you."

~~~

Ronja still came to the pit to commune with Bastraal. Though the demon had acquired access to this world and could touch her both physically and psychically, old habits died slowly and painfully.

The altar in the subterranean room just felt right to her after all this time. The mixture of rock and soil, bone and blood, it conjured powerful communions. And she'd knelt before the dais for so long.

As she tread from the stone floor of the dungeon, her bare feet cooled even further when they sunk into soil. Bastraal had first come to her in a cold, dark cave, so the atmosphere here put her at ease. The dank chill relaxed her, helped her open herself to him.

A biting current rippled through the air, across her cheeks, and as it did, a message swelled in her mind. Bastraal was here. He'd come to her.

He always did.

The message was not a request but a command, and in response, Ronja gripped the sides of her black silk gown to drag the material slowly up her legs. Over the hillsides of her hips. And finally past her shoulders to be thrown aside.

Bastraal ordered her to bare all, and she did so without pause.

Letting her head fall back, she felt the arctic caress of his dark power whispering against her skin. He'd caused her pain in the past, that was true, but only when rightfully deserved. He was here in the human world now, thanks in large part to her efforts, so she expected no mistreatment.

And to her, daughter of the ancient north, the painful cold was akin to mother's milk.

"Hmm. You are so good to me, Bastraal." When icy fingers latched onto her hand to pull her forward, she let the beast guide her down the last few steps to the pit.

Beast? Yes. In her world, the term was an endearment. And the demon she'd helped to free was her dearest love. Except . . . perhaps now . . .

"Thank you for bringing my brother back to me, my lord. When I saw his face after all this time, I knew," she put her hands over the freezing pressure points as the demon raked a frigid claw over her flat stomach, "his return to the earth could have only been a gift from you."

More appendages—for she couldn't rightly call them hands—

wrapped around her thighs, her back, and she gasped as power rushed through her. She threw out a hand to steady herself, but the gesture was captured by more of the demon's essence.

He flowed around her, encompassing her body. So this is why he wanted her naked. How wonderful to feel him again.

The true contact was much more powerful than she'd imagined. The coldest, blackest waters of the deepest lake cascaded over her skin, and the hedonism, the intensity—was staggering.

She cried out when he lifted her into the air, his form cradling her, supportive as she floated several feet above the dank, sodden ground. What would he do to her? Should she be afraid? Or excited?

Her vile imagination turned to things even she had never done, and her body ran hot, responding instantly. Could Bastraal be missing the fleshly pleasures from this realm? Could his disembodied spirit recall the slow-building warmth of arousal? The muscle-clenching explosion of orgasm?

Soon another surge of energy flowed into her, but the cold had been replaced with an indescribable sensation. Every neuron in her body was being stimulated. They came to life all at once, like a city after a blackout.

Another signal to the back of her brain. A question. "Yes, Bastraal. Anything for you. Anything. You've given me back what I feared never to have again. For my brother's re-incarnation, I owe you everything. I owe you all."

The next wave hit and her body convulsed. Pleasure and pain shot to levels previously unknown, and for a split-second, she feared she could die after all.

Her nerve endings pulsed, and her cries reached crescendo when he pushed farther, doing things to her body she couldn't comprehend. The cruel strength, the incredible power . . . she came on a swell of the blackest evil and screamed her ecstasy.

When she was lowered to the ground, she sensed a similar

relief in the demon. And now that he was sated, it seemed he would turn again to pillow talk. He whispered in her brain, crooning to her of agony and grief.

Two of her favorite things.

"Yes," she whispered, writhing as the force still thrumming inside her stroked and pulsed. "I understand."

Eventually, Bastraal moved away from her, and she settled against the packed earth. Soil that had felt cool before now burned in comparison to her master's touch. For a moment she simply breathed, luxuriating in the last few tendrils of dark magic quivering in her veins.

Then her eyes snapped open.

Vengeance, he'd murmured. "Yes." Ronja stared at the cement ceiling far above her. Payback.

It was time she made the coven understand how far Bastraal's reach extended. What Ronja was prepared to do to them.

And how dirty she was willing to play.

15

Kylie felt as though something was inside her head scraping at her sinuses by the time they got back to the island. But that's what she got for holding in the tempest of tears that demanded release.

She and Quinn had found his car, suffered a tense and silent drive back to the mainland house, and now she was stepping off of the boat at last. She was back on the island, where she could run and hide.

Which was apparently her new thing.

At least Joseph had offered to bring them and had chatted throughout the trip. He'd been curious about what she and Quinn had found in the forest, but Kylie had ridden near the bow, letting Quinn give their friend the details.

All but one. Her moment of brutal humiliation.

Quinn had given Joseph the simplified version of the bizarre building and the stone yard out back, but his voice had been flat and lifeless. Tired.

"I wonder why planes never spot that rock?" Joseph was keeping the boat steady as Quinn disembarked after Kylie. She was already walking up the pier, and only heard one word floating on the salty sea air. Magic.

The very same magic that was ruining her life.

Just keep walking. Keep walking. She was going to get as far away from Quinn St. Germaine as she possibly could, and she didn't care what anyone said. She was not going to work with him anymore.

She tripped over a fallen branch, and then turned to stomp it into pieces. *And I will die before I ever kiss him again.*

Cutting through the woods took no time at all, especially in her agitated state. She gave a whole new meaning to the idea of power-walking, and paid no mind to the snaps of energy popping all around her.

Her turbulent emotions were siphoning electrical charges from the air, the humidity, the environment in general. Her body collected the juice until she was overloaded, and the energy was forced to leap back out.

Anna was opening the double doors when Kylie bounded up the stone steps of the mansion. "What's wrong?" she asked. "I could feel a disturbance the moment your feet hit the island."

"Ask your brother." Kylie didn't mean to be rude, but she was all out of patience when it came to Quinn. She couldn't help the feeling of betrayal clamping down on her heart like a mousetrap.

A trap. Ha! Isn't that essentially what Quinn had accused her of? All these years, she'd bided her time and pushed aside any hint of normal, young-adult lust. All because she'd wanted to wait for the right man.

Because she'd wanted to be in love.

Then that mysterious force had summoned her to Savannah, to this island, where she'd discovered she was a witch. Oh yeah, and fated to save this hot, humid, flat city.

Magic and Fate didn't seem to give a rat's ass about her needs. And neither did Quinn.

A creeping awareness gave her pause, and she stopped in the middle of the foyer. Had she done any better, really? Been any more considerate? Had she ever asked him what *he* wanted?

Biting her lips, Kylie resumed her stride but at a much calmer pace. Everything was all jacked now. She hadn't lied to

Quinn, exactly, but she had willfully denied him information.

Her chest felt like it was collapsing. She'd really screwed up, and for a minute there, just a moment, when he'd filled her and looked down at her that way . . . she'd believed he loved her too.

Then he'd gotten upset. Again. And she was running out of a lot more than just patience. She was out of hope. She was hollow, broken. What more could she possibly give?

When she entered the great room, Willyn, Hayden, and Shauni were all in a row on the green velvet couch. They were watching a movie with canned laughter, a comedy. Not unlike the current state of Kylie's love life.

She tried to tamp down on the acrid taste of envy. These three were the nice girls of the coven. All of whom apparently deserved to be loved.

"Hey," Shauni called out.

Kylie gave a quick wave and hurried past them to the staircase. She knew begrudging her sisters' happiness was unfair and only a result of her fury over Quinn's rejection. His latest and greatest denial. But honestly, she only had herself to blame, because she was the one who just kept going back for more abuse.

Her eyes blurred as the tears made a push for escape. *Damn!* Why did she keep going back?

"How'd it go?" Willyn asked, standing up to come around the couch to intercept Kylie.

"Uh . . . um, we found something, but I really need to get into dry clothes first. We got caught in the thunderstorm." And an emotional hellstorm. "But Quinn should be right behind me. He'll fill you in."

"Oh. Okay." Willyn leaned forward as if about to ask a question, but she retreated instead, smiling softly before going back to the couch. As she sat, she spoke quietly to Hayden and Shauni.

They can all probably guess what's wrong with me. Shame

suffused her cheeks, warming her face. Quinn was always what was wrong with her.

And she felt like the biggest fool in the world for throwing herself at him. She clenched her eyes and shook her head, shaking with embarrassment. How was she supposed to live here with him now? See him every day?

She could never meet his eyes again. A sob twisted her chest, right beneath her sternum. But she wouldn't let it out. Not yet. Not here where someone might see or hear.

If any one of her sisters gave her a sad look or used that tone women do when they sympathized, she would break down and bawl, adding another layer of mortification. So maybe things *could* get worse.

She jogged up the stairs, hoping to reach the privacy of her room where she could shower and cry all she wanted. But as she rounded the landing and had one foot on the next set of stairs, a commotion filled the lower level. A man's voice was yelling. Was that Mr. Attinger?

It was. And he was shouting for Willyn. Willyn. The nurse. The healer. *Oh no.*

Taking two steps at a time, she ran back downstairs and saw Anna rush into the great room. "What is it?" she cried. The leader of the coven stopped, stared, and then broke into a run, her alarm causing Kylie's skin to prickle with dread.

One hand on the banister, Kylie hit the slate floor and sprinted down the hall toward the back. She saw the others gathered there, midway down the corridor. Mr. Attinger, white-haired from age and white-faced from terror, was carrying his wife in his arms.

Kylie heard the front doors burst inward, and she knew it was Quinn. Then Viv's and Claudia's concerned voices carried down from the hallways above.

"What happened?" Willyn asked, helping Mr. Attinger ease his wife to the floor. His arms were shaking. He must have carried her all the way from their house on the backside of the estate.

Mrs. Attinger's eyes were open, but she wasn't speaking.

Her husband stammered, "She . . . she was making us some tea, and I heard a clatter. She yelled for me." The poor man could barely speak, clearly distraught. "She said, 'Something's in here!' and when I got to the kitchen, she was staring into space, her hands waving in front of her."

Willyn was assessing Mrs. Attinger as she listened to the story. Kylie saw her lift both of the woman's arms, instructing the older woman to hold them up. The left one dropped immediately to the floor.

Willyn repeated the process. Same results.

"Then she turned around to look at me." Mr. Attinger was on the verge of crying. "And her eyes were so wide. So scared. She tried to talk to me, but her mouth just twisted up. Gargled sounds—" Here he broke off, unable to continue. "Please help her, Willyn."

In full medical mode, Willyn nodded quickly. "How long ago did this happen? I need as close to the actual time as you can tell me."

"No more than . . ." the older man looked up, thinking. "About six minutes ago. I brought her straight here."

"You did exactly right." Willyn pointed at Viv. "Remember the time."

"Got it," Viv said."

Then Willyn looked to Quinn. "Is Joseph gone with the boat?"

"Yes."

Kylie looked at the man she'd been doing her best to despise only minutes ago, but her heart wrenched to see him in such torment. Overwhelmed by fear. Mr. and Mrs. Attinger had raised him and Anna since their parents' deaths. They were his family.

"Then call Claire and Joe. They need to bring the other boat if Joseph isn't there by the time you reach them."

Quinn pulled his cell phone from his pocket and used his trembling finger to press a button. He eased back toward the great room to talk.

"Mrs. Attinger?" Willyn was speaking to the woman still lying on the floor, whose terrified blue eyes stared straight ahead. "Can you speak?"

The noise emitted was horrible, and Anna dropped to her knees beside the woman who'd been as much her mother as housekeeper. "We're here. All of us. We'll fix it, Mrs. A. We'll fix it."

Anna and Willyn stared at each other, but it was to her patient that Willyn spoke. "Mrs. Attinger. You're having a stroke, but it's good that your husband was there with you. I know it's scary right now, but we have time. What you're experiencing right now . . . may not be permanent."

Another stab to Kylie's gut. *May not be?*

Paige and Lucia had come down by now, so the entire coven was there. They all watched, likely feeling as helpless as she did. Mrs. Attinger was dear to each of them.

"Can't you heal her, Willyn?" Paige was rubbing the back of her neck and shifting on her feet.

"I don't want to take a chance with this. It's too delicate, and if I missed something . . ."

"We understand," Anna said, still holding onto Mrs. Attinger. "I trust you."

Kylie heard Quinn speak into the phone, his anguish twisting her heart. Because she knew his was breaking. "Joe. We need a boat. It's Mrs. A." He thrust a hand through his sable hair. "Joe, you have to hurry."

~~~

The lengthy hours in the Emergency Department waiting

room had been a special kind of torture for all of them. Only Mr. Attinger had been allowed into the treatment area with his wife, but he'd come out to brief Anna and the others on any development, any new information.

The spry and maternal woman they all adored and depended on had indeed suffered a stroke. Kylie glanced to Willyn, caught her eye, and nodded her thanks. She'd made note of the time for a reason, and since they could pinpoint the onset of Mrs. Attinger's symptoms, the doctor had a window of time to work with.

Apparently, there was a medication that would break up the clot—after a CT scan had ensured it was a clot causing the stroke and not a bleed—and because they had an idea when the problem began, they could treat her with that medication. If they'd gotten her to the hospital too late for treatment . . .

Kylie rubbed her face, refusing to let her imagination wander that way.

She and the others had arrived at the hospital shortly after the ambulance. That had been late afternoon, and now it was well after midnight. Mrs. Attinger had finally been assigned a bed in the Intensive Care Unit, so they had relocated to a newer, less crowded waiting area.

The doctor had warned there might be a variety of side effects while she recovered, but if she continued to do as well as she was now, they would move her to the neurovascular floor the next day. Willyn seemed okay with the plan, so the rest of them were as well.

Kylie sat in a blue vinyl chair, grateful the lounge here was more comfortable than that of the ED. Quinn and Anna had been allowed back to visit when Mr. Attinger came out.

The older man had experienced seven levels of Hell tonight. They all had. And with the worst behind him, he finally dropped into a chair and let his head fall forward into his hands. When his shoulders began to shake, Kylie made a move toward him to offer comfort.

But when he lifted his white-topped head, he was smiling. "I think she's going to be okay. They got to it in time."

His eyes found Kylie, so she smiled and bobbed her head. "Absolutely. You were her hero today, Mr. A. You saved her."

"We all did." He extended a hand, so she rose and went to his side. He grasped her fingers. "With the immediate danger having passed, you have to promise not to let this distract you." He scrunched his brows at her. "She wouldn't want that. You've got to keep your eyes straight ahead. Finish your trial."

"I will. I promise." *As soon as I figure out what I have to do.* Her hand went automatically to her amulet. For the sake of the coven and the city itself, Kylie was determined to hear the stone's pure, clear song.

He was right. She had to stay on task.

And dear, sweet Mr. Attinger. How had he known she needed his permission? His approval.

When the older man patted her hand and sat back, Kylie found herself staring at the ICU doors where Quinn had gone with his sister. He too had been devastated.

Shaken up and apprehensive, his usual calm had vanished, replaced by confusion and fear. Until the nurse had told him and Anna they could go back to see Mrs. Attinger, he'd been quiet, pensive, and unwilling to speak to anyone.

Kylie knew him better than he gave her credit for, and she understood why he was taking this so hard. *Oh, Quinn.* How was she supposed to be angry with him when he was beating up on himself this way?

With a gentle glide, the double doors swung open an inch at a time, releasing Quinn and Anna from the secure medical unit. Quinn veered over to speak to Mr. Attinger, who was still holding Kylie's hand. "The nurse said you could come back one more time, and then they would have to enforce normal visiting hours. But she also said the next place they'll move

Mrs. Attinger will be less strict. You can even sleep in the room with her."

Joy bloomed in Mr. Attinger's face. "Thank the Lord." He stood and thumped Quinn on the shoulder before gripping him in a tight hug. Then the older man let go with tears in his eyes and walked over to Anna.

Cupping her cheek, Mr. Attinger grinned at the woman who'd been like a daughter to him, and then the two shared soft words. Afterwards, he went inside with a young woman in blue scrubs who'd been holding the door and waiting for him.

Quinn started to move away, but Kylie gripped his arm. She had to say one thing to him. "Quinn. This wasn't your fault."

He frowned, shook his head, and tried to pull away. She held on. "It was *not* your fault, Quinn."

Now he jerked his arm hard, turning all his pent up emotion her way. Well then, if he needed to vent, she could take it. For him.

"You heard what Mr. Attinger told Willyn," he said harshly. "Something was in their house right before she had the stroke. Something I allowed to get in. So yes, it *is* my fault."

His eyes raked her up and down, misery colliding with disgust. For himself? For Kylie? "I had a job to do—one fucking job—and I didn't do it. Instead, I was at a party, getting drunk so I wouldn't think about *you*."

"Quinn—"

"No." He shook off her rebuttal. "Then today, I went with you, when anyone else could have gone. And after what happened between us, I wish I'd listened to Paige. Then we wouldn't have let ourselves do something so stupid."

He clenched his jaw and glared at her. "If I'd stayed at home, then maybe I would have found a way to repair the wards completely. So far, I've only been able to block humans." His hands curled into fists. "Not demons. And we all know exactly what was in that room with Mrs. Attinger. We know what caused her stroke."

With every second he grew more incensed, his neck so tense she could see the muscles cording. "I let Bastraal onto our property, and he attacked Mrs. Attinger. Whether he caused it directly or not, she had a stroke!" He slammed a fist to the center of his chest. "I almost got someone I love killed!"

As soon as his voice rose to a thunder and everyone in the waiting area looked at them, Quinn seemed to draw it all back down. He sucked all the fury and blame back inside.

Though he spoke quietly now, the impact of his words was greater than if he'd raged. "And all because of you. My messed up feelings for you."

"That's not fair." Kylie could barely whisper, too stunned and horrified by the blame he cast. "Neither of us could have known—"

"We should have known." He drilled a finger into his chest. "I should have known."

He released a slow, controlled exhale. "Fuck, I did know. The protection spell's been offline for weeks, and I've been trying to keep you at bay, so I could focus on repairing it. So I could concentrate on what's important. So now, Kylie. Please. Now that you and I have done our worst, will you just . . ." he stared past her, "please just leave me alone."

"Fine." The word was quick and sharp, but it was all she could think to say. "If you want to beat yourself up over what happened between us, then go ahead. But we did not cause this, Quinn."

Though even as Kylie denied the guilt, shame began to swarm.

Had she pulled Quinn away from his duties? He was their best researcher and had insisted on being involved. He'd wanted to go with her to find the property.

Kylie whirled and headed for the elevators. She heard Viv call her name. "I'm going to get us coffee," she said, throwing up a hand but refusing to look back.

Maybe Quinn was right. He had tried to keep his distance, but Kylie had never let up. She hadn't been able to. She thought they were supposed to be together.

Tears burned her eyes, turning the white tile floor and the wide blue line on it to watercolors. Her head felt packed with cotton. She couldn't think straight or make sense of anything.

No matter how she picked things apart, she found no answer. Had she been so stubborn that she'd set events in motion that had hurt Mrs. Attinger? Was all of this her fault? And if she entertained the notion, it was no wonder Quinn was doing the same.

When the bell dinged and a sob broke from her chest, she prayed no one was standing behind the elevator doors. But people probably cried a lot in hospitals. And these days, Kylie just seemed to cry a lot, period.

She heard her name again as the doors began to close. Viv ran up but not in time to get a hand inside. Kylie tried to sound cheerful. She tried to pretend everything was fine when she called out to her friend, "I'll be right back."

16

"Now where are *you* going?"

Quinn's head jerked up in response to the question. Viv was striding toward him as he headed for the hospital elevator. "I need to get home and repair the wards," he said. "I've let this go on for too long. I've had almost two months to get them fixed, and there's no excuse." He brushed past Viv as she held out a hand to stop him.

"Hold on," she whirled around and came after him.

Quinn jabbed the button over and over again to call the elevators, but he wasn't escaping that easily. Viv was there beside him again. "I'll go down with you," she said.

"That's not necessary. I know my way." He couldn't seem to stop the frustration from snaking its way into his voice. He wasn't really angry with her, or for that matter, with Kylie either.

No, all his hate was self-directed. Just one more reason he needed to get away from everyone he cared about and get home where he could be by himself. Where he could concentrate on the task he'd left incomplete.

And if he had to work until dawn—it would be dawn in a couple of hours—well then, if he had to work all day, so be it. He wouldn't stop until his family was protected again.

Viv didn't say anything else but walked onto the elevator with him in silence. Once they made it to the main floor, Quinn hooked a right, expecting Viv to go in the opposite direction toward the cafeteria. Instead she walked with him.

A hospital at midnight seemed one of the quietest places on earth. The air felt ominous, heavy with the smell of worry. Empty halls were filled with nothing but the artificial light that bounced from sterile white floors and walls.

Then a man carrying a plastic tray with vials and implements to draw blood hurried from a side passage, nodding to Quinn and Viv as he passed. "Are you going to walk me all the way out to the car?" Quinn groused to his unwelcome escort.

Viv shook her head. "No. Just until you tell me what's going on with you. You've become a brother to all of us, Quinn, and I can see when you're hurting. When you're blaming yourself." Her gray eyes grew shrewd. "And I expect that's exactly what Kylie said to you before."

"Doesn't matter. I know what I should have done. What I now have to do. Everything else is just extra bullshit that gets in the way." They passed the gift shop, dark and locked up tight until morning.

The electronic doors of the main lobby swooshed open, the sound like a pent-up breath exhaling softly. Quinn slowed, noticing a man and woman that stood outside in the drive where cars normally picked up or dropped off patients. The couple looked at him and smiled.

Then the man's face morphed into that of a monster, mouth open with a leer that revealed fangs.

Quinn halted abruptly and grabbed Viv's arm. "Do you see that?"

Her brows clashed together, and she reached over her shoulder for her sword. Which she didn't have. "Yes, but the question is, how do *you*?"

"I don't know." A blast of fresh rage burned through Quinn. "He let me see it. But why would he do that?" He started to step forward.

Viv grabbed his arm this time, pulling him with her as she backed into the lobby. The doors closed in front of their faces as the man and woman approached.

"I don't have an herb bag," Viv said. "Do you?"

"No." Quinn understood immediately. If they couldn't douse the people with Ethan's special herb mixture, there was no way to tell if demons had possessed two innocent human bodies, or if the beasts were pure evil.

"We have to call the others," Quinn said. "These two must be here to finish what Bastraal started. You go on up, I'll do what I can here."

"No way." Viv was already on her phone, speaking into the small cell. "Shauni, we've got demons here. Two coming in the front entrance. We don't have weapons. We don't have herbs." Viv listened briefly then said, "Good. We'll do what we can."

She shoved the phone in her pocket. "Ethan has a bag with him. He's sending it down." She shifted her eyes to Quinn. "Thank goodness someone was thinking tonight."

Quinn agreed. How had they all managed to come without protection? Easy answer. Because they'd been distraught over Mrs. Attinger.

He spread his legs, ready to fight with magic if he had to. These bastards weren't getting near Mrs. Attinger, lying defenseless in her hospital bed. *We'll be her defense. I owe her that at the very least.*

The door swooshed open again to admit the man and woman. Both of them revealed their true nature now, their misshapen and oversized heads bearing short, curved horns, their maws wide and hungry.

They growled in a threatening manner, but all that did was piss Quinn off even more. He stood his ground. "You aren't getting past me, but you did show up just in time." Pulling fire from the air, he held the flaming ball at chest level between his hands. "Because kicking some demon ass would make me feel a whole lot better."

Viv had called her blue light and had it loaded, prepared to use the coven magic if the monsters tried to advance. Innocent human bodies or not, they couldn't get inside the hospital. Far too many other people would be in danger if that happened.

The man wore cargo pants the color of soot with a tight black t-shirt. The woman, oddly enough, was in a floral sundress. They would blend right in with the human populace. Until they showed their ugly faces.

When the male made his move, Quinn was ready. He dismissed the flames he'd conjured, opting instead to lunge forward. Lowering his center of gravity, he rushed to meet him.

They came together like two rams, and though the demon was huge, Quinn was pumping pure adrenaline and fury. He lifted the man off the ground, so they both careened to the side to collide with the wall.

The demon began squeezing Quinn, trying to crush his ribs, so Quinn reached for the fire again, shoving it into the center of the beast's back. The demon bellowed his rage but stayed locked onto Quinn.

Suddenly all the overhead lights went out, leaving only the pale glow of emergency floor lights. The disturbance cost him a moment of attention, and that was long enough for the demon to head-butt the side of his face.

Reeling from the throbbing ache in his temple, Quinn heard the female demon cry out. He saw her movement in his peripheral vision. But a flash of blue stopped her in her tracks. Viv was throwing her magic, heading off the woman's attempts to leap into the fray.

Trying something different, Quinn raced through the various spells stored in his mind. He'd been practicing magic since his youth, but tonight he'd been overrun by his need to fight like a man. To expend his rage with brute force.

"*Caecus.*" He'd always preferred straight Latin over Anna's secret language, but then, he was the linguist in the family. This time as he said the word for 'blind,' he pressed his hand over the man's eyes. *"Caecus!"*

With a sound more like a scream than a yell, the thug pushed away from Quinn, thrashing his head about as if he could shake off the blackness cloaking his vision.

Quinn took the opportunity to drag in a breath, but as soon as he'd inhaled a deep gulp of oxygen, he felt the stabbing sting in his left side. The demon had been moderately successful, it seemed.

Well, Willyn could make him right again, and what were a few broken bones when it came to protecting the people he loved? He took a step to head off the female as she jerked toward him, but something flew between him and the demons.

Quinn watched the blur take form in the soft, dim light. Paige. Yeah, that made sense. She'd probably run down the stairs, her body much faster than any manmade elevator could ever be.

She held an herb bag in one hand. A knife in the other.

When she held the curved weapon toward the man still shaking his hideous head, the blade glowed brilliant crimson. He was all demon.

"This just isn't your lucky night, pal," Paige told the beast just before driving the knife into his throat. Sending blue light through the blade, she streamed it into his foul body.

As Quinn watched, the demon burst into a cloud of ash. When the particles drifted his way, he swiped his hand through the air to clear his eyes and stared at Paige. "I guess I should say thanks."

She hiked a knowing brow. "But you were really enjoying pounding on him? Sorry about that, but I think we all want a piece of a demon tonight."

She jerked her head toward the female who remained. Then she tossed the knife to Viv. "Share and share alike."

The woman was hissing like a snake and bearing long, sharp fingernails. Viv ranged close enough to see the knife turn red once more, but she chose pure magic as her weapon, no blade needed. And her flash of cerulean light created just as much ash.

The raven-haired physicist blew out a breath and turned. "They might not be the only ones here. And what's with the lights?"

Paige nodded. "The others went out in teams of two to sweep the other entrances. Ethan and Lucia, Shauni and Michael, Hayden and Trevor," she grinned, "and Claudia and Cole. At least all that pairing up has increased our ranks."

Quinn normally appreciated the woman's disdain for all things romantic and often felt the same. But tonight he couldn't find humor in anything.

His world was crashing down around him. His logical, balanced, well-ordered world, where he'd always known what was coming his way. And what he should do about it.

Until Kylie.

He coughed to clear both his throat and his mind. "Look at all this ash." He moved toward the doors until they slid open.

He raised his hands, palms facing the opening. Air always had been his favorite element. Deceptively light, yet deadly if used the right way.

He raised a gust of wind, and the gray particles lifted, sweeping out to blend into the night. He rarely used his magic in front of others but was making up for lost time.

His face fell into a scowl as he focused again on the two witches with him. "Why did they come here tonight? They must have tracked us, but if they think they're going to touch her again—"

"Easy. Take it easy." Paige made a calm-down motion. He must have looked as near nuclear-detonation as he felt.

Viv was on her phone again, checking in with the others.

Lucia and Ethan had gone back to the Emergency Department, but that area was secure. Claudia and Cole reported that the east portion closer to The Heart and Vascular Institute was clear as well.

Shauni and Michael were at the opposite end now, near the parking garage. As yet, there were no other signs of anything demonic. Viv met Quinn's eyes after she clicked off. "I'll go to the cafeteria to let Kylie know what's happened. She was going for coffee."

Not trusting himself to speak, he nodded. "We'll wait here."

Milling around the front entrance, Quinn glimpsed a teddy bear inside the gift shop, a huge pink balloon attached to a stick that proclaimed, "It's A Girl!" For some reason, his stomach churned.

Perhaps the thought of innocent babies somewhere in the sprawling medical facility? If the Amara had their way, they wouldn't stop at hurting the coven. The city of Savannah would become a blood bath, and eventually, Ronja and Bastraal's vile reign would spread beyond the city borders.

He pulled his stare from the fluffy pink bear. *I can't let anyone else down. What good did I do spending all those years preparing, waiting, if I can't see my duties through to the end?*

He met Paige glare for worried glare, but only one lone person entered the doors. A twenty-something-year-old guy carrying a bag of fast food—burger and fries by the smell of it. Midnight snack for someone working the late shift?

Paige looked to Quinn and shook her head as the young man walked inside. She brushed close to him, all the while watching the blade of her knife. No response. The man wasn't a demon in disguise.

The only other passerby was a janitor sweeping his way along the corridor behind them. He stopped to incline his head before carrying on.

Paige shrugged to Quinn as if asking his opinion. He frowned, considering the complication. "Lots of people work here or are visiting. We can't go running up to each of them with a knife to check their status."

Crossing his arms over his chest, he leaned against the wall. "Anna, Willyn, and Dare stayed upstairs to watch over the Attingers?"

Paige mimicked his pose on her own wall. "Yeah. They'll let us know if they need us. I mean, that's got to be why those jackasses came tonight, right? To make sure they finished what Bastraal started?"

Quinn tightened his lips, pressing them together as he mulled it over. The demons had seemed eager to fight. Why hadn't they just slipped past if they'd wanted to find and hurt Mrs. Attinger?

He was beginning to get a bad vibe.

Viv returned then, her breath hitching slightly. "I don't want to alarm anyone, but Kylie wasn't there. I called up to Anna, and she didn't come back to the ICU area either." She darted her gaze between him and Paige. "And I can't get her on her cell."

"Shit." Quinn cleared his mind and made a plan. "Paige, we need a witch on the doors in case other demons try to get inside. Tell them to send the men to the cafeteria. We'll split up from there to search. Anna and Willyn need to stay in the ICU waiting room."

He looked at Viv. "Is Nick here yet?"

She nodded. "He just texted me that he's here. I'll have him cover the parking garage on his way in."

"Good. Thanks."

"No need to thank us, Quinn." Paige was unusually gentle when she spoke, drawing his gaze back to her. "We care about her too."

"I know you do." He gave a sharp nod and started down the hallway, following the thick blue line until it became orange.

The stripe led him toward the rear of the building. Toward the cafeteria.

He took a walk through the food lines to check for Kylie, with no luck. By the time he was back in the dining room, the other guys had shown up.

Michael held up his own phone. "Nick just called and said he's driving through all the levels. No sign of her so far. Then he's going to check the garages out back."

Quinn nodded. "Good."

"And Willyn will keep calling her phone." Dare came over and clapped Quinn on the shoulder. "Don't worry. She'll turn up." The look in the male witch's eyes made Quinn uncomfortable.

Then his throat closed off unexpectedly, forcing him to clear it with a harsh cough. "Yeah. Yeah, I'm sure she will. But why isn't she answering her phone?" He glanced around at the empty tables. "If she's ignoring us just because she's mad at me . . ."

"Don't." Michael gave him a sharp look. "She wouldn't do that, and you don't need to take any more responsibility for what's happened." The tall blonde man stepped closer, a somber expression in place. "You didn't cause any of this. And neither did she."

Quinn's neck flamed. How many of them had heard him berate Kylie? The disgrace he felt told him how badly he'd handled that conversation. "You're right. It's been a long night." *And a day of surprises. Of mistakes.* "Let's just find her."

They broke into groups. Dare and Michael would scout the offshoots of the hospital floors, in case she was wandering around taking time to recover from . . . well, everything.

Trevor would go with Ethan, and Cole with Quinn. So at least two of the pairings had a gun, and the others had a witch or someone who could detect demons. Fire power at every front.

As the others went on their way, Quinn and Cole ducked through the side door just outside of the cafeteria where Shauni still stood sentry.

"Anything?" she asked upon seeing them.

"Not yet." Quinn wanted to encourage her, to bolster her as he always tried to do with the women, but he couldn't summon the energy. Or the faith that everything was going to be all right.

With every step his blood rushed faster in his brain, pounding his eardrums. A demanding cadence of fear and dread. Where the hell was Kylie?

Shauni waved a hand as they pushed through the doors. "Keep your guard up out there. Something's . . . not right about all of this."

"We will," Cole told her, but Quinn could only think how much he agreed with her. That bad vibe was getting stronger.

"That must be Nick." Cole indicated the tall garage to their right. A single headlight was trawling slowly through the bottom level. Nick's motorcycle.

Still taking his time, he disappeared behind the mammoth wall of concrete and came back into view on the near side. Quinn and Cole were crossing the grass, scanning the open area as they did. Cole waved Nick over, and they met on the road encircling the facilities.

"Anything?" Nick yelled over the rumble of his bike.

"No." Quinn shook his head.

"I'll take a ride through the others." The pub owner who'd bound Viv's heart gave Quinn an encouraging look. "She's here somewhere. Don't worry."

Quinn gritted his teeth and lifted a hand in acknowledgement. Why did all the guys keep telling him that? "I'm not worried," he said abruptly.

Cole gave him a funny look. "Okay."

They crossed the back side through the ED parking lot. Lucia was staring out as they went by. They waved to her but shook their heads in the negative.

Even from that distance, Quinn could see her shoulders slump.

"She's probably just listening to her music." He stopped suddenly, slamming his hands together. "Of course." Laughter that was more frantic than relieved pushed out of his gut. "Why didn't I think of that? She always listens to her iPod when she's upset. She's probably just got the volume turned up and can't hear us calling."

Did he sound a little unnerved? Panicked? Why should he? The idea was perfectly plausible.

But that bad vibe was strumming in his gut like an out-of-tune bass guitar. "She's fine," he said with more conviction. "She's okay."

His cell phone buzzed in his pocket. In one move, he had it out and saw Nick's name on the screen. As he answered and casually raised the cell to his ear, he trained his eyes on the far-away parking garage. A single headlight shone on the second level.

"Quinn . . . I—" Nick faltered, pausing long enough to send needles skittering down Quinn's spine. "I've found an amulet back here. The middle stone. It's yellow."

Quinn clenched his eyes shut as his stomach plummeted. He answered in a rough, uneven voice. "That's Kylie's."

17

The blue metal door slammed against the concrete wall and bounced off from the force after Lucia sprinted from the stairwell. The other witches followed closely, all except Willyn, who'd remained behind to guard the ICU and the Attingers.

Ethan and Dare had returned to the hospital unit as well, with Trevor and Cole as backup. With badges and magic standing guard, the rest of the coven would take the search for Kylie to the next level.

Because she obviously hadn't disappeared of her own free will. There was no longer any question in their minds. She'd been taken.

Quinn and Nick still stood around the amulet. Chain broken, the silver necklace lay discarded on the cracked concrete of the parking garage. "Hurry." Quinn motioned Lucia over. "They might still be close."

Not wanting to interfere with any of Kylie's essence that might still be channeling through the amulet, the men had left it on the floor. Lucia paused to stare, blinking. "This is the first time any of us have been without our amulet since the night of the selection ceremony. Unless there was a purpose, but I can't see any reason why she would have taken hers off."

Quinn nodded with grim understanding. Magic and the amulets had done the choosing, the silver pendants becoming talismans for the women. Connecting them to each other and their united power.

Now Kylie had been cut loose and was out there on her own.

Lucia's bottom lip quivered, so Quinn spoke firmly. "Lucia. Let's go." He had to jar her from the emotion that was welling up, preventing her from performing. Lucia could find anything that was lost, inanimate object or living creature.

And right now, one of the most precious things in Quinn's life was missing.

Why am I acknowledging that now? Why couldn't I have . . . Shaking off the whirl of insane thoughts in his head, Quinn focused instead on the Spanish woman and the necklace she now clasped in her palm.

"I've been trying to get a bead on her since we first realized she was missing," Lucia said, brown eyes full of angst. "I had hoped the amulet would trigger something." She shook her head and glanced to Anna. "But I'm not getting anything. I can't even tell she was here. It's as if . . ."

"What?" Quinn barked. "As if what?"

Lucia's voice shook. "It's like she doesn't even exist."

Despair swamped Quinn, the pressure inside his chest cavity causing actual pain.

"Let me try." Anna took the necklace from Lucia, rubbing the stone lovingly as she closed her eyes and concentrated.

After several ragged heartbeats, Quinn touched his sister's arm. "Anything?"

Anna's rigid posture collapsed. "No. Nothing. It's like Lucia said. Kylie is being blocked from us, and the force behind this spell is strong. Incredibly powerful."

Ramming his hands into his hair, Quinn tossed back his head and walked a wide circle. "No. No. All of this was done on purpose. The Amara brought us all here. That's why Mrs. Attinger was attacked."

Anna too put a hand to the side of her head. "They knew it would get us all off the island. That we'd come to the hospital with her."

"You're saying they wanted to take Kylie?" Paige stalked forward as the other women listened intently.

"Or one of us," Lucia said. "They drew us here where we were completely unprotected. Then all they had to do was wait."

"No." Anna shook her head. "They knew she'd be alone. Tyr saved up his energy to do his one great psychic trick. They saw her alone downstairs, near the cafeteria."

Quinn groaned. If he hadn't argued with Kylie, she would never have left the way she had. She wouldn't have been by herself.

"They sent the demons, because they knew we would do exactly what we did." Paige plowed a fist into the wall. "Split up to defend the entrances."

Shauni stepped forward, her arms wrapped around her midsection. "But how did they get her outside?" She swept her hand out in an arc. "Out here?"

"By force," Quinn said, his body revolting from the growing horror of what Kylie had gone through. What she was still going through. "When the lights went off. That's when they made their move. If anyone happened to see them, Scarlett or Ronja could have spelled the person so they would forget."

Claudia bound her red hair in a ponytail as she spoke. "If Lucia and Anna can't find her with their magic, then we have to start a search. On foot. By car. By whatever means necessary."

She'd recently faced the demon himself, in a dream-like world stuck somewhere between the present and the past. Claudia had experienced the beast's cruelty firsthand, and her face was now as white as the washed-out concrete walls.

Quinn wondered if he looked the same, because he felt like his soul was being torn slowly from his body. They were all thinking the same thing. The Amara had one of the Savannah Coven members.

And no mercy would be shown.

"The plantation." Quinn's heart suddenly hammered back to life. There wasn't time to worry about his own feelings or how Kylie's abduction was affecting him. "It's Ronja's stronghold. They'd take her there."

Paige shrugged, her eyes fierce with aquamarine fire. "What choice do we have? I'll see you there." In a blur of movement, she was gone.

"Damn it, Paige. Wait!" Hayden lunged toward the swinging stairwell door, but Paige was likely already crossing the ED parking lot with her super-speed. She'd been one of the people who'd driven to the hospital, so she would have her car.

Anna snapped out an order to the others. "We have to keep our heads. No one acts alone, got it?"

Rarely had there been such tension crackling through the air between the witches. Not since the very beginning, when they'd all been getting familiar with each other. And with their magic.

Quinn stared hard at Nick, then let his eyes track to his bike. "Can you take me on that thing?"

Nick was already handing him the helmet. "I only have one."

"Keep it." Quinn tossed a leg over the motorcycle.

The engine roared as the machine sped down the ramp to the first-level exit. Over the grinding noise, he heard his sister's furious yell. "Quinn!"

He didn't look back.

~~~

Paige was pacing back and forth across the country road when Quinn and Nick idled to a stop. Her white-blonde hair was in disarray and looked as if she'd been attempting to pull it from the roots.

"I can't get closer!" She hurled an angry hand toward the drive that led to the white plantation home. "The fuckers have some sort of force field up!"

Quinn clenched his jaw. It was to be expected, but being stopped so far from the house was a heavy blow. Was Kylie in there? Was she hurting? Or being hurt? "They've got a protective spell."

"Isn't that what I just said?" Paige was on a tear, stomping around like a caged wildcat.

Quinn understood her, because like him, she carried a load of responsibility around with her. As the witch who was physically strongest and fastest, she felt it was her job to keep the others safe from bodily harm. But she put too much on herself.

Quinn's steps staggered when he pictured Kylie's face. She'd told him almost the very same thing. So sweet and unguarded, doing anything she could to ease his burden.

And he'd only struck her down, lashing out because of his own guilt.

Quinn went as far down the drive as he could, until he sensed the throbbing magic shield. Logic and reason could go to the devil. He still felt like he was to blame, both for Mrs. Attinger's attack and now for Kylie's disappearance.

If he'd had the wards up. If he hadn't been so hard on Kylie. None of this would have happened. In an act of self-castigation, he slapped his open palm to the invisible wall. And was thrown ten feet backward.

The burning jolt up his arm was no surprise, but he'd felt the need to test the strength of the barrier. Now he had, and the situation was far worse than he'd imagined. Scarlett and Ronja weren't the only supernatural creatures fueling the spell.

Bastraal had lent his vile power to the cause.

Quinn was still on the ground when two cars rolled up behind Paige's vehicle and Nick's bike. Anna swung out a passenger door and ran to Quinn, chewing his ass the entire way. "Don't you ever go off half-cocked like that again!"

The head witch then whirled on Paige and jabbed a finger in her direction. "You either!" Running her hands down her white peasant blouse, a style she favored, Anna drew a breath and spoke more calmly. "If we lose anyone else, we'll only be weakened. The only way we'll be able to help Kylie is together."

She walked over to Quinn, but instead of lending him a hand to rise, she crossed her arms over her chest. She was still in a pique. "How bad is it?"

"Bad." Quinn rocked forward to his knees and stood. "Bastraal's involved with this protection spell. And you can bet he's helping block Kylie from us."

Anna moved away from him and stood as close to the impenetrable force field as she dared. Her eyes dilated as she focused her gaze.

Quinn knew the danger she faced, opening herself up this way so near the Amara plantation, but he trusted her to pull back when she had to.

"I don't feel her," Anna said finally. She turned and sought out Lucia. "What do you think?"

Lucia didn't look to the sprawling white house with its alabaster columns and wrap-around porches. Instead, she closed her eyes to search the area. Then she opened them and sighed. "I know she's being blocked, and I can't be sure. But I don't think she's here."

Anna nodded. "I agree, but I wanted to have you back me up." She looked over her shoulder at the house again. The night was still. The sky clear. The surrounding forest was without sound.

"No." Anna's whisper was barely perceptible. "She's not here."

Marching back to the invisible wall, Quinn glared toward the lovely home, the elegant pillars and plantation-style grace. All of it shrouded in evil. His hand trembled, so he clenched it and made a fist. "Then where is she?"

~~~

Kylie was awakened by hard, piercing pressure in her side. As her eyelids fluttered their way open, she was confused by the shadowy gray that stretched out before her. Her vision cleared, but still no answers came.

Where am I? The points of pain beneath her were due to a rough stone floor. In the corner, she noted the masonry met up with a wall of the same construction. Craggy rocks had been joined with mortar, a hand-hewn job from the looks of it, with dried drips of cement-mix on several of the stones.

Alarm sprang to the front of her addled brain. She didn't know this place.

Rolling onto her back, she saw a cement ceiling above her. Her muscles ached, but only from having slept on the uneven floor. She tried to bring her arms down, but they met resistance halfway there. Her wrists shot with needles of pain. "What the . . .?"

Dropping her head back to look in the direction of her arms, she saw shackles around her wrists. She was chained, the links threading from the cuffs and out through iron bars. Bars?

Now panic set in fully, and she tugged against the chains, squirming onto her stomach to get a better look. She was surrounded by tall black rods on three sides, the stone wall on the fourth.

Then her recall kicked in, and her last memory returned. It chilled her very bones. The Amara had been there, at the hospital. They'd attacked her, and Scarlett had shot her red dust into Kylie's face.

Then there had been nothing. She must have passed out.

And now Kylie had woken to a nightmare. She was in a holding cell, a prison, captured by her worst enemies. Tossing her head around, she studied the room beyond the bars, but only the dimmest light emanated from a small electric lantern in one corner.

She could make out the outline of a door about eight feet away. Wooden planks, indicative of recent construction. Other than the door, everything was stone or metal. She was cut off from the outside world and couldn't tell if she was on a walk-in floor, higher up, or beneath ground level.

The rattle of keys clanked against the other side of the door. Her short reprieve was over, and unless Lucia and the coven had somehow found her, the person on the other side of the door would bring nothing but trouble.

With her body still flat on the ground and eyes straight ahead, the first thing she saw was a pair of black riding boots. Then she trailed upward, following the line of fawn-colored jodhpurs and a white tucked-in blouse. Of course, the anachronistic Scarlett stood there.

The witch had no sense of modern style.

"She's awake," Scarlett said to someone outside the door, and then the panel swung wide as she entered. Ross came next, the shape-shifter who was ruled by his own insanity, followed by Beth. The young girl Willyn had once tried to save.

Finally, the woman who ran the Amara's morbid show stepped inside. Ronja.

Kylie felt the first true stab of fear.

The immortal *seiðr* wore a shiny dress of midnight blue, as if she'd come straight from the opera. Kylie had no idea what time it was, and the absence of windows gave no indication whether it was night or day outside.

"It's Kylie, isn't it?" Ronja's smile and demeanor were that of a genteel hostess greeting a guest. But Kylie wasn't returning the etiquette. She remained silent.

"Oh, you don't have to answer. I'm well aware of the package I requested." Ronja glided closer to the cell. "The most important of gifts, delivered at long last." She tossed a scathing look to her fellow Amara members, reminding them of past failures.

Now a predatory gleam entered her stony blue eyes. "I've dreamed of this time, when I would have one of you at my disposal. All alone with none of your *sisters,*" she narrowed her eyes, "to save you."

Kylie trembled inside, trying to push past the terror and make a semi-lucid plan for when they came for her. Because they *would* come, and they weren't going to be nice about it. She had to be ready to defend herself.

But how to get out of these cuffs? Her telekinesis wasn't nearly as strong as Viv's, but she might be able to manipulate the inner workings of the manacles.

Ronja spoke sharply to Ross then, diverting Kylie's attention from her escape plan. "Lift her." The blonde queen of darkness smiled in an awful way as the shifter moved into the shadows.

He turned on another lamp, barely brightening the dank area, but it was the wheel he cranked that sent both awareness and apprehension into Kylie's gut. The chains began to rise above her head, and just as they began to tug at her wrists, Ross stopped to adjust the metal links on the outside of her prison.

He looped them over a large hook before returning to crank the wheel. Despite her struggles, Kylie was raised up, up, onto her toes, with her shoulders wrenched back and pressed against the black bars. A squeak and locking sound issued from behind her as Ross completed his modifications.

"You remember Beth, I'm sure." Ronja floated her hand toward the younger woman. The innocent blue eyes and brown schoolgirl braid did nothing to hide the malevolence that made up the girl's core.

Beth grinned with only one side of her mouth, and for the first time, Kylie sensed there was more to the little stray than her ability to cause nightmares. During Willyn's trial, Beth had brought a great deal of anguish to her life.

But Kylie felt sure she was about to be the recipient of a

different kind of torment. Beth was emitting a low, creepy giggle, and pain was a promise in her eyes.

"Beth is more than a mare, as you'll soon see." Ronja stood back and gestured for Beth to open the cell door. "And I'm actually grateful your ghost-talking friend convinced Sylvie to leave us. Sadism comes much more naturally to young Beth. As it turns out, it was she who was always meant to be our seventh female."

Kylie tested the width of her hands against the shackles when Beth stepped inside with her. She couldn't get loose fast enough and would have to rely on her magic. But could she take on all four of them?

"Both her strength and her powers get stronger when she inflicts pain," Ronja said, her voice light and instructional. A schoolteacher happy to be sharing her knowledge. "And I promised her she would get first crack if we ever caught a coven member."

Beth sidled up to Kylie. "I remember you. You always had a big mouth."

Kylie was too terrified to put that big mouth to use; instead, she waited until the girl's hand landed on the side of her face. Then she channeled her lightning to the point of contact, enough to throw Beth to the opposite wall of bars.

But the only one who got stabbed with electricity was Kylie. She cried out when the skitter of heat shot back at her.

Ronja and Scarlett both laughed, and then one of them started clapping. Ronja. She stopped the applause long enough to wrap one arm around Scarlett's neck and pull her in for a deep kiss. When she drew back, she purred, "I knew you'd do it, my darling."

With mirth still lifting her words, Ronja faced Kylie, peering through the bars. "Did you silly witches actually think you were the only ones who could play with metal and magic? You won't be able to call forth your lightning bolts or that revolting blue light while wearing those cuffs."

Kylie was struck with terror now, a jagged spear that tore through her middle. She was truly vulnerable. In the hands of the Amara, with no weapons, no magic, and worst of all, no one to help her.

No one who would step in when things got out of hand. When they got too rough.

Digging deep for courage, or at least the appearance of such, she narrowed her eyes at Ronja. "What do you want?"

Studying a long black fingernail, Ronja angled her head to the side. "Oh, I want something from you all right. But tonight?" She dropped her hand and fixed her stare on Kylie. Her smile was slow, sinister. "Tonight is just for fun."

Beth laughed in Kylie's face now. "Don't worry, pretty girl. This is only your first session." She patted Kylie's cheek and stepped back to stand with legs apart. "So I'll start with my fists."

18

Weather earlier in the day had brought rain, making their excursion into the deep forest even more miserable. Quinn barreled toward the fence of stacked posts and leapt over. He called to those who'd accompanied him, "Almost there. This is the last place I can think of."

He could scarcely believe he and Kylie had been here only yesterday. That he'd had her in his arms, that he'd finally made love to her. It all seemed like a dream now. One he yearned for, but was unable to recapture.

If he'd known then what was to come. What would happen.

His throat burned with regret. So many things he could have done differently, said better, or said at all. But it wasn't too late, he reminded himself with force. It couldn't be.

Crazed emotions bounced in his head, crashing into each other until he couldn't think, could only move. He had to keep moving, keep searching. Or go mad.

If he stopped long enough to truly consider what might be happening to her . . .

"Quinn?" Hayden's hand was on his arm. "Quinn. Which way from here?"

He'd stopped walking, lost in imagined nightmares, and hadn't even realized. "That way." He gestured. "Straight to the center." His shoes crunched across nature's detritus, dead leaves and pine needles from last season.

At this point they'd all been awake for over thirty-six hours, but still, they pushed on. After leaving the plantation, they'd traveled to the only other place in Savannah where members of the Amara had been known to congregate.

The daytime staff at the vamp bar had been light, but Anna had still been forced to cast a spell, enchanting the manager to let them enter and search the premises. Both Trevor and Cole had gone along, though no warrant had been issued. But no warrant had been needed.

The search had been off-book, and if they'd found Kylie, there would have been no arrests.

Quinn flexed his fingers. No one involved with her kidnapping would be walking away. Only blood and death was coming for whoever had taken the youngest member of the coven.

And Quinn was eager to dole it out.

After their failure at the vamp bar, they'd decided to split into teams, spreading out to visit any and all possible locations. Ronja's property holdings were on the list, as were Dalton Morne's and any place a portal had been found.

The random sites had once been powerful epicenters where the darkness had broken through, invading this world. So they would be investigated, even if the chances of Kylie being there were slim.

Quinn and the others were simply running out of options, and a physical search was all they knew to do. The Amara had taken Kylie, of that they were positive, but Ronja and her demon had hidden her well. Not only concealed from sight, but veiled by magic.

Leaving Quinn and his friends all but helpless.

Even Anna was in a panic, though she did her best to hide it. Every once in a while, Quinn caught his sister rubbing her thumbs against her palms, a sign she was trying to stay calm. And her anxiety filled him with an unsettling dread.

If the coven's strongest witch couldn't locate Kylie, and if

Lucia couldn't track her, then what was left to them? Would they ever find her at all?

Quinn's back and neck throbbed from restrained rage. With every hour that passed, his hands, his arms, every muscle in his body seemed to twist into steel cables. He had bloody, violent vengeance in mind, and his entire being ached to deliver.

"We're close," he said, recognizing the terrain. They trudged onward but at a swifter pace. None of them had stopped for any reason, even for more comfortable clothing or shoes. But no one complained.

Every minute Kylie was in the hands of the Amara was a minute too long. And the desperate disquiet was growing amongst the group.

While the teams were combing the entirety of Chatham County, Willyn and Dare had stayed behind at the hospital with the Attingers. A call had also been placed to Claire and Joe, warning them to keep their heads up. The yellow house on the mainland was fully protected, but Willyn's small son was in residence.

Only one thing would be worse than what they were going through now. The loss of the child they all adored . . . No, it just didn't bear thinking of.

Footsteps began pummeling the ground now as they ran, and as they grew closer, Anna pointed out the trees with peeling bark. She said something aside to Shauni but Quinn didn't hear.

He called to Shauni. "Anything from the birds?" Shauni had sent out some winged scouts to scour the lands from above.

"No, I'm sorry, Quinn. Either she's not here, or the animals are being blocked too." A shadow crossed over her eyes. She was in the same state of distress as the rest of them.

So he only nodded and turned back to the house as they approached. He was the first to trample up the wooden steps and burst through the cherry-red door.

The chapel room was as empty as it had been before and still as eerily clean. "There's only the attic," he said to Ethan as his friend barreled in behind him. No one quarreled about man versus woman or witch versus non-gifted human. This was every person for him or herself, and whoever found Kylie first, then all the better.

"I'll go up with you," Ethan said, and when Quinn met his stern, dark gaze, he thanked the goddess his friend could cover his emotions. If Ethan showed an ounce of sympathy, uttered one word too soft with compassion, Quinn was afraid he just might lose it.

Like two buffalo, they stomped up the steps, but this time Quinn took extra care with the corners and walls, searching for any hidden space or passageway he and Kylie may have missed the first time.

After five minutes of banging on partitions and pulling at loose boards, he and Ethan faced each other. "Nothing here." Ethan nodded one time and went back downstairs.

Deflated once again, Quinn followed behind.

The others had been of the same mind, searching every square inch with diligence. The large number of them made the work quick and thorough.

"Take us to the rock face you told us about." Anna was unyielding, her expression controlled, but she couldn't quite mask her worry. It wasn't often Quinn saw his sister look so frazzled, so unkempt, and completely out of sorts.

But weren't they all? He put a hand to his sternum where a massive weight seemed lodged. Would the coven ever be whole again? Would he?

He couldn't think about that now. The loss of Kylie was too great, and he didn't even want to consider that it might be permanent. The very idea would be the final shove, and he'd go flying into the abyss.

He was no longer wracked by guilt alone, but by an absence

so profound, he simply couldn't put it into words. *Just keep moving. Keep breathing.*

Keep looking for her.

He didn't hold onto anyone this time when he burst through the perimeter of shrubs, but he waited just inside as the others pushed their way through.

Hayden surveyed the area, her mouth pressed into a grim line. Quinn wondered what she saw, or sensed.

While he and the others had gone to the vamp bar, Hayden and Trevor had scoured local cemeteries and graveyards. She'd encountered ghosts, as she always did, but none of the spirits had told her anything useful.

She walked forward now, as if pulled by an invisible string. Quinn and the others fell silent, watching as she traversed the field of great stones. Some were large but flat like dolmens, and for all they knew, they *were* tombs of some kind. But who or what did they contain?

Reaching a hand up to a tall, jutting rock formation similar to those encircling Stonehenge, Hayden put her hand near the rough surface, hesitated, then pulled away. She turned guarded eyes back to Quinn and Anna. "This place is sinister. I can feel it sucking at me, my power. As if it's porous and wants to . . . absorb me. My life or my magic—I can't be sure."

"Then come away," Ethan said. "Trust your instincts."

Frustrated and sick with worry, Quinn made a sharp motion with his hand. "The cavern is over there. I'm going in." Just as he and Kylie had before. Just yesterday.

Damn it! The need to turn back time was making him insane. He should never have let her out of his sight.

He cursed himself as he walked. He'd never had time to research the markings they'd found inside the cave either. The inscriptions in the stones.

God, it felt like an elephant was sitting on his chest. He had so many obligations, and he'd let them all fall.

He'd let Kylie fall too—in so many ways—away from him and straight into danger's path.

He'd decode the mysterious writing as soon as they returned to the mansion. If legwork failed and they couldn't find her, then he'd turn to what he knew best. What he did best. Magic. And dead, forgotten languages.

He'd conjure the devil himself if that's what it took. And as he entered the black mouth of the rock, that possibility seemed far too real.

Though vast, the cavern was easily canvassed, since he could make out each wall. The interior was domelike in structure, and as he called fire from his hand to light the space, he could see everything within.

Kylie wasn't here. Another failure. Icy daggers pierced him as he grudgingly turned to leave the cave.

Anna and the others were in deep discussion when he exited and crossed the clearing to them. He sidestepped the huge, spherical slab of dark rock that glittered bizarrely. There was a certain depth within the stone, a sense of endless evil.

And as he hurried past, he felt sure it was the black, oozing heart of this malignant place.

Anna was shaking her head with two fingers at her temple when he rejoined them. Her exasperation was almost palpable. "I don't see anything."

Quinn watched his sister as she heaved a weary breath and pinched the bridge of her nose. Gathering composure, she said, "Let's make a circle."

"Here?" Ethan stabbed a finger toward the ground. "That's not a good idea. If Hayden's right and this place is some kind of . . . vortex for evil, we can't risk opening ourselves up to be drawn in." He waved his hand. "Not without your full circle. The entire coven."

Quinn stepped up. "They might not ever have their complete circle again if we don't find Kylie." He jerked his head to

Hayden and Shauni. "The three of us and Anna. Ethan," he told his friend, "you can keep an eye out. Watch us for any signs that something's wrong."

Anna took his hand and reached for Hayden. "I just want to try to harness what's here, if I can. Dark or not, the magical concentration of the site might show me a psychic pathway to Kylie."

Quinn narrowed his eyes. "Smart. Bastraal and Ronja blocked everything benevolent in our world, but they probably didn't think of their own kind."

"Exactly." Anna waited until Quinn and Shauni joined hands, and again as Shauni completed the link with Hayden. "Ready?" she asked.

They all nodded in the affirmative.

"Just channel what magic you can to me." Anna let her lids drift closed. "I'll do the rest."

Just before he shut his own eyes, Quinn caught sight of Ethan's worried scowl. But still the demon hunter stood his ground and readied himself to be their lookout—their guardian and protector.

As Anna went under.

Sending his strength and every ounce of power he could muster, Quinn let his magic flow to his sister. He could feel Shauni's blowing through him as well, her pure green energy full of kindness and love. But today it was tainted by a desperate, bottomless grief.

Anna's fingers clutched his more firmly and she gasped. "Show me," she whispered. "Take me to my lost sister."

Her breathing became heavy and labored. Her grip on him grew tighter, and Quinn felt her sway. Keeping his eyes shut tight, he concentrated on giving her more, giving all that he was if that's what she required.

Pain began to slice at him in small, careful strokes, but he ignored the sting. He held firm. Though he was supporting

Anna, seeing her through, ultimately, Quinn had to stay strong for Kylie.

The slices continued, changing to jagged, rending tears into what felt like muscle, flesh, internal organs. When Hayden cried out, Quinn knew the women were enduring the same agony.

"Show me!" Anna screamed, and the ground beneath them gave a faint but definite rumble.

"That's enough. You have to pull out." Ethan's voice, speaking low but with severity, somewhere in Anna's vicinity.

"I'm almost there. I can feel her!" Anna's fingernails bit into Quinn's skin, but he only shoved more power toward her, denying his own discomfort. Warmth trickled over his upper lip, but it wasn't until his chin ran with blood that he acknowledged the copper taste.

"Anna. You've got to come out now, or you'll lose your circle for good." Ethan's voice was rising and the earth was vibrating. "You're losing Quinn, Anna! You've got to pull back!"

No! Quinn tried to shout, but he couldn't make the necessary sound. He wanted to scream at his sister to keep reaching. *Don't let Kylie go! Don't stop!*

Now he was the one clinging to Anna's hand, as well as Shauni's. His fingers were set like stone, clenched. He felt someone prying at the connection. *Don't. Don't!*

"Let go now, Quinn." Not Ethan's voice but Anna's. "Take your magic back into yourself." She was rubbing his brow with one hand, and then he felt her other slip free from his grasp.

With the connection severed, a burst of energy rushed back into him. His eyes opened. "No," he croaked. The fierce sting of loss rushed alongside his returning power.

Angling his head, he saw Ethan still working to loosen his other hand, the one still fastened on Shauni. But the circle was no more, the magic now faded, so Quinn released her. Shauni lowered to the ground, kneeling to catch her breath and recover.

Still dazed, Quinn dropped his eyes to find that he was also on his knees. At some point, he must have collapsed.

"Did you see her?" He looked up at Anna as he tried to stand but only wobbled for his efforts. He was spent of all strength.

Anna's eyes were deep pools, her pupils still dilated. As they were whenever she allowed her gift to take over. "I . . . caught a glimpse. But I couldn't get a location."

"What did you see?" Quinn took the hand Ethan offered and strained to stand. He was completely tapped out. "Anything might help us narrow down the search."

"I'm sorry." Anna shook her head.

Just as he was about to push her for more, Hayden pressed a hand to her mouth to block the gasping sobs that were building.

"What is it?" Ethan asked as Shauni and Anna both closed rank and put their arms around Hayden.

Shauni struggled to speak, because Anna had her head buried against Hayden's shoulder. Finally, the animal-whisperer battled back her own tears long enough to say, "We saw her too. Hayden and I got pieces of Anna's vision."

Quinn's body was depleted, but he felt the freezing cold as it shot into every particle. "Tell me." He wiped the blood from his face, smearing it over his cheek. *"Tell me."*

"We got an image of Kylie's face. Only her face."

Quinn waited, his breath lodged in his throat, strangling him.

Shauni's eyes were filled with sorrow. "Quinn. She was in pain."

19

Gloom and stillness reigned over the mansion when they returned. No one spoke to fill the void, each too consumed by their own desolation. And there was nothing to say that would make any of it better.

Noiselessly they all dispersed, some to the kitchen for food or drink, while others trudged upstairs to bathe or to fall into whatever peace they might find in sleep. Many of the women, Quinn knew, would crawl into their respective corners to cry.

The only options left to them for the moment, as even those who were gifted with magic had to crash at some point. So they would rest, recharge their weary bodies, and then continue with the hunt.

Somehow, they would. They had to.

The last angry words he'd thrown at Kylie echoed back to Quinn constantly. Every hour that passed while she was missing.

Missing. Gone. And likely having horrible things done to her. The bleakness and powerlessness of that fact overwhelmed him, swallowed him whole until he was tempted to lie down and fall away into oblivion.

He'd been so hard and angry before, taking his own self-recriminations out on her. He was the one who'd chosen to leave the house when it was unprotected. Kylie had even suggested he stay behind to work on the wards.

But he'd insisted on accompanying her. Then when things went to hell and Mrs. Attinger was attacked, he'd taken the easy mark, unloading his guilt on Kylie. Because she'd been there. For him.

He was a heartless, shortsighted bastard.

How could he have ever called her childish or selfish when he was the one? He'd been naïve, only concerned with his own interests. So he'd pushed her away with cruelty. Like he'd always done.

Falling into the brown leather chair, Quinn dropped his head into his hands. Now she was gone, and he might never get the opportunity to undo all the wrong he'd done.

What he wouldn't give to see Kylie now, to tell her that he'd lied. He'd covered up the truth, about so many things.

He longed to tangle his hands in that mass of golden curls. If he got the chance again, he'd meet those hazel eyes with honesty, and for the first time, undisguised emotion. He'd tell her how he felt and admit that their powerful, sizzling chemistry had evolved into . . . more.

He slammed a fist into his open palm. Even now he balked at the words. But nothing he'd dreaded before came close to what he was enduring now.

He had fallen in love with Kylie. He loved her.

And the deeper he'd sunk, the harder he'd struggled, lashing out at anyone who came near. Especially the one sweet girl who'd been pulling him under.

As his eyes bore holes into the wood paneling of his walls, a sound carried to him from below, down near the bottom of the door. A repetitive scraping noise.

He stood and edged closer, listening, then leaned his forehead on the wood panel. He recognized the plaintive but insistent scratch. Opening the door a crack, he allowed entry to the only other one he could stand to share company with right now.

Sassy pushed inside and circled behind Quinn, staring up at

him the whole time. She didn't meow or make any noise. She simply watched him.

With his temper somewhat alleviated, he sat in the brown leather chair, despondent. As if she'd been waiting for him to do just that, Sassy moved to sit in front of his leg. Then she leaned her small golden head forward and rested it against his shin.

The act was more than he could take, and a furious grief welled in his chest. "I know," he said, his voice a croak. He reached down to rub the curve of her back. "I miss her too."

Anguish rolled from his center to every part of his body, as if the deep, constant ache was trying to find its way out. Only more lay beneath to take its place. His heart held an endless supply of suffering.

A soft knock at the door and Quinn lifted his head. Anna, it had to be. She was the only one who'd attempt to talk to him at a time like this. Except for Ethan, maybe, but the tap had been too gentle.

He didn't answer or go the door. It eased open anyway.

"Go away, Anna." He was too spun up with anger and sorrow, still too irascible, and feared he would take it out on his sister. He'd misplaced his worries and resentment before and had hurt Kylie. He was desperate to not repeat the mistake.

"I won't stay long. I just wanted to make sure—"

"That I'm all right?" Quinn rasped, pent up emotion squeezing his throat. He could hardly even breathe, let alone talk. "Well, I'm not. Nothing is all right. And we," he swept an angry arm toward her, "all of you, the most powerful witches I know, can't do a damn thing about it."

"We don't know that yet." Anna stepped into the room and closed the door. "We've done what we felt necessary. All we knew to do was search, because time is critical."

Quinn thought of the hours since Kylie had gone missing. All the long, agonizing minutes that she'd been in their hands.

"Don't. I can't talk about it."

"We'll turn to other ideas now, Quinn. We'll use the power you spoke of."

The compassion and misery in Anna's tone belied her words of encouragement. Of hope. Quinn couldn't take it. His skull seemed to tighten, squeezing with a burning pressure that centered behind his eyes.

He didn't know what was happening, had no idea he was crying, until Anna knelt beside him, taking his hand between both of hers. "Oh, Quinn. I can't stand to see you hurt this way. And I bleed inside when I think of Kylie." She was crying too, but doing her best to stop the flood.

She was trying to be strong for him. "I don't deserve your sympathy," he said. "I did this. I sent her away."

"No. The Amara were watching and waiting. There would have been another opportunity." She grabbed his chin and jerked his face to meet hers. "Do not blame yourself. I need you, now more than ever. You can't recede into guilt or remorse. You shove that all aside and keep your head straight."

Her hands gripped his tighter. "I can't do this without you, Quinn. This is the closest we've all come to . . ." She swallowed and closed her eyes for a moment. Then, composed, she said, "The coven is close to falling apart. You and I have to be the binding center. We have to keep it together, no matter how difficult it becomes."

"Just like we always have." He didn't care about the tears now. They were cleansing, a release, and he was able to listen more rationally. "You're right. You're right."

He sat back against the leather. "I just need a few minutes to get cleaned up and changed."

"Okay. Me too." Anna wrapped her arms around his neck and gathered him close. "We haven't tried everything yet." Her voice trembled. "And I'm not giving up."

"No. We won't give up." Quinn clenched his eyes but couldn't shut out the images that flew at him. Kylie being hurt or bitten by Carson. Poisoned and choked by Scarlett's red magic. Mauled by one of Ross's beastly forms.

Goddess, what would they do to her? What were they doing to her now?

Had he really told himself he could live without her? That he'd actually prefer it? Now he knew, too late, that being away from her wasn't better at all. It was like living without the sun.

He let his sister cling to him, needing her comfort as much as she did his.

No foreign, exotic lands called to him anymore. No adventure tempted. And they might never do so again. Because it made no difference where he went or what he might see.

None of it mattered anymore. For the whole world had gone dark.

~~~

Blackness. Kylie blinked and opened her eyes wider, still disoriented by the enveloping gloom. Then she tried to move. "Ohhh." Lines of pain lanced through her arm when she lifted her elbow, and her lip split as soon as she opened her mouth to groan.

Then she remembered.

She was in the cell on the stone floor. Recovering from Beth's brutal assault. Sensation rocketed back into her limbs and torso, every fiber and cell alive with agony. The malicious young woman had spared no part of her body.

Though at the end, she'd concentrated on Kylie's hips and thighs, where there was less chance of delivering a fatal blow. Because Ronja wanted to keep Kylie alive.

What did the Nordic witch want from her? Well, whatever it was, Kylie wouldn't deliver.

Cold from the floor had seeped into her muscles, and as

much as it pained her, she had to start moving. Blood flow and loosened tissue would help chase away the prickling soreness, and would also warm her up.

The next attempt to move made her suck in a jagged breath. She felt like a corpse in full rigor.

With no way to discern the extent of her injuries, she gently tested one limb at a time. Slowly. At least she'd regained consciousness, which was a good sign. No concussion, she hoped.

But when she tried to sit up, passing out again didn't sound half bad. Her back convulsed when she moved, so many bruises and contusions her flesh felt three sizes too small. She didn't have to see her body to know it was discolored and swollen.

Maybe she could conjure a little healing magic. Or at least a small anesthetic spell. Anything.

But when her power rose up, it only backfired, shooting tiny darts into her arms, which were already tender from abuse. Those damns manacles, charmed to act as some mystical lodestone, attracting her magic before spitting it right back into her.

Our stolen weapons. Kylie had sudden recall of the last portal she and her friends had destroyed, the demon entry point that had been used as a lure. During Claudia's trial, they'd been attacked out in the woods, dosed by Scarlett's poisonous fumes, and had lost a dagger and a sword to the Amara in the process.

Both blades had contained stores of the blue magic unique to Kylie and her sisters, a handy source of power when it was time to kill a few demons. The coven had suspected something that day. They'd presumed Ronja and her deviant crew had wanted the weapons for a reason.

And now Kylie knew the purpose. Ronja had managed to turn the coven's magic against them. She'd harnessed its power for use in her own black spell, creating a repellent metal to block not only Kylie's special gift, electricity, but also the protective blue light of the coven as well.

The words "Oh shit" kept repeating in her mind, but they just didn't sum up her problems accurately enough. She was in real trouble here, unable to free herself, unable to see—since they'd removed or powered off every source of illumination—and at the mercy of a woman who would show her none.

A verbal chant, then. Maybe she could send her magic out away from the chains and into the space. What had Quinn said that day when all of the lights had gone out?

Illuminaria. Yes. That was it. With that one word he'd lit candles, as fire and flame came most naturally when called. The element most easily summoned and controlled.

And Kylie could use some easy right about now.

On her first endeavor to speak, her throat scratched, as if the walls of her windpipe were glued together. She worked up as much saliva as she could, swallowed, and tried again. "Illuminaria."

She waited for brightness, wondering if her eyes had to adjust. Soon it was apparent nothing had changed, but at least the spelled handcuffs hadn't bit back at her. Swallow, swallow, moisten the throat, and once more with vigor. "Illuminaria!"

Zzzt! "Ouch. Ouch." Okay, that time the manacles had heard her. So a verbal incantation was a definite no-go.

For long, tedious minutes, she stared into the void and struggled for an idea. A plan. The Amara would return eventually, and Kylie had no reason to think the next time they visited would be any better than the last.

And if what Beth had said could be believed, each "session" would be worse than the previous one. The cruel mare who gained power from pain had already taken her turn, and she'd chosen a physical torment. Punches, slaps, and kicks.

Kylie grimaced in the dark when she remembered the sounds. That had been the worst. The revolting orgasmic groan Beth had uttered with every draw of fresh blood.

With her sense of sight out of commission, Kylie easily picked up on muffled voices that seemed to echo from a great distance. Shortly after she'd first heard them, a shaft of orange appeared on one wall as the door to the room cracked open.

Then with a burst, the wood was kicked all the way open, infusing the space with light. What Kylie had longed for only moments ago now seared her eyes. And how appropriate, she thought when her vision returned, as she saw who stood in the doorway.

Searenn. The Droehk.

The hoodie of her gray shirt sat back on her head, revealing a pair of eyes that must have been sent from the devil himself. One pale blue, one black as pitch. "Sleep well, witch?" The woman's voice was like gravel through a sieve.

Kylie didn't respond, wouldn't give Searenn anything to work with. Not a single piece of information, no matter how small.

"It was my idea to lower you back to the floor." Boots clomping across the floor, Searenn kneeled outside of the bars and stuck her hand through.

Kylie didn't flinch, she wouldn't allow herself to, but the freakish woman only trained her mismatched eyes on Kylie's hair. Then she lifted a long, curling lock and rubbed it between her fingers. "I wanted to let you rest." She stood. "So you'd be ready."

For what? Kylie shivered inside and could feel the tremors growing stronger, making their way out. She didn't want any of her captors to see her terror, but the panic was there, and no amount of bravado could override her mounting fear.

Ross was back again, along with the Native American man called Tyr. And that was one human being who lacked any trace of a soul. When Kylie looked into his eyes, she saw vacancy. A complete lack of recognizable emotion.

The two men stood off to one side, allowing plenty of room

for the queen's entrance. Ronja strolled inside, dressed today in tight pants and a high-collared shirt of navy. Today? Tonight? Kylie couldn't tell.

Last of all, Scarlett entered, like a lady in waiting trailing after her superior. The red-headed witch smirked down at Kylie and moved to stand with Tyr and Ross. Were they here to participate? Or only to watch?

Kylie's stomach caved in on itself as nausea twisted and turned. She hadn't eaten since before she and Quinn had gone to investigate the strange building in the woods. The vile preacher's place of unholiness.

But hunger wasn't the cause of her internal revolt. Imagining what was about to happen—and simultaneously trying not to imagine—filled her gut with unspeakable dread. *I won't scream. I won't break.*

"I never took you for the silent type," Ronja said, drawing a chuckle from Scarlett. "In fact, from all reports, you're the talkative one, the brash one." She gave Kylie a look of disdain. "Young and impulsive."

The stony blue of Ronja's eyes grew ever colder, if that were possible. "Your lack of experience and patience are why we picked you." She tossed a hand. "That, and the fact it was your turn at trial. Actually, I couldn't have planned this better if I'd tried."

Kylie held her tongue but couldn't prevent her glare of hatred.

"You see?" Ronja pointed at her and laughed. "You're so emotional. And we've barely even begun." Glancing over to Searenn where she stood apart from the others, the blonde seiðr notched her chin. A signal of some kind? A direction to do something?

Kylie couldn't help herself. She let her gaze roll to the Droehk, tracking her every move.

Searenn unzipped her hooded shirt with one slashing pull.

Removing it completely, she tossed the article to Ross. The shifter caught it one-handed and hung it over his shoulder.

Holding out her arms, Searenn let a tiny smile curve her lips. "Let's see. Which one should I choose?" She studied the swirls of blue and black ink on her arms, shoulders, and even her stomach and sides as she lifted the skimpy tank she sported.

"You see," Ronja began, "You are, without a doubt, the coven's weakest link. And I will get what I want from you. Now that Beth has . . . tenderized you for the rest of us," the witch narrowed her hard stare, "we can get down to the serious business."

She spoke low to Searenn. "Make it a good one."

"I think I've finally decided on," Searenn touched a finger to her right forearm, then higher up on her shoulder, "this one." She leered at Kylie. "Oh, yeah." A sickly green smoke began to swirl around the Droehk. "You're going to enjoy this."

Searenn's ancestral ability was a mysterious and obscure language. Passed down in secret for millennia, the magical writing tattooed all over her body had but one purpose.

Kylie's spine stiffened as waves of terror raced up her vertebrae. The singular gift possessed by the Droehk was the ability to summon and command demons.

Like a pear gone bad, the fumes building around Searenn were a nasty blend of pale green and gray. Kylie could feel her bones seeking to press into the cold stone floor. She hunched her way back and into the bars, forcing herself into the safest, most distant place.

The deepest, most primeval part of her was trying to hide. So she couldn't be seen by whatever was forming in the mist. So she wouldn't be touched.

Terrified of what Searenn was calling forth, her instinct was to flatten against the floor, the back wall, or the corner where it met steel bars. But she was tethered in place, with only a foot or two of slack in the chains that held her fast.

The shape of a head morphed into being, wider and more triangular than a human's. The beast's skull was widest at its crown, where it branched into thick, round horns. Though still only outlined by smoke, the slow-curling projections were visible.

And when the creature opened its misty mouth, green fire erupted.

Searenn held both of her hands out with her head lolled back on her shoulders. She was shaking as she pushed the demon into formation, but when her face came forward, she was smiling. "Hot as a blowtorch and sharp as a blade. His tongue gives a kiss you'll never forget."

Still attached to its master, the monster swiped a hand through the air, eager to get to Kylie. To its victim.

"And claws sharp as razors." Searenn laughed. "But the wounds he leaves will heal instantly." She thrust her hands toward the ceiling and the demon roared free. "So he can spend hours and hours with you." She shrugged. "As long as the pain doesn't stop your heart."

When Searenn jerked her chin down, the gray-green devil slithered through the bars and into the cell with Kylie. Her entire body clutched, but she couldn't escape. She had nowhere to go.

When the first stab of its blazing tongue went through her leg and deep into tissue, she clashed her teeth together, grinding them to create a barrier to sound. *I won't scream. I won't!*

The burn was unbelievable, and her body quaked despite her determination to control it. The best she could do was keep herself from crying out, but the visceral response to the scorching pain in her bones was unavoidable.

The demon withdrew its flaming tongue then, only to flick it closer to Kylie's face. She jumped this time, unable to prevent her reaction.

And she would swear the thing smiled at her. Just before

dragging a sharp finger down her cheekbone.

Flesh, adipose, and other connective tissues sliced open and spread, splitting the side of her face from the corner of her eye to her jawline. Whimpering moans whirled in her chest, her body's instinctual urge to release her agony in a scream.

But as soon as she felt the warm trickle of blood, her flesh began to knit back together. The high-pitched crackle of her own healing made Kylie's insides heave. She gagged once. Twice. Unable to hold back the retching convulsions.

But still, she made no other sound.

"I can stop this." The whispered statement didn't penetrate the haze of her mind until Ronja strode forth and spoke louder. "Tell me what I want to know, and it all goes away."

Don't listen to her. She's all lies. Knowing she couldn't hide the anguish living within, Kylie shut her eyes, clenching them tightly.

Another jab of the excruciating fire, but this time, it was in Kylie's pelvic region. The bone-melting invasion pierced all the way through her until her back burned as well. Noises erupted from her lips, a shaking, quivering sound produced by the involuntary contraction of her abdominal muscles.

"Where is the dagger?" Ronja called out the demand in her haughty tone, but beneath the arrogance, a vein of anger. Impatience.

Kylie would hold out if it killed her. Pissing Ronja off would be her motivating force.

But when the tendons above her knee cut so swiftly and cleanly she felt her quads retract, Kylie finally howled. The pain was unbearable, and just as the tissue started to sew back together, the demon struck out at her other knee in the same way.

Her upper teeth were literally biting down on her lower lip, her chin. She fought to regain control, to manage some restraint.

A heavy breath on her neck made her turn to the opposite side. The demon was doing something to her hair. His smoke was covering her body, taunting her, threatening.

Kylie's breath came in ragged gasps. She was overcome, unable to process thought or action beneath the torturous attack. The heat of the beast still hovered beside her, above her.

Suddenly and without warning, his sharp, flaming tongue stabbed into her ear to puncture. White starbursts exploded in front of her open eyes as her heels pummeled the floor. She screamed.

And screamed.

"Where is the dagger?" Ronja demanded. "Tell me now! Bastraal has combed every inch of the St. Germaine estate."

A low, keening moan filled the air. Kylie barely registered the sound as her own.

Then more words flew from Ronja's twisted lips. "Back him off, Searenn. She can't tell me anything when she's like that."

Kylie cried noiseless tears. Like what? Were they talking about her? Blood pounded in her ears, her head. And if she'd thought the sound of her skin repairing itself was awful, her ear drum mending was like a thousand metal claws on a wall of steel. Reverberating. Screeching.

"Take this reprieve and catch your breath." Ronja was standing near the cell, glowering down at her through the black bars. "Then tell me where the dagger is. The one your Spanish witch brought back from Peru. That bitch Anna thinks she's smarter than me, but I *will* find it."

The aches that Kylie had concerned herself with before were now a welcome relief. Absent the deep cuts or flames that impaled her, mere bruises were almost a pleasure.

But she had no idea what Anna had done with the dagger, only that it was hidden. That it was cloistered away. Safe.

The silver dagger with onyx stones would one day be used

against Bastraal. It was the only weapon that could kill the mighty demon. The only one that could destroy him for good.

The thing torturing Kylie now was a common underling, so she curled her fingers and channeled fortitude. What would happen to the world if more of these creatures were released? Chaos and horror would ensue if these monsters were set upon innocent people.

So Kylie had to remain silent. Yes, she'd probably scream again before this was over, but she wouldn't tell them anything. Even if she'd known anything to tell.

A roar of frustration broke free from Ronja. "Searenn, more!"

Kylie glanced to the Droehk before she thought better of it. Then she looked into the smoky eyes of the creature that still floated above her. With a brutal swipe, he hacked across her shoulder at Searenn's command. Then again as it healed, and again.

Finally Kylie wailed out, the cry turning into sobs as the demon kept cutting. He moved methodically, one limb, one area at a time.

Never ending, yet never-fatal agony.

At one point, Kylie's head lolled to the side. She noticed that Ross had repositioned himself and was closer to the cell. He stood with feet spread wide, his arm crooked up. *What is he holding? What is he doing?*

Her stomach clutched again. What more could they possibly do to her? This torment was beyond imagining, and she was sure she would pass out soon.

She couldn't wait.

The onslaught of cuts and burns—both superficial and deep—continued as the demon switched between claw and flame. But still she forced her eyes to focus on Ross. Finally her vision cleared, and she saw what was in the shifter's hands.

Oh, please, please. No. Kylie turned her face away when the scorching heat pierced her side. When the next convulsion hit.

She bit down on her lip as well as the whining moan that begged for release. With renewed determination, she resisted the urge to yell. Hiding her reactions as much as possible, she tried to diminish the sickening images her torture must surely create.

She tried to downplay the incredible pain the Amara were putting her through.

Because they were filming it.

20

Quinn heard the knock and whipped his head up to glance around. He was in his office, at his desk. Rubbing one side of his face and his gritty eyes, he called out, "Come in."

The door opened enough for Paige to stick her head inside. "Sorry to bother you." Her brow furrowed as she looked him over. "Oh, you were sleeping. Now I'm really sorry."

"It's that obvious?"

She lifted a shoulder, her expression grim. "We all have to rest. Even we can only go so long without."

Quinn nodded. What she didn't say was that they all felt guilty for even the briefest nap. For eating, sitting, just being around each other. Everything seemed like a luxury now. Like blessings.

Because none of them could be sure Kylie had anything other than . . . discomfort. He rubbed his eyes again, hard enough to hurt and make blue bulbs flash behind his lids.

Again he told himself not to think of the possibilities. All the horrible possibilities. If they were going to help Kylie, they had to work to find a way.

Rolling in misery or self-recriminations did no one any good. Least of all her.

Now Paige was pointing at his desk and the books spread over the surface. "Tell me you didn't sleep here all night."

"No. When we came back last night, Ethan and I hit the

books for a while, then I got a few hours' sleep in bed. I got up around three this morning. Must have dozed off again."

He looked past her to the clock on the wall. "It's almost four?" Panic stirred. The last time he recalled being awake was a little after noon. He'd lost over three hours to sleep, and that was time Kylie couldn't afford for him to waste. "I need to get back to it."

"Okay, but I came to tell you two things. One, Mrs. Attinger is doing a lot better. Leaps and bounds. Willyn says that stuff they used, that stuff, the ATP—"

"TPA," Quinn corrected. "Tissue plasminogen activator."

"Yes, that." Paige quirked her mouth to one side. "They gave it to Ms. Attinger in time. At this point, they don't think she's going to have many residual effects at all."

Relief poured into Quinn like a cooling balm. "That is good news."

"Yeah." She stepped closer. "The second thing is that Anna has an idea. About Kylie." When Quinn started to speak, she held up a hand. "Hold on, I'm telling you what I know. We have to wait until sunset. Evidently, whatever she did at the evil playground yesterday sparked some ideas about using alternative energies."

"What is she talking about?" Quinn had been scouring papers, textbooks, and old journals for any hint of a locator spell that could break through the Amara's shields.

"You'll have to ask her." Paige turned to go.

"Wait. I want to run something by you. We feel strongly that Mrs. Attinger was attacked by Bastraal, and that's gotten me thinking about something. The other day, Sassy was hissing like crazy up here in the hallway. I thought she was looking at me, pissed at me for some reason, but now I wonder—"

"If she wasn't sensing the demon," Paige finished. She rammed her fist into her other palm. "Son of a bitch!"

"What?"

"When I got home last night, I could hear Tiger-Lily all the way down the hall howling from my room. She was locked inside, and I never close my door when I leave for that very reason." Paige shoved her jagged blonde bangs aside. "She bolted from the room and darted up and down the corridor, growling the whole time. Like she was looking for something."

"I knew it." Quinn blew out a breath of frustration that puffed his cheeks. "Another sign I missed. Another mistake."

"Hey." Paige's voice demanded his attention. "You're going to have to stop that."

Quinn only stared at her.

"Stop blaming yourself for every little thing. None of us saw this coming. Anna's the seer of the coven. You think she's not kicking herself too? Maybe even more than you? Guilt is a useless emotion that will only slow us down and burn up brain cells we should be using to find Kylie."

Quinn dropped his gaze to the multitude of research materials on his desk. Hadn't he just berated himself for the very same thing?

Paige's eyes softened then, as much she ever allowed them to. "So cut it out, all right? This isn't your fault."

"I know."

"I hope so, Quinn. I really do." Paige opened the door again and started to step out. She stopped and looked over her shoulder. "If Bastraal has been coming around," she crinkled her brow, "then why the subterfuge? Why didn't he just attack one of us?"

"He did. Mrs. Attinger."

"Yeah, but that was to get us all to the hospital where the Amara would have a chance to . . ."

"To kidnap one of us. To take Kylie." Quinn cringed. Voicing her name hurt every time. "I still believe that was their intention." Scraping his thumb over his chin, he added, "But maybe they wanted us out of the house for another reason.

Why, though? Spying?"

Lost in calculation, Quinn stared straight through Paige as he ran it all over in his mind. Then he leaned back in his chair as the answer coalesced. "He's looking for something."

Encouraged by insight, he nodded. "It has to be the dagger. That's the only possible thing he could want."

"Shit." Paige ran a hand through her hair. "Then we have to make sure it's hidden. Really well."

"Don't worry." Quinn stood, deciding he needed to stretch his legs and find a cup of coffee before he delved back into the books. "If I know my sister, it already is."

Joining Paige in the hallway, Quinn thought of Anna and her cryptic ways. What did she have planned for later? He tossed a puzzled look to Paige as they walked. "So why do we have to wait until sunset?"

~~~

As the last bright line of day vanished on the horizon, Quinn stepped outside. The scent of burning wood rushed over him and with one whiff, he was thrown into autumn nostalgia. The air, however, was still heavy with heat and humidity, and the illusion of fall dissipated quickly.

In the middle of the yard, halfway between the side of mansion and the surrounding forest, the witches had gathered and stood in multiple small groups. Orange and yellow flames leapt, popping and crackling, from a bonfire that was blazing strong.

He hadn't spoken to Anna since Paige's visit, trusting that his sister would come to him if she needed his assistance. To his mind, working on individual projects simultaneously just made more sense. She hadn't sought him out, so he'd seen no reason to deviate from his research.

Ethan and Lucia stood together, the Spanish woman in a

sleeveless dress of crimson. As Quinn took in the scene, he noted Hayden wearing a gown of the same style, but hers was pale pink. Both of them held what looked to be black robes in the crooks of their arms.

Turning his head, he saw Shauni in emerald, Paige wearing turquoise, and Claudia gowned in the color of peaches. They were all dressed in ritualistic garb, and while their apparel answered one question, it raised even more.

What exactly was the ceremony being performed? And why outside with a fire?

The heart of the coven's power was in the oldest section of the home, the dome-shaped great room with its massive pentacle overhead. That was where most rites and rituals were carried out, so Quinn puzzled over the location. And the bonfire.

Searching for Anna's signature royal blue, he found her speaking with Viv donned in purple and Willyn sheathed in white.

Quinn's step faltered as a swift and merciless shock of pain caught him off-guard. One color was glaringly absent, the bold and glorious gold of the sun.

Kylie's color suited her so well, and he was suddenly overcome with the need to see it. Here, where it belonged.

The nine were now eight, and the earth seemed off-kilter. How could this ritual succeed if the coven wasn't at full strength? Their youngest member was missing. The brightest of them all.

He didn't hear Ethan's approach and only came back around when his friend touched his shoulder. "Hold it together, Quinn. They're going to need you for this. They'll need both of us."

The image of Kylie faded then, as if her smiling face had blown away with the wind. "Right." Quinn cleared his throat. "Need us for what?"

"I'll let your sister tell it. I only know they want us to join the circle—you, Dare, Michael, and me. Any of us with even the smallest hint of magic."

"That won't make up for Kylie." Quinn loosed his irritation, drawing a frown from Ethan.

"No, nothing will take her place." His friend held his dark gaze on Quinn. "But tonight, it's about power." Ethan removed his hand. "And love. The strongest magic of all."

Nodding because he didn't trust himself to speak, Quinn glanced again to Anna. His sister was staring at him, and when he met her eyes, he saw the question resting there. Kicking up his chin, he let her know he was ready.

All over the lawn cats strolled or reclined. Though they often served as the coven's second line of defense, sometimes—he had to admit—they were actually the front line. When Quinn looked at Sassafras, she lifted her head in what was, he believed, a gesture of acknowledgement.

Damn, he liked that Sassy cat. For some of the same reasons he'd fallen for her human. Straightforward and not afraid to speak her mind—such as it was with cats—and a boundless energy that enlivened anyone lucky enough to be in the vicinity.

I have to see her again. I have to tell her I love her. He shook as he fought the urge to curse the cruel universe. To threaten the gods and others who bore destiny down upon the heads of helpless mortals.

But then humility rushed back in, and he offered his prayers to the goddess instead. *Please, please. Let her be safe.*

Staring into the cloudless sky, he followed a beam of the moon all the way back down to the ground. But as the others moved in to encircle the pit, each and every face was burnished only by firelight.

Another pentacle had been created on the ground with the bonfire as its center. The lines weren't cast in chalk or salt but inlaid with hundreds of rounded stones. Solid, weighty. Impervious.

What was his sister up to?

Studying the stones, he wondered who had helped Anna set up. But then he surveyed the other men gathered, each with a serious countenance, and was certain she'd had all the hands she'd needed.

Nick was with them again tonight, as he had been since the moment he'd found Kylie's amulet. Trevor and Cole were present as well, with Michael and Dare rounding out the male flank.

Rarely were they all able to get together, but since the . . . abduction . . . they hadn't been apart. Claire and Joe had taken up posts at the hospital, but with a strong protective spell laid down by Anna, Mrs. Attinger and her visitors were secure. Just as Joseph was protected at the yellow house where he stood sentry over young Tadd.

So the witches and their men could focus on the search.

Noticing that each point of the pentacle glistened beneath the flames, Quinn kneeled to inspect Anna's handiwork. There were lumpy white chunks he knew well—magnesite, to aid psychic clarity. Given Anna's clairvoyance, the mineral was one of her favorites.

He also noted orange crystals of citrine for success. And hematite, a deep and polished gray with a high iron content, which was said to increase knowledge. Quinn figured they needed plenty of both.

In greater numbers were the clear shapes of quartz crystals. These would connect the physical dimensions to those of the mind. As he studied the last, stones he didn't recognize, Anna moved to stand beside him.

"Thunderstone," she explained. "Those are Ethan's idea. An obscure rock found only in certain parts of Africa." She waited the space of three heavy heartbeats, then added, "They help to summon evil spirits."

After shooting her a look of confusion, Quinn stood. "And you do this, why?"

"Yesterday at the stone yard, what I saw—what I used to help me see—it wasn't pure. And I know that's the only reason I was able to get a link to Kylie." Anna folded her arms, rubbed one elbow. "I can't always call up what I want or need to see. But we were lucky."

Quinn gestured. "So tonight you're using everything at your disposal. People, stones, crystals." He stared into the licking flames. "But why the fire?"

"That last vision . . . it was like swimming through tar, terribly difficult to manipulate. The smoke from our fire," she looked up, following the gray wisps as they floated, "that is the conduit of my choice. Light and airy, able to travel far and swiftly. I'll have greater control."

"And you dare summon evil to help your circle, because you believe it will mask our presence again. That it will get us to Kylie." Quinn nudged one of the rounded rocks with the toe of his shoe. "Even with the extra solidity, and the larger circle, it's risky."

"And worth the inherent threat. If we can't even save one of our own, Quinn, then what good are we? Besides, I can handle it. No. *We* can handle it." A thread of pure determination ran through her voice. "We are the Savannah Coven after all."

Anna gave him a steely stare and firmed her lips. Then with a twirl of her hand, she indicated they should begin.

The women all put their black robes on over the colorful dresses as they tightened the circle. Befitting symbolism, Quinn thought, since they were cloaking their light magic with spirits of the dark.

Michael stood next to Shauni while Ethan went to Lucia, and Dare to Willyn.

"I think we should use everyone," Quinn said abruptly, indicating Trevor, Cole, and Nick. "They all care about Kylie too, and as a wise man once told me," he stared at Ethan with a wry smile, "love is the strongest magic. And the most formidable."

Anna inclined her head. "You see things I cannot." The look she gave him was trusting. "That's why I need you. Why I always have."

Without question, the three men fell in line, each going to stand beside the woman he loved. All of the cats found their witch as well, Cuileann to Shauni, Ivy to Anna, and grouchy Kiko with Viv.

When Sassy chose Quinn to align herself with, he pinched the bridge of his nose to stifle the tears of loss and fear that begged to flow. Even the cat recognized his connection to Kylie.

He only prayed he hadn't thrown away his last chance to show respect for that bond. To honor their destiny.

The fire burned stronger now, flames soaring into the air, while embers settled below to shimmer with the bright orange of heat. After everyone had joined hands, Anna put Kylie's amulet around her neck. The bright yellow center lay next to her own gemstone of royal blue.

Quinn watched, hoped, and prayed as his sister lifted her face to the night sky. Then again when she lifted her voice. "I open the door to the moon gate and beyond, for myself and the spirits I travel among. I offer the key of the otherworld, as it is mine by right. My mind is free as it flies with the smoke. It sees what I seek as it flies on the night."

The first ripples of magic awoke inside Quinn as Anna continued. "Let sight be one with the air, fire, earth, and sea. This is my will, and so shall it be."

Now the ripples grew to pounding waves. They flowed from the center of Quinn's body, and the middle of his mind. Soon he felt the strength of others streaming with his until mere trickles became a tidal flood.

Unlike their small circle at the stone yard, tonight their greater unity formed a shield. There was no pain, no loss of control, only the intense magic of the coven, supported by the men who held them up.

This time when he pictured Kylie's face, he used it to open more doors inside of himself. To give more magic to Anna's mental pursuit. He thought of Kylie and her golden hair. Her bright and inquisitive hazel eyes.

Her image was the strongest talisman, and he could feel it giving him strength.

"Find our lost sister," Anna said, and Quinn knew she was sending the smoke. "Take me to her. Show me what I seek."

A new intensity began spreading throughout the circle, spinning in one direction. The whirling energy was benign but increased its strength with every revolution.

"I am one with the darkness. One with the sky. I see all."

Quinn didn't like the sound of that, but as long as Anna only meant her vision was joined with evil, then he would lend her his magic. For Kylie. They would use all tools available. Any mechanism. Because like Anna said, they were the Savannah Coven.

Their souls could resist the temptation.

"South." Anna's word was sharp, intended for the people in her circle. She was giving them information. "Southwest. Inland. Over marshes and city sprawl."

Yes. You can do it, Anna. Keep going. She was tracking the smoke as it flowed to Kylie.

"The trees . . ." Her words trailed off. She sounded confused. "Ahh . . . North now and down to the trees. The trees." Anna drew a deep, raspy breath.

Quinn was still comfortable as the magic spun around them and through them. The night was calm, the sky littered with stars. And the cats, sensitive creatures, still seemed unaffected.

So what was going wrong?

"South again." Defeated, disappointed, Anna relayed what she was seeing. "I can't get past the canopy of the forest."

"Keep trying." Quinn knew he shouldn't speak, but he could

hear his sister's surrender. "Try again."

The power started to slow, as if an engine had been turned off. "It's no use." Anna broke the connection.

Quinn turned to see her drop her hands from Claudia and Michael, but the anguish in her gaze was for Quinn. "We must have caught Bastraal's attention yesterday. I'm sorry."

"What does that mean?" Quinn released his grip on Hayden and then Willyn. "We should have been able to slip by undetected."

Anna shook her head. "Kylie is blocked completely now. She's been cut off from any outside force, good or evil."

"We can try again." Quinn grabbed onto Hayden, waving for Willyn to move back into the circle. She had stepped away, closer to her husband Dare.

"No. It's a waste of time. And time is the only thing we don't have enough of to spare." Anna took off Kylie's amulet and stared at it before closing her fist around the silver necklace.

"What do we do now?" Quinn demanded. "This was our best shot. The best idea that any of us could come up with."

He knew his voice raged, but he had nowhere else to release the frustration. "If we can't find her physically or psychically, if our best and most devious magic won't work, then what the hell is left to do?"

Anna put a hand to her brow. "I don't know." She shook her head, voice breaking when she said, "I just don't know."

21

"It's almost sunset." Anna's aggravated voice carried through the thick tension permeating the library where Quinn and Ethan worked. When Quinn ignored her, she threatened, "If you don't get some sleep, I *will* put a charm on you."

Quinn threw up a hand. "Leave me alone, Anna. We're still looking for a way to find Kylie. To break the cloaking spell that's hiding her from us." He flipped a page, only mildly concerned when the fragile vellum tore on the edge. "And we will find something."

He pictured the youngest witch and her sunny smile. *We have to find something.*

With a sound of disgust, his sister marched out of the library. Tempers had been running high since the bonfire's dismal failure, and Quinn and Anna were no exception. In fact, they'd been biting at each other ever since.

Doubt about the prophecy, second-guessing his actions, fear for Kylie, and that his whole life had been a waste. These things battered at Quinn every waking minute. They ate at him. Wore him down.

But he would keep pushing through, until they found her. Without her, none of the things that had once been so important meant anything.

For a moment the lines in front of him blurred. He lost his train of thought, too caught up worrying over outcomes he'd never dreamed possible.

Could he have been wrong all along? He hated to even entertain the notion, but could the coven be destined to fail? How cruel would it be if the woman he loved—a fact he was admitting far too late—was the one witch fated to break the chain? To be defeated in her challenge?

He scrubbed his eyes with the heels of his hand, fighting the gritty sensation that threatened to pull him into sleep. He couldn't stop now. He couldn't give up on her. None of them could.

If positions were reversed, Kylie would never give up on any of her sisters or friends.

Or Quinn.

He flipped the next page to scan its crooked, hand-written script. He felt trapped in a maze of terror and doubt, and every wrong turn led to another disappointment, another letdown. None of them knew what to do, and frankly, his confidence and optimism were taking serious damage.

"I can't find any mention of Bastraal," Ethan said, striding over to where Quinn sat. He held a great black book in his hands, scoured its interior, and then closed it soundly. "Not him specifically."

"He's had Ronja at his beck and call for a thousand years. She either killed any who knew of Bastraal or destroyed anything they might have recorded about him. We've gathered everything we've been able to find over time, as have those who came before us, my ancestors."

Ethan pressed a fist to the book after setting it on the gleaming mahogany table. "It never hurts to take another look." He frowned. "I only wish I'd found something, noticed anything you may have missed."

Quinn's head and chest were both being squeezed. The only question was which one would cave in first.

Everyone always gave the same responses, the clueless and

useless replies. *Maybe. We don't know. What do we do next?* No one had anything positive to say, and that included Quinn.

They were all lost. All of them. Kylie was depending on them, and they were chasing their magical but inept tails.

"What about that village you mentioned?" Quinn asked. "The one from Sri Lanka that was mysteriously wiped out. Weren't there stories of a demon in a woman's body? Destroying everything and killing everyone?"

Quinn rolled his shoulders back and stretched. It was creeping into evening, and he'd been hunched over the desk all day. "She sounds like she could be one of Bastraal's kin. Hell, his sister."

"Yeah. There were stories, but that's all I've got, hearsay dealing with the woman after she attacked the village. But if they managed to defeat her or learn about where she came from, what she was," Ethan sighed and rubbed the back of his neck, "there's no remaining evidence. Not that I can find. No information on Bastraal's power or how to counteract his spells."

Trailing his stare over the walls of books, Quinn felt the now-familiar sense of depression. Of defeat. The library held too many books to count but not nearly enough were on the subject they needed. He and Ethan had gone through almost every pertinent reference. They were still empty-handed.

A clatter at the doors had Quinn jerking around in his chair, ready to tell his sister to leave him the hell alone. He'd sleep when he was—

No. He wouldn't say that. Wouldn't utter anything even close to the words *dead* or *death*.

But Anna hadn't returned to harass him. Shauni was there, her face milk white, eyes huge and shattered. "Come in here. Now." She twisted her hands. "Anna got a message."

"A vision?" But Quinn's question floated to empty space. Shauni had fled back the way she'd come.

Quinn and Ethan locked eyes. And then they ran.

Anna was coming down the wide staircase when they burst into the grand hall. The rest of the group was pouring in from above, out of the kitchen, and from the opposite wing of the mansion.

"I . . . I didn't open it." Anna was stammering, in much the same dazed state as Shauni.

"Open what?" Quinn hurried to her, his gaze locked onto the blue laptop she carried. He took it from her, gently, and moved to set it on the coffee table in front of the long couch covered in green velvet.

She'd gotten an email, and when Quinn read the title, the words shook him to his core.

Lost something?

Fear congealed at the base of his skull before it raced down his spine. He could guess who'd sent the message. The Amara.

When he studied the body of the message, a fist of apprehension curled in his gut. There was an attachment.

A video.

As if immersed in water, Quinn's movements were slow and rubbery. He slid his finger over the touchpad and watched as the cursor drifted to the untitled attachment. With a deep, bracing breath, he double-clicked to open the video.

At first he didn't know what he was watching. The view was closed in, cropping out any identifiable object. And everything was so dark.

Slowly the film zoomed out, and he began to make sense of the images. They focused and cleared until he understood what he was looking at.

Quinn went numb as shock flooded his system.

His back muscles clenched so violently they felt fused into place. As were his lungs, until his involuntary need for oxygen made him draw a burning breath.

Kylie. She was chained in a cell with some sort of . . . smoke creature above her. "A demon," he said hoarsely now, unaware of the room or people around him.

His sense of reality was confined to that dark prison cell. To the torture chamber. "They used a demon on her."

The video played its gruesome footage, but he had no idea how long they watched.

"Turn it off," Willyn cried when Kylie let loose a horrific scream. "Please."

"We have to watch." Quinn made himself stare, though his spine ached from the spasms in his back. "There could be something useful. They sent it for a reason."

A hand fell on his shoulder. "Let us deal with it, Quinn." Trevor was beside him on the couch. "You can trust me and Cole. You don't need to see this."

As brave as he'd tried to be, as much as he'd been driven to help her, to find her, Quinn simply couldn't bear to see any more. Finally he tore his eyes from the screen. His only answer to Trevor was to rise from the couch and walk away.

Willyn had already run from the room, as had a few of the other women. They were all too close to this, and Trevor was right.

There was no need for them to witness Kylie's torture.

Anna remained in the grand hall, stunned and in shock. Her eyes were riveted to the laptop monitor.

Paige and Viv were still there as well, stoic in their stances. But if their expressions conveyed emotion, they too were sick to the heart.

"Where is the dagger?"

Quinn's head swung swiftly back toward the sound of Ronja's voice. "I knew it," he said, voice thick with rage and despair. "They want the dagger."

In a swift move, he went to Anna and grabbed her arm. "So let's just give it to them. If we don't, she's dead."

Paige spoke up, her lips shaking with unspent fury. "We

can't do that. Look at what Kylie's endured to safeguard the dagger. If we just give it up, we dishonor her and everything she's done to protect it. To protect us and the innocents."

"But giving the Amara the dagger could save her."

A tear rolled down Anna's cheek. "And it would doom the world. You know this, Quinn."

Hands gripped in his hair, Quinn spun away in an attempt to control the wrath boiling over, afraid he would burn anyone standing too close. This was all so wrong! It wasn't supposed to happen this way!

The prophecy had been his entire life. Now it would be his destruction.

And Kylie's end.

Viv covered her mouth with her hand and began to cry softly.

It was too much. Quinn was going to explode on something, someone. He wanted to hurt those who'd hurt Kylie. If he were able, he'd wrap his hands around their throats and squeeze the life out of their putrid bodies without blinking an eye.

He knew all about the balance of nature and the universe. How what he sent out would come back to him. But he didn't care. He would mete out bloody justice if he had the chance, and would give the bastards as much pain as possible.

But that bitch Searenn wasn't here—her and her monsters that stabbed and burned. *Oh, Kylie's face. Her tears.* He had nowhere to vent this overwhelming anger, the kind that turned sane men into monsters.

He needed to hit. To maim. To murder.

In an aggressive lunge, he grabbed the laptop, ripping it from the coffee table to throw across the room. The lightweight computer smashed into a wall and broke apart, metallic missiles firing in every direction.

He roared his outrage. "Fuck this! All of this!" Whirling on Anna, he clenched his shaking hands. "Fuck the prophecy, and the goddess and her—"

"Quinn!" His sister made a fist and thrust it downward. "Stop this!"

"I will!" He surged forward, his finger trembling as he pointed. "That's exactly what I'll do."

His voice was calmer, but deceptively so. "Screw Fate and this damned prophecy. If this is what Kylie deserves, what any of us deserve after all we've done, then Fate, the goddess, the spirits, they're all worthless bastards."

He grasped his face with both hands, then tore them away again. Madness welled in his head.

Looking at Anna, he rasped, "And you can add me to that list too. I was as cold-hearted as any of those pitiless gods. I treated her so . . ."

He turned away, covering his eyes with his fists. "I hurt her. I sent her straight into their hands. Now look what they're doing to her!"

"No." Anna took a step forward. But he shoved a hand at her.

"Just back off," he warned. "I'm done with this prophecy. Nothing else matters until we find her. Do you hear me?" Then he lifted his face and fists to the rafters. "Do you hear me?!"

A cell phone rang out as if in response, its light and airy tinkle incongruous and out of place in the emotional scene. The sweet song seemed to mock Quinn's rage.

Paige swiveled her head, trying to locate the source. Once she had, she stomped across the room to a sidebar. "It's your phone, Anna." She snatched the cell up and stared at the screen. "It's Claire."

Anna wiped at her wet cheeks. "Answer it." Then she hurriedly added, "But don't tell her about this."

Anger and misery still pulsed within Quinn. The unbelievable heartbreak and sense of helplessness dragged on his sanity. So he concentrated on breathing. On calming down.

Paige nodded and spoke into the cell phone. After a moment of hushed conversation, Quinn heard her say, "Yes, ma'am."

When she was finished, the blonde warrior rejoined them in the middle of the room. "She says we all need to come to the yellow house. She has something to tell us. Something important."

A tiny, insignificant place in the deepest, darkest corner of Quinn's soul flamed to life. "About Kylie?"

Paige sighed. "Yes. But she wouldn't say anything over the phone. She wants us all there."

The miniscule flame grew, but Quinn wouldn't call it hope, not yet. Not until he heard what Claire had to tell them.

His voice was somber when he said, "We'll need both boats."

~~~

The kitchen was crowded, as they'd known it would be with this many people, but Claire just waved a hand at the coffee pot. "I've made plenty, and can always make more. We're likely to need it." She notched her chin at the island of creamy marble. "Sit."

"Where's Joe?" Michael asked, easing into a corner to lean against the counter.

"He's at the hospital standing guard. Mr. Attinger is still there too. He's sleeping on a cot and won't leave." Claire shook her head but smiled with admiration and love for her old friend. "He just won't leave."

Quinn was glad Mrs. Attinger was recovering so well and so quickly, but he had no interest in the coffee or small talk. He only wanted to hear what Claire had to share with them.

He couldn't stop seeing the green smoke. The awful things that creature did.

Shaking his head to force out the terrible pictures, he shot an intense look to Claire. But when he opened his mouth to speak, she jabbed a finger at him, effectively shutting him up. Then she repeated the act with Anna.

Claire had swatted their bottoms as many times as Mrs.

Attinger had, so Quinn and his sister both knew the look. The tone. And that finger.

"First off," Claire began, still heated with ire, "you should have told me everything from the very minute Kylie went missing."

"We—" Anna started.

"Everything." Claire eased onto a stool and sipped her coffee, her expression smoothing into one of frustration. Which was far less worrisome than her anger. "I had to find out about this place in the woods, this *stone yard*, as you call it, from Dare. And then it was only through an offhand remark."

She leaned toward Anna now, her forehead creased. "Girl, do you forget who I am? What I've seen? I may not have magic," she tapped her head, "but I have knowledge, especially when it comes to this land and its history."

Quinn flushed as the distinct feeling of foolishness spread through him. "Claire, you're right. We should have come to you. You taught me most of what I know about local lore and legends." He sat back and dropped his hands to his thighs. "I've just been so caught up."

"I know, and that's why you're both forgiven. Plus, I wasn't thinking clearly either, so worried about Mrs. Attinger and Kylie." She grimaced and then tapped an unpolished fingernail to the marble. "But now you'll listen to me."

Offering a brittle smile to all the others standing around her kitchen, Claire said, "Go on and get a drink, and a chair if you need. This is a crowded house for sure, but you should all hear this."

A few filled mugs and others found a seat. When silence reigned once more, she began her tale. "My father's people came down from the Yamacraw, a tribe that was here before the city of Savannah was even born. All different kinds of people were flocking to the area then, trying to get a foothold. British, Spanish, and the Creek tribes who wanted to trade with the foreigners."

Claire set her mug down and ran a finger around the rim. "Other folks came too, taking advantage of the wild lands and burgeoning turmoil."

Her eyes got a faraway look. Her voice grew hushed. "There were rumors of a place back then. A place with many strange stone markers and a tower of rock." Her mouth was grim when she looked to Anna. "Sound like somewhere you know?"

"The stone yard." Anna brushed her cheek as if chasing a stray lock of hair.

"I say rumor," Claire continued, "because people would go off looking for it every now and then." She gave a careless tilt of her head. "None ever found it."

"The same as it is now," Dare interjected before gesturing to Quinn. "Joseph also mentioned that the place wasn't listed on a map or in any records. He wondered why people flying over in planes didn't report it."

"Because not everyone can see it." Shauni summed up the line of thought and ran a hand down her raven-black braid.

Quinn suddenly felt chilled and decided he'd take a coffee after all. He stood. "Not everyone is meant to see it."

Claire was quiet as he poured some of the steaming black brew for himself. When he sat at the island again, she spoke. "They say a young girl came screaming into the settlement one day. This was years later, after the Yamacraw had spread themselves out to other lands."

She sipped her drink as everyone watched and waited, rapt with curiosity. "The girl told of terrible things, atrocities. Mutilation, rape, murder." Claire closed her eyes and drew a shaky breath in through her nose. "Things she said were happening at the tower of stone."

The kitchen crackled with nervous energy and the unspoken imaginings of all gathered around to listen. The room was filled with light, but the environment seemed dark, tainted with illusions of brutality and carnage.

"Of course, people searched, but they never found this place. They chalked it up to the girl's trauma, a knock on the head. Something. Anything but what it really was." Claire stared at Quinn. "I don't know when this preacher built his church out there. In fact, I haven't thought of the story of that girl or that tower of rock for a long time now."

Quinn drummed his fingers on top of the island. He glanced aside to Anna, wondering whether or not they should tell Claire about the video. Why cause the older woman any more anguish than she was already dealing with?

Before he got a chance to nudge Anna or draw her attention, they heard the front door open and close. Footsteps, more than one set, were tromping down the hall.

Claire looked over Quinn's shoulder to the door, her face expectant. Then she shifted her soft brown eyes back to him. "There's another reason I called you here tonight, and I can honestly say we all dropped the ball on this one. Myself included."

"How? What do you mean?" Quinn glanced back quickly. Who was here?

He stood to meet whoever was coming toward them, but was baffled when only Joseph stepped into view. "Joseph?"

Then another person trailed in behind his friend.

Her hair was straight to her shoulders and a light, glossy brown, with bangs cut evenly over her eyes. Eyes that Quinn recognized instantly.

The hair was new, as was the prim and preppy striped boatneck shirt she wore. But some preferences were bone deep, as evidenced by the painted on jeans and spike-heeled boots.

"Thank you for coming," Quinn said on a breath, and he sent Joseph a look of comprehension. Of gratitude.

Claire hadn't overstated anything, because they'd done more than just drop the ball. Hell, they hadn't even been in the game. Their tunnel vision had blocked out alternative means, unconventional sources, and people they hadn't considered.

None of them had thought of her. Their last and final chance to find Kylie was now standing before him. Someone who'd once been privy to Amara secrets.

"Thank you," he said again, but this time, the heartfelt appreciation was directed toward their unexpected guest.

In reply, Sylvie simply nodded.

22

Each breath streaming in and out of her lungs brought stinging, radiating pain. Yet Kylie let herself breathe a sigh of relief as she watched Tyr tread across the expanse of her darkened prison, open the creaky door, and finally, blessedly leave.

When the bolt turned behind him, she closed her eyes. She lay as still as possible, hoping the agony would begin to recede.

Tyr had once belonged to a Native American tribe, and he'd looked the part in his mid-calf brown pants. Of course, wearing so little served a practical purpose too. It made it easier for him to wash off the blood.

Her blood.

She almost preferred the vicious demon Searenn had conjured to what Tyr had done to her. At least that monster's wounds had healed.

Tyr's knowledge of blades and burns and how he applied them was somehow more heinous. He too was a beast from the depths of Hell. Each time one of the Amara visited her, she thought the torment couldn't get any worse.

And each time she was wrong.

Rolling onto her side took great effort, but her back had been too abused to remain in the supine position. Her skin felt as if it had been put through a grinder.

Once on her left side, breathing became a little easier. So she opted to rest that way for a while, maybe recover a little. If she didn't bleed to death first.

She could barely drag in the much-needed air but did her best, clenching her teeth against the shooting jolts of pain. She didn't know how long she'd been trapped here in the cell, but the sessions were taking a toll.

She often vacillated between blurred reality and nightmare-filled patches of sleep, unable to tell one from the other. It was also becoming harder to differentiate between sleepiness, physical exhaustion, and her body's instinctual need to protect and preserve by passing out.

She'd lost a lot of blood at Tyr's hands, and the evidence was still pooling around her body. Small rivulets spread outward, like wine colored fingers seeking to escape. Just as she would do if she could move.

The Amara had given her no food or water since her abduction, and she could feel her body . . . changing, as if her skin and muscles were stretching and tightening. She was well past her original state of frenzied fear. She was far beyond worry or concern.

At least for herself.

Regrets, however, clung to her like the sticky mixture of dirt, grime, and her own drying blood. With nothing to do but think or doze between her visitors, Kylie found herself in a type of mourning.

She grieved for all of the things she'd lost, loved ones she'd never see again. Her parents, her sisters of magic . . . and Quinn. But even more, she ached for things she would never have. Sweet happiness that she'd come so close to tasting.

Quinn. Love. And the coven's victory over the Amara. Everything would fail now. Ronja had come back at them with all she had, and now the coven would pay dearly for their actions.

Sure, they'd all known Ronja would be good and pissed

about Dalton Morne's arrest. That she would be insulted by the witches' arrogance. But that's exactly what they'd wanted.

They'd anticipated her fury and maybe even some backlash. Kylie winced when a gash on her leg scraped over rock.

But this. She moaned. They'd never expected this.

Kylie stared at her limp hand, the fingers that could only curl because they had no strength to open. Her fingernails were broken, torn, and blackened by whatever filth coated the floor.

There had been moments—she shivered to recall—when she'd clawed at stone and dirt in her pitiful attempts to gain some leverage. To get away from whoever was in the cage with her, bringing more and more of the agony. The suffering.

There was no escape, she understood that now. But in the midst of such incredible pain, her body just took over. Her mind went blank, wild in its need to block or break away from the hurt. She was grateful when it worked.

Tyr seemed to have left for the time being, but she still listened intently. For his footsteps or any others.

The fear of his return, or the return of any of the Amara, was its own brand of torture. Psychological warfare that made her jump at every scratch or bump that ricocheted through the building around her.

Unable to lift her head, Kylie strained to hear past the rocked-in walls of the room. But there was no sound, only her own ragged breaths. A lone lantern still burned on one side of the gloomy chamber, so she could at least be glad Tyr had forgotten to turn it off.

This might very well be the last place on earth she would ever see, and the thought saddened her. The dusty, moldy chamber was drenched in shadow. And it stank. The space reeked of blood, sweat, and the unique pungency of her own terror.

Deep in her chest, another moan began to build, but she hadn't the energy to give it life.

She would die soon. She knew this. She'd accepted it.

But when the aches became too much, as they were now, she simply willed herself to slip away, into her only real means of escape. Unconsciousness.

But soon, she would truly be set free. Soon she would have the final relief.

There was no way she'd survive another "session" with the Amara. And given her current condition—the number of serious wounds, how much blood she'd lost, and her lack of hydration—Ronja had to know Kylie was fading.

And was not concerned.

Kylie wouldn't—couldn't—give them the information they wanted, so her death deprived them of nothing. In fact, it was a victory.

Wishing only to be free of the stink, the darkness, and the awful pain, Kylie relaxed when oblivion beckoned. She willingly followed the black tunnel that meant she was fainting and prayed for a long stretch of serenity.

As she drifted off, she began to see things. Bright and colorful, like the most vivid fantasies. Maybe they were even hallucinations, but she didn't care. She welcomed them.

In her current half-dream, she found herself suddenly staring into the sun and azure sky. The blue was so pure and true, it couldn't be real. Wrapping her arms around her waist, she let her head fall back and relished the warmth on her skin.

It had been so long since she'd seen the sky. Since she'd experienced daylight. Too long she had been in the dark.

"Hey there." Quinn's voice rolled through her, rich and deep. The familiar timbre pulled her gaze away from the sky and straight to a smiling set of eyes that rivaled the brilliant depths of sapphires.

"Where have you been?" She held out her hand to him, smiling when a yellow butterfly landed briefly on her wrist before zipping away. And then she angled her head, hoping to flirt a bit with her handsome Quinn.

"I've been looking for you," he said, entwining his fingers with hers. His touch wasn't electric, as it had often been, but comforting, and so much warmer than even the sun.

Still holding her hand, he turned and began to stroll with her through the field. Wildflowers were everywhere. How had she not noticed them before?

And in the distance, she could hear the ocean. The clean winds and mysterious depths always reminded her of him. Of Quinn.

"I'm sorry," she said. "I've been waiting for you, but the trees were in my way. They were keeping you from me." The words didn't make sense to her, but what ever did in a dream?

"I know." He lifted her hand to his lips, the kiss miraculously soft and tender. "But I'm here now, and everything is going to be all right."

Her breath rushed out, painlessly now, and she squeezed his fingers. She wished they could stay this way forever. "But it won't be, Quinn. I know that, and I know it's why you're here. I've been given one more chance to do what's right."

His brow furrowed. "No, Kylie—"

"It's okay," she whispered, cutting him off. "I can see so clearly now, and I owe you an apology. I never should have pressured you. I shouldn't have had such expectations. That wasn't fair, and I was only thinking of myself. Not you. Not really."

She stopped and put a finger to his lips. Inhaling the sweet scent of honeysuckle, she trailed the back of her knuckles over his cheek. "Love, real love, is selfless, Quinn. I never asked you what you wanted, only pushed my own needs at you. Always wanting. Demanding."

She stepped into him, leaning her head against his shoulder. When his arms stole around her, true and unassuming joy flooded her heart. "I should have loved you better, and I'm sorry."

"Please, Kylie. Just let me hold you."

"Always. If I could." She rested her palm over his heart, letting the thrum of it pulse through her. She would never forget this moment, real or imagined. "I'm so glad I could tell you this. Be happy, Quinn. That's all I want."

Suddenly, the field and sky were shrouded in darkness. The blue sky was gone, overtaken by churning clouds. The dark gray masses were strangely silent but rushed overhead like quicksilver.

The field of flowers was gone too. And when she looked, so was Quinn. Her heart dropped. "Quinn! Where are you?"

The sweet smell of honeysuckle dissipated just as quickly, and in its place, the nauseating mix of mildew, waste, and blood rushed back to her. Instead of her previous bliss . . . there was dread.

"Oh, no you don't. Not yet." A raspy voice rattled Kylie's brain just as the woman's hands rattled her metal cage.

Awareness fell over her again, and with it, the pain. Her body was past hunger, consumed only by weakness and the last tiny spark of will. Her lingering desire to live.

Kylie's very skin was almost too heavy to bear, but she managed to open her eyes to slits. A scuttling movement caught her attention, and she watched as a long, flat insect crept across the dirt and stone she lay upon.

The silvery bug stopped at the edge of her blood. And began to feed.

"Over here," the female called again in a sing-song voice. "We brought you a present."

Male laughter followed, and the meaning of the words registered. Kylie bolted awake to clarity. Searenn and Ross had returned and were standing in the corner.

Between them they held a man, a young man judging by his baggy shorts and t-shirt emblazoned with the promise to live fast and die young. His head hung forward so that long blonde hair fell down to shade both sides of his face.

Kylie didn't speak. She didn't know what was going on, what this new game of theirs was, but she was afraid to reveal any reaction.

While Ross supported the groaning captive, Searenn exited the room, returning shortly and dragging a cheap wooden chair with her. Together, she and Ross shoved the man down and proceeded to tie him up.

Oh no. Don't let them do this. "I don't know where the dagger is." Speaking rubbed Kylie's raw throat. The tissue had been chaffed by her seemingly endless screams. The ones that had ripped from her while Tyr had done his work.

Ross leered at her, his unholy blue eyes practically glowing with perverse desire. "If you do know where the dagger is, you'll tell us to save this idiot." He flicked the guy's ear and received a muffled yelp in return. "But if you don't," he shrugged, "what's the loss, really?"

Ross and Searenn shared a grin as she said, "It will still be a good time."

The man's head lifted marginally, and then he shot fully upright. His eyes darted around the room before landing on Kylie. He blinked several times before he recoiled, face twisting with disgust. "What is that?"

Kylie's stomach sunk even more. Did he mean her?

The prisoner glanced at Ross and then Searenn. "Where am I?" He struggled to free himself from the ropes. "Are you going to do that to me? Why? I don't even know you!"

Kylie's appearance had to be horrific to cause such panic. "Shhh . . ." She tried to calm him, but he was hysterical.

Ross drove his fist into the side of the blonde man's head. "Damn, shut up already." The shifter hooked a thumb at the pitiful guy, who was now blubbering. "Too bad he's not the one who knows what we need. He's already broken, and we haven't even started yet."

"I can't tell you what I don't know." Kylie begged with her eyes. "Please don't do this."

Searenn only sneered and jerked her sweatshirt over her head. She perused her arms and the repulsive ink on her arms.

"No. No." Kylie could barely move, but she tried to sit up, to use the chains still shackling her to hoist her body.

Searenn had already found her tattoo of choice and had her hands out in front of her. The glowing mist that emanated around the Droehk wasn't green this time. It was blood-red.

A ripping noise thundered in the room as the air itself split open, allowing a child-sized creature to push through the opening. It clawed its way out in a gangly manner, with arms that were longer than its legs.

Once liberated from its small, tight portal, the demon rolled fully black and soulless eyes around its new environment. It sniffed the air and panted, his gasps high and mottled by what sounded like phlegm.

Searenn pointed to the hapless figure tied to the chair. "There," she directed.

The demon's black eyes shifted, landing on the unfortunate hostage. To Kylie's horror, the monster scrambled over, its limbs long and looping like a chimpanzee. It covered the ground quickly, throwing itself at the poor man's leg. The creature wrapped itself around his calf.

And began to chew.

Shrieks bounced and vibrated off the stone walls, ear-splitting wails of anguish and horror.

"Don't! It won't do any good!" Kylie pulled against her chains to no avail.

The screams were the worst kind of torture, and honestly, if she could reveal the dagger's location to save him being . . . eaten alive, then she would. God help her, she would.

"Please. Please." She was crying now but no tears flowed. She had no water left in her to spare.

She couldn't stop this. She couldn't help the man. And as the pitiful screams of misery and terror pierced her ears, her mind, she wasn't even able to lower her hands and block the sound.

As the guttural smacking and growling continued beneath the hideous cries, Kylie prayed she would just go back under. That the dream of Quinn would come and save her again.

As the man screamed and screamed—just as she had before, she prayed for the sweet release of unconsciousness. Hearing another's suffering was so much worse than enduring her own. And at some point, she began to pray for death.

The man's . . . hers.

Whichever came first.

~~~

Once Sylvie and Joseph joined the group, everyone relocated to the den where there was more space. Sylvie sat in a butter-toned wingback that perfectly matched the begonias atop the coffee table.

"Joseph's filled me in," she began, "and first I want to say . . ." she readjusted in the chair, "that I'm truly sorry about Kylie."

Quinn waved his hand as if brushing aside her concern. "You aren't with the Amara anymore, Sylvie, and we know how hard you've worked to change." He took a seat on the end of the couch closest to her chair. "We're just grateful for any help you can give us."

She nodded and visibly relaxed, blowing a breath out her pursed lips. "Okay then." She put both hands on her knees. "The only other place I know of that you haven't already checked, is a building, a house, rather, over in Bryan County."

"Southwest of here," Anna said, lips flat and regretful. "Maybe my vision was originally headed in the right direction after all."

Sylvie look chagrined. "I'm sorry. I don't have an exact address, and I only went there one time. At night."

Trevor spoke from where he stood with one arm propped on the mantle. "If you can get us close, Cole and I should be able to narrow down the properties."

"Do you remember what the house looked like?" Quinn asked her.

Sylvie met his eyes with cool and open honesty. Her fashion sense wasn't the only thing that had changed. Her demeanor was different too, as time with her grandmother had been good for her.

Joseph's devotion hadn't hurt either.

"Pretty much." Sylvie's eyes rolled to the side in thought. "Run-down, rotting, broken windows. Oh, and a wooden staircase that runs straight up to a door on the second level." She lifted her hand and performed a zigzag motion. "That stuff they use on roofs, the up-and-down sheet of metal."

She bit her lip, concentrated, and finally snapped her fingers. "Corrugated sheet metal. The bottom floor was encased in that stuff, like an extra layer."

"That's good." Cole was jotting notes on a small pad. "Do you remember the route you took? I know it was at night, but anything will help."

"Well, we were headed west, so naturally we took I-16. We didn't get off until the exit that takes you toward Georgia Southern University." She looked at Quinn and nodded. "You know the one?"

"Yes."

"We didn't go toward the campus, but took a left instead. We stayed on that road a few miles." Frowning, Sylvie stood and began to pace. She nibbled a fingernail. "I can remember a weird sign. I think it was yellow, but I definitely know it said something about popcorn."

Quinn perked up. "Paulson's Mart. The building was

demolished years ago, but for some reason, that sign still stands."

"We turned right just past there." Sylvie clapped her hands, then dropped them as bleakness covered her face. "After that, it was a bunch of twists and turns. But I remember there wasn't much else around. Maybe that will help."

While Cole continued to notate Sylvie's directions, Trevor gave his keys to Hayden, asking her to retrieve a map from his car.

Then he zeroed in on Quinn. "Can you pull up some satellite imaging on a computer? We can get a better lay of the land, maybe get lucky and find the house."

"I'm on it." Quinn rushed toward the foyer, but Joseph was of the same mind and had already beaten him to it.

Stopping long enough to give Quinn a look of encouragement, Joseph said, "We're getting close. I know it." His face fell into serious lines again. "I'll get my laptop." Then he dashed up the stairs.

Moments later, they had the Internet pulled up and were searching the satellite images as requested. It wasn't hard to find the intersection of I-16 and GA 67. Then it was only a matter of progressing the search down the road.

At last, Quinn tapped the screen. "There's the sign and the empty lot with the concrete slab where Paulson's used to be."

They followed the first road past the faded yellow advertisement for popcorn and took the screenshot down to street view. After that, the search slowed to a frustrating crawl. So much so, that Quinn was overrun with impatience and beads of sweat broke out on his brow.

But they had to be thorough. They couldn't rush. Or they might miss the house they were looking for and would have to start all over again.

A glance at the window told him the sun had set hours ago. They'd lost more time traveling to the mainland, waiting for everyone else to arrive. And now this.

The closer they got to finding this house—that Quinn truly believed was Kylie's prison—the edgier he became. She'd been missing for two days now, but a new sense of urgency was flogging his back like an incessant whip.

In the back of his mind, he kept hearing *Hurry. Hurry. Hurry.*

But all he could do was search each painstakingly slow-loading frame at a time. They had to zoom the images in for every twist and turn, and Sylvie hadn't lied when she'd said there had been a lot. They had no choice but to follow each street to the end, backtrack to the beginning, and then start again.

More coffee was made, and Claire kept food and snacks coming. Everyone sensed the night ahead would be long and treacherous.

Just when Quinn felt ready to explode, Sylvie tapped his shoulder. "That looks familiar. Keep going, but slow, so I can take a good look."

Finally they came to a structure that made her eyes light up with recognition. "I think I remember that doghouse and the big tree."

The second structure they zoomed down on made her even more certain. Small details were the only thing that helped the trail emerge from the thick spread of trees and shrubs that all looked alike.

"Keep going down this road," Sylvie said, her voice thrumming now.

Quinn did as she instructed and switched the camera angle when she asked him to.

He zoomed in on the next structure, and behind him, Sylvie sucked in a breath. He could see for himself that the house matched her previous description, so he didn't give her time before looking over his shoulder to meet her wide eyes.

"Sylvie," he demanded, "is this it?"

23

"This is it," Sylvie said. She stood between Quinn and Trevor on the gravel road as they studied the dilapidated structure in the moonlight.

"This place is disgusting." Quinn's voice was low and threatening. "It's practically falling down." As his words echoed, a night owl called out, asking who dared to trespass.

He couldn't stand the idea of Kylie being imprisoned in such a place. Especially given the attack she'd endured, and anything else that had been done to her.

His ribs seemed to squeeze inward as fury surged. He'd kill them all, Ronja included, if he had to spend the rest of his years searching for a way.

If Kylie came out of this okay . . . No, he'd seen some of what they'd done. Even if her body had been somehow left unscathed, her memories would never be hers again. Not completely.

He started forward, veins bulging on the backside of his clenched hands, on his forearms. Yes. He'd make sure that immortal bitch paid dearly. One way or another.

But first, they had to make sure Kylie was safe. Quinn could sense her here, in the air somehow, in a way he hadn't at any of the other places they'd searched.

Trevor gripped his arm. "Wait. We do her no good if we go in half-cocked. We don't know what we're walking into."

"Ronja's not here. I can tell you that." Quinn surveyed

the unkempt grounds flanked by tall trees and wild growing shrubs. "She wouldn't stay out here for any length of time."

"Too remote?" Trevor asked.

"Too dirty," Quinn and Sylvie replied as one. They shared a quick smile, half-hearted on both parts, considering what lay before them.

"Looks like those steps are the only viable entry in front." Quinn chin-notched toward the decrepit wooden stairs. "We should send Paige that way. She's lighter and can jump faster in case those steps start to give way."

The house had been painted a light color at one time, but the coats had peeled away, leaving faded wood as the primary shade.

"Let's go back and regroup with the others," Trevor suggested.

Quinn knew he was right, but the urge to race up those stairs himself and break in the door was pressing in from all sides. "All right," he said grudgingly. "But let's make it fast. I can't leave her in there much longer."

Chunks of rocks crunched beneath his boots as they walked, and though the summer night sweltered, he felt better prepared in the heavy shoes and jeans. "She could be critically ill by now. Wounded, with an infection."

Quinn was growing more anxious by the second. He was sure they'd found the place where Kylie was being held captive.

Back down the road, the cars and the rest of the group waited. After a brief planning session, they decided a small tactical team should go in.

Cole and Trevor would be a part of it, as they had experience carrying out raids. Anna would go for magic, Lucia to help locate Kylie, and Willyn in case they found her in bad shape. Paige would also go because . . . well, because she was Paige.

And of course, Quinn. No one even suggested he stay behind. They knew better.

The seven members of the team moved quickly and quietly

back to the house. They surrounded it, with Trevor, Anna, and Willyn creeping around back, while Quinn and the others targeted the front.

After the two allotted minutes had passed that Cole and Trevor had agreed upon, Cole nodded to Quinn. "Time to go in. If the others hadn't found a way in, they would have rejoined us by now."

And that was all Quinn needed to hear. "I'll lead." He couldn't wait long enough for someone to test the sturdiness of the steps, even lightning-fast Paige.

Cole started to speak, then allowed, "Fine." The cop waved a hand to Lucia. "You go next and try to get a lock on Kylie."

"I feel her," the Spanish witch answered but with a frown. "It doesn't seem strong enough, though."

Quinn didn't over-examine what Kylie's weakened vibe could mean. He wasn't wasting any more time. He had to find her, whatever her condition.

He couldn't stand not knowing, trying to guess what she was going through. His overworked imagination and the pictures it conjured—those were what tortured him.

Cracked and dried steps groaned under his weight, issuing a warning as he ascended. He only hoped they held out long enough for him to get inside.

When he tested the rusty doorknob, it turned easily in his hand. The seventies-style door, with its diamond-shaped window in the center, opened with a creak.

Using stealth, Quinn and the three behind him entered the dilapidated house. He and Lucia went left to clear the room as Cole and Paige veered right.

Lucia fired her hand up with blue light, a sign in the dark for Paige, telling her the room was secure. Paige returned the signal.

Still separated from the others, Quinn and Lucia went through a musty dining room that boasted a metal folding table and broken-down chairs of the same low quality. They exited through a different door and met up with Cole and Paige again in a centralized hallway.

"Clear," Cole said.

"Us too." Quinn stilled, holding his breath when low, creeping steps sounded in the rear of the house. They all listened intently, breathing in the stale stench of the decaying building, and waiting for whoever was in the back to show themselves.

A pale blue glow let him know the noises were from the other team, and either Anna or Willyn was coming down the narrow hall toward them. "There's a door in the kitchen." Anna's voice floated to them, and then she came into view. "It leads down."

"To a basement," Quinn inferred, gaining a solemn nod from his sister. A low drone suddenly surrounded the house, and he realized the rain had come again. Lifting eyes to the ceiling he said, "At least it will help cover our movements."

Silently they followed Anna to the back of the house. Trevor and Paige were positioned on either side of the interior door.

A latch lock was on the wooden panel but no padlock or chain held it shut. Whoever had secured the door at one time had now left it open, as if the threat of injury—or escape—was no longer a concern.

Quinn felt the perspiration on the back of his neck run cold. If Kylie was down there, why wasn't she still locked in tight?

She was a powerful witch. She could find a way out, eventually. Unless . . .

Not caring what the next strategy might be in anyone else's mind, he pushed the door open and started down the stairs. The old wooden steps went straight then veered left halfway down, following the structure of the walls.

He heard Cole call for him to wait, so he paused long enough for the cop to catch up. Lucia was right behind him.

Her eyes met Quinn's. "What I'm sensing is straight through there." She indicated a tunnel, a man-made corridor of cement blocks and stone. The structure was out of place, as if part of a room had been built inside the subterranean space.

At the end, Quinn could make out another door. He felt as if icy insects were crawling down his back. The door was carelessly ajar. *Kylie.*

He rushed ahead with the others on his heels, forcing his way into the room before giving himself time to register the meaning of the lax security.

The first thing he saw was the cage. No, it was a cell, made of metal bars with chains snaking across the floor inside. His eyes struggled to adjust to the dark as he searched frantically for Kylie. *Where is she?*

With a word from Anna, the dark compartment lit up. She called forth the first available light source, and two electric lanterns cast a dim glow into the gloomy chamber. But they gave off enough illumination for Quinn to see that the cell—the entire room—was empty.

Kylie wasn't there.

He went to the cage and grabbed onto the bars, shaking the metal poles as if he meant to rip them from the mortar in which they rooted. No one tried to calm him or tell him to stop. Wisely, they let him spill his frustration as he would, without interference.

He spun around to inventory the rest of the room. To scope the corners and the entire length of the floor for any hidden lever or door. But he found nothing.

"She was here," Lucia said, staring at the empty prison cell. Her arms arrowed straight down by her sides, stiff as rods. "The blood . . . the blood left behind." She gulped. "It's hers."

"Oh, God." Willyn's wide eyes fell to the congealed liquid, now a dark and thick maroon. "There's too much. She's lost too much."

Trevor was inspecting a chair near one wall. Bits of flesh and more blood surrounded the wooden legs on the floor. "What did they do?" he asked.

As a homicide detective, Trevor had seen multitudes of savagery. But even he was repulsed by the scene they'd discovered in the basement.

Quinn pounded his fist on the stone wall. And then he pounded his own emotions into submission. He couldn't lose his shit now. They had to keep pressing on, because Kylie was still lost.

But she was coming home with him. No matter what.

"Lucia, can you get a bead on her now?"

"I . . ." Lucia put her hands out, exhaled, and closed her eyes. Then they popped back open. "Yes! She's being taken somewhere else. And she's already a long distance away."

A bright explosion of hope went off inside Quinn. "They aren't cloaking her anymore? You can track her?"

"Yes. But we need to go now, before the distance is too great."

Paying no heed to the noise they created, the bunch of them ran back up the stairs and through the dusty rooms. They clambered down the rickety front steps and bolted through the tiny yard, past the trees—disturbing a murder of crows that scattered and screamed—and down the road toward the cars.

Unrelenting rain had turned the black night into a swirling mist. When Quinn saw the rest of the group, he would have yelled for the others to get in the vehicles. He would have told them they had to leave.

But Claudia rushed forward, drawing their attention. "Anna," she cried. "Your phone rang while you were gone."

They'd left their phones behind so no inadvertent rings would give away their approach. All for naught, since the place had been empty.

"I answered when I saw it listed as private. I just felt I needed to." The red-haired woman's face was so stark and pale, her eyes were like twin bruises against the white. "It was Ronja. She told me to deliver a message."

Anna skidded to a halt next to Quinn, panting, as were the others. "What is it? Lucia can track Kylie now. We have to go."

"She won't need to." Claudia shook her head. "Ronja said we would find Kylie at the lighthouse on Tybee Island. That we can have her back now."

Claudia reached out and grasped Anna's hand. "She said . . . that they were done with her."

24

Not everyone had made it in time to board the first boat with Quinn. As he'd sprinted down the flagstone paths at the yellow house, he'd yelled to Joseph to start the engine. His old friend had been waiting for their arrival and was at the wheel, ready to go.

Anyone who hadn't made it to the docks yet had been left to follow in the second boat. Because Quinn wasn't waiting.

Now as they raced over the water, he stared bleakly at the horizon. The search had used up most of the night, and sunrise was peeking over like a shy little girl at a windowsill. He silently urged it to come out. To show its face.

He welcomed and needed the light.

But for now, they were stuck in that predawn illumination, a sad lavender-gray like twilight in reverse. Still, he could make out the spear into the clouds that was the lighthouse on Tybee. Jutting into the somber skies, the black and white landmark called to Quinn, just as it had so many sailors in centuries gone by.

Here. Come to the light. Here is what you seek.

He gripped the side rail of the speeding watercraft and hoped beyond hope that Ronja, for once in her despicable life, had been telling the truth. With his gaze fastened on the island, Quinn searched for Kylie, for any sign of activity in the early morning hours. The stillest hours, before life began to stir.

Over dunes, through waving palms, and past the few rooftops, he focused his sights on the upper catwalk. His heart stuttered when he saw a figure standing there, just beneath the rotating light.

Using the set of binoculars Anna handed him, he adjusted them to bring the image into sharper focus. "It's Ross. The shifter."

Something hard lodged in Quinn's chest as he perused the scene. Another person lay crumpled at Ross's feet. So still, unmoving. Long hair spilled over the edge of the walk, but it wasn't the glorious gold he associated with Kylie. It must be some other poor woman.

Relief and disappointment were dual fists rapping inside his head, but as the boat drew closer to the coast, he realized his mistake.

Stomach clenching and breath frozen in his chest, Quinn struggled to accept what he was seeing. "He has Kylie. She's up there with him."

The beautiful blonde of her hair was simply so dirty and matted that it looked brown.

Ross turned and stared toward the approaching craft, straight into Quinn's eyes, it seemed. Then the shifter grinned and kneeled to Kylie's unconscious form. He lifted her into unnaturally strong arms.

"What's he doing?" Joseph yelled from behind the wheel. He had the boat at full throttle.

"I don't know." Quinn kept the binoculars trained on the shifter, terrified to let Kylie out of his sight. "But whatever it is, I don't like it. I don't trust him. Or Ronja."

As everyone riding with Quinn stared, transfixed, Ross lifted one leg to stand on one of the middle rails. He wobbled precariously with Kylie in his arms.

Several of the women gasped and Anna shouted, "Viv!"

"I'm ready," the other witch called back. Viv's special gift was telekinesis, and if the vicious shifter threw or dropped Kylie, Viv would catch her in a cradle of air. She wouldn't let her sister fall to the hard-packed sand.

Ross was laughing, enjoying his unstable perch. The man was insane, always had been. Just as he leaned too far forward to recover his balance, two giant wings sprouted from his back. The rest of his shape remained human, and he still gripped Kylie to his chest.

With a wingspan of at least seven feet, the appendages had to belong to a condor or some other great bird. They would easily carry Ross's weight. As well as the limp woman in his arms.

With a roar, the shifter launched himself from the deck of the lighthouse and soared out over the beach, over the water, and away from the boats.

"No. No!" Quinn yelled, just as Joseph steered after Ross in pursuit. "Where is he taking her?"

To his horror, he saw that the insane shifter wasn't fleeing with Kylie at all. Instead, he flew straight up, higher into the air. And then he flung her body away from him, letting her unconscious form plummet toward the ocean below.

Viv's hands were up, ready to send out her invisible safety net, but a shockwave hit the boat broadside, sending the vessel into a hard keel. All of its passengers went flying as one side was thrust upward before crashing back to the water. The entire craft rocked back and forth, making it difficult for anyone to regain balance.

Viv's scream wasn't one of fear or pain, but of fury. "Damn it!" She was clawing at the vinyl of one of the rear seats, trying to regain her footing. "I lost her!"

The boat righted itself, and despite the continued rolling motion as it settled, every pair of eyes was trained on the retreating man-bird. Quinn darted his eyes over the choppy surface. Where was Kylie?

Ross gave a triumphant whoop before compressing himself into the form of a sleek, black raven. He flew in an arc, back around and toward the mainland, cawing, cawing as he flew.

And the cruel sound was laughter.

As they fought to get their bearings, and Joseph tried to throttle forward again, the second boat roared past them.

"What just hit us?" Viv shouted over the roar of the engine.

Anna whirled around, searching the water and then the coast for the cause. The hit they'd taken hadn't come from any wind shear or rogue wave. Quinn had felt it too.

They'd been attacked by magic.

When Anna's eyes tightened, Quinn followed her line of sight. A tall blonde woman in a breezy gray dress stood with the wind in her hair. Ronja. When she was sure Anna and Quinn were looking at her, she smiled and gave them a salute.

Then she turned slowly and strolled out of sight.

Quinn felt as if the cold ocean had risen up to take him. He shivered. Ronja's body language, the smug gesture, the way she'd waited for Anna to meet her evil stare . . .

"Get to Kylie," Quinn barked to Joseph. "Now! Hurry!"

By the time they caught up to the other boat, Michael and Dare were hanging over the far side, pulling Kylie from the water. Quinn was on the very tip of the bow, ready to jump off when Joseph swung them around to ease up beside the other craft.

They had Kylie out of the water now, and Quinn almost stumbled from the shock. Her face was so pale. Her lips were tinted blue.

"Put here down here." Willyn directed the two men to lay Kylie out on the open floor. Quinn summoned every reserve of strength he had and continued forward. He knelt beside Kylie's knees while Willyn put her fingers to the young witch's neck.

Quinn knew. He could feel it. But hearing the confirmation from their healer almost caved him in. "No pulse," Willyn said, falling immediately into the role of experienced nurse. "No respirations. I need help here. Michael," she snapped, "you know CPR."

"Yes." Michael assumed the position to deliver breaths as needed.

All Quinn could do was stare, stunned and terrified. Kylie was too white. Too cold. *Please, please. This can't be happening. This isn't the way it's supposed to end.*

Willyn began chest compressions in quick succession. Quinn heard her counting to herself, and when she said, "Forty," she nodded to Michael, who then blew two times into Kylie's mouth.

"I can help." Had he said that? The words were but a breath over his lips. He had to do something, but when his mind began to crack again, he knew Kylie was getting the best care from Willyn and Michael. He would only be in the way.

Quinn did the only thing he could do and took her lifeless, icy fingers in his hands. He tried to warm them up. "She's cold. She's so cold. Get her a blanket."

Michael raised somber eyes to Quinn and nodded. "After. We need access to . . . we need to be able to touch her."

Willyn finished another repetition, and Michael blew again.

Willyn stopped to check Kylie's pulse. Her breathing.

Quinn almost flew apart when she shook her head and said, "Nothing." She put hands over Kylie's heart again. And began to pump.

"Take her other hand," Quinn told Lucia, barely recognizing his own voice. It was so flat and empty. "She's cold."

Lucia's eyes were overflowing, but she nodded at Quinn, the slightest whimper slipping from her throat. She took Kylie's other hand, holding the small, delicate fingers between her own.

He tried to ignore Kylie's physical condition, because his heart fractured with every glimpse of the savagery she'd been exposed to. Her poor, sweet body. Every inch was swollen and discolored with bruises, gashes, and—he swallowed against revulsion—multiple types of burn marks.

"Come on. Come on!" The outburst erupted from Willyn, and Quinn thought he heard her sniff. Was she crying too?

"Willyn," Quinn said, abruptly jarred from his horrified trance. "Use your magic. Heal her."

"I can't." She gasped the words between compressions.

"You're our healer. It's your gift." Quinn shifted and put one foot on the floorboards to lean in and plead with her. "You can fix this!"

She didn't answer, only kept working.

As if out of nowhere, Ethan was suddenly beside Quinn. "They're doing all they can."

"No, they aren't. *We* aren't. The coven is strong. Their magic can save her." He grabbed his friend's shoulder and knew he was squeezing too hard. "Why won't they?"

"Just wait. Hold on." Ethan's deep brown eyes were fierce, as if he was sending Quinn strength. Sharing all he had to give.

Why would he do that? Quinn was fine. They'd found Kylie, and Michael and Willyn would save her. That's what had to happen. Right? Didn't he and Kylie deserve their happy ending like everyone else?

He concentrated on Kylie's legs, rubbing his hands over her shins and calves, sending as much of his heat and magic into her that he could manage. He went back to her fingers for a few minutes.

Because he just couldn't let go of her hand. Not for too long.

Murmurs flew between Willyn and Michael. Whispered words, and then finally, sobs.

Quinn ripped his gaze up to search theirs. Michael wouldn't look at him, but stood and turned to envelop Shauni in his arms.

"What's happening?" Quinn reached for Willyn's shoulder and shook her. "Why did you stop?"

"We should t-t-take her to the island." Lucia was shuddering, barely able to speak. Ethan had gone to her, had supportive hands on her back. "Maybe we can do what Quinn said."

"I don't know. I don't know what to do." Willyn shook all over, her face colorless. At last, she dragged her blue eyes to Quinn. "There's nothing more I can do for her."

"What are you saying? You can heal her!"

Willyn shook her head, tears rolling forth. "I can only heal if I have a life force to work with. Kylie's . . . is gone." Now she wept openly. "I'm so sorry. I think she was—" She looked out to sea, then back to Quinn. "I don't know how long ago her heart stopped."

"Back to the island," Quinn said to Michael. "Get us there. Do it." Heedless of anyone else's grip on Kylie, he gathered her in his arms and pulled her onto his lap. "Take us home. We need to get her warm. Get to the great room." He shook his head. "I'm not giving up."

He felt the cool touch of his sister's hand on his cheek, felt their shared and soothing magic flow from her palm and straight down to his soul. He pulled away from her. "No. You promised, Anna. You said you wouldn't give up."

"Quinn."

"No! I have to take her home!"

Drawing in a shaky breath, Anna locked her stare with Michael's. "Will you take us to the island?"

"What about a hospital?" he asked.

Willyn stood. "If we do that, we'll have to leave her."

Anna nodded with firmness. "For now, we take her home."

Michael went to the wheel and started the boat. Quinn couldn't separate the sounds of crying and cursing from the two vessels as they started to move over rocky waves. He may have heard Paige's threat of violence to the Amara. And was that Viv wailing? Or Claudia?

Quinn readjusted Kylie's head so it rested on the softest part of his arm. "I'm not giving up yet, Kylie. I'm not letting you go." He looked up with gratitude when Lucia brought a blanket to spread over their youngest, brightest witch.

And just that way, close to his heart, he held her as they sped across the stormy sea.

His mind was on Kylie and how different she felt. So light and slack. No energy zipping through her or from her eyes. Her once-pink lips were ashen.

He tossed one last glance to the beach they were leaving behind. And his soul almost broke in two when the bright, warm glow of the lighthouse . . . winked out.

25

Crying. Quinn couldn't take the crying. The women were falling apart one by one, and their lack of faith, their acceptance of Kylie's death, was simply smothering him.

He wouldn't believe her short, beautiful life was over. He couldn't.

"Almost there," Michael said, steering the boat into port. Shauni's boyfriend was being kind in his calm and stoic way, but he couldn't comprehend the gaping hole that was growing inside Quinn, expanding with every second that Kylie lay there without breathing. Without moving.

I'll get her to the great room. The coven's magic, it's very heart . . . that will save her.

A jolting shudder threw them all forward abruptly. Quinn tightened his grip on Kylie's cold, lifeless form. "What's going on?"

Another shudder surged from below the boat, an insistent mechanical cough and choke. "I don't know." Michael scowled. "The engine's dying."

Gauging the distance to the pier, Quinn stood unsteadily with Kylie still in his arms. "Just coast her in. Just get me close." He'd swim Kylie home if necessary.

But a gust of wind blew from astern and gave the boat the necessary momentum. The craft eased close enough for Michael and Ethan to leap out. As soon as they had the boat tied down,

Quinn was moving.

"Let me help." Ethan reached for Kylie, but Quinn shook his head.

"I've got her." The sentiment felt like much too little now. His rescue coming far too late. "She's not heavy." His feet hit the dock and he began to run. His words were true, devastatingly so, because he barely felt Kylie's weight.

As if the force that made her who she was had flown.

No! I won't allow it! And if he had to die to visit the gods themselves, he would see this injustice righted. Or at the very least, avenged.

In his fury, he spoke silently to them now. *Don't let her be gone. You owe her more than this. You owe the coven.*

And damn you all, you owe me.

Quinn wasn't the strongest witch on the island—under normal circumstances—but today he channeled from his deepest wells of power. Eyes focused on the double-doors of the house, he slammed them open with his mind.

He took Kylie inside, heading straight for the great room and the power yielded by the sacred pentagram.

He heard a rustle behind him. Paige had followed, her speed allowing her to catch up to him. "Get her amulet," Quinn directed.

With a flash, Paige was gone.

And Sassy was flying down the stairs like a golden streak of lightning. The cat knew her mistress had returned.

By the time Quinn traversed the long corridor that led to the ancient dome-shaped room, Paige had returned with Kylie's necklace.

"Wait," she told Quinn. "Let me get the altar."

He nodded, grateful for the help. She had the door open when he approached, and her strength made lifting the huge marble dais a minimal task.

She positioned the altar in the center of the room, directly beneath the intersecting beams. Below the giant star he prayed would give Kylie life.

In Paige's eyes, Quinn saw a reflection of his own pain. And his own desperate hope. This had to work and they both knew it.

He lowered Kylie's limp body onto the altar. Behind him, he heard the others filing into the room.

Brushing her hair from her pale face, he took her icy hands and crossed them over her stomach. Then he drew a shaky breath.

With a lift of his eyes, he met Paige's anxious stare again before opening his hand expectantly. Kylie's amulet was warm in his palm, in stark contrast to the coldness of her skin.

"Hayden," Lucia asked in a reverent whisper. "Have you seen her?"

"No," the medium answered. "But that isn't a bad thing. If she's gone . . . If her spirit's gone ahead," Hayden's voice cracked, "then she went with peace."

Ignoring the exchange of words, as well as the implication, Quinn carefully fastened the silver chain around Kylie's neck. He nestled the pendant with its gleaming yellow stone on her chest.

And he waited for magic.

He couldn't command it to do what he wanted, nor could the coven. They were led by destiny and had been granted the power to fulfill the prophecy. But they were not gifted with immortality.

The witches could be killed.

And resurrection of the dead was a forbidden use of their gifts. Manipulation of a soul was unnatural, and ultimately cruel to all involved.

"Come back to us, Kylie." He stroked the back of her hand. "We need you."

Heavy silence hung over them all as they gathered close.

Even the sobs and muted cries had stopped.

Quinn didn't know what to do other than follow his instincts, so he leaned down and kissed her lips. They were so cool, so light in color. "Kylie, come back. *I* need you."

Silence spread, the atmosphere heavy with anticipation, and a horrible suspense. He could practically feel the prayers and pleas floating from the others. Their combined sorrow and entreaty created a force of its own.

But still no breath stirred in Kylie's lungs. Her lids didn't lift or flutter. Her head rested listlessly to one side.

A brush against his leg told him Sassy was there. Knowing of nothing else to do, he bent and lifted the cat, placing her next to Kylie.

Sassy settled against Kylie's side and curled into a ball. She didn't purr or make a sound of any kind.

"Anna," Shauni said, "is there nothing we can do?"

Quinn only held Kylie's hand, needing to be close to her. His sister shook her head, but he'd already known the answer to Shauni's question. The amulet had made no difference. The pentagram and the source of the coven's power had caused no change.

And neither would any spell or charm they might cast.

Reality and awareness began to permeate the air, settling on their shoulders and ripping at their hearts. Quinn was certain the others were being crushed by the truth, accepting it slowly, just as he was. They had nothing left to try.

Kylie was gone, and they couldn't bring her back.

"Damn it," Paige said before storming out of the great room. Someone else cried out and ran, with more footsteps following after. But Quinn only continued to caress Kylie's hand. He wasn't ready to let go.

More movement confirmed some of the other witches were leaving as well.

Shauni and Lucia came to stand on the other side of the

altar. Shauni touched Kylie's cheek, and Lucia murmured something in Spanish. Quinn didn't understand the words, but he heard the love and grief in her voice.

Next Willyn and Claudia came, staying only long enough for each to put a hand on Kylie's arm. Her poor, abused arm, still stained with blood and grime.

Claudia began to cry, so they also exited the room.

And finally, Anna was there. The only other person left under the great pentagram—that awesome force—that could do nothing to save Kylie. "You can take some time," his sister said, "but then we'll have to—"

"I know." Quinn cut her off, grateful for the privacy the others were giving him. The solitude. So he could say his last goodbyes.

"All right." Anna took Kylie's hand and astonished Quinn by breaking down. Her shoulders shook and tears flooded. His strong, determined sister finally snapped.

"I'm so sorry, Kylie." She looked up to the massive wooden beams, then down again to her young friend. "This never should have happened to you."

Quinn couldn't look at Anna. He couldn't bear to share this wrenching loss with her. Not yet.

A wall still stood inside of him, and he couldn't let it crumble. He was still in a certain amount of denial. But it was straining in the face of this awful truth.

Anna walked softly and left him then. There was nothing more to say.

All that had been Kylie was gone. There was no more warmth, color, or laughter. Only coldness, where once there had been summer.

As he clutched Kylie's hand, he listened to his sister's receding footfalls. He heard the gentle closing of the door.

And as that wall finally collapsed, he let the tears fall.

~~~

Anna passed mahogany walls and the art that hung there, things she had known since her youth. Her feet dragged over slate flooring, but nothing registered. She was trapped in her own consuming grief.

The hum, the mystical vibration of the nine, would never come to her home again. To her heart. The coven would never be whole.

They had lost.

She felt ultimately responsible for anything that went wrong, any injury to her friends, to her loved ones. And what had been done to Kylie was horrific. What she'd suffered had surpassed nightmarish or barbaric.

Anna shuddered, trying to keep her eyes straight ahead. She wandered aimlessly, then stopped to lean against a wall.

And Quinn. She curled her fingers, nails sinking into her palms. His agony had just begun, as all of theirs had.

Strange, fleeting thoughts were in her head, untethered recognitions of her surroundings and the women and men spread throughout the grand hall. But she could barely command her legs to walk.

Tragedy affected people differently, and she sensed a range of reactions as she finally entered the main area of the mansion. The meeting place with the well-used green couch and huge television that Kylie had loved.

Kylie. They'd all come together here, for fun and frivolity, fights and strategies. But no more.

Anna searched the faces of her sisters for comfort, for answers, and the impossible chance that one of them would tell her this all was but a dream.

No one did.

Viv and Claudia—who were so often the ones that held up under emotional strain—were both desolate, crying harshly and holding on to the men they loved.

Willyn too was inconsolable, and Anna presumed their gentle healer was wracked with guilt, just as she was. Willyn hadn't been able to revive Kylie. But that had been beyond her control.

They'd done all they could, and this loss was not their fault.

But Anna knew logic paled next to the bright burn of regret. She knew too well, and was blinded by her own reproach.

If only they'd found the house sooner. If they'd thought to contact Sylvie. If they'd gotten to the lighthouse ten minutes earlier. Five minutes? One?

How close had they really come to finding Kylie alive?

Anna saw Shauni and Hayden share a glance. One of mutual understanding that they needed to hold it together. Because no one else was.

Anna was a shell. She felt the lack of control and gladly relinquished it to her friends.

Paige wasn't crying either, but she was still nowhere close to calm. Fury came swiftly to their warrior. It was her preferred balm for pain, and anger helped her to defuse the hurt.

"What do we do now?" Paige demanded of Anna.

When Anna sat on the couch, voiceless and without expression, Paige turned to Shauni and Hayden. "We can't just keep her here like this."

"We won't," Shauni said. "But for now, we have to think. Decide rationally." She clenched her eyes against burgeoning tears. "We're all so upset right now."

"Well," Paige strode in long, angry steps to the antique rotary phone on a side table. Always one for tradition, Anna's family maintained a landline. "We have to call her parents."

"Just wait." Hayden held a hand to her stomach.

"Wait for what?" Paige thrust a hand through her short blonde hair. "Angels? A miracle?" Her laugh was thick with scorn, with resentment. "Or maybe magic? What good did it do her?" She swung an arm to gesture down the hall.

Then she stared in that direction, toward the great room. Where Kylie now rested.

When no one answered, Paige picked up the receiver.

"Just wait a minute, damn it." Hayden had passed her point of control, covering her face to scream into her palms. Trevor hurried over to take her in his arms.

"Paige is right." Anna felt herself speak but was still floating inside herself. She struggled to rein in the overpowering grief, and to acknowledge the solid reasoning that Paige had already reached.

"We should call Kylie's parents," she continued. "Kylie was their child." Anna stood. Nodded to Paige. "She was theirs before she was ours, and they have a right to know."

Shauni, clutching Michael's arm for support, stepped forward. "But what if something happens? What if . . ."

Anna shook her head. "There's nothing we can do. She's beyond our ability." She shifted her eyes to Paige. "The number is there in the book."

A wine-colored address book lay next to the rotary phone. All of the witches had listed familial contacts in case of emergency.

None of them had ever dreamed the information would actually be used.

Paige dialed, and everyone held their breath. Her back visibly stiffened as she waited, listening to the receiver as the call went through.

At last, she must have connected. "General Worthington? My name is—hello?" Paige frowned before reaching to press down the switch hook over and over. "Hello?"

She faced Anna, confusion marring her brow. "The line went dead."

Frustration welled in Anna's chest. She was holding on by the thinnest thread of sanity.

What else could go wrong? The coven had failed, lost the fate of Savannah to those who would destroy it all, including the innocent people who lived there.

Kylie was dead.

Quinn was destroyed.

And now the phone wouldn't work.

Running a hand up her neck and uttering a frustrated oath, Anna went to where she had tossed her purse in a chair. She retrieved her phone. "I'll use mine. What's the number?"

But when she swiped her thumb over the screen of her cell, it remained black. No emission of light or sound. "What is this?" She shrugged at Paige. "Mine is dead."

With her face still wet and red from crying, Viv turned within Nick's arms to pull her own phone from a pocket. Her face revealed her bewilderment. "Mine too."

A ripple of dread rolled through the room, its presence palpable.

"So is mine," Willyn said.

Hayden nodded as well.

And as they all glanced around the grand hall and at each other—perplexed, uneasy, and with a growing sense of fear—the lights overhead suddenly flickered. Then they all went dark, as did the lamps on various tables.

The glow emanating from the kitchen died, and with it, the low hum of the refrigerator and air-conditioner, sounds so monotonous they weren't detectable until they disappeared.

"Something's happening." Anna went rigid, sensing a current of magic as it cascaded through the mansion.

"Could it be Bastraal?" Lucia asked. "Has he come back?"

"If he has," Paige clenched both of her fists, "then he won't ever leave again. Not if I can help it."

No one made a sound, their senses on alert as they searched the grounds and rooms with their own tendrils of power. Anna could feel something churning, working, growing, but she couldn't identify the source.

Her heart tripped over itself, and she gasped when Quinn's voice echoed down the corridor. His booming yells ricocheted off the mahogany panels, over the stone floors.

Transfixed, Anna stared. Then she broke from her daze, and as one, she and her friends began to run.

Quinn wasn't just yelling. He was shouting Anna's name.

~~~

Anna burst into the great room a few steps behind Paige. They were both brought up short by the brilliant strike of white and gold crackling through the air.

"It just started," Quinn said. He stood a few feet from where Kylie still lay on the altar.

Anna noted Sassy's new location as well. The cat was far away from the stone dais.

"It's so hot." Quinn looked up when another line arced from the ceiling straight to Kylie. His face showed his puzzlement and shock, but also his increasing hope. "It's Kylie's. I know it. The lightning, the energy, it's just flowing into her."

Viv wiped her eyes, the great pools wide now with exuberance. "That's why we lost the phones. The power."

"And the boat." Knowledge dawned on Willyn too. "The power, it's all trying to find its way back to Kylie."

"No." Quinn's denial made them jerk their heads in his direction. But despite the severity of his tone, a slight smile began forming on his lips. "It's not just *going* to Kylie."

He looked to Anna, tears in his eyes. "She's calling it back to her. She always said she was one with electricity." He laughed. "And she's not done yet."

A huge boom reverberated in the room as a jagged streak of blinding white shot straight from the center of the pentagram above Kylie. The lightning struck the center of her chest. It streamlined straight to her heart.

Anna stared, amazed, feeling more blessed than she had in far too long. Their youngest one was a fighter. Stubborn and strong-willed.

Kylie wanted to live and was causing the energy from every source in the immediate vicinity to coalesce, to bind together for increased amperage.

Another huge hit of the pure white and Kylie's entire body jumped on the table.

"Will that hurt her?" Shauni asked.

"No." Willyn had her hands clasped into a ball that she held beneath her chin. "It's like a defibrillator, only her magic doesn't need a rhythm to jumpstart. It's shocking her, restarting her heart."

Quinn stood watching, rubbing his jaw, combing fingers nervously through his hair. Anna could hear his whispered pleas. "Come on. Come on."

Despite the intense heat and bright illumination, the coven and their men, along with Anna and Quinn, all edged closer, forming a circle around Kylie.

Sassy still sat near the wall, her tawny eyes fixed on her human. Patience and confidence rolled from the feline, and Anna's soul simply leaped. "Yes. You're the strong one, Kylie. You can wait anything out and make it come around to your way."

Casting a glance at her brother, who was so painfully in love with the golden-haired girl, Anna laughed out loud. Yes. Kylie could do it if anyone could. Just look how she'd brought Quinn around.

Another pounding jolt of energy targeted Kylie's center, a thunderous clap echoing in its wake. Kylie's body bowed with the force and her mouth fell open. She drew a deep, ragged breath.

Everyone went perfectly still. The air still snapped and sizzled.

Then Kylie's eyes opened, and she inhaled again.

As Anna, Quinn, and the ones who loved her watched, Kylie blinked her eyes and continued to breathe. Her heart was beating. She lived again.

And as Kylie brought herself back from the arms of death itself, the sunny stone of her amulet sang out. The most beautiful sound Anna had ever heard decisively confirmed Kylie's victory.

26

Kylie rose to consciousness as she had so many times in the recent past. As she climbed, the ache and burn of her injuries returned with a vengeance.

But this time, she felt another presence behind the crushing pain. A pleasant and uplifting sensation. A sweet and very familiar . . . hum.

It was the energy of the nine. Her sisters. She would've cried if she were able, because somehow, someway, she'd been miraculously reunited with her coven.

A higher-pitched, crystalline sound resonated all around her, and it took her a moment to comprehend what she was hearing. The song of her stone carried from where it rested against her chest. The tune was warm, clear, and as brilliant as a gem.

She had no idea what had transpired or how she'd been brought home, but somehow, she'd completed her trial.

Blinking rapidly, she cleared her vision and was greeted by the long and ancient beams that formed a pentagram. High above her on the ceiling was the revered symbol of the goddess.

She was in the great room of the mansion. On the St. Germaine island.

The breath that seeped from her almost wept with relief. She was home.

The sheer joy of seeing the faces of her sisters diminished all the pain and misery of the last few days. She let the comfort of their presence wash over her and reveled in it.

Because she'd been hurt and sad for so long.

In spite of the throbs and twinges she felt, Kylie tried to sit up, to move her legs. But as soon as she put real effort into the attempt, an immobilizing spasm shot through her left side.

So the nightmare wasn't completely over yet. Something was broken.

"Willyn," she croaked with a tight, dry throat, unashamed to call on her friend for help. Her body had suffered so many attacks and still had the wounds to prove it.

"I'm here. Just lie back." Willyn put her hands to Kylie's shoulders. Then, starting near her head, Willyn simultaneously searched for injury while channeling her healing magic to the places that needed it most.

Some of Kylie's agony receded as her friend made a slow path from head to toe. "Thank you," she whispered.

"That will get you through for a little while." The coven's healer held onto her hand. "But we have some work to do." Turning to Hayden, Willyn made a request. "Can you make us a couple of your green juices?"

"Absolutely." Hayden sniffed and sent a loving smile to Kylie. "Instant energy, coming right up." She winked and hurried away.

Kylie sighed. They did have some work ahead of them and would both need vitamins and minerals to recover their strength throughout the healing process.

"We're so glad you're finally safe, Kylie." Willyn's light blue eyes watered. "So glad."

Kylie let her lids fall as memories ambushed her. "I was in the dark," she said suddenly, blinking again as she shivered. "I wanted out."

"You're here now." Claudia stepped closer. "You saved yourself Kylie, even when we couldn't. The coven couldn't pull it off, but you did."

Kylie pondered the statement as her head fought to clear. "The Amara. Scarlett, Ronja, and Tyr. All of them. They told me I was the weakest one of us, and that I'd be the ruin of the coven."

"And you just shoved those words right back down their fucking throats." Paige crossed her arms over her chest and grinned like a villain.

One by one, the witches spoke to Kylie, each coming close to give her a quick, soft touch as if to assure themselves she was really there. Kylie was still having a hard time believing it herself.

So much had happened in such a short time. Recall of the events leading up to her abduction had her snapping her head up to find Anna. "Mrs. Attinger. Is she—"

"She's fine." Anna put a hand to her chest, then used it to wave away a fresh well of tears. "Okay. I'm all right." She sniffed. "Everyone is okay now. She's wonderful. So are you."

Kylie had never seen Anna emotional and rattled, not like she was now. So she worked up a grin just for the head witch.

Then Kylie's gaze traveled, seeking out a similar pair of deep blue eyes. And without fail, he was there.

Everything inside of Kylie gave one great sigh to see Quinn again. His sexy jaw was dark with stubble, and his eyes were an even more startling blue because they were rimmed with red.

Quinn had been crying.

Her impulse was to reach for him, but the memory, the fantasy she'd experienced while on the nasty floor of that cell came back to her. She'd learned something about herself in that dark and lonely prison.

And she would cling to that lesson for Quinn's sake. Because she loved him, truly loved him. And from now on, his needs would come first.

So instead of holding out her hand for him—as she yearned to do—she simply remembered his face from the dream, his kind words, and how thrilled she'd been to hear them. Pulling from that moment of bliss, she smiled at him and said, "Hey there."

"Kylie," he began, stepping forward. But he stopped and shook his head. "I'm so sorry."

"No. Don't say that." He'd heaped the responsibility for what had happened to her onto his shoulders. Just as he did with everything else. That accountability was part of why she loved him so, but she wouldn't let him punish himself.

"I was the one who wanted a coffee," she said, trying for a joke. But when she laughed, something seemed to slice through her thigh. She clenched her eyes shut and sucked in a haggard breath.

"We're not quite done with that leg yet." Willyn put her palm on Kylie's thigh. It felt swollen, thick, and hot. "The femur is fractured. Pretty badly."

Lifting her arm to test its strength and to feel for any other breaks, Kylie abruptly dropped it back to the table when she saw her skin. Astonished, she realized the full extent of what had been done to her. She was covered in lacerations and marks.

Knowing what the rest of her body must look like, especially through the rips and tears in her clothing, Kylie spoke to her friends. And to Quinn. "I'm so glad to be with you again. All of you." She swallowed. "But I'd like to do this with Willyn. Alone."

Shauni and Claudia nodded their understanding.

"Yes. We'll see you soon," Lucia offered as she backed away.

Hayden had returned with two green juices and two bottles of water. "Plenty more if you need it."

"Thank you," Willyn said with a grateful smile.

As the women retreated, Sassy leapt back up to sit by Kylie's head. Another rush of tears tried to flow when the cat greeted her with a purr and licked her cheek. "Oh, my pretty girl." Kylie relished the tiny kiss. "You can stay."

Only Quinn hovered as the others filed out. He inched closer to Kylie, as if he too longed for contact. "We did everything we knew to do."

"I know that." Kylie cherished seeing his face, hearing his voice. "Everything is going to be okay now, Quinn. I promise."

He offered her a crooked smile, his eyes crinkling at the corners. "Yes. It will be."

With a glance to Willyn, Quinn turned and made his way out. Kylie's battered heart trailed along after him.

But she would keep her love to herself. She would guard his well-being by guarding her desire.

"Ready?" Willyn's question pulled Kylie from her lovelorn musings. "The sooner we start, the better."

"Let's go for it," Kylie said, again searching for levity she didn't quite feel. Her face collapsed into sad lines as the stark reality of her condition overwhelmed her.

"Willyn?" her voice shook with brand new tears. "The cuts, and . . . burns. I know this sounds trivial, especially after everything, but—"

Willyn shushed her, eyes soft and warm. "I won't leave a single scar." She leaned down and lightly put her cheek to Kylie's forehead. "We'll fix it, sweetie. We'll take it all away and make it like it never happened."

Choking down a mix of sorrow and gratitude for Willyn's intuition, Kylie nodded when her sister drew back. "Okay then."

"Okay." Willyn put her hands on Kylie again, starting with the broken thigh bone.

As the beautiful and much-welcomed magic swam into her, Kylie closed her eyes and wished Willyn's words could be true. The wounds on her skin would heal, as would those on her psyche.

Kylie would make sure of that. She refused to let the Amara have even that small triumph.

But her life would never again be like it was before. As much as she might wish it, Willyn couldn't take it all away.

Parts of her would never completely mend. Because she would never forget.

~~~

Beneath the amazing happiness zinging through his every particle, Quinn could still feel the weight and drag of sleep deprivation. He was riding high on adrenaline, a shot to his system that had everything to do with Kylie.

She was alive. She was home at last.

And he would never take her presence or her love for granted again. Not many men were as big of a fool as he was, needing to be put through this kind of hell before having his stubborn-ass eyes opened.

He loved Kylie to the ends of forever. And starting this minute, he would prove it. He'd show her.

And he had a lot to make up for.

Ethan met him at the elevator. With a cocksure grin on his face, the demonologist grabbed Quinn and gave him a class-A man-hug. "Damn, Quinn. *Damn.*"

"I know." And when his eyes stung a little in response to his friend's shared excitement, Quinn didn't even feel embarrassed.

"Since Kylie's going to be with Willyn for a while, I expect you'll be knocking back on your mattress."

"Not just yet." Quinn hit the button to call the elevator. "Kylie's here, but she's still not safe. Not as safe as she needs to be. None of us are."

Ethan tilted his head back and released an *ahhh* sound. "The protection spell." He walked into the car with Quinn,

"Why don't you get some rest first?"

"No. No way. I won't sleep until that demon bastard and all his brethren are blocked from this house."

"I hear you." Ethan nodded. "You want some help?"

"No, but thanks. You go keep Lucia warm. And get some sleep yourself."

"That's one directive I can follow." They stepped out on the top floor and veered in the same direction, but Ethan kept walking when they got to Quinn's door. "But seriously," he said, taking slow backward steps, "come get me if you're stuck."

"Will do." Quinn waved his friend away and let himself into his room. He shut the door behind him, leaned against it, and let his head *thunk* against the dark oak.

Now the relief could come. *Thank you. Thank you.* He blew out a breath.

And the thanks were for whoever was listening.

Opening his eyes, he glanced around his office. He still had a job to do, and one solitary but elusive piece was missing.

The protective wards weren't complete, but if he could put it all together and figure out the formula, he would be able to reinstall the coven's own version of a force field.

He rubbed his face as exhaustion created black spots before his waking eyes, like inkblots that came and went randomly. He pushed away from the door and stared at the open book on his desk, remembering the last reference he'd been pouring over.

He had no idea how he was awake, how any of them were, but symbols and ancient words seemed to float through the very air as he looked at—looked through—the dark leather of his office chair.

And then, in the depths of his delirium, the answer simply swam by.

He had the solution, he was certain, and it had probably been there all along. Just buried under his normal, logical mindset.

Good thing he had Kylie to shake him up once in a while.

Good thing he had her at all.

With a weak smile, he began making notes in his head. All he'd needed was a complete lack of sleep, a mind-breaking loss, followed by an incredible infusion of joy.

His laugh was hoarse as he moved to his desk. Hallucination or not, he'd finally found the last part of his spell. So everything was back in place. And all was right in his world again.

Almost.

~~~

The following morning—as most of them, including Quinn, had slept a good fifteen hours— he knocked on his sister's chamber door. At her call to enter, he stepped in to find her in her private parlor, sipping coffee from a ridiculously feminine cup with tiny flowers and curly-Qs.

He raised one brow but said only, "The wards are up. All of them."

Anna smiled at him over the rim of her cup. "Yes, I know. I felt them resume yesterday afternoon. The power actually woke me." With her own brow-lift, she added, "Good job, by the way. I knew you would figure it out."

"Yeah, well, just wanted to let you know." Inserting his hands into the pockets of his dark cargos, Quinn asked, "How's Kylie doing?"

"Good. She's doing really well. Still sleeping. Recuperating." Anna pulled a napkin from her lap and dabbed her lips. Always the genteel lady, Quinn thought, taking tea in her elegant blue boudoir.

And sudden love for his sister was a quake beneath his feet. Here he'd always thought he'd been the one supporting her. This week had shown him the flip side.

Nudging aside sentimentality, Quinn coughed. "Is Kylie

awake? Do you know?"

"I don't think so."

They both fell silent, Quinn studying the floor while Anna studied him.

"You're wondering if you should go to her," she said. "If you should tell her how wrong you've been."

Quinn's eyes snapped up to hers.

"Oh, no question about it." He rocked on his heels. "I just wonder how she'll be . . . you know, after this. I don't want to push too soon."

He didn't elaborate, and Anna waited patiently. Like pulling teeth with a silver string.

Oh, what the hell. His sister always seemed to know everything anyway. Quinn shrugged. "But then again, after all these months, all the time I wasted, I just can't wait to talk to her. To tell her exactly what I feel."

Anna hummed, with question or doubt, he couldn't tell.

"*Everything* I feel," he amended. "Every truth I've ever kept from her, about my life, my fears, my plans."

When Anna only crossed her arms, he added, "And yes, I want to tell her I love her." He grimaced. "So much it makes me feel stupid."

With a scowl, he tipped his head toward her. "Happy now?"

"Yes. Very."

Because the sun was out, and Kylie was tucked up safe in her room with her golden Sassy-cat, Quinn laughed in the face of his sister's teasing.

"Right." He opened her door to leave. "Since she's sleeping anyway, I'll be gone for a couple of hours."

"Heading to the mainland?"

"Yeah. I've got to take care of something." Quinn gave her a sly grin as his gaze drifted over her head and through her windows to the green trees and gardens beyond. "I've been remiss in certain areas, and I have one task that's long overdue."

27

Kylie reclined against an abundance of pillows and released a long breath of pleasure and appreciation. She was amazed by how much the simple things in life could mean. Particularly after they'd been wrenched away.

Like the soft texture of the striped yellow comforter she lay upon, sunlight coming through the window—she might never pull a shade again in her life—and the sweet rumble of a cat by her side.

She ran a hand along Sassy's curved back, delighted when the feline stretched and trembled. Golden eyes blinked up at her, and Kylie experienced a sudden rush of emotion. "I missed you," she whispered, scratching beneath the small golden chin.

"I missed so much." Choking down the melancholy, she gave thanks again for her renewed life. Her very existence—along with all its little gifts.

Then she reminded herself to call her parents. She longed to hear their voices, even her father's stern tone.

A knock on her door brought her around, so she cleared her throat. "*Entre*," she called out in the French pronunciation.

The door cracked open and Quinn stepped in. Breathlessness overtook her when he came into view, and just seeing his face made her tingle, made her feel as if she were alight and glowing, just like those sunbeams she'd been admiring.

But her newfound responsibility made her tamp down the

excitement. After all, nothing had really changed since before the Amara had taken her. Other than her own perspective.

And she would maintain her decision to show Quinn how different she was. He deserved to have peace of mind as he followed his own destiny. She watched his mouth break into a hesitant grin, and her stomach turned over.

Yes, he deserved to have everything.

"How are you feeling?" He walked to the center of her room, tentative and even a little fidgety. She smiled, because he seemed so large and masculine in her frilly bedroom, a white armoire on one side, and a vintage painting of sunflowers on the other.

"Believe it or not, I feel great. Willyn's special touch and about . . . oh, eighteen hours of sleep, and I'm practically a new woman." *In more ways than one.* She sat up straighter, tucking her legs in lotus-style.

She thought he might join her on the bed, make an offering of friendship, so then she could reciprocate. But he remained standing, intently rubbing one finger of his left hand.

Now she was seeing the second St. Germaine sibling in an unusual state of agitation. This was definitely a week for firsts.

Well, whatever Quinn was feeling, she certainly couldn't invite him to sit on her bed. That might be misconstrued, and she wanted no misunderstandings between them. Not anymore.

She should do them both a favor and get it over with. "Quinn, about the night in the hospital—"

"Wait." He stepped forward as if he might come to her, but then he rerouted to the window to stare outside.

Kylie's heart actually hurt to look at him, so stoic and serious, almost broody, with his handsome face gilded by the sun.

Caught up in the striking picture he made, she jumped when his voice finally sounded. "I'll cut to the chase and tell you that I was wrong to say the things I said to you." Though he spoke to her, his gaze was still on the scenery outside.

His sights dropped from the sky to the estate grounds below. His shoulders lifted and fell with his sigh. "I let my own guilt turn me inside out, and all the anger I had for myself got directed at you instead."

Kylie gripped her pillow. "I know."

He angled toward her, perplexity straining his expression. When he would have replied, she cut him off this time by throwing her legs to the side of the bed to stand. "You felt responsible for Mrs. Attinger," she said. "I understand that, and I'm not angry."

"But I hurt you." He furrowed his brow.

"Oh, Quinn." She shook her head. "We hurt each other, just in different ways." *Time to make the cut.* "But things have changed, and we don't have to do that anymore."

He scowled. "What do you mean? I don't want to hurt you. I never did."

"I realize that now." Crossing one arm over her stomach in a reflexive gesture of self-comfort, Kylie offered a kind expression, a mask to her real emotions. The ones that wanted her to run to him and wrap herself up in his arms.

Pulling fortitude from pools of strength she didn't even know she had, Kylie continued. "I had a lot of time to think when I was in . . . that place."

"You don't have to—"

"Please. If nothing else comes from that experience—other than having to die and bring myself back to finish my trial—then at least I learned something about myself."

Quinn faced her fully now, concern wrinkling his forehead. "And what's that?"

Oh, this was going to be hard. "My trial is over, Quinn, and I had it all wrong. You didn't have to fall in love with me for me to succeed."

"But, Kylie—"

"No. Listen." She interlocked her fingers, squeezing until

they ached. "You used to call me a brat, and I was. I really was," she added quickly when he began to shake his head. "All I could see was what I wanted, what *I* thought should happen."

Her laugh was short and merciless. "I never cared that you didn't see things the same way. I just kept pushing, sure you would eventually fall in line."

He pressed his lips together. But was that a smile playing around the corners of his eyes? No matter. She had to finish this. To say it all.

"I never considered your dreams or desires or even that you might have any that conflicted with mine." She firmed her mouth, resolved to make him understand. "And that's not love. It's selfishness. I don't want to be that way anymore."

For a split-second, she felt the warmth of love for him shine from her eyes. So she squelched it." I especially don't want to be that way with you."

"Kylie—"

"You're right to want your own life. Your own dreams." She waved a hand when he opened his mouth. "I see that now. I know where you were coming from."

Now he smirked before grabbing her wagging hand. He tilted his head. "Am I ever going to get to talk?"

Deflated by his happy reaction to what was breaking her heart, Kylie shrugged. "Go ahead."

"I was wrong before too. I was narrow-minded and had tunnel-vision."

Kylie blinked, her chest fluttering. *He'd been wrong? But he couldn't mean—*

"I can have more than one dream, can't I? One doesn't have to exclude the other." He edged closer to her, still holding her fingers between his.

"I can have them both." The blue of his eyes was so warm, so steady and clear. "And I want them both."

Yes! "No."

He pulled back his chin, surprised. "I can't?" And then he actually laughed.

Rubbing her forehead and taking a moment to clear her mind, Kylie pivoted and moved away, giving herself room to think. "Look, Quinn, I know you were scared while I was gone, but I won't take advantage of your jumbled emotions. You were not responsible."

She whirled on him. "And I am not your obligation."

Keeping the bedpost between them for good measure, she went on. "We should just take some time to settle down. You were worried about me and probably had some guilt mixed in too, but that's not the same as love."

Quinn scoffed and made a face of annoyance. "With all due respect, and to throw your own words back at you," he leaned in for emphasis, "don't tell me how I feel."

"Would you just listen?" This was not what she'd imagined. Not at all. Was it the man's quest in life to always be confusing her?

"It's no secret that I love you, Quinn, but the difference is, I now know what that really means. I know what I have to do."

She swallowed, wishing her heart would stop pounding. Wishing things were different. "It's because I love you . . ." *thump, thump, thump* in her chest, "that I'm letting you go."

Quinn's brows shot up to his hairline, but after the brief moment of shock, he said, "The hell you are." His sexy mouth turned fierce. "You don't get to make all the rules."

Her mouth fell open, so he added, "But neither do I. That's what compromise is all about." Sighing, he gave her an abashed half-smile. "And it's time we *both* tried some of that. It will be an adjustment, considering how badly we've both behaved in the past."

"Hey—"

"But, since we both love each other, I figure we'll manage all right." He came around the end of the bed.

Kylie took another step back.

"I don't know if you and I being together was ever a part of your challenge, Kylie." He stalked her one more step. "But I did fall in love with you. A long time ago. I was just too scared to admit it."

Elation and love poured through her, so pure and unfettered she would swear she floated off the floor. "Quinn, oh . . . but I can't . . ." She rubbed her belly as the burn of need and fear of loss flared together. "I love you, but—"

"You can't trust me yet," he said. "You can't put faith in my love. I understand that." Quinn closed in, and her mixed, confused emotions froze her to the spot.

Between that and his mesmerizing eyes, she couldn't escape.

"I spent so much time and energy beating down my feelings for you," Quinn said. "I used logic or resentment, anything to deny the truth. But it never really worked, not completely. If it had," here he smiled again with chagrin, "I probably would've been a lot nicer to you."

His voice gentled, as did his eyes. "Loving you is easy, Kylie. And about the best thing I've ever decided to do."

She couldn't move. Couldn't breathe. How long had she dreamed of this?

But what he was offering seemed so new, so fragile. And he was right. She was afraid to believe in it. Maybe she didn't possess the faith.

"I'll go now and give you some space." He cupped her chin and brought his lips to hers slowly for a sweet, chaste kiss. The tenderness in his touch almost made her cave.

"And one more thing," he said, severing the connection and backing up to the door. He opened it and stepped out into the hallway.

Then he reappeared. With a huge bouquet.

The roses were bright and cheery, the satiny petals glorious in her signature yellow. So beautiful. And so elegant.

"I'm sorry about the flowers I put out before." He handed her the vase, of the finest cut crystal.

When she stood there immobile, speechless, Quinn touched her cheek. "You deserved these all along."

~~~

Austere. That was the word that leapt to Anna's mind as she was led into Ian Keller's office. She eyed the plain and sleek desk. Tidy, modern, yet reserved. And not to her taste at all.

Through the windows, she saw the charm of a typical downtown square. Locals and tourists alike traversed the brick walkways, sat upon the benches to enjoy the amazing trees that towered like giants. The ancient oaks stood as sentinels to their city, and even now, the leaves of one dappled the expensive carpet at her feet with sunlight.

That too, though, was a dull and stately gray. Anna had come to the law offices on her own, well under the radar of her friends and family. With all that Kylie and Quinn had gone through, and the fact they were still dancing around each other, she'd chosen to take this duty upon herself.

On a chance, she'd come to speak with Ronja's new lawyer, heaping hopes and optimism on top of wishful thinking that he might just be a man of reason. One of honor.

If so, her plan was to introduce doubt, and to convince him that Ronja wasn't being fully honest with him. She would allude to the Nordic woman's immoral nature, and explain how helping her acquire the property she sought would lead to his involvement in illegal activity.

Vile and evil-borne activities, the likes of which he couldn't imagine.

That was the basic outline of her plan, and a very thin skeleton it was. She was banking on Ian Keller's goodness. Or at least a desire to not be arrested, as Dalton Morne had been.

She didn't have to wait long for the man to join her, and soon the sound of the office door closing alerted her to his presence. Standing to greet him, she turned, and was taken aback by the look in his eyes. He studied her as he might a moldy growth he'd discovered on his lunch.

Anna dropped the hand she'd been about to extend. This might go even worse than she'd imagined. "Mr. Keller," she said coolly.

"Ms. St. Germaine." He matched her tone. "I'm afraid I haven't been informed of the reason you needed to see me." He kicked up a blonde eyebrow. "But I understand you were very insistent."

Taking a seat and hoping he took her cue to move to his own chair, Anna crossed her hands primly in her lap. "My request is unorthodox, that's true, but I feel the need to bring certain facts to your attention."

His blue eyes roamed over her, and then, as if making a snap decision, he turned and walked swiftly to his seat. He sat down in an abrupt manner. "Very well."

With an expectant expression, he leaned on his desk with his forearms. "I don't have much time."

Planting a smile on her lips, Anna channeled as much grace as she could muster. Despite his golden-boy good looks, the man was severely off-putting. And cold.

Perhaps Ronja had found another of her ilk after all.

"I came in regard to a client of yours. Ronja."

He stood again. "I'm not at liberty to discuss clients." He seemed in such a hurry to get rid of her. Had Ronja already warned him? If so, why had Anna ever been allowed into his office in the first place?

She stayed in her chair, unwavering. "I'm not here to ask questions. But you should be aware of her true motives. And why she wants that land."

"I do know why." He came around the desk and stuck his

arm out toward his door. "Now, if you'll please—"

"Ronja hasn't told you everything." Anna's fingers clenched on the armrest of her chair. "And if she has, then you already know what you'll be party to. If not," she continued, "you should hear me out. Because you have no idea what you're risking."

When he remained silent, she pushed her advantage. "Your reputation, your career, maybe even your license to practice may be at stake." *Not to mention your soul.*

The stalwart man made a sound in his throat but only stared at her in silence. He was tall and more than a little intimidating, looming over her as he did.

Anna was running out of time, so she decided to lay it out for him.

"Ronja is part of a group that . . . practices in the occult. The property has a dark history and that's why she wants it. She wants to revive a . . . well, the closest name for it would be a cult."

He lowered his brow, appearing doubtful. "That's hardly illegal."

Anna paused, squeezing her hands. How much should she risk telling him? "But what she and her group have planned *is* against the law. The laws of man and nature."

He held up his hands. "I'm not going to ask what you mean by that last part, but I am curious about your involvement. Why do you feel such a strong need to insert yourself in another's private matters?"

Anna stiffened. "Let's just say Ronja and I go way back."

"Well, if you truly believe all of this, you need to take your information to the police. You forget I'm Ronja's counsel. I can't help you."

Anna stood, slamming her open palm onto his too-sleek desk. Hard and unyielding, like Ian Keller. "If she gets this land, she'll do terrible things." Then she pointed at him. "And if you help her, I'll be around to remind you of that fact."

As if a steel curtain had been lowered, the lawyer simply shut down. "I think you should leave. You're clearly unstable."

Anna gaped at him. "You are aiding a woman who plans to commit murder. And worse."

"What could be worse than murder?"

The way he cocked his head and smirked ignited something inside Anna. Not to mention that he'd called her unstable.

So she took a leap. "Ronja believes she can kill a person and sacrifice them to a demon." *Because she can.*

"Demon?" The way his eyes widened would have been comical if not for the immediate arrival of his anger. "That's it." It was his turn to put hands face down on the table. "Leave now, or I'll have you removed. I think you might qualify for a psyche eval."

Anna drew herself up. "I don't appreciate your mockery."

"And I don't appreciate your lunatic rant. Now, I have serious business to . . ."

His statement trailed away as his gaze locked on Anna's right hand. The one she'd balled into a fist. "What's that?" He stared. "What are you doing?"

Anna felt the heat and tried to calm her magic. The man had infuriated her, and after the last horrid week, she was emotionally beat up, wrung dry, and apparently, still out of sorts. She'd lost control.

Something she never did.

Should she try to explain away the strange blue glow? Or should she use it to her benefit? The coven was at war, and they were fighting for human life.

At the very least, she would give Ian Keller something to think about. "Now do you see what you're dealing with?" She opened her palm and let the ball spread and flicker.

"Whether you believe what I'm saying or not is immaterial. There are things at work in this city that you and most others do not understand. Forces you can't comprehend. But I'm telling you this," she snapped her fingers and extinguished her power, "if you help Ronja get that land, hers won't be the only bloody hands. Yours will be covered as well."

His features hardened, and she couldn't tell if he'd checked out or was just cloaking himself in denial. Whichever it was, the man was removed and aloof once again. "As I said before, I can't help you."

"Please." Having tried reason and shock, both of which had failed, she now held her arms out in supplication. "You don't understand."

"No," he snapped, "*you* don't understand."

"Please, you can't do this."

Ian Keller straightened slowly. Then he shook his head. "It's already done."

28

Surging on disappointment because Ronja had been allowed to buy the property and irritation with the arrogant Ian Keller, Anna stormed into the mansion when she returned home. She barely caught herself before she slammed the doors behind her, managing instead to guide the oak into place with a soft *snick*.

She wouldn't improve the situation by revealing her pique to anyone—warranted though it may be. Her role was not only to educate and lead the coven, but also to encourage and sustain morale.

Taking a breath, she pressed her fingers to her throat. *For the sake of the goddess, think of what's been returned.*

Kylie was safe and breathing. Quinn would find his happiness, she felt sure. And the coven was whole once again, able to continue the most crucial of battles.

Even if there were still setbacks. Like today.

Ronja's acquisition of the property was not the end. Anna and her sisters were not yet defeated.

Still, Anna's inner witch cringed with dread. The land would definitely bear its part in her future. Ever since she'd stepped onto the putrid soil, she'd felt that certainty in her bones.

Death and sorrow would be meted out in that place. And Anna would be a central component.

Enough of the dark thoughts, she silently berated herself. There was still one more trial before her own, so she should think of more positive things. If she could.

But that Ian Keller. *Ooh!* He had been maddening, Refusing to listen to reason, even after he'd seen her power.

She'd revealed her most guarded secret, and the stiff lawyer had acted like he saw magic in his office every day. The entire ordeal had just rubbed her the wrong way, and she regretted her impulsiveness.

Recent events had taken a greater toll than she'd let herself acknowledge, and her first order of business was to restore personal balance. How could she maintain equilibrium with the coven and life in general when her own emotions were running amok?

Luckily, no one was around to notice her foul mood. And she would set herself to rights before anyone did.

Meditation. That's what she needed. A long hot bath, a cup of chamomile tea, and a trip to serenity. In that order.

Attempting to use up some of her agitated energy, she took the stairs up to her room—all three flights—and slipped inside her door without ever being seen. A massive feat in a house filled with so many people, even if the mansion was vast.

Dumping her cotton dress in the laundry basket, she went to her garden soaker tub and turned on the hot water. She poured in bubble bath and scented oil from exotic Schizandra berries to help her handle mental stress.

Pinning her hair up, she slipped into the warmth and luxury, settling in with a moan of satisfaction as the day began to melt away. Intent on forgetting all about the Amara and their brand new team member, she let the drone of running water calm her.

Hands resting at her sides, she immersed herself in the assuring heat. And as contentment stole over her, she exhaled the last vestige of tension. She closed her eyes.

Twenty minutes later and much more relaxed, Anna was in her favorite robe of sapphire-blue, hair down and brushed out, and her favorite lotion applied. She'd decided to skip the tea, sensing she would be better served by some inner peace.

Now that her body was calm, she would see to her mind.

Near the rear of her room, there was a table. Long, made of teakwood, and aged until almost black in color. Primitive scenes were carved into the wood, evidence of the piece's age.

Above the table hung a mirror in a plain silver frame. She employed it for reflection, both outer and inner. Tonight, though, she had a preference for flame, so she lit the array of candles and enjoyed the spit and hiss.

Through an open window, she had a view of the indigo sky. There, the waxing moon was a mere sliver away from full. The lunar beauty called to her, holding sway over her mind just as it might the tides.

So she would use that controlling essence. She would let it guide her.

Along with her blue gazing ball, tarot cards, and candles, colorful bottles also decorated the antique table. She enjoyed the shine of amber, ruby, and cobalt as she made her choice. The gem-hued bottles held more essential oils, her favorite scents for clairvoyant travels.

She reached for lemongrass, because her goals were now clarity and vision. Putting her finger to the bottle, she caught a large drop on the tip and distributed the light scent to her pulse points. Her wrists, elbows, and neck.

Taking a seat on a silken ottoman, she set flat feet on the floor. And then, looking again to the bright white moon, she opened herself up to flight.

Instantly, a pool of impossible blue formed in her mind's eye. It was her favorite imaginary place when she needed to go somewhere calm. Emerald grasses waved at the edges, and a red bird perched on the branch of a tree.

The surrounding forest was shadowed and dim, but the darkness didn't unsettle her. Rather, it was tranquil, familiar.

Sporadic yellow dots lit up the hidden recesses and floated amongst the trees. Fireflies or fairies, she was never sure, and preferred to leave that a mystery.

With slow steps, she approached the natural pool, its bottom covered with clean white stones. They were bright and shining, not a speck of dirt in sight. This was *her* fantasy, after all.

As she slipped naked into the water, she took her consciousness down, down, easing into a sleep-like state where pre-cognition came most easily. When the water was at her shoulders, she let her legs rise and her head fall back. She floated in the dreamy blue. Then, as she had in her previous bath, she closed her eyes again.

And was startled by a loud and vicious yell of laughter.

When she stood to find the source, she was no longer in her favorite pool but at the edge of a forest. The woods were those of her island where they butted against the sandy beach.

Boisterous shouts and more laughter rang out, and she turned to spy movement farther down the shore. People were walking, apparently having just disembarked from a boat.

She stepped out of the shelter of the oaks and pines, growing more fearful with every step. More rowdy sounds flew at her, vulgarity and riotousness.

But it wasn't until she caught a flash of red hair that she turned to a statue of ice. Bright red hair in the moonlight. Scarlett. She and Tyr were on the island. With Ross, Carson, and Jack.

The Amara had come to Anna's home.

They carried weapons, and cruel-looking chains, similar to those Anna had seen in Kylie's cell. The ones the younger witch had explained held magic. An enchantment designed to work against the coven. To contain and block their power.

Searenn was strutting over the sand as well, but the only weapon she carried was her skin. Her tattoos went with her everywhere and held hundreds of demons that awaited her beckoning.

Panic flashed and Anna stepped forward, but she came up short when she met with an invisible wall. Ramming the flat of her hand against the barrier, she bristled with alarm.

The Amara had to be stopped.

The coven, her friends, none of them were prepared. *I have to tell the others. I have to*—whirling in the beige sand, she felt the entrancing light of the moon on her face and looked to the heavenly sphere for direction. *How do I get home?*

She had a sense she'd seen this moon before, but it hadn't been quite the same. Where had she been then?

Home. The word was a mantra now.

Home. But it was also an answer.

Home in her room, that's where she'd seen this same moon. But it hadn't been seated this far to the west.

What she was witnessing now—the Amara invading her island—it hadn't happened yet.

Not yet. But soon.

With a gasp, Anna woke up and found herself still staring at the moon, but her view was once again from her bedroom window. The white body was still in its original position, not like it had been in her vision. But definitely the same as the one she'd seen on the beach.

"It's tonight." She leapt from the ottoman and ran to the room nearest hers. "Kylie!" She banged on the door.

The oak panel swung open, revealing a wide-eyed Kylie. "What's wrong?"

"I wanted to make sure you're okay." Anna ran a trembling hand over her loose hair. "Sorry. Sorry. I'm a little out of it."

"You mean you just *came* out of it. A vision." Kylie rubbed Anna's arm. "Your pupils are still like black moons."

"Moons. Yes." Anna was still semi-drowsy despite the surge of anxiety.

"Anna!" Quinn was rushing down the hall toward them. "I

heard you all the way in my room. Are you okay?"

"Yes. But I had a vision." Now that her head was cooler and her breathing slower, she told them about her meditation and what she'd seen. She summed it up with, "The Amara *will* attack. Tonight."

"They believe the circle is broken," Quinn said. "And that the coven magic has been weakened."

"Because they think I'm dead." Kylie's grin was surprisingly malicious. "That means we have the advantage."

~~~

Kylie peered out the kitchen window as she drank a glass of water. "How long do you think we have?" she asked Anna as her friend finished an apple. Apparently, each of them had their own pre-battle rituals and preparations.

Shauni and Michael had locked themselves in her room for a half-hour, while Paige, Quinn, Ethan, and Dare had cloistered in the library plotting. Nick, Cole, and Trevor had joined in as soon as they'd arrived.

"Less than an hour now." Anna tossed the core in the trash and sidled up next to Kylie to take a look outside herself. She studied the sky and said, "Yes. We're almost there."

"We should get into position then." Kylie was still upset over Mrs. Attinger's stroke, but she was grateful the housekeeper and her husband were still off-island. They'd be safer that way, far from any collateral damage that might result from the coming conflict.

The wards might be protecting the mansion again, but Bastraal had blown them away once before. He should be barred from entry to the house, but no one wanted to take the risk.

Quinn had assured them he'd added an extra kick to the spells this time. And even the evil underworld bastard Bastraal couldn't break through.

Which is why the coven and the men were taking up posts around the island. They wanted— were even eager for—a chance to face off with the Amara. Like Kylie, they were ready for a fight.

"Everyone's here," Quinn said from the doorway. He glanced to her, and his eyes softened, almost imperceptibly. Then he retreated, leaving her and Anna to follow.

As they trailed him to the grand hall where the others were waiting, they heard Paige ask, "Are you sure the runes will work?"

"I'm sure." Quinn eyed the warrior with the angel's hair. "Are you sure *your* part will work?"

"Of course." Paige looked offended. "I know what I'm doing."

"As do I," Quinn shot back. But then he and Paige shared mutinous grins.

"Those two are enjoying this entirely too much." Anna crossed her arms and sighed.

"Yep." Kylie lifted on her toes twice in a row. "But I have to tell you, Anna—I'm pretty pumped too."

Her animated movements caught Paige's attention, and the soldier's expression fell into an intense stare.

Abruptly, she set aside the dagger she'd been holding and marched over to Kylie. She wrapped her super-strong arms around her.

"Paige?" Kylie caught Anna's gaze over the warrior's shoulder, but the head witch only shrugged.

Paige breathed in and out before releasing Kylie from the bone-crushing hug. Her voice was ragged when she said, "It's just good to see you bouncing again."

With a loud cough, she became the tough girl once again and returned to the table in front of the velvet couch. She picked up one of the black two-way radios. "These have a range of twenty-four miles, so we should be good to go."

"Let's head out," Dare said, apparently as thirsty for a good brawl as Paige and Quinn.

The entire coven community was present, with all the men throwing their muscle behind the coven. Joseph and Sylvie had wanted to help, but someone had to stay with Tadd on the mainland.

Sylvie had gotten teary-eyed when Willyn had asked her to care for her son, giving the hoodoo woman the ultimate indication of trust.

Perusing the area and all those who were "suiting up," Kylie went to Paige and gestured to the others. "Well, that's one good thing about all the love stories and happy endings."

Paige grunted. "What's that?" She was scowling, as she usually did when the words *love*, *romance*, or even *hooking-up* were used. She was rather anti-destiny in that sense.

"With all the guys, we really outnumber the Amara now."

"Yeah, well." Paige shrugged. "There is that."

Viv overheard the caustic response and laughed. She slipped the straps of the scabbard over her shoulders that would house her two swords. Then she jerked her chin to Anna. "Do you think this Ian Keller is the type to get his hands dirty?"

Anna shook her head. "I don't think so. He's a slick one, though. Like Dalton."

"Great," Kylie said. "Another perv."

"I'm not sure." Anna's eyes grew distant, thoughtful. "I'm not sure he's as bad as the others or knows what he's gotten himself involved in. He was difficult to read."

"Well, if he does show up, he'll wish he'd stayed in the safety of his courtrooms." Trevor holstered a weapon, but he was sticking to his trusty Sig.

"Move out!" Paige yelled, her mouth kicking up in a grin. "How I've missed saying that."

Rolling her eyes, Kylie chuckled with Anna and Viv. But still they followed orders, each falling in with their assigned group.

Given the length of the island—shaped like a kidney bean that narrowed at one end—two teams would situate at distant points along each of the longer sides. Two teams on the east, and two teams on the west.

The narrow tip at the north consisted primarily of marsh, abundant with cord grass. A boat landing there was unlikely, but Nick and Willyn would be stationed there to keep a lookout.

Divided into seven teams, the plan was to monitor the seas for the Amara's approach. Anna hadn't been able to pinpoint the specific beach from her vision, though her sense was that it was on the southeast of the island.

Anna would be in one of the groups on the eastern side with Shauni and Trevor, while Cole and Hayden would be stationed farther south. Then at the southern tip, Kylie, Dare, and Lucia would keep watch.

Now as Kylie secured a hunting knife on her thigh strap— one imbued with her special blue magic—she lifted her eyes in the direction her group was bound. The tall hardwoods and pines were densely packed, the underbrush thick with woody vines and sparkleberry.

She and the others would navigate the forest until the palms and magnolias gave way to sand. Then they would meet the open expanse of the coast.

Ethan and Viv headed out to her right toward the docks. Farther past them, Claudia and Michael would hold a more northern position.

In addition to the human surveillance, Shauni had also called in the Air Force. Her version, anyway. Ospreys would help keep the night watch, literally giving the coven a bird's-eye view.

But Quinn and Paige, they were the surprise element and would wait in the center in Quinn's Bronco. As soon as they received word of the Amara's approach, they would dispatch to the designated location.

And would lay their traps.

Kylie grinned as she edged through the shadows. No wonder Quinn and Paige were so excited. They were both getting to play Army.

Then her smile faltered and fell. Because this wasn't a game. Not at the heart of it.

Beneath the bluster and talk of payback was a very real need for revenge. Each and every one of her friends was consumed with a certain amount of bloodlust. Even Shauni, Willyn, and Hayden, the gentlest of the witches, were ready to dole out some retribution.

They all wanted vengeance for what had been done to Kylie.

As for herself? Returning some of the pain she'd been given didn't sound half-bad. The only question was who she would strike first.

She shivered suddenly, not only from her racing adrenaline, but from the wind that rushed from behind her. The south-blowing gale brought fog on its current, mists that had arisen from the marshes. The fog rolled onward, intermingling with tangled branches of oaks and the dangling gray beards of moss.

Soon they heard the low static of ocean waves, and Dare pointed out a stand of three wide-trunked oaks. "Those will make good cover." So just inside the forest edge, the three settled in to wait.

"Ready to try the charm?" Lucia asked.

Kylie nodded with vigor before undulating her hands for flair. As her eyes flickered closed she said, "*Noctis visum.*" Then she opened them again to check the results.

"That is coolness," she whispered, taking a look around at the sharper, clearer, and now green-tinted world. She waited for Dare and Lucia to mimic the incantation, chuckling when they had the same reaction.

"I've got to hand it to Paige." Dare stood and examined the depths of the forest. "This is one badass spell."

"Yeah," Lucia agreed. "Leave it to her to think of it. Even if the Latin isn't quite right."

Kylie chuckled, amazed by how far she could actually see, the details she could make out. Far out to sea, tiny white caps bobbed in the ocean, and nearer to their position, fiddler crabs scrabbled over the nighttime beach.

She and the others didn't need a set of goggles, just those two little words of magic. Because *noctis visum* was a fairly literal translation. For night vision.

29

Barely any wind blew across the interior of the island, but Quinn and Paige had the windows down anyway. With the ocean blocked by impenetrable brush and forest, the dark road where they were parked was still and silent.

Until the radio in Paige's lap crackled to life. Claudia's voice came over the channel. "There's a boat headed our way. Michael and I see two figures, but can only identify one. Ross."

Paige depressed the button on the receiver. "You sure it's only two?"

"As far as I can tell, the other person . . ." Claudia paused, and when she came back on, her tone was both disgusted and tense. "Hold on. I see her now. *Valentina.*" The name came out tight with implication.

"We're on our way," Paige said. Then she added, "Try not to kill her before we get there."

"No promises."

Quinn laughed beneath his breath as he started the engine. Valentina was the Amara's resident succubus, and during Claudia's trial, she'd used her wicked wiles on Cole. She'd made Claudia doubt Cole's honesty and his love for her, even if only briefly.

Still, the slight hadn't been forgotten, and Claudia would enjoy putting some hurt on the pretty and poisonous Valentina.

The tires of the vehicle rolled softly over a mixture of sand

and soil, and since he and Paige had settled in the center of the island to wait, Quinn felt sure they would arrive in plenty of time. The ex-soldier had crafted some simple but effective traps, and they were both eager to put them to use.

Quinn had come in on the magic side of the plan, putting together a host of runes from the magick languages. And as he pictured the damage they would cause, his veins pumped with both blood and retaliation. He couldn't wait to see those Amara thugs run and scream.

And burn.

The interior road only took them so far, and when they came to the end, they jumped out to grab black duffels from the back seat. Inside were the implements they required.

"Coming in behind you," Paige said into the radio, alerting Claudia and Michael to their presence.

No one wanted any friendly-fire incidents.

"Better hurry," Claudia came back.

Michael met them halfway down the trail. He gestured behind him. "If they maintain the course they're on, they should come this way. I can't imagine they'll choose to pick through the undergrowth when there's a path already here."

"That's what we're banking on." Paige nodded to Quinn, and he dug into his bag. He pulled out a small burlap sack that clinked and rattled in his hand. The runes he'd created specifically for this purpose.

Using a similar alloy to that of the coven weapons, he'd created metal discs, imprinted with the runes of choice. Once in place, the runes only needed to be activated. And if disturbed
. . .

Quinn gritted his teeth and opened the bag. Pouring several of the discs into his hand, he quickly found the symbols he wanted. Two discs, each with the runic representation of *Feoh* followed by the Hebrew letter T for *Teth*.

Paige held a spool of wire in her hands. With the efficiency of the trained soldier she was, she promptly attached the end of the trip-wire to a tree on one side of the path before unwinding the spool as she backed over to Quinn.

He waited until she had the second end in place before telling Michael, "Okay, nobody walks this path until I give the all-clear." Then he grinned with evil intent. "Or you hear a lot of screaming. Whichever comes first."

"No big boom?" Michael asked, only half-joking.

"No." Quinn gripped the runes in his hand, his upper lip curling into a snarl. "An explosion would be over too quickly."

"Uh, then I'll make sure Claudia knows." The blonde veterinarian with a soft heart and courage of steel jogged back toward the beach.

Quinn placed the metallic discs on both ends of the wire, putting his finger to the center of each once it had been secured. Then he chanted a single word three times. The engravings lit up a bright, sizzling white before burning out and fading again into obscurity.

Moonbeams struggled to reach the forest floor, but with Paige's night-vision spell, Quinn was able to see just fine. The two of them huddled behind the concealment of shrubs. Far enough away for their own protection, yet close enough to enjoy the spectacle that was about to unfold.

"Now will you tell me what those marks mean?" Paige had been hounding him ever since he'd come up with the idea for enhancing the booby-traps with magic.

"Trust me." Quinn kept his voice hushed. "You'll appreciate it better if it's a surprise."

She grumbled and readjusted her position. "Don't like surprises."

When he would have replied, Quinn stilled instead, listening for sounds down the trail. He'd thought he'd heard voices.

Paige confirmed the suspicion when she whispered, "Shhh," beside him in the dark.

So far, there'd been no other reports of incoming attackers, but if the trap worked as it was intended, this section of the island was going to get noisy. Anyone else coming in this way would know their secret invasion was blown.

A man's voice echoed through the trees. "Damn bugs. Why the hell would anyone want to live out here?"

Quinn recognized Ross's disagreeable tone and found irony that a man who shifted into animal shapes had a problem with insects.

"It's not like they sleep out here in the woods." A female this time, Valentina. Based on the proximity of their voices, they would both be within range.

He and Paige both focused on the path from their location in the bushes, and as the Amara members came into view, Quinn's gaze fell to the wire he knew was there but couldn't quite discern. With a shift of his head, he caught the slightest glimmer. The thin stretch of metal was still in place.

And Ross the maniac was about to fall all over it.

The shifter had his mouth open to speak again when his left ankle twisted beneath him and he went sprawling. Valentina kept walking, still unaware of what had brought him down.

The enchanted runes didn't discharge with an ear-splitting detonation, but Quinn knew the sinuous hiss would be just as harmful. And a hell of a lot more terrifying.

As soon as it took full form.

Quinn watched as Ross scrambled to his feet, but the shifter didn't notice the streams of red whirling from both sides of the path. His female companion had, though.

"What the hell?" Valentina jerked her head between the two shapes as they materialized. The mists grew and morphed into red silhouettes until two giant figures were flanking the intruders.

"Hey, Paige," Quinn whispered aside to her as she observed with a grin. "Those symbols you asked about? The rune *Feoh* can be used to represent fire."

The blood-hued magic had created two bodies, both long and massive as they circled Ross and his friend. The mystical creatures spread huge, ominous wings as they zeroed sightless eyes in on their targets. Those who had tripped their wire and become their prey.

"Are those—?" Paige shuffled her feet and stood higher for a better view. "Holy shit, Quinn. You were right about the surprise."

Quinn nodded. "The Hebrew *Teth* refers to a serpent." The first blast of fire scorched Ross from head to toe and sent the shifter clambering backward as he shouted.

Laughing cruelly, Quinn stood. "What better example of fire serpents," he eased out of the woods and crossed his arms, "than a couple of dragons?"

Paige revealed herself as well, but their unwelcome visitors didn't notice. They were too busy trying to escape the flying fire-breathers that swooped and dove, torching their victims with each pass.

The vapors that formed their bodies sparkled like a million red gemstones in the sun. The dragons were stunning, agile, and deadly.

Quinn didn't know how adept Ross and the succubus were at healing, and frankly, he wouldn't mind if they both fried to death. But they were doing their best to avoid that fate, sprinting down the path and back toward the ocean.

Immersing in the water would provide some protection, but regardless, the first objective had been met. These two were done for the night and wouldn't be attacking anyone.

Soon Quinn and Paige were joined by a chuckling Claudia and amazed Michael.

"Quinn, I'm forever in your debt," Claudia said, holding her stomach from laughing. "You hit Valentina right where she lives. Her vanity." She hooted again. "I'll never forget how she looked running wide-eyed with half her hair singed off."

Quinn was overpowered by his own smile and rolling laughter. "Did you get a picture?"

"No. Darn." Claudia snapped a finger. "Wish I'd known I'd need a camera."

The radio on Paige's belt squawked suddenly, sidelining the thrill of the trap's success. An exchange came over the open channel.

"Paige, this is Willyn. We've spotted another boat."

"Roger." Paige looked askance to Quinn, and at his nod she added, "We're on our way."

"That's two vessels coming in close together." Quinn retrieved his duffel from the bushes. "They're headed toward the marsh?"

"Looks like." Paige lifted her chin as she asked Michael and Claudia, "You guys coming with us?"

"Yes." Claudia was already moving. "They aren't likely to use this same landing point."

Quinn began to jog and so did the others. "That's what I'm afraid of."

"What do you mean?" Claudia asked.

"Staggered arrival times in separate locations." He shared a knowing look with Paige. "It feels orchestrated."

Since they were already close to the northern tip, it didn't take long for them to make their way to Willyn and Nick. Fortunately, the island road went straight to the marsh, terminating near their location.

"The boat's painted a dark color," Nick said as soon as Quinn was at his side. He and Willyn were still within the shelter of the forest. "Just there." He pointed, and Quinn scanned the dark ocean.

"I see it." Narrowing his eyes as the watercraft glided behind a clump of trees, Quinn growled low. "Damn. Lost them. "

The marshes were like a living, growing labyrinth, and

after a summer of heavy rain, the cord grass was high and green. Interspersed with plant life, channels of water curved and meandered. Whoever was on the boat had slipped up a waterway behind a jut of land covered by forest.

"Let's go." Paige made as if to return to the truck, but Quinn stopped her with a hand on her arm.

"Wait. I know where they're headed." He met her stare in the shadows just as clouds blotted out the shiny moon. "There's only one way to get from where they are now to the main portion of the island."

"A good place to set a trap?" the warrior asked as the other four crowded around to listen to the plan.

"The perfect place. And we can go on foot. In fact, we don't have a choice."

The six of them set out immediately, walking at a brisk pace. Quinn was certain they'd have plenty of time to get set up.

Until he heard the thin, mechanical buzz. "Shit."

"What's that?" Willyn stopped to listen.

Nick was the one who answered. "They brought a dirt bike." And he would know, being a cycle enthusiast himself.

Without taking another second to explain, Quinn broke into a run.

"We can set another wire," Paige said, barely winded from the exertion. "I can be quick."

"Maybe." Quinn was envisioning the area ahead, filing through his memory for natural resources they might be able to use.

When he finally saw the fork in the trail, he let himself relax. Judging by the motor humming from across the open marsh, they still had a few minutes.

As he scanned the land for a place to lay the wire, Paige jerked her hand up to point. "I just caught a glimpse of them. One bike, two riders." Her brow creased. "Another two-man team. They might just be decoys, in case Anna picked up on the

Amara's presence. "

"Smaller groups to draw our attention and divert our forces?" Quinn looked down the long pass, a narrow strip of land that traversed the marsh. This is where the bike would have to cross.

"Yeah. But they didn't count on Anna being able to predict their assault as far in advance as she did."

Quinn felt his neck tense with renewed fury. "They assumed she'd be too distraught over Kylie's death. That she wouldn't see them coming in time." The thought of the alternate scenario that could have been—the one where Kylie hadn't come back to him—only fueled Quinn's need for vengeance.

He pictured that disgusting video and how helpless Kylie had been. Restrained, both physically and magically, while the heartless sons of bitches had gathered around to enjoy her pain.

His hand tightened around the strap of his bag. "I have an idea."

But he'd have to work fast.

"Forget the tripwire." He gestured to Paige's duffel. "Do you have the chain?"

"Yeah." She dug in the bag before hefting the weighty coil with one hand.

"Let me have it." Quinn opened his own sack, the one that held his runes. He withdrew two metal discs, both with another Hebrew letter inscribed on their flat surfaces. This time the symbol was *cheth*. Its everyday meaning—*fence*.

Using his magic, he fused a charmed pendant to each end of the chain before tossing the silver links back to her. "Think you can throw this across the path at the midpoint before they get here?"

Paige gave him a look that might as well have said "Seriously?" Then in a flash, she was twenty yards away, laying the chain across the lane so the bike would run over it, and was back beside him before he could even get his fingers around another silver piece.

"Nice." Quinn nodded to her.

Paige only shrugged.

"What are you planning?" Claudia had edged closer to study the medallions in Quinn's palm.

"I left some of these blank, just in case we had to improvise. Like with the chain. We knew we might need it but couldn't predict which spell would best serve us based on the scenario."

The sound of the engine grew, urging Quinn to work more quickly. He pulled out a hand-engraver with a round grip. His inscriptions wouldn't win any prizes for penmanship, but their magic would work. And that's all that counted.

They were still visible, and the Amara were getting close. He made himself scarce along with the others, hiding behind trees so the riders wouldn't see them and slow the bike too soon.

Paige's night-vision spell was coming in handy. In the darkness, he chiseled more runes on the discs with swift scratches.

"Hurry it up, Quinn." Paige was shaking her leg, watching the narrow trail. "There's the headlight. They're on the last stretch and coming this way."

"Here." He handed her and Claudia the medallions. "Use your fire to weld these onto some of Paige's throwing stars."

"You mean my demon spurs?" She grinned. "I like the sound of that better."

"Whatever. As long as they can be thrown." Quinn turned to Nick and Michael. "You guys want a piece of the action?"

"Hell yeah." Nick was primed, and he had his own sordid backstory with the Amara. They'd murdered his friend Jen. Now the set of his features and the glow in his whiskey-hued eyes were nothing short of pure vindictiveness.

Michael patted the knives on his belt. "You know my aim is true."

"Whatever these symbols do, Quinn, get ready to make it happen." Paige distributed the barbed metal balls, each of them embedded with a rune. "Because the bike is about to hit the—"

An indescribable sound blasted across the previously-silent marsh, a reverberation of both solid *thud!* and metallic destruction.

"—chain," Paige finished.

Two bodies were splayed across the dirt path, but one of them was already recovering and sitting up.

"Just hit them. One time is all it takes." Quinn burst from the underbrush, ready to fire up his retired pitching arm.

Like a band of outlaws, they rushed the hapless Amara members, who had run full-speed into the chain's mystical barrier. The invisible "fence."

Quinn raised his arm, ready to throw, when a black-haired figure tried to stand.

Jack. The female was equally as fast and strong as Paige. Damn. But Quinn knew he'd inscribed the right rune for this job. And that Jack was the perfect recipient.

He nailed her on the first try, and while her instinct may have been to look down at whatever had pierced her side, she only stared straight ahead, arms dropping to her sides.

And as if someone had yelled, "Timber!" she keeled over like a rigid redwood.

While Jack was falling, Nick lobbed a spur at the other Amara member. The one still on the ground. Long but tangled blonde hair declared the woman to be Carson, but the lean-muscled Amazon didn't attempt to rise.

Then again, she couldn't if she tried.

"What did you do?" Claudia's mouth hung open as she skidded to a stop, observing the stock-still women. "They're completely out."

Quinn walked over to the chain and pulled it to one side.

"They're alive. Just immobilized."

Stopping next to Carson's stiff figure, he nudged her hip and rocked her slightly. "Just checking," he told her, sure her features would contort with rage—or terror—if she'd actually been able move her facial muscles.

"What now?" Willyn looked at the two murderers with loathing, hands twisting in front of her. "How long will they be like this?"

"Long enough for us to clear the rest of the island." Quinn recalled his previous plan and why he'd thought of immobility in the first place.

Because Kylie had been chained down. Because she hadn't been able to defend herself as she lay in the cold, disgusting slime of that cellar.

"But we won't leave them like this," he said.

"No?" Paige cast him a puzzled glance.

"No. Like I said about the explosion," he went to Carson and grabbed her forearms, "that would be too easy."

Dragging her off the dirt until she was partially immersed in the muck of the marsh, Quinn watched as water engulfed the Amazon's legs and lower body. "Don't worry, you won't drown." He kneeled and spoke into her frozen face. "But remember this moment."

He noticed the glint of fear in her eyes as the moon escaped from the clouds to shine down. "And *never* come to my island again."

He stood, rank with bitterness and filled with ire. These two deserved worse. They all did. For Mrs. Attinger and for Kylie.

But he wouldn't kill two women who couldn't even fight back.

That was the downside of having morals. Of being human. But it was also what separated his kind from soulless bastards like the Amara.

So he'd take what vengeance he could and be satisfied. For now.

Nick had pulled Jack to the other side, off the strip of land and into the marsh. The pub owner seemed a little too pleased to lord this moment over their adversary. But Quinn knew where he was coming from.

Even morals had to crack once in a while.

Nick's eyes curtained their gleam and shifted to Quinn when the walkie-talkie on Paige's belt crackled again. The two men exchanged a worried stare.

Just as Paige had suspected. The Amara were attacking on various fronts.

"We've got more heading our way," Hayden reported through static, an interference that shouldn't have existed.

Quinn's gut tightened. Because that meant strong magic was coming toward Hayden and Cole's position.

"We see them too." Dare's deep voice joined in. "We're en route."

Without further discussion, Quinn turned and made for his truck. The others were right with him, and none of them needed to ask why his face had hardened. Why he'd fallen into a severe and determined silence.

As soon as they arrived at the Bronco, he slung himself inside, revved the engine as Paige, Michael, and Claudia climbed in, and made a hasty three-point turn in the sandy dirt before the last door had closed. Nick and Willyn were in another vehicle and would follow close behind.

Quinn hoped they kept up, because he wasn't slowing down.

Kylie was on Dare's team, and they were moving to intercept more of the Amara on the southern part of the island. And Quinn was on the north, the farthest point from the woman he loved.

The most dangerous members had yet to show themselves, so that meant Kylie could be headed straight into Ronja's path. Or Scarlett's, Tyr's, or Searenn's. None of which were good options.

And they all had magic to fight with, unlike the four who'd been derailed by either dragons or paralysis.

Quinn felt as if he had his own serpent of fire lodged in his chest. Squeezing the steering wheel, he roared down the road, veering at the split that would take them to the inevitable standoff.

Kylie wasn't going into battle without him. She would not face those bastards alone.

Not again.

And he'd give up everything to ensure she never had to.

He knew now that he would make any sacrifice for Kylie. To keep her safe, free from pain. Hell, even just to keep her happy.

The road took them through monstrous live oaks, whose crooked arms and Spanish moss hung over the road to create a canopy. Around the backside of the estate they raced, closer to Cole and Hayden's position.

Soon the Bronco skidded to a halt, as close to the rendezvous point as they could drive, so everyone jumped out. Michael had his throwing knives—and was terrifyingly accurate with the sharp blades—while Claudia had opted for a sword and dagger.

Searenn would likely be part of the assault squad, so the weapons were infused with coven magic. The only firepower that would kill the Droehk's demons.

Quinn had taken a sword as well, more than ready to engage the Amara or their summoned monsters.

A short trip through the woods took them to the beach, and given the dense underbrush, the clear path of sand would be the quickest route to Cole and Hayden. With every step, Quinn prayed he made it first. That Kylie wasn't already immersed in battle with the Amara.

Only Hayden was waiting at the rendezvous point, and she hurried from the trees to greet them. "The vessel we saw veered south, so Cole went with the others. We're only a minute behind."

"I'm going ahead," Paige said before shooting off into the shadows.

The moon hung high in the sky, adding a pale blue blush to the already green-tinted sand and sea. For the first time, Quinn wished for even half of Paige's speed.

As it turned out, though, he and the others didn't have to run far before they caught sight of Paige's blonde hair shining like a torch in the dark.

She was with Trevor and three more, though he couldn't make out identifying features. When he drew closer, he recognized his sister's form. Her long brown hair was secured in a braid, and she was the only witch without a weapon on her back.

But then, she didn't really need one.

She, Shauni, and Trevor had come up this side of the island to arrive before Quinn and his group. Still running, he perused the coastline for any sign of Kylie, but she wasn't there yet.

His gut released but only marginally. Then the low rumble of a motor floated to him on the ocean wind, and he saw Anna turn to face the approaching watercraft.

So much for subterfuge. His sister was striding boldly across the beach to meet the boat, announcing her presence to those who dared attack her land. Her family.

She stopped midway to the water and stood with legs spread, arms loose at her sides, and fury in her posture. No wrathful goddess ever looked as menacing as his sister did now, with the wind kicking up around her, whipping her clothes against her body.

Magic. Quinn could almost smell it. And he most certainly sensed it, prickling through the environment as Anna clashed eyes with the woman riding in on the boat's bow.

Ronja stood just as proudly, but the smile she wore was smug.

The vessel was small enough to coast to shore, and Tyr leapt out to pull it up onto the sand. Then the hulking man helped Ronja step down with the deference of an underling who knew his place.

Quinn slowed his speed when he drew near, he and the others surrounding Anna, providing her support and coverage.

Unfortunately, he'd assumed correctly. This boat contained the strongest of the Amara.

Ronja glided with a malevolent kind of grace, her eyes locked on Anna's face. "Well, well. Look who saw me coming." The witch wore a long black dress that shimmered silkily in the moonlight. Her battle-wear was strangely apt.

"You've gone too far, Ronja." Anna held her ground, unflinching as the Nordic witch moved closer.

Finally, Ronja stopped. She held out her hands. "I acknowledge no boundaries, Anna. For me, for one of my strength," she narrowed her eyes and laughed viciously, "there's no such thing as *too far*."

"You've broken every creed set down for our kind. You've defied every law outlining the prophecy." Anna took a step forward. "But what you did to Kylie—" Her voice tightened with rage until she fell silent.

Ronja fluttered her eyes. "What do you mean? Oh," she feigned surprise. "You're talking about that little witch of yours. *Tsk. Tsk.* You really should have trained your girls better. She apparently wasn't up to the task."

"You've become a monster, Ronja. Taking what doesn't belong to you, murdering innocents, setting your demons loose to do what they will." Anna held out her hands. Light glowed within her fingers, but this magic was deep blue like sapphires. It belonged only to her.

She angled her open palms toward Ronja, the mystical equivalent to lifting a sword. "Now it's my turn to break some rules."

Ronja chuckled, clearly unafraid. "If you kill me, the prophecy will be forfeit."

Anna's voice was as cold and sharp as a knife. "Who said anything about killing?"

Turning to the side, Ronja put a hand on her hip, all but dismissing her adversary. "Oh, but I forgot. You've already lost. The prophecy is no more, now that your circle is broken. But," she continued," I don't see why you and I can't still have a go at each other."

With a jerk of her wrist, Ronja lashed out at Anna with a whip-like streak of putrid green.

Anna easily deflected the strike with a pulse of her own magic that expanded before returning to rest idly in her hand.

"I see you've been practicing." Ronja faced her fully, her smile gone, replaced by an ugly sneer. "But all for nothing, Anna. I beat you. Your little witch is dead. Your coven is destroyed."

When the wind grew in intensity, Quinn sensed the arrival of a new force. One that carried a bright and sizzling heat. Pure and free. Wild.

He sensed the power of lightning.

Kylie exited the shelter of the forest, and her approach caught Ronja's eye. She walked through the line of her friends and moved to stand with Anna.

Far out to sea, strikes of lightning announced Kylie's arrival. They echoed her rage when she met Ronja's cold blue eyes.

They struck and rumbled when Kylie said, "Guess again."

30

Ronja's expression betrayed her shock. Her mouth worked soundlessly, like a fish that had been tossed onto the dock. For Kylie, that moment alone was priceless.

"You were dead," the Nordic seiðr finally spat before swinging her gaze back to Anna. "You brought her back! You broke the very credos and governances that you wave in my face!" Ronja stabbed a finger at Anna.

"We didn't bring her back." Anna still held her magic at the ready. "She brought herself back."

"And you told me I was weak." Kylie took slow, measured strides closer to Ronja. "I'm so happy to have proven you wrong."

As much as she thrilled to gloat over the black-hearted witch, Kylie was keeping an eye on the others moving in behind her. Scarlett had disembarked from the boat, fanning out on one side behind Ronja as Beth and Searenn went to the opposite.

Tyr had edged farther out, and with a glimpse, Kylie noted that the rest of her own team, Lucia and Dare, had emerged from the brush farther down the beach. The Native-American brute had them in his sights.

Ronja whirled to face Kylie, and with the motion, she called more of her power. A horrible green and violet cloud, like a third-day bruise, rose up to swirl around her. "You little bitch. I *will* kill you."

Kylie shrugged, but in the distance, lightning seared the skies. "I've kind of been there. You know, done that." She opened her arms and created a light show of her own as radiant bolts of golden energy darted and snapped.

"But you're more than welcome to try for a repeat." Kylie felt the heat of vengeance sear beneath her skin. "I'm not chained down anymore, and magic is mine to use as I will."

The first clap of thunder had Beth snapping her head around, scanning the ocean and the skies above. Murderous clouds were rolling from the north and south, as if summoned from outlying areas. They collided into one massive brewing storm.

Kylie met Beth's stare when she hazarded a glance her way. There was a sweet taste of payback when she saw fear in the mare's eyes.

"You're still no match for us," Scarlett said, adding her own haze to the flowing magic. "I never had a turn with you." She sent a gust of her poison toward Kylie. "So I'll take mine now."

Kylie had always been one with energy, just as she'd told Quinn, but now she felt the connection on a deeper level. Before, she'd always had to think about what she wanted to do, but when Scarlett's fumes blew her way, it was as if she and her magic were partners in a dance.

They moved in sync, and their rhythm was lethal.

Tiny bolts of lightning, hundreds upon hundreds, skittered through the air. Acting as one unit, the electricity engulfed Scarlett's noxious cloud and lit it up with so much wattage, Kylie could smell the burn from where she stood.

The crimson particles were arrested mid-flow, frying to a deep brown before dissipating into the wind. Kylie laughed at the redhead's stunned reaction. "You were saying?"

Scarlett curled her pretty, painted lips, circling as she walked farther from where Ronja and Anna still faced each other. She lifted a hand and threw some old-fashioned magic at Kylie instead, invisible but solid.

The blow hit Kylie mid-center. She let out an *oof* but didn't lose her footing.

Surging on her own rise of power, Kylie would have scorched Scarlett where she stood, but Quinn's voice caught her attention. He wasn't interfering—he'd only spoken low to someone else behind her—but the realization that he was close by slowed her reflexes.

Ronja must have sensed Kylie's hesitation, or seen her eyes flick to the side, and she took the opportunity to double-up on the punch Scarlett had landed. With a thrust of her hands, she sent a wave of magic to Kylie.

And a dozen invisible knives entered her body, the enchantment slicing as deeply and surely as metal.

Still doubled over, she heard Quinn's expletive, but behind his outburst, another voice. Paige. She was telling Quinn to wait.

As Kylie lifted her head and started to stand, she saw Ronja preparing to deliver another round. But a flood of vibrant blue rammed Ronja in the center of her chest. She lost her purchase momentarily, but dug her feet into the sand, leaning into the force as she screeched Anna's name.

Tyr released a roar when he saw Ronja under attack. He ran down the beach, kicking up sand as his muscular legs pumped. His face was distorted with rage as he barreled straight for Anna.

And like a linebacker from Hell, Trevor came at him from the side.

Tyr might have possessed mystical power, and he may have borrowed immortality, but the detective was bigger, stronger, and faster. He aimed all that strength at dead-center mass and took Tyr down hard.

Tackling the man, Trevor tumbled with him into the surf. As soon as they erupted from the waves, the two took turns pounding on each other.

Kylie glanced to Anna and Ronja, still dueling with magic and pressing at each other. Searenn, Beth, and Scarlett were all watching the two hulking men fight in the ocean. So as she regained the breath that had been knocked from her by Ronja's assault, Kylie turned as well.

Both men's faces were bleeding from physical blows, but it wasn't long before Tyr pulled out a punch Trevor couldn't return. He struck with magic, and whatever supernatural jolt he used sent Trevor flying backward, far out into deeper water.

All eyes but Anna's and Ronja's turned to where he'd gone under, waiting. And when his blonde head re-surfaced, Hayden let out a cry of relief.

Then she turned her fury on Tyr. As she walked into the rolling surf, her caramel-colored hair floated around her, lifted by wind and her own swirling power. "Tyr, I thought you might show up tonight, so I invited some friends. They've traveled a long way, and they'd really like a word with you."

The Amara members were all familiar with the witches and each of their unique gifts. Tyr's bronze skin actually blanched as Hayden hit on what must have been one of the mighty warrior's deepest fears.

Spirits. Most Native-American tribes held a deep respect for the afterlife and for those who had crossed over.

"Two of your ancestors have returned," Hayden explained. "And they aren't pleased with the side you've chosen. Not at all."

Hayden nodded into what appeared to be empty air, but when Tyr covered his face with his hands and bellowed in horror, Kylie knew the ghosts were there. She watched as Tyr struggled with invisible attackers, yelling and pushing with his legs as he tried to keep his head above the surface.

And she smiled when those attackers drove him under the water. She felt retribution fire inside of her when he didn't return. When the ghosts kept him down.

One of her torturers was suffering now, enduring the agony of drowning. But Tyr had likely been drinking Ronja's immortal blood, and he'd be back to cause more trouble. Eventually.

But for now, for this fight, he was no longer a threat.

Kylie turned her attention to the remaining Amara women, each of whom had participated in her torture, or at the very least, had cheered from the sidelines. Quickly summing up the amount of danger each one represented, she chose to disable Searenn first.

Her presence wasn't the actual threat, but the demons she might summon at any moment were.

"Hey," Kylie called to Scarlett, sending an unexpected bolt of lightning straight to her heart when she turned her way. The blow was only a setback, but would provide just enough time for Kylie to focus on Searenn.

As if sensing her plan, Shauni and Lucia stepped up to distract Scarlett with a few tricks of their own. The red-haired witch cursed and twisted as Lucia threw flames. Scarlett deflected each one, but between the bursts of fire, Shauni slipped in to deliver jabs of power.

When one of Shauni's hits threw Scarlett off-balance, the cruel woman shouted and took a few steps back. Kylie felt victorious, and she shared a ferocious grin with Lucia.

Scarlett was retreating. They were beating the Amara back.

Angling her head at the sound of new voices, Kylie saw Ethan and Viv running up the beach. The last team was here now, just in time for the main event.

By the time she returned her attention to Searenn, the Droehk had begun to chant. She had her shirt off and was channeling one of the beasts she kept on a chain.

Maneuvering her way behind Anna so as not to create crossfire, Kylie flung a yellow streak of electricity at Searenn. The impact stopped Searenn's recitation, but the woman only sneered, her one-black and one-blue set of eyes clamped to Kylie. "Is that all you've got?" She laughed. "You'd better hope not."

Kylie sent another bolt her way, just to wipe that smirk off her face. "Don't worry." She stood with her legs shoulder-width apart and spread her arms. "That was just the warm-up."

Behind Searenn, the clouds began to glow. Slivers and streaks of lightning coursed through the billowing veil of gray.

When Kylie let her head fall back, channeling her gift as she never had before, the strikes became jagged lines of white and gold that split the very sky.

Winds from the sea rushed over them all as Kylie called both storm and gale. The energy in the air fueled her magic, and as it increased, she returned even more to the atmosphere.

Kylie. Her magic. And nature's gift of lightning. The three worked together in a cycle of ever-increasing power.

Images flashed into Kylie's head. Beth's pummeling fists, Searenn's sadistic demon, and Tyr's relentless cuts.

All of her fury detonated into one massive pulse of electricity. And she drove it into Searenn.

The Droehk screamed as she flew through the air, landing farther down the coast on the hard-packed sand. Her body thudded, leaving gouges in the sand before she went limp. Waves crashed over her as she lay still as death.

Kylie saw the scorch mark in the center of her torso. She had done that, but the sight of her violence didn't raise an ounce of pity or remorse.

Movement erupted in her peripheral vision. She jerked her head in that direction, but Beth was already running.

The young girl was sprinting, her face twisted with anger. But she wasn't coming for Kylie.

Instead, she was gunning for Anna, who was still slamming her magic into Ronja's.

The mare who so enjoyed causing pain now channeled her

strength and plowed into Anna's side. She tackled the coven leader much as Trevor had Tyr only moments before.

Anna's surprised cry was a knife to Kylie's stomach, and her hands jerked reflexively.

The sequence of events that occurred next felt like slow motion, but despite the painfully sluggish reality, Kylie couldn't stop what was about to happen.

She saw the stony blue of Ronja's eyes shift toward her. She sensed Ronja's coming attack.

But Beth had hit Anna like a wrecking ball, and Kylie's tiny moment of concern for her friend cost her. Her magic still surged and snapped, but she'd broken the connection for one split-second.

This time when Ronja fired, Kylie couldn't block quickly enough.

The Nordic witch shoved both hands through the air, and a tidal wave of magic literally rippled toward Kylie. Lifting her hand in an overdue attempt to protect herself, she discharged a burst of lightning.

Her power was headed directly toward Ronja's, an inevitable combustion of lethal forces.

And Quinn dove into the middle of it all.

A scream tore from Kylie's throat when she saw him flying to intercept the strike meant for her. His body seemed to hover briefly, vibrating from the immense power he'd absorbed.

Then reality crashed back to its normal speed, and he dropped like a rag to the beige sand.

Chaos erupted on the beach as every witch and friend of the coven fell into a free-for-all. They'd all hung back to let Kylie fight for herself against her tormentors, while Anna expended her own vengeance against Ronja. But once Quinn took such a deadly hit, multiple battle cries rose into the stormy night.

And Hell was loosed upon the Amara.

Kylie didn't pay much attention to the commotion. She

trusted her sisters to guard her back.

As she fell to her knees and cradled Quinn's head in her hands.

"Quinn. What have you done?" His eyes were closed, but his face was scrunched up, as if he were in pain.

Groaning, he tried to sit up, but Kylie put her weight on his shoulders. "Don't move."

Her voice wobbled, so she swallowed and tried again. "Just lie still." She stroked his brown hair, his face, his chest. "What were you thinking?"

Popping one eye open, he muttered, "I was protecting you."

"And now you're hurt." She kissed his forehead. "We'll get Willyn. Just—"

"No." Quinn opened both eyes now and latched onto Kylie's wrists, smiling as he halted her incessant patting. "I think I'm okay. It hurt for a minute, but the dull ache I had is fading."

"You're in shock. There's no way you caught both mine and Ronja's magic without any damage." A tear dropped onto his cheek, and she realized it was one of hers. "You idiot. I didn't come back from the dead just so you could kill yourself."

Against her protest, he rolled to his side and sat up. "All I could think of was to make myself a shield. For you. My magic flooded just before I launched." He put a hand to his sternum. "I'm still burning some, but . . . I think it protected me."

He switched to rub the base of his skull. "But pulling out that much magic at once is going to leave me with a mother of a headache."

A hole opened up in Kylie's chest, and just as swiftly, it filled with an overpowering warmth. A bright and blazing sensation that could only be love. "Quinn." She threw herself into his arms. "I'm so sorry, but . . . I love you."

She felt his laugh rumble where their bodies pressed together. "I'm sorry too."

Pulling her head back to look at him, she trembled, wondering if he'd changed his mind again. "Why are you sorry?"

"Because I love you too, and it's taken me way too long to tell you."

"Are you sure?" She snuggled against him, then leaned away again. "Are you *really* sure?"

"I'm positive. But if *you* need more time—"

"No," she said suddenly. "Hell to the no. I don't want to wait a single minute longer." She pressed her smiling lips to his, ignoring the battle that was dying around them.

"But don't you ever throw yourself in front of a blow that's meant for me," she chastised. "Never again."

"Always." Quinn's eyes were fierce, despite the grin he still wore. "I will always take the hit for you. If I can." With his hand on the side of her face, he held her and locked his blue eyes on hers. "Don't you understand, Kylie? If you suffer . . . then so do I."

That pesky catch was in her throat again when she took his other hand between hers. "Then I guess we'll have to take good care of each other."

They clung together on the sand as the lightning diminished and the storm began to clear. The moment was perfect, despite the battle-scars left on the beach. But nature would take care of the marks they'd left. She'd wipe them clean with rain and wind.

A shadow blocked the moon and Kylie sensed another person hovering close. "I hate to break this up," Paige said, "but I thought you'd both like to know that everything's clear. Ronja bitched the whole way, but Scarlett convinced her to give it up. At least for now."

With a guilty smile, Kylie bit her bottom lip and stood, still holding onto Quinn's hand.

"Thanks," Quinn told her, but his eyes were still on Kylie.

A flush crept over her skin, a heated sensation that was all because of Quinn.

"Oh for—Will you two just get a room already?" Paige gestured down the beach. "It's not like we're in the middle of a war or anything."

"Right," Quinn said, his mouth kicking up on one side.

"Okay." Kylie whispered, as she thought about Quinn's mouth.

Without checking on anyone else, and fully trusting in their friends to finish up, Kylie let Quinn guide her over the sand and back toward the cars.

As they hurried away, Kylie heard Paige muttering. But instead of her usual grousing about love, the soldier surprised her by saying, "About damned time."

31

They stumbled into the mansion, and Kylie pushed the button to call the elevator. But she used her magic, as her hands were too busy touching Quinn. They fell against the wall as they waited, and she was lost beneath his searching hands, his oh-so skilled tongue.

Kylie was grateful the house was empty, because she and Quinn were finally combusting. And they were putting on quite a show.

With the *ding* of the car's arrival ringing in her ears, she walked backward until she hit the wall. Quinn's mouth was still plastered to hers, creating a hot, unbearable need that ripped through her.

The throbbing lust was heady, thrilling, and very, very welcome. He pressed her into the wall and lifted her, so her legs naturally encircled his hips.

Then he slow-rolled those hips in a way that should have been illegal.

The coil of lust cinched even tighter. "Hurry," she said on a raspy breath. "Hurry."

With her legs still around him, Kylie simply held on when the door opened on the top floor. Quinn turned to carry her out and showed no indication of tiring as his long legs took them down the hall to his room.

Her romantic heart hammered when he kicked the door

open and carried her in.

This time when the male scent of his chambers enveloped her, she relished the feeling of belonging. No longer would she wish for Quinn's love. No longer would she be kept at arm's length.

Oh, she was still determined to make his needs and desires a priority, but if she truly wanted Quinn to have the best in life—then no one in the world was going to love him better than her.

As one, they fell to his bed, and Kylie's delighted laughter rang out. But her heavy-lidded glance to Quinn drew a low, primal growl.

Her breath got stuck in the vicinity of her throat. *Oh, my.* Still another side of him to enjoy. The bookish brainiac had gone rogue.

And she absolutely loved it.

His tongue teased hers lightly, and then he delved deeper, with strong, possessive strokes. When he paid equal attention to her neck, her breaths started to come in short, quick pants.

There was no shyness or hesitation on Kylie's part this time. And Quinn seemed more than happy to give her what she wanted—all she'd ever asked of him.

And what she desired most in the world was to have him love her. It only seemed fair, since he'd owned her heart almost from the beginning.

When they were both naked from the waist up, Quinn slowed the frantic pace abruptly. He pressed the firmness of his chest against hers and hissed out a breath. "I will never get used to how good you feel."

"Good," she said, wiggling his jeans down and over his hips. She ran both her hands over the curve of his lower back, and then she pulled him against her, gasping when he added a thrust to the motion.

When he kissed his way up her neck, she met his gaze. "But I bet we can feel even better."

The primal sound he made had Kylie's breath catching and her body shivering with delight. And glorious anticipation.

Quinn's bedroom was a shadowed sanctuary with a slice of moonbeam as the only light. Luxuriating in the feel of his hands on her skin, his fingers seeking secret places, Kylie simply let go when his mouth found her breast.

He nudged her pants down over her hips, as she had done to his, but gently, reverently, with lingering strokes. Finally they were skin to skin, and the fires flamed as their shared magic swirled.

But Quinn wasn't done with her yet. He looked up through his hair that had fallen over his forehead and gave her a son-of-the-devil smile. Then he softly raked his fingers down her side.

She'd always thought of his hands as strong yet elegant. And now, as he worked, she added naughty to that list.

Her breath caught on a moan. Released. Yes, naughty . . . But oh-so nice.

Gripping his broad shoulders, she pulled him back up to her, missing the warmth of his chest against hers. Then she dragged her fingers down hard pecs, over rigid abs, and to the flat of his stomach. When she gripped the hot velvet length of him, her world went white-hot with need.

His mouth was on her collarbone then, and who would have thought the small hollow would be such an erotic spot? She lifted her hips in response and pulled his greedy lips back to her own.

He kissed her like a man who'd starved years for human touch, but when she whimpered from the ache inside, he slowed, became more tender. She sensed a change in their tempo, and a sudden surge of emotion.

Again he tasted her mouth, but his tongue on hers was wondrous instead of wild. She combed fingers through his hair—such a rich brown, cool and silky.

When he lowered his forehead to hers, he surprised her by

speaking of those emotions she sensed rampaging through him. His tone was sedate. "You know, I used to be afraid of loving you. I was terrified of all that would entail. Commitment, sacrifice, obligation."

Kylie lay beneath him, feeling his heart beat against her, into her. She listened, knowing this was something he had to say.

"I thought you would only tie me down, that love would hold me back." He lifted his head, and the honesty in his stare floored her. "But just the opposite is true."

Quinn grazed her lips with his. He softly touched her hair. "Kylie, you've set me free."

In the half-light of the moon, Kylie was sure she felt the sun, and the kiss they shared then was one of promise. Quinn wasn't simply accepting her. He was giving himself.

Slowly now, they discovered each other, testing and tasting each new curve and angle. Sighs competed with growls as they rose again on overpowering desire.

When he re-positioned and pressed against her core, Kylie felt that fluttering tug in her belly and the light-headed euphoria only he could bring. Then he drove into her and held himself . . . just there.

Digging her fingers into his muscles, she let her head fall back, blinded by the rush of ecstasy as he filled her. And more as he began to move with slow, languid strokes.

Her blood swam with pleasure, her body tightened deliciously, wickedly. Higher and higher Quinn took her, until they both were flying. When Kylie felt herself reaching for the peak, she tightened her hold on him.

Here, at last, was her Quinn. His strong arms surrounding her, his angel-blue eyes caressing every inch, and his heartbeat under her palm, thudding just for her.

This time when she said it, her heart throbbed with every word. "Quinn, I love you."

Intense blue eyes held hers. "I love you, Kylie."

And after all this time, after all the heartache, it was just right.

~~~

The following morning, Anna was in the kitchen enjoying a quiet moment. With a book in one hand, coffee in the other, and a cat in her lap, all was right again with the world.

She noticed the word *trounced* as she devoured the love story and chuckled to herself. It wasn't every day one used such a term, but last night—she sipped and grinned—the coven had mightily trounced the Amara.

So she and her friends deserved some downtime. And Kylie most-assuredly deserved her safety period.

She frowned then, thinking again of Ronja. Few rules were revered in the Nordic witch's mind. She might still practice the magic of her kind, but her soul had long ago been consumed by a demon.

Ronja's master, Bastraal. Sighing and re-immersing herself in the Victorian era, Anna was determined to forget about the Amara and their powerful beast.

She would be facing him soon enough. Only one more trial stood between her and the battle she'd been preparing for her entire life. So she would take her coffee hot and dark while she could.

Anna picked up her mug again, but halfway to her lips, she paused, fingers clenching on the handle. She had a flash of insight, a vision of . . . a bird?

She couldn't be sure, because all she'd caught was a glimpse of wings. Huge wings. And visions weren't always literal.

One thing was certain, though. They were about to have a visitor.

Unalarmed, she stood and made her way through her home.

She crossed the foyer and opened the front door only seconds after the bell had chimed.

The man standing on her doorstep was neatly dressed, but even with the creased khaki pants and casual polo-style shirt, his carriage and demeanor spoke of a militant discipline.

When she was met by familiar hazel eyes, she understood why. *So those are the wings I saw.* She smiled in greeting. "You must be General Worthington."

"I . . . yes." He nodded, his features rock-hard, revealing nothing. "I apologize for my unannounced visit, but I am under the impression my daughter is in residence?"

"She is." Anna stepped aside, waving him into the foyer. "Please."

With measured steps, he entered and perused Anna as if unsure of what to make of her, what her role was in Kylie's life, and what his daughter was actually involved in.

Anna smiled reassuringly.

Granite, she thought as they walked through the house. The man was made of granite. Not just the set of his features, but from head to toe.

Rigid. Unyielding. The very picture of appropriate.

And this was *Kylie's* father?

Paige came out of the kitchen just as Anna and the general reached the grand hall. "Paige," Anna said. "This is Kylie's father, General Worthington."

Paige straightened in response. "Sir." She nodded. "It's an honor to meet you."

The man inclined his head, and with that one gesture, he acknowledged Paige while releasing her from the tension rolling over her. Chain of command was still ingrained in the coven's soldier, and she showed respect where it was due.

"Why don't you go up and let Kylie know?" Anna raised a meaningful brow to Paige.

But their guest had other ideas. "If you don't mind, I'd rather find her myself." He strode across the floor to the staircase.

"Um . . . it's no trouble—" Paige began, but the man waved her words aside. And Paige didn't argue. Instead, she offered, "You'll find her on the top floor."

They watched as the stoic man climbed the stairs, and Paige lost her rigid posture as soon as he disappeared from sight. "Oh, shit," she said, though her eyes danced with mischief. "I would so not want to be your brother right now."

Anna bit her bottom lip, trying to stop the grin. Paige's delight was infectious. "He'll be fine. He's a grown man."

"A grown man in bed with the general's daughter," Paige replied. Then she lowered her voice. "This is going to be good." She made a move for the staircase, but Anna grabbed her arm and tugged her back.

"Aw, come on, Anna," Paige entreated, her face twisted up with curiosity. "I don't want to miss this."

"I know." Anna flashed an impish smile. "Which is why we're taking the elevator."

~~~

Quinn had his shirt in his hands and was watching Kylie stretch beneath the covers when what sounded like a giant's fist pounded on his bedroom door. After tossing her an I-don't-know expression, he moved through his office to answer.

He had no idea who the man was or why he looked so surly, but when the stranger saw Quinn, his face grew even more severe. If that were possible. "I must be mistaken," he said through a clenched jaw. "I was directed to this door by a man who said I could find my daughter here?'

In a whirl of confusion, Quinn shook his head. "What man?" he beetled his brow. "Your daughter?"

"That's the one, sir," Ethan called from down the hall. When Quinn leaned out to ask him what was going on, his friend ducked around a corner. Along with Paige and Anna.

Then it struck him, and Quinn felt the blood in his head drop to the floor. "Your . . . daughter?"

The man's fierce eyes drifted past Quinn. Then he barked, "Kylie!"

"Daddy!" Kylie leapt from his bed, and was—thank the goddess—wearing pajama pants beneath Quinn's t-shirt.

Still in a state of shock, Quinn echoed, "Daddy?"

"Kylie," the man said again before turning his livid stare back to Quinn.

Quinn had faced down witches, shifters, and a plethora of other fearful beings, but this situation had him backing up. Several steps in the space of a heartbeat. "Sir," he said, fumbling for the appropriate words. What were the appropriate words?

Kylie rushed to her father and put both hands on his chest. "Wait, Daddy. You don't need to be upset."

The man eyed Quinn as if sizing him up for measurements. Probably for the hole in the ground where he would make Quinn disappear.

He curled his lip. "Clearly."

Feeling more than a little exposed, Quinn pulled his shirt on. This was Kylie's father, a man he would be getting to know a lot better. So he needed to salvage this really, really awful first impression.

Clearing his throat, he stepped forward and put his hands on Kylie's shoulders. He pulled her gently aside, but almost changed his mind when she sent him a sidelong glance of worry.

Hoping the general wasn't actually packing a weapon, Quinn held out his hand. "Quinn St. Germaine. Welcome to my home."

One tawny brow hiked up as the man studied his proffered hand. He leveled Quinn with a stare.

Turning his head to Kylie, the man scowled at his daughter.

Rubbing her hands together and pleading with her eyes, Kylie said, "I would have brought him home to meet you, but

I've been kind of . . . busy."

The general returned his glare to Quinn. "Apparently."

Quinn gulped. The man was hell with one-word implications.

Trying not to flinch, he waited until the general released a heavy sigh. At last, he grasped Quinn's hand and shook.

But the grip of steel did squeeze a little harder than necessary. And it did hurt. A little.

Kylie's father was accepting the peace agreement. But was backing it up with a warning.

Emitting a relieved laugh-sigh combo, Kylie hugged her father. But with a new tone of concern, she asked, "What are you doing here?"

He crossed his arms when she stepped out of the embrace. "I received a strange phone call. It got cut off, and there was no follow up call to explain. I recognized the area code."

He tilted his head and locked his sights on his errant daughter. "And since you didn't see fit to contact me either, I decided enough was enough. You've had your year off from college, young lady, and it's past time you told me just what is really going on."

"Oh, well . . ."

"Your father's right," Quinn said, taking her hand to show both support and unity. "We should tell him everything. He's your family."

Kylie stared at him for long seconds, and then her smile bloomed. "All right. But he already knows the basics." She turned back to the man who was still partially glowering. "After all, he was the first person I ever shocked."

The man grunted, and a touch of what might one day become a grin played at the corners of his mouth. "Hmph. Your terrible twos. Don't remind me."

With a softening of his eyes, the general studied Kylie. And abruptly, he hardened again to fix Quinn with a glare. "I expect you'll participate in this conversation?"

"Yes, sir."

"Good. And let me make this very clear up front. No lies, no mistreatment." He stepped closer. "Trust me, son. You don't want to be in my crosshairs. And I *will* protect my daughter."

Quinn held the man's gaze while he held Kylie's hand. "With all due respect, sir," he steeled his own countenance, "that's my job now."

The general's eyes narrowed as he nodded slightly. "Hmm. I suppose we'll have to see about that." Then, "Kylie," he said shortly, "I'll see you downstairs. Now that I know you're safe, I'll make my apologies to the young lady who greeted me."

He moved to Kylie and kissed her on top of the head. Finally, the man's shoulders relaxed, and Quinn felt a fast and tight kinship. If there were anyone else who worried over Kylie as much as he did, it would be her father.

In fact, he might find some pity for the general. He glanced aside to his little bolt of lightning, imagining what her teenage years must have been like.

Without another word, her father exited the room and left them alone. Quinn pushed out a breath of relief. "Well. I'm awake now."

Kylie laughed and threw her arms around his neck. "I know, right?" She lifted on her toes and kissed his lips. "Don't worry. I think he likes you."

Rubbing her arms, Quinn moved in closer. "*That* was him liking me?"

"Consider the situation," she said, veering her eyes back to his bed. The rumpled covers. Then down to her ensemble which wasn't entirely hers. "But you were great." Her eyes became dewy. "What you said was perfect."

Putting his hands to her waist, Quinn tugged her to his chest. "I meant it. You're my priority now."

"And you're mine." She put her head on his shoulder briefly before lifting her eyes to his again. "I do want to finish college, but I want to travel with you too. Maybe there's a way we can do both."

"I don't have to travel anymore, Kylie." He tucked a finger under her chin. "Nothing in this world is as exciting as a single day with you. If I have you," he wrapped a long golden curl around his finger, "I have all I need." *Wildflowers on a sunny day.*

"Aw, sweet-talker. But I saw your list, and . . . I kind of got excited about visiting China."

Quinn's head fell back as laughter rumbled. Then, leaning down to brush her mouth with his, he murmured, "Anywhere." Another kiss. "As long as it's with you. Only two more trials, and the prophecy will be fulfilled. Then we'll do whatever we want. Together."

Quinn quirked his mouth to one side. "That is, assuming your father allows me to get anywhere near you."

"Oh, he'll come around. I'll work on him." Kylie twirled a finger in the center of his chest. "I can be persistent."

"Hmm."

"And stubborn."

Quinn simply raised a brow.

"Especially when something is important." The corners of her lips tipped up playfully, and Quinn couldn't keep his mouth from the pretty pink bow. Then her cheek.

When he dipped to her neck, she gasped. "Quinn."

"Kylie," he teased.

It was going to be a beautiful day. His golden girl was in his arms, and she wasn't going anywhere.

She giggled when he squeezed her backside. Her hazel eyes warmed as she leaned into him. Her voice was soft as velvet. "I'll fight to the end . . . when something is worth the effort. When it's worth the wait, I won't give up."

Wrapping her up like his own little present, Quinn cocked his head and grinned. "You don't say."

If you enjoyed this book, we would love to read your review on your favorite retail or review site.

Thank you!

Suza Kates writes both paranormal romance and suspense. She lives in Savannah, Georgia with her family and three ridiculously spoiled cats.

For more on Suza and her books visit

www.suzakates.com